1018462048

PB EVE
Everson, John
Sacrifice / J

S0-ASX-737

CLINTON LIBRARY

CRITICS RAVE ABOUT JOHN EVERSON AND
COVENANT

"*Cove...* ...
Everso... ...g
it, yo... ...ely
worthy... ...gue

"I've waited four long years to read *Covenant* and it was well worth it. Everson has taken a classic genre plot and given it his own spin. This is how horror is done RIGHT."

—*The Horror Fiction Review*

"You might even begin to wonder with writing this good, if Everson agreed to his own covenant in order to create this devilishly dark and terrifying tale."

—Pagan Pulse Magazine

"Truly entertaining no-frills horror, which is a damned good thing."

—Horror World

"Equal parts dark mystery and supernatural horror, *Covenant* is a white-knuckle reading experience that will keep you guessing and gasping."

—Creature Feature

"Everson allows the storylines to unfurl, carefully layering each of the individual character's arcs as he crosses genres ending up with a nice blend of mystery and horror."

—*Dark Scribe Magazine*

"John Everson has written a powerful tale as readers wonder whether it is a coincidence, the supernatural, or a serial killer behind the suicides."

—*Midwest Book Review*

"Everson sets up his story well, fleshes out Joe Kieran as a character readers can root for, and truly sets him against a pitiless, horrible evil."

—Shroud

DRAWING EVER CLOSER

The ring was growing wider now, and she could feel her strength increasing. Soon, she would be able to draw the final razor and with the blood of her final victim close the knot to open the door.

With every kill, Ariana felt her power increase, and the gap between the worlds grew more transparent. As she stared at the walls in the hotel rooms she killed in, she could see them fade sometimes, and see the movement just beyond. Shadowy, indistinct. But growing stronger. The Curburide were out there, waiting. Their hands reached out to her, their faces begged for release, going in and out of focus like the gasp of an unborn baby in the hazy sights of an ultrasound. She could hear their whispers in her sleep.

"Soon," they promised. "We will be yours to command. You will be ours…"

Other *Leisure* books by John Everson:

COVENANT

Sacrifice

JOHN EVERSON

Thompson-Nicola Regional District
Library System
300-465 VICTORIA STREET
KAMLOOPS, BC   V2C 2A9

LEISURE BOOKS NEW YORK CITY

For Geri
Love is Sacrifice.

A LEISURE BOOK®

May 2009

Published by

Dorchester Publishing Co., Inc.
200 Madison Avenue
New York, NY 10016

Copyright © 2007 by John Everson

All rights reserved. No part of this book may be reproduced or transmitted in any form or by any electronic or mechanical means, including photocopying, recording or by any information storage and retrieval system, without the written permission of the publisher, except where permitted by law.

All persons in this book are fictitious, and any resemblance that may seem to exist to actual persons living or dead is purely coincidental. This is a work of fiction.

ISBN 10: 0-8439-6019-1
ISBN 13: 978-0-8439-6019-8
E-ISBN: 978-1-4285-0669-5

The name "Leisure Books" and the stylized "L" with design are trademarks of Dorchester Publishing Co., Inc.

Printed in the United States of America.

10 9 8 7 6 5 4 3 2 1

If you purchased this book without a cover you should be aware that this book is stolen property. It was reported as "unsold and destroyed" to the publisher and neither the author nor the publisher has received any payment for this "stripped book."

Visit us on the web at www.dorchesterpub.com.

1018462048

ACKNOWLEDGMENTS

This novel is a travelogue of sorts, which allowed me to re-visit some of my favorite places with one of my oldest fictional friends. While I've tried to ensure geographical accuracy (as well as travel times), I've taken some liberties in the name of fiction and foggy memory. The rest I blame on MapQuest.

Behind every novel, there are a thousand conversations that mold and shape the author to write what he does. It would be impossible to track or thank everyone for their influence but I must note a few:

Special thanks to Shane Ryan Staley and Bill Breedlove for be-lieving, when my faith was gone. To Don D'Auria, for giving this book new life. To Robert Cichowlas and Mateusz Ban-durski for bringing it to Poland. And to my Street Team, for spreading the word.

For friendship, encouragement and support: Dave Barnett, Bill Gagliani, Dave Benton, Paul Gifford, Martin Mundt, Lo-ren Rhoads, Maria Alexander, Brian Yount, Jade Paris, Edward Lee, Brian Keene and everyone at Shocklines, The Horror Mall and Twilight Tales.

For my loyal readers and *Covenant* fans, especially Kathy Ku-bik, Peg Phillips, Sheila and Joan, Lauren and Brenda, Mis-sy, Whitney, Martel, Giovanna, Deanna, Raymond Brown, Rhonda Wilson, Louise Bohmer, Chris Hanson, Tim Feely, Jess Kaan, Audrey Shaffer, Jen Vickers, Nerine Dorman, Eric Morgan, TigerLady, Terri Beirness, Sheila Halterman and John Palisano. I hope you'll find the wait was worth it!

Sacrifice

Prologue

Goose bumps peppered Ted's skin. The temperature dropped every step forward. The air swam with palpable presence, as if he was walking through a liquid current of clammy spiderwebs. Ted shivered, but kept moving.

It had all happened down here. His sister Cindy had finally told him the story after he'd badgered her enough. A spirit had lived inside this cliff, a spirit that had killed and killed and killed again. It had demanded sacrifices from the town of Terrel for more than 100 years. But now it was gone, along with that reporter from the *Terrel Times*.

Ted had come, pressing through the dank, cobwebbed caverns, to see where it had all happened.

Once, these cold stone corridors had been the basement beneath the old lighthouse. Terrel had been a minor port, back in the day, and its lighthouse had stood high on the cliff above the town, warning errant ships away from the deadly pillars of stone gouged out of the bay like crippled fingers. The lighthouse was long gone, but the stairs leading down into the cliff remained, hidden beneath a pile of remnant boulders and rotting beams.

Ted shone his flashlight back and forth, catching the watery glint of the cool gray walls on the right and left, its light sucked away into the endless black hole ahead. His narrow beam was swallowed by that blackness, but he continued on, step by step, into the void. There was no sound besides the soft shuffle of his feet on the uneven floor, and the whisper of his jeans in motion. Ted had never felt so alone and cut off; at times, he had to remind himself to breathe.

The flash struggled to pry through the darkness, and then suddenly, Ted saw a reflection, an answering flicker, bounced back from the black. There was something ahead. He yearned to hurry up, to run ahead and see what was there, but forced himself to move slowly, carefully, panning the spot across the floor a few feet in front of him to make sure he didn't trip over a rock and break a leg. He didn't think he could crawl all the way back down the tunnel and up the stairs to the outside world. Even if he could, it wasn't likely he could flag anyone down for help from the top of Terrel's Peak. It was not exactly the center of town.

Heart pounding harder, Ted continued his slow, measured walk, occasionally flicking the flash up to eye level to look far down the path. The reflection grew with every step, a twinkling prism of blue-white light. The corridor walls narrowed. It tightened until his shoulders almost touched the rock on either side of him and he wondered if he was really just walking into a claustrophobic dead end.

And then the wall to the left disappeared, his flash meeting only blackness as he raised it up and down. He swung it to the right and there, too, the walls had disappeared. The air was even colder here, its taste on his lips salty and dead.

He brought the flash back to dead center and was almost blinded. The room exploded in a prism of sparkling light, reflecting off the object in the center of the cavern. The walls all around were visible now; more passages led to and away from this room.

This was it! He had found it! The chamber of crystal that his sister had described.

A pedestal—a rocky altar—of watery blue crystal rooted in the center of the room; it reflected his light in a blinding feedback loop to the azure mirrors that cut into and out of the walls all around. It was like standing in the center of a gigantic geode.

Ted walked to the center and reached out to the crystal altar with his left hand. He stopped, inches from its glassy surface. Would a jolt of blue fire scorch him for his intrusion? This had been the seat of the demon's power. Did any still remain, like a battery poised to spend its last electric jolt?

He tapped a fingernail on the cool, hard surface, but nothing happened. With his palm he traced the latticework of its surface. There were spots of darkness blotting out the window to the crystal's core. Rusted, gritty spots led away from a deep dark stain near the center of the flat surface.

Dried blood.

Sacrifice and soul-binding had occurred here.

Ted stepped away from the stone and twisted, clockwise, admiring the sparkle and flash of the room. This was nature's disco, and he the only dancer.

He grinned and moved to the edge of the room, peering into each corridor that led to places deeper inside the cliff.

His flash disappeared without meeting any reflection down the first two paths. They seemed endless. Then he found a side room. The corridor wound around the outside of the circular chamber, and ended in this half-hidden cubby. He walked to the end, and found a small ledge, like the surface of a desk. A look at its contents said it had been used for just that, once.

This was probably where the keepers of the old lighthouse had come to for safety during the fury of a North Atlantic storm, he thought. They would have stoked up the giant searchlight, trained its saving, warning beam towards the ocean and then crossed their fingers that any wayward ships could see it. And then, as the structure groaned and shivered in the treacherous winds, they would have fled to safety below. To here.

The shelf held a couple of old, small bottles, and what looked like chicken feathers, in a pile to one side. In the center lay an old, rotting book. It was bound in reddish brown leather, and Ted could see without even flipping, that its pages were yellowed and mold eaten.

The Journal of Broderick Terrel it said on the cover.

He opened the book to a random page and smiled. *This* was

what he had come for. This was why he was here. The script was faded and hard to read, but its import was clear:

"I have called a demon from hell," the author had written in an early entry.

Ted set down the flashlight to shine sideways across the pages, and read on.

Part One:
Leaving Home

The rewards of a successful Calling are riches and hedonistic fulfill-ment beyond any man's wildest dreams. But the path to union with the Curburide is long. He who chooses this path must be committed to the Calling in both heart and soul; there is no turning back. To waver on the path means not only death, but eternal damnation. Once the Calling has begun, and first blood spilled, the Caller be-longs to the demons called Curburide. If the Calling is successfully completed, they will also belong to the Caller—a mutual symbiotic bond is forged. But if the Curburide detect weakness, doubt or insin-cerity in the Caller before that bond is complete, beware . . .

—Chapter One, *The Book of the Curburide*

Chapter One

If the lights went any lower, the woman would have been indistinguishable from the shadows. She was dressed all in black.

All.

Even her hair was covered in a shiny skullcap ending in two pointy faux cat ears. The only skin showing was her face, but when lights flickered across the costume, her obsidian body rippled with dark reflection.

Ryan Nelson eyed the woman from heels to head and, without even realizing it, licked his lips.

Un-fuckin'-believable.

Four-inch stiletto-heeled boots merged seamlessly into glossy black bodysuit and arm-length vinyl gloves that showed every flow of flesh and muscle beneath. Not that she moved or flowed. He had been sitting next to her in the club for an hour so far, and had yet to see her do more than bat an eyelid.

The latex catsuit was not unusual. It was Sunday night—and more importantly, Halloween—in Austin, Texas, and a catwoman was the least of the odd sights he'd seen so far. Driven by the wild college crowd of the University of Texas, which nestled just blocks off the state capitol steps, the city had been forced to close off a several block stretch of Sixth Street, downtown Austin's main drag. A wild mix of college kids and locals paraded down the asphalt, in costume creations dredged from some pretty twisted and bloody imaginations. Mascara-smudged vampires leaned out of every open bar window as if this were Amsterdam's red-light district. Ragged witches French-kissed bile- and gore-streaked corpses. And when they came up for air, they all peered over second-floor balconies to watch the parade of other homemade horrors on the street below. At least three "Sons of God" pulled giant wooden crosses behind them as they trudged down the street. Ryan was quite sure that the original walk that had inspired the "Stations of the Cross" celebrated in Christian churches around the world had not used a cross with handy tote wheels screwed into the base.

While there certainly were many costumes of greater extravagance, Ryan's favorite so far had been an older woman. She had been dressed in ripped and mud-crusted rags. She'd walked along the crowded street with a rope tied around her waist. Hanging from that rope, with twine knotted tight around their tiny ankles, were a half dozen baby dolls. At least, he assumed they were dolls. From the smears of blood across their tortured, wrinkled faces, he wasn't sure, and he hadn't stepped close enough to confirm or deny the atrocity.

Early in the evening, he'd spent a couple hours shivering outside with the mob in the chill, unseasonable wind and laughing at the bizarre imaginations of his neighbors, until he finally left the street and slid into the comforting black confines of Elysium, an outwardly nondescript, black-walled goth club around the corner on Red River. His own facial white paint and the pale threads in his black and white striped hobo suit glowed electric blue-white in the black light of the club. As he passed through the entryway, a girl in a purple corset, torn fishnets and a bloody ax lodged in her skull caught his eye, flashed a red lipstick smile of appreciative recognition and yelled, "Beetlejuice, Beetlejuice, Beetlejuice!"

He grinned back and bowed, appreciating her recognition, then moved to the bar where a blood-spattered cheerleader in a gold and blue ultrashort skirt poured him a Vampire's Kiss.

The DJ was mixing ambient, ethereal Delerium as Ryan né "Beetlejuice" found a chair along the dance floor to wait for the evening's band lineup to start playing. He took an empty seat next to the young "catwoman" and silently whistled his appreciation of her getup.

Over the next few minutes, as the disco ball and a couple

of red and blue spotlights worked in tandem to swirl a mind-numbing pattern across the floor, alternating from psyche-delic circles to swimming neon tadpoles, Ryan snuck looks at the silent feline. He wondered if she was with anyone. She seemed to be sitting alone, and wasn't drinking. She stared straight ahead across the floor, without expression. Cat's eyes.

Over the course of an hour, she didn't uncross her legs or move the gloved hands from her lap. The black whiskers penciled on her cheeks didn't so much as twitch. She was a statue, cool dark eyes trained at some point just above the floor. There, impossibly thin men both in drag and wearing tight leather pants with fishnet shirts along with uniformly chubby women in combat boots and pink or blue hair and various shredded bits of spandex, netting and twines of chain moved in a disconnected, colorfully jerky ballet to the beats.

"Wild night, eh?" Ryan said after awhile, staring straight at catwoman's face. Her expression didn't change. She didn't answer. He shrugged and sipped his blood-dyed drink, averting his eyes to the floor.

Murder Box, a local band, picked up their instruments at last, and Ryan abandoned his seat to get closer to the stage, nodding at the industrial guitar grind and bleating synthesizers as an Edward Scissorhands look-alike thumbed the bass, spiky black hair bobbing in time. A young goth girl wrapped in tantalizing curtains of gauzy black swiveled her bared hips and teased the audience as she fellated a microphone above the pounding beat.

After the set, he bought another drink and looked for a place to rest until the headliners came on, a Florida darkwave act. He slipped between a variety of ghouls and black-clad, black-eyed patrons and found himself back again at the edge of the dance floor, at the same empty seat next to the catwoman.

He sat.

She didn't seem to have moved.

"They were pretty good, didn't you think?" he asked.

Her head tilted ever so slightly to almost meet his gaze, and then returned to face forward, still saying nothing.

Ryan drew up his death clown charcoal-ringed mouth and sighed. Talk about ice-queens. But she was gorgeous, in an arctic way. It was one thing if she didn't want to be picked up—he'd been there. But she could at least be polite. The more he thought about it, the more it steamed him. A simple shake of the head, the barest acknowledgement of his existence, would have been enough. Purely out of spite, he leaned over her shoulder and struggled to keep a straight face as he dropped a line patently designed to piss her off as much as her silence had annoyed him.

"Do you come here often?" he asked.

No answer.

Not even a flicker of response.

Ryan sighed and presently went back to watching the goth boys and goth girls pirouetting to the gloomy self-flagellation of The Smiths. The dance floor was slowly filling, as people began to elbow their way in closer to the stage, eager to be in place for the next set.

And then she spoke.

Her voice was cool, like her eyes, but her meaning was clear.

"Do you want to take me out of here?"

Ryan turned abruptly to face her. Had she said what he just thought he heard? For the first time, her face was actually turned towards him, eyes trained fully, unblinkingly on him, awaiting his answer. Her pale lips were drawn tight.

"Huh?" he said.

"I asked if you wanted to take me out of here?" she repeated, her voice a delicate shard of deadly beautiful crystal, high-pitched and thin enough to break.

"Now?" he asked.

She moved, for the first time all night, stretching provocatively while running both black-gloved palms down the shining suit. Ryan stared as her black-gloved fingers traced the lithe ridges of her tightly visible rib cage and then reached down over the spread of her thighs. Her outfit groaned like the creasing of a tight leather couch as she stretched, catlike in her chair, and then opened both eyes wide to meet his growing interest.

"Yes," she said. "I need to go. Now."

It didn't take him long to consider. Visions of his hand unzipping that tight vinyl flooded his mind. Ryan jumped to his feet. He bent and offered his arm. Catwoman smiled and nodded, gracing his forearm lightly with a cool vinyl finger. She rose with a slow but audible crunch. In her heels, she was as tall as he was, and in mincing steps she strutted next to him through the crowd of goths and out the doorway. From behind them, Ryan heard someone again call out, "Beetlejuice, Beetlejuice, Beetlejuice!"

"I think someone just wished you away," she said.

"Looks like it worked."

"I'm just up the street, at the Marriott," she announced.

"Cool." He led her down the street, through the crowds of gaudy painted faces and gales of drunken laughter. Her steps clicked like sniper shots against the pavement, and she said nothing more until they had passed Stubb's and some burnt-out warehouses and turned the corner to arrive at the Waller Creek bridge near the hotel.

In five minutes, he was trailing her up the stairs of the hotel's rear courtyard, across the polished granite-tiled lobby, and up the elevator to room 618. She flipped a light switch, and Ryan saw that she had rearranged the room, piling the mattress and frame of one of the two double beds up against a wall.

A ring of what looked like pebbles littered the ground where carpet marks indicated that the deconstructed bed had stood not so long ago. Catwoman turned and pressed her face to his, drawing his breath out in a hard kiss. She stared wide into his eyes.

"I like the floor," she said, and drew her tongue from his chin to his ear, biting briefly at the lobe.

"Why don't you get out of those clothes, make yourself comfortable," she hissed. "I'll be right back."

She disappeared into the bathroom, shutting the door behind her. Ryan shed his hobo coat and tie, and kicked his shoes to the side of the bed. He sat down on the bed she hadn't dismantled and waited, grinning expectantly when he heard the run of water in the next room. He imagined her coming out of the bathroom wearing only a towel, hair let down to flow in loose curls of raven gloss over bare shoulders.

His imagination was wrong.

She returned still fully clad in vinyl, still gloved and skull-capped.

She walked over to him, and planted one leg between his feet while handing him a warm, wet cloth.

"For your face," she offered. "Can I take your shirt and pants for you?"

"Can I take your catsuit for you?" he retorted. She lifted her chin.

"Boys first," she said, looking down her whiskers at him. "I'm shy."

He laughed at that, but took the cloth and rubbed the character makeup from his face with vigorous wipes. Then he stood and unbuttoned his shirt and pants, letting them fall to the floor.

"And what do you keep in there?" she asked, nodding at the growing bulge in the pouch of his underpants.

"You don't waste time, do you?"

She grinned, and touched a pink tongue to her upper lip.

"Do you want to waste time?"

He kicked his underwear off and stood naked, hands on his hips.

"Does it pass?" he asked, confident, though starting to feel a little uneasy. This was definitely a weird one. Would she be a frigid mannequin beneath him, or would she truly become a catwoman?

She nodded. "It'll do."

Hands behind her back, she circled him, inspecting. He shivered as a cool nail scratched down from the top of his neck to the crack of his buttocks. She slid close, kissed him with her entire body, wrapping around him like a coat from behind, biting at his ear, whispering as she pinched his nipples. Her hands slipped down to move between his legs, kneading and gripping at the flesh swelling with desire.

"I need your help," she purred in his ear.

He moaned.

"I need a big, strong man to help me open the door," she purred again, and he made as if to turn around. Her hand gripped tight and held him facing forward. "I need you to give it up for me," she said, slowly withdrawing her hands. Then she wasn't there at all, and Ryan felt a chill as her voice commanded, "I need you to stay right there."

He rolled his eyes and continued to face forward, wondering if he should make a quick and apologetic exit. Catwoman really was some kind of freak.

Behind him she whispered something. Something he couldn't hear.

"What?" he asked, but her voice didn't pause.

He turned around and saw the woman had dropped in a crouch on the floor. Her forehead touched the ground and she mumbled and whispered to herself.

He felt a knot form in his belly and shook his head. In a heartbeat he'd made up his mind. Last straw.

Ryan began to step backwards, noting the location of his clothes out of the corner of his eye.

Her head shot up at his silent retreat.

"Wait," she hissed. "I need your help, I'm not done."

"Well, I'm done," he said. "Thanks for the memories."

He reached for his shirt and she pounced, knocking him off balance and then pushing him to the floor on his back.

"Whoa," he said, grabbing her by the shoulders to hold her back. "I don't know what you're into, but I don't think I'm the right one for you tonight."

She slipped her arms inside his and pressed her palms to his chest. She leaned in, breath warm and sweet against his face.

"You're done when *I* say you're done," she said. Her words weren't warm and sweet at all.

He pushed against the floor with his elbows and tried to rise, but then her lips pressed wetly to his and he hesitated, involuntarily responding to the force and erotic liquid heat of her touch. A cool finger reached around his shoulder to ruffle the back of his hair. He smiled and slipped his tongue between her teeth. And then something hurt as she drew that caressing hand around his throat . . . pressing deep with cold pressure.

Something pinched his throat, and a confusing alarm of ice and fire rang inside Ryan's skull. Then the pain blossomed and he coughed at a tickle across his larynx . . . and then there *really* was pain . . . and warmth spilling out across his chest and shoulder. He tried to scream but Catwoman pressed his head to the floor and drew the second razor secreted in her palm across his neck from the other direction, severing his windpipe and vocal chords in one deep slice. A spray of blood spattered and beaded across her protective vinyl bodysuit. The pain was all consuming and he struggled against her weight, but every movement was excruciating. The room blurred instantly. Ryan struggled to look at his killer one last time, his brain crying silently, *Why?*

She pressed him firmly to the floor and waited. His own blood dripped back down onto his lips, cascading from the jet escaping his throat to dribble impotently down the shiny black vinyl of her chest. The taste of iron from his last blood slipped into his mouth and clouded his last shuddering sight as it pooled in his eye sockets.

"Beetlejuice, Beetlejuice, Beetlejuice," she said with a smile, and licked a spot of blood from her pencil-drawn, smeared whiskers.

"Now you're done."

Chapter Two

They're coming.

The voice was in his head, but that still didn't prevent Joe Kieran from answering it out loud. He was alone in the car, and in the middle of nowhere. Nobody was likely to hear.

"What the hell are you talking about now?"

Joe didn't respond well to the occasional intrusions of Malachai, his indentured spirit. It wasn't like the invisible demon ever meant him well.

"Who's coming?" he asked. The irritation oozed from his tone.

The Curburide. Somebody is calling them. I can hear it.

"And I should care about this because . . . ?" Joe asked, keeping his eyes on the road and his foot on the pedal.

He had miles to go before he slept. Nebraska was a long state. A long, uneventful, incredibly even-planed state. It played tricks on you, as the road unwound straight to the horizon, crossing and recrossing the damned Platte River, as if you were going in a circle, not a line. The Platte River was like the Styx—unless you were Charon, you could never escape crossing it.

Because whoever is calling them is strong. They can hear. And they are answering.

"So?" Joe asked. "What am I supposed to do about it?"

Nothing.

Joe watched the orange-fire tongs reaching low over the horizon, watched the light stretch and grab one last futile time before fading into a memory of sunset's oblivion.

"Then why even bother to tell me?" Joe asked again.

Because I thought you'd want to know.

Joe didn't say anything.

I thought you'd want to know that you don't have very much time left to live.

The demon in his head began to laugh, louder and louder until Malachai's invisible power manifested itself physically, cracking the Hyundai's aging vinyl ceiling until it dripped dusty blood over his head.

Joe sneezed and shook his head in irritation. The demon had a penchant for the dramatic.

They'll kill you and everybody you've ever known.

Images of Angelica and her daughter, Cindy, flashed before his eyes. He'd left them both behind in his flight from Terrel. It was Malachai's fault that he had gotten close to each of them, and Joe's fault that the two women had been brought back together, 18 years after Angelica had given Cindy up for adoption in a vain hope to save her child from the grasp of the demon.

Thanks to Joe, Angelica's effort and estrangement had almost been in vain. But in the end, Joe had also saved both of them from Malachai's enslavement. The demon had held an entire town in thrall, thanks to a century-old covenant. The creature had holed up in Terrel's Peak, a cliff just outside of the seaport town, and demanded blood sacrifices every year to protect the townsfolk from an even worse fate—an incursion from the Curburide, a howling scourge of sadistic succubi that would have, if they'd had their way, fucked and flayed the flesh from every living being in Terrel. While Malachai had kept his bargain and protected the town from the Curburide, he had also struck a side deal to serve his own sadistic ends. A deal which would have resulted in Cindy's death, had Joe not managed to uncover the demon's real name and bind its service to him.

But in saving Cindy from the clutches of the demon Malachai, and also freeing Angelica, Joe had taken on an awful burden. The demon was now locked in servitude to him. The terms of the contract bound Malachai to Joe, and required that he do whatever Joe asked if he was to continue to have access to the earthly realm. One of Joe's first commands had been that the demon would not harm him or those he loved. But Joe had no doubt that the spiteful creature would do its best to quietly put him in harm's way, for when Joe was dead, it was unbound again. Free. It would then be able to swindle some other unwitting soul to strike a new covenant. One that would give Malachai all the advantages.

Part of him was ready to grant the demon its freedom. Part of him was ready to just lie down in the center of the road and wait for a semi to come along and cleave him in half. Let it all hang out.

Life hadn't turned out the way he'd planned. Joe had landed a plum job at the *Chicago Tribune* right out of college, and had taken to big-city reporting like a hound to a rabbit trail. He loved uncovering city hall corruption. He had broken the story about the police superintendent and his connection to the Colombian drug lord, Anabi Urubu. In a matter of months, Joe had put together a network of street kids who traded all sorts of information with him. He'd put the bust on a school principal for child pornography, and gotten a city ward boss put away for his dealings with the mob.

Joe had taken to the game with relish, never realizing that his girlfriend, the woman he intended to marry, was also in bed with the wrong crowd. And one of his exposé pieces on corruption in the district courthouse had landed her in jail for graft and forgery. She'd refused to see him after her indictment, and his fervor for turning over stones had soured. He suddenly didn't want to know what people hid in their bottom drawers and back rooms. He didn't want to know who they saw after dark, down by the alley at 83rd and Halsted. He didn't want to do anything but watch his own backyard. Play it safe.

Stay home.

The stories dried up, and his street network disappeared. It only took a couple missed visits to make those kids turn skittish and taciturn. One day, Joe went home from the paper, threw his clothes in a suitcase, his books and CDs and papers in a couple boxes, and got in his car and drove. He'd driven to the end of the world, the East Coast town of Terrel, right on the ocean. Ironically, in his desperation to escape the million minor sins of the big city, after only being in the tiny town of Terrel a few weeks he'd discovered a ring of murders that was bigger than any small-time crack dealer and welfare department grafter. He'd gone from mundane, selfish thievery to malevolence that transcended generations.

He'd lost a thieving girlfriend from his bed and gained a deadly demon in his head. Hardly a bargain.

The last bloody rays of sunlight faded without further conversation, and Joe's world contracted to a thin ribbon of yellow-striped asphalt. He rubbed his eyes, squinting into the headlight-burned night, and decided to call it a day when a green sign flashed by advertising OGALLALA, 2 MILES. He'd been on the road for nearly 12 hours, and it was time for a rest. He was humming a Creedence Clearwater Revival song when he pulled off the exit and headed for the center of town. The last place he'd gotten gas at hadn't been big enough to call a "town" in his estimation. It had consisted of a graying general store that seemed more a giant moldering growth on the pavement than a planned structure, a Clark service station with orange, rounded pumps from the 1960s and a tilted rusting grain silo. It was essentially a crossroads where soybean farmers met on Friday nights.

He hoped that Ogallala would prove larger. It appeared as a bold spot on his Nebraska map, which was a good sign.

He was in the "downtown" area in minutes, and pulled up to a small brick façade that boasted in simple blue neon, BRILL'S. A Budweiser sign glowed in the window.

Joe killed the engine and stepped out of the car into the crisp night air. He hadn't realized how stuffy the car had gotten until he stepped out of it with a groan of stiff joints. His stomach turned over and he realized that not only was he stiff, but he was starving. He pushed open the heavy wooden door and stepped inside.

Brill's was a good-sized bar, with two pool tables off to one side, and a long bar on the other. He could see the grill behind the bar to one side, and a healthy selection of whiskies, vodkas and gins against the center wall.

"Evening."

The voice was heavy and husky, but friendly. It came from a big man behind the bar, moving out of the shadows and into the red glow of a Pabst Blue Ribbon sign.

"Hi," Joe said, pulling up a stool at the bar. Only one other stool was taken. A thin, grizzled man nursed something amber over ice at the end of the bar.

"Quiet night, eh?" Joe offered.

The big man nodded, drying his hands on a stained white towel. Joe saw he'd been washing glasses in a small sink when he'd come in.

"Not much going on here on a Tuesday night," the man said, and held out a hand.

"Frank," he said. "Frank Brill. You just off the highway?"

It was Joe's turn to nod.

"Then you'll be wanting a meal and a room, yes?"

Joe smiled. "You nailed it."

"I can handle the one; you'll find the other about two blocks down. Prescott Hotel. Not a bad place for a night."

Frank pulled a menu out from beneath the bar and set it in front of Joe.

"You can look at this if you want, and Jenny will rustle up anything from here that you want, but"—he leaned forward conspiratorially, after glancing over his shoulder at the double doors in the back of the grill area—"I'd stick with the hamburger and fries if I was you," he whispered.

"Done," Joe said, pushing the menu back. "Got anything on tap?"

"Miller, Bud, Coors," Frank said. "What can I pull you?"

"MGD," Joe said, and glanced up at the TV flickering above them in the corner. A female news commentator with overly red lips and smallish eyes was mouthing cheerily as footage of a black body bag being carried to an ambulance played in a small window next to her sickly happy face.

"You hear about this nutjob?" Frank asked, thumbing at the screen as he pulled a beer from the tap.

Joe shook his head.

"Third stiff they've found so far, and each in a different city."

"New serial killer?" Joe asked, and took a healthy swallow from the heavy pint that Frank passed over.

"Apparently." The burly barkeep shook his head and grimaced.

"If the murders have been in different cities how do they know it's the same guy?" Joe asked. The beer slid down his throat and took away the imaginary dust of a day of travel.

"Same scenario in each place," Frank said. "Real freak show. All three bodies have been found in hotels, in rooms rented by a woman with black hair. She apparently picks 'em up at a bar, brings 'em back, strips 'em and then slices their throats. The police aren't saying what else she does, but it must be pretty twisted, because they're saying each killing was done exactly the same way. When the second one happened, they knew immediately it was done by the same person. She's cutting up more 'n just their throats, I'd guess."

Frank looked away from the TV and called to the back: "Jenny! Burger and fries up!"

"I've been on the road the past couple days," Joe said. "When did this all start?"

Frank picked up a glass near the sink and started toweling it dry with the dirty rag he'd wiped his hands on a moment before.

"San Francisco," he said. "A week or two ago. Then Phoenix. This one that they're talking about was last night. Down in Austin, Texas. Poor schmuck still had some clown makeup left on his face from Halloween."

"Creepy," Joe said, and took another swig.

"Make you think twice about who you go home with after last call, that's for sure," Frank said, turning away. "Excuse me."

The bar owner shuffled into the back with a stack of glasses, and Joe noticed the old man at the end of the bar was staring at him. The guy looked at least 65, with long silver-speckled black hair matted around his ears and collar. A two-day growth of beard salt-and-peppered his wrinkled, sunken cheeks. His eyes were black in the low light of the bar, but Joe could see clearly that the man was grinning.

"They're coming," the man said, head nodding vigorously. "Oh yes," he said, getting up from his stool and moving quickly to the exit. His eyes never left Joe as his hands pushed the door open. "They're coming."

Joe's heart leapt.

"Who's coming?" he asked, but the man was already through the swinging door of the entryway. Joe jumped off his stool and went after the man, pushing through the swinging saloon-style doors and pressing his shoulder to the heavy wooden outer door that he'd come in through.

The air was cooler outside, and the handful of streetlights did nothing to blot out the velvet black sky awash with pin-pricks of light. There were a couple cars parked on the main street, but the lights in the shop windows on either side of the bar were out, and there was no sign of the old man. The breeze tickled the hair on the back of his neck.

"Who's coming?" he murmured to himself, and stepped back inside.

In his head, he heard only laughter.

Chapter Three

Ariana stepped off the St. Charles Street trolley and sighed. It was a typically hot, sticky day, but she was right where she wanted to be. In the heart of New Orleans. The center of voodoo, albeit overrun with tourists. She stepped quickly across the street and into the welcoming neighborhood of the Garden District. She had some time to kill, before she found some*one* to kill.

Her steps clicked in staccato time on the uneven sidewalk. She had ditched her latex before leaving the hotel, but was still wearing her black spike boots with the more sedate blue jeans and a black tee. While you could wear basically anything in the Quarter without drawing a stare, Ariana did not want to draw undue interest here. She'd picked up a new latex bustier with plenty of useless yet intriguing chains and zippers at Dark Entry, a fetish boutique on Bourbon, and thought she might model it for the denizens of the Shim Sham club later tonight. She'd modeled it for herself back at the hotel, and liked what she saw. Her thighs warmed at the thought of using it as bait tonight. Thinking of having a man's head nestled between her legs, unknowing of the sacrifice he was about to make, was all she thought about anymore. Which was funny, because initially, just a week before, she had never believed she could go through with it. She had trawled for weeks before finally acting. And then, just a week ago at the Cat Club in San Francisco, she'd found the perfect mark. She'd been at the club before, a curious wallflower enjoying the scent of withheld sex and unspent desire, but this time, she was there to participate. It was Sunday, and the leather-whipped crowd took over the club and acted like it was a Friday. They even staged a mini bondage demonstration on the upstairs level. The perfect spot for the man she needed to find, to begin her Calling.

She had read the passages over and over again. The ancient book was very explicit, but also very convoluted, its diction archaic and at times confusing. She wanted to get it right. There were incantations to say, and rituals to perform. Done out of sequence and the Calling wouldn't be heard.

And so, after sitting at her kitchen table and reading the chapter on Calling a dozen times, Ariana had slipped out of her business clothes from another stale day at the bank, meticulously smoothing and hanging her blouse and skirt in the closet. And then, still clad in a black silk panty and bra set, she had reached into the back of her wardrobe, behind the camisoles and fluffy white blouses and conservative black and cream-colored jackets, and pulled out her tight black leather pants. They didn't come out often, and she worried that she might no longer be able to squeeze her thighs into them. But she needn't have worried. Ariana easily slipped one long calf into the long hole of a pant leg, and then stepped in with the other, shimmying the pants up high and tight around her pelvis, until she could barely breathe. Then she pulled a filmy black mesh shirt from the same hidden spot in the back of her closet, and pulled it over the curve of her black bra. The lace edging of the bra remained easily visible, but still somewhat obscured by the crisscross holes of the cotton top, and she nodded at the revealing, teasing effect in the mirror. Reaching into a drawer by her bed, she pulled out a silver-studded black leather collar, and matching wristbands.

From her dresser, she retrieved and draped a silver cross on a black string over her head, and then poked in a pair of skull earrings. She stopped in the bathroom on the way downstairs, and pulled a razor blade from between the Tylenol and the decongestant bottles. Slipping it into the zipped pocket of her leather pants, Ariana slid into the backseat of the waiting cab.

"Clubbing tonight?" the cabbie observed, and she didn't deign to answer.

"Cat Club," she said. "On Folsom."

He took the hint, and didn't make further conversation, so she gave him a $3 tip when they got to the curb of the club.

The black lights made the white of her skin look blue, and Ariana danced in the half-empty center of the club's downstairs, waiting patiently for the space to fill with more freakily garbed frolickers before she made her way up the dark stairs, into the bondage half of the evening. A gay boy in tight leather, waist chain and a mesh top gyrated wildly in one of the cages suspended 10 feet above the black paint of the converted warehouse dance floor. Across the other side of the space, two blondes in raven leather minis and matching bras did the shimmy and dip with each other in the second cage. You could almost taste the cherry of their lipstick.

Ariana stayed on the floor, quietly swirling and twisting to the gloomy sounds of The Cure and the industrial pound of Skinny Puppy. When the DJ announced the start of the fetish parade upstairs, Ariana blended into the crowd heading up-wards, and then picked her spot at the side of the small stage. She watched as a brunette in a red mini and fishnet stockings bent over and exposed a wide, white ass to the crowd, while a dominatrix in knee-high black boots and a latex bodysuit twirled the strands of a spanking flail, and then proceeded to smack the brunette in smooth circular motions across her ex-posed behind. The woman grunted and called out at each slap, but when she turned her face towards the crowd, it was with a slack expression of ecstasy.

Ariana stepped away to order a coke at the bar and re-turned to watch a buff boy in a ripped T-shirt bend over for a workout by the dominatrix. She enjoyed watching him shiver and grip the restraints tighter with each ever-louder crack of the whip. His back soon glistened with sweat and angry red stripes covered his skin when he left the ring. A fat, balding executive type took his place, eagerly stripping down to a pair of white cotton briefs and letting his hairy white gut hang out as he bent over to accept the strap from the club's master of discipline.

Ariana stifled a laugh and shook her head, waiting for the right man. He turned out to be already standing next to her. As the fat man on the stage screwed up his lips and rolled back his eyes at the attention, the fair-haired, blue-eyed guy beside her leaned over and whispered, "I could never embarrass myself like that in public."

"Ahh," she returned coyly, "but could you do it in private?"

He'd slipped a hand around her waist almost instantly, and suggested, "I could be convinced."

That had been just a month ago. Ariana smiled as she walked confidently and alone down the sidewalk of the Garden District, remembering his first advances, and subsequent screams. He *had* been convinced. And she had paddled his ass red and raw with a rolled-up magazine, thoughtfully provided by the hotel, before she had drawn the razor across his neck and kissed him a bloody good night on the floor.

He had been her first, and he had been amazingly easy. He had allowed her to tie his wrists together, and had begged for mercy when she told him to get down on his knees with his hands behind his back. "Kiss my feet!" she had yelled when he started to look up at her.

He had thought it all a game until the spots of blood rained down on the toes. He was busy kissing, and the warm hint of something strangely amiss had made him ignore her commands and try to twist his head upwards to see what she had done. But by then it was too late. His jugular was spraying her calves with his life, and he trembled with shock and fear and confusion as she said the words:

"I call you in death, as you ravaged in life
I call you to breath, as you gasped for all strife

Your wants and needs I beg you fulfill
Your victims so near to suck and to kill

Break the veil
Come inside the earth to rule
Break the veil
Hold the heart that beats in each fool
Slip inside my mind and ride
I call thee, call thee Curburide."

Was it coincidence, or had the hotel lights dimmed as she'd spoken those words, and drawn her razor a final time across his throat, in the midst of the circle of the 16 bones, and the 21 pebbles?

She couldn't be sure of that, but Ariana *had* been sure that she'd felt the oily electricity of the Curburide's feathery kiss on her forehead, as she leaned to kiss the blood from her first victim's own lips, spotted like freckles across his face. He struggled no more and she mounted him only then, long after his spirit had fled. She rode him clumsily in a last homage to his burgeoning life, and in a calculated perversion to appease and interest the Curburide.

She'd gained their attention, she thought. But it would take more sacrifices to gain their trust. And feed their power. Ariana stepped quickly down 1st Street and admired the bougainvillea-covered brick walls and wrought-iron gates. She stopped before the long iron filigree that extended from the gate of one home, where a perfect pink rose hung on a thin, pale green branch, just in front of the gate's black bars. Two red-bricked pillars flanked the gate and a flagstone walk led towards a beautiful collection of topiaries and flower beds. The rose seemed to guard the entrance, offering both beauty and the warning of thorns.

The mansions here were beautiful, decadent, and she could almost taste the old money. She strode on easily from manse to manse, admiring the quiet formidability of them, the ageless-ness, the decaying porches and proud Grecian columns. This was old New Orleans.

Old, rich New Orleans. She breathed in the lightly scented air and smiled. Today, the rich. Tonight, the decadent.

What a feast she would have.

Joe pulled down the covers of the old, flowered comforter and stifled a sneeze. He wondered if the sheets had been changed on this bed in the past three years. He could almost see the bedbugs crawling down to the foot of the mattress to escape the light.

He'd downed his burger and beer at Brill's in record time, being the only person in the joint, and checked in at The Prescott, as Frank had suggested, just a few minutes shy of 9 P.M.

The hotel turned out to be a converted home, and the Prescotts seemed nice enough people, though Joe really didn't want to sit a spell and chat in the parlor with them. After listening to Mrs. Prescott's recipe for perfect piecrust, he excused himself and pulled the door of his second-floor suite shut, turning the old copper lock behind him. He didn't bother to unpack his suitcase, except to pull out a tube of toothpaste and his brush. He wouldn't be staying past the morning.

In bed, he followed every crack in the ceiling with his eyes, and counted the daisy blooms on the wallpaper next to him. But it didn't help. He couldn't get the words of the old man out of his head.

"They're coming."

You heard it here first, Malachai whispered in his back-brain.

"So they're coming, what am I supposed to do about it?" he whispered, the musty taste of old sheets tamping across his tongue.

Nothing at all, Malachai soothed. *Nothing at all.*

Joe considered. The spirit had stopped the incursion of the dream demons once before, if the journal of Broderick Terrel was to be believed. Joe had stood in the damp bowels of Terrel's Peak and read that tome. Read of how Broderick had bargained with a demon named Malachai to stop the Curburide invasion and save his precious coastal town of Terrel, in exchange for one blood sacrifice every year.

"How did you do it?" he whispered into the black room. "How did you stop them before?"

With hate, came the reply. *Hate . . . and blood.*

Joe slipped into troubled dreams.

Chapter Four

Austin, After Ariana

In room 618 of the Austin Marriott Capitol Hill, Jamie Gartside was also having problems sleeping. He'd had a long day, meeting with clients north of the Loop, and then a long dinner with copious margaritas at a Tex-Mex place near the arboretum. The hotel room swayed unevenly when he'd first walked in, and now the bed seemed none too stable either.

He hugged a pillow to his middle and moaned. If only Rachel were here. She could have stroked his head and whispered in his ear the way she always did when he felt just a little wonky. She would have lulled him into dreamland.

Not tonight. She was 1,000 miles away at home, taking care of Dennie, their six-month-old. And she'd be none too pleased, he bet, if she knew that he was lying here bloated and buzzed after a night of "business" partying, while she was stuck home with a colicky kid. If she had been here, she probably wouldn't have caressed his brow and whispered sweet nothings. "She would have told me to kiss her ass," Jamie muttered.

There was a noise by the window.

A scratching, clawing kind of noise. Dull, muted, but not far away.

Jamie peeled his eyes open and struggled to sober up. The window at the left let in a faint stream of moon or streetlight that brightened the shadows in the center of the room, but did nothing for its corners. He stretched out an arm towards the light, slowly, trying not to make a sound.

But he couldn't reach the switch. Not without hanging halfway out of bed.

Crrrraww. Crrraw. Crrreeech.

The noise grew louder, more insistent. It was here with him in the room. In his haze of inebriation, Jamie panicked. What if it was a rabid bat, stuck in the drapes of the room and just waiting to bite him? There was a whole flock of bats that came out from beneath a bridge in the center of town. The damn city actually advertised it as a tourist attraction, instead of killing the vile things. What if one of the dirty creatures was here, in the room with him? Just waiting for its moment to strike?

Slipping out of bed on the far side from the window, Jamie crawled to the edge of the bed and found one of his black hard-heeled dress shoes. The scratching continued, and it was definitely coming from the window. He crept quietly across the floor, stopping right in the middle of a wide, faint stain in the otherwise mauve carpet. But the floor was not his concern. He could see the shadow of something flickering there, right in the center of the window, blotting out the light from the street below. It shifted and moved, spread and contracted.

It was a bat. He knew it.

Damn if the thing was going to bite him in the middle of the night as he slept! He was not taking a 10-inch needle in the belly for a month to ward off rabies. No way. He'd kill the sumbitch first.

Jamie nodded. One good smack to the head, and it was good-bye bat, hello free room (he could imagine the manager's face as he pointed out the dead animal and ranted, "How dare you put me in a room with a rabid animal!").

Gripping the shoe tight by the toe, he tapped the heel slowly against his hand and considered. Two steps to the window, stand, and smack. Four moves, three seconds.

3-2-1.

Jamie launched himself at the gripping, waving, growing shadow in the window, and raised his arm to smash the creature hovering there.

But as he brought the arm and shoe down, he gasped.

The creature had no wings. It had no face. It wasn't really

black, but shimmery, silvery, translucent. It wasn't a bat at all. It looked like . . . a ghostly hand.

And as he landed the blow of his shoe against its knuckles, it didn't squeak or cry out or fall to the floor.

Instead it reached out and grabbed him, stretching long fingers out and bearing down hard around his neck. Jamie's eyes bugged out and he stumbled forward, cracking his head against the glass and gasping, trying to call for help.

But the glass didn't break, and the hand held fast. It lifted him up off the floor and dangled him there, as if to admire him head to toe. Then it pulled him into the invisible crack near the window that it had slipped to earth through. It had followed the Calling and found a chink in the armor of the universe there.

The hand disappeared back from where it had come, pulling its prize, Jamie Gartside, away from all that he'd ever known to someplace else. Someplace outside of this world entirely.

Chapter Five

The Quarter was already alive at 8 P.M. when Ariana set boot to cement and stopped at the start of the strip. This time, she was in full dominatrix regalia, shiny black corset cinched tight at her middle, encouraging the slinky sway of the equally skin-tight leather that bound her ass like a vise. Ariana loved the constraints of good fetish-wear, and loved the sidelong, slack-jawed looks it brought her when she stalked down the street, all obsidian-deadly curves above her dangerously spiked boots.

Bourbon Street was a hive of human activity, with throngs of walkers moving up and down from bar to bar, restaurant to restaurant. The flesh barkers were out at the front of their clubs, hooking in the unwary with promises of skin and show-girls. Farther down the strip, she could hear the cheers from a crowd gathered around one of the clubs, probably the Cat's Meow, she thought. The girls there would be lifting T-shirts and unbuttoning blouses to the cries of "show us your tits," all for the reward of strands of worthless beads. Bourbon was the Mecca for the voyeur and exhibitionist, and the coin was beads—though the girls flashing and flipping their mammaries about wouldn't have needed anything in exchange. The exchange of beads just provided a convenient, codified excuse for being bad in public.

Absentmindedly, Ariana fingered the string of turquoise and green beads around her own neck and moved forward. She'd not be earning any strands of these, tonight, she thought. She'd bought this pair in a cheap souvenir shop, determined to look at least a little the part of a tourist, despite her distinctly left-of-center outfit. Hell, even if she wanted to accede to the crass call of "show us your tits" by a crowd of frat-minded males, it would take her five minutes just to uncinch and release herself from the tight hold of her outfit. Still, she swung the beads around her neck. She had to look like she was in the right mood, even if she obviously was not a bumpkin tourist from the heart of Ohio.

She wandered the strip for an hour, swaying to the sounds of raw blues and funky Dixieland from a variety of open-to-the-street bars, and downing a frozen drink from one joint that featured churning vats of alcohol Trojan-horsed in icy swirls that bled from virtually every color of the rainbow. Finally, she turned off the main drag and sidled into the Shim Sham.

The lights in the front bar of the club were low, a strand of white plastic skulls with glowing orange lights for eyes draped in low swoops across the mirror of the bar. A stocky boy in an LU jersey sat in the corner at a round table studying an economics text, while a couple chatted up the bartender, a slim twentysomething with too-black hair, and a dozen piercings in her ears and nose. Conversation at the bar stopped when Ariana walked in, but she only nodded and kept going, paying the cover at the back door and stepping through to the wider room in back reserved for live bands and their paying audiences. Another long wood plank bar took up the whole back wall here, surrounded by a mix of tables and chairs right up to the barrier of the small stage. She bought a gin and tonic and leaned against the wall at the side of the room, out of the line of traffic. The back room was already packed, and it didn't take Ariana long to find her mark. Or, more accurately, for him to find her.

"Hey," he said. "Nice night, huh?"

He was tall, dark-skinned, ebon-haired. Wet, brown eyes. Italian, she guessed. Carried himself well, proud. Thought he was something. She ignored him, staring straight ahead. Nothing encouraged persistence as much as being ignored.

He stood next to her quietly for a moment, sipping a Shiner

Bock and stealing sideways glances. Ariana bided her time, staring straight ahead at the empty stage. The DJ was playing something industrial; the band wouldn't be on for another hour.

"You from around here?" he finally hazarded again, staring hard at the side of her face.

She fed him her profile and concentrated on the motions of a fly spinning lazily over the clouds of smoke rising from the cigarettes burning a few tables ahead.

"I love this place," he volunteered. "It's so seedy, but so much fun."

Ariana bit her tongue to keep from smiling. It was going to be a shame to slit his throat.

"I'm Ray," he said, sticking his hand out to brush his knuckles with hers.

She had to give him one thing—he had nothing if not persistence. Maybe the old saw should say persistence killed the cat.

Ariana sighed and turned to take Ray's hand.

"I'm Air," she said.

"I'd like to be breathing you," he shot back. He was fast.

"That can be arranged," she promised.

"So, you're a California girl, eh?" he asked on the way back to her hotel.

"Born and bred," she said.

"I'm looking forward to breeding you myself," he grinned, and she shot him a dirty look.

"Be nice," she warned.

"Okay, okay," he said, looking sheepish. "Vapid pleasantries. I can do that. Let's see . . . what do you do for a living?"

Ariana grinned, and rubbed his thigh.

"These days," she said, "I travel a lot."

"So you're here on business?"

"Sort of. What about you?"

"Real estate," he said. "My company owns some buildings down here. Home is Cincinnati. I'm here 'til Wednesday, doing management reviews, process evaluation, you know, paper-pusher stuff."

He looked away from the road, directly at her, with clear, naked intent.

"How long are you in for?"

"I'll be leaving in the morning," she said, and watched his face fall a little.

"Then we'd better make tonight count."

"Oh, I intend to."

He talked fast, but he learned slow. Ariana had him naked on the floor, wrists tied behind his back and had begun invoking the Curburide before he began to get nervous.

She hated to sacrifice this one, he was so dumb, and yet so cute. And hung. She licked a lip as she stared at the burgeoning tool between his legs, but mentally shook her head.

There would be time enough for that. Time enough to sit on all the men she could ever want.

"Um, are you some kind of voodoo queen or something?" he asked as she whispered the invocations, kissed the floor at his feet and then stared up at him through heavy lids.

"Something," she agreed, moving closer. She could see him testing the strength of the rope around his wrists. Trying oh-so-hard to be unobtrusive.

"Baby," she whispered in his ear, "I am *something* else. I'm your worst nightmare."

"Ugh," he said, a look of shocked surprise spreading across his face as the circulation suddenly changed course from his brain to his lap. He was seated in the center of her stone and bone circle, in a Sheraton this time, and with just a flick of her hand, he was suddenly bleeding all over his most prized possession.

Ariana felt a small bit of remorse over that. It *was* a fine prize to behold, though it lost a bit of its cocky pride when the warm rain of Ray's heart began to drench its mushroom head in hot, salty blood.

His eyes bulged like poached eggs when Ray saw the dark pelt of his well-toned belly and groin suddenly painted in spurts of crimson, and felt the white-hot slit of Ariana's razor release the veins and muscle on the other side of his neck seconds after the first cut.

He was so shocked by her attack that his first instinct wasn't to fight, but to question.

"Why?" he gasped, but she punched him in the forehead with a balled fist and then straddled his head, holding him to the floor with her legs scissoring his gouting neck and her crotch smothering his cries for help. Her legs felt warm and slippery, and his legs kicked and thrashed behind her, trying to unseat the scissor of her thighs. But she would not release her grip, and in moments, Ray went from breathing her in to not breathing at all.

Ariana looked behind her, when the body was finally still, and her heart fell as her worst fear was realized. The night truly had turned into a downer.

Not all corpses stay stiff when their lives bleed away.

She stripped off her latex and lay down next to him, the blood pooling warm against her skin, and tried to imagine what it would have been like to ride him. Her fingers slipped easily into the wet cleft of her sex and as she looked at the slack, bloody penis lolling against the dead man's thigh, she moaned. She'd never, ever know. Her breathing quickened and she found herself humming an old favorite as she built toward release.

"It's a shame about Ray," she murmured and then squeaked a gasp of pleasure as her fingers grew sloppy wet. When the tremors subsided, she bent over the corpse and kissed the cooling lips.

"I might like you better if we'd slept together," she giggled. Then with her fingers she drew a large red X over the corpse's chest in his blood. Then she reached for her razors and set to work.

Chapter Six

Sagebrush and sepia can make for a lulling combination when the horizon unrolls in an endless procession of same. Especially after a night of very little sleep. Joe was an hour into Colorado on I-80, but fighting to stay awake. The sky was a sleepy gray, and the dead grasses bordering the highway trembled and shook in his wake. No Doubt was on the radio, barely rising above the static of the plains, reviving a disco groove. Joe wasn't dancing.

Stifling a yawn, he slapped a hand on his left cheek, and then did the same to his right, a little harder. Would've looked funny to anyone watching, but nobody was tailgating him. The pain kept him alert.

"Damn," he mumbled, and peeled his eyes open, staring hard at the horizon, searching for mountains.

He wanted to direct Malachai to make him stay awake, but the demon would no doubt interpret the command in a way that would ultimately be unpleasant for Joe. While the creature was bound to do his will, if there was a loophole in the commission of that will, the demon would find it. The first time Joe had tried to benefit from the powers of his "genie," he'd been at home, thinking of how much he didn't want to cook. Finally he'd said, "Malachai, get me a good ham for dinner."

A moment later, he'd heard the angry release of aggressive air, and turned around just in time to avoid being gored by a wild boar in his own kitchen.

Somehow, after dodging behind table, couch and end tables, and eventually ripping open the patio door and standing aside, he'd managed to free the furious, angry beast and save his own life in the process.

"How could you do that?" he'd asked the demon afterwards. "You promised not to hurt me, and you nearly killed me."

The demon had laughed wickedly inside his ear.

I didn't hurt you, I gave you what you asked for. A good ham. Believe me, if you'd just killed the beast, you would have had the best ham you've ever tasted.

"Yeah, well, the beast almost killed me! You're not supposed to hurt me," he'd complained, and again the demon chuckled.

I didn't do anything but give you what you asked. If the pig had gored you, it wouldn't have been my doing.

Joe had quickly learned that if there was any way the demon could misinterpret his wishes in a way detrimental to Joe's health—without actually directly causing him harm, of course—then the spirit would jump at the opportunity.

Joe was far better to Malachai dead than alive.

He thought back to the time when he'd first told Cindy about his new symbiotic relationship with her former captor and she'd questioned his veracity.

"Show her that you're real," he'd said to Malachai. Instead of materializing, the demon had levitated Cindy in the air, holding her by one foot and allowing her head to dangle over the bonfire they'd built on the beach. She'd screamed in pain and Joe had leapt across the fire, bowling her out of the air to land both of them in a tangle in the cold sand.

Joe didn't ask the demon favors anymore, unless he was desperate. And had thought out his questions very, very carefully. And for the most part, the demon left him alone.

You just gonna pass by? A familiar voice grated in his head.

"Huh?" Joe asked, and then saw a flash of yellow pass by the car on the right.

If you were paying any attention to the road, you might have noticed a kid hitchhiking back there.

"What, are you my mother now?" Joe replied, kicking his foot out at the brakes and sending the car into a slaloming skid.

I wouldn't claim you as any bastard of mine.

"Screw you," Joe mumbled, and looking into the rearview mirror, began to back up towards the hitchhiker behind them.

You would if you could, Malachai promised. *You don't seem very picky. I recall a certain mother AND daughter that you couldn't keep your hands off of . . .*

Joe ignored the bait, and focused on the reflection of the teenager in a yellow smiley face T-shirt and too-large blue jeans that was growing larger in his rearview mirror.

He couldn't be sure under the baggy clothes, but he thought it was a girl. She had a navy blue knapsack over her back and a baseball cap on her head, rim facing the wrong way. He stopped the car, and rolled down the passenger window. The kid leaned over and looked inside.

"Can I hitch a ride with you, mister?" Her voice lilted above the drone of the engine, and Joe had no doubt as to her sex.

"Depends where you're going," Joe said, a little apprehensive about picking up a hitcher, no matter how innocent this kid may have looked. The cardinal rule of journalism was to distrust everyone—if your mother told you something, check it out. The cardinal rule of the street was trust no one if you don't have a gun. And right now, Joe didn't even have a rusty nail file to protect himself if he was ambushed somehow.

"Denver. Or at least a few miles closer. It's a long walk."

"That it is," Joe admitted.

"You mind some company?"

Joe considered the fact that he'd almost gone off the road a couple times in his struggle to stay awake, and finally shrugged. The last road sign he'd seen still said more than 100 miles to Denver.

"Get in."

The kid tossed her backpack in the backseat, and slid into the shotgun seat with a smile.

"Thanks, mister. I've been walking for days, it seems."

"Where you coming from?"

The kid blanched.

"I don't think I should tell you that."

Joe shot her a glance.

"If I tell you, you can always call back there and tell people where to find me. If you don't know, you can't send me home."

There was some intelligence to that. Joe let it be. For now.

"Can I at least have a name?"

"Oh, sorry," the kid grinned, showing two buckteeth and a spread of freckles in the process. She held out her hand. "I'm Alex."

"And why does a kid called Alex, from Somewhere, U.S.A., want to hitch to Denver?" Joe asked.

"Actually, I'm going beyond Denver," she said. "I'm headed up into the Rockies."

Joe looked the kid over again, taking in the pug nose and freckled skin, and the curly red hair struggling to escape its confinement beneath her hat. She looked no more than 15, and hardly seasoned enough to go hiking alone in the mountains. Maybe he could help. Or at least wheedle out some more information so that he could call someone who could.

"Buckle up, then, my girl. We're heading to the mountains!"

Alex grinned, and settled back in the seat. After a minute, she stared at the radio, currently pumping out an old slab of Deep Purple. She reached around the seat and dug a hand inside her backpack and Joe froze, split between watching the road and watching what she was pulling on him.

"Do you like Blink-182?" she asked, and he let out a breath.

"Go for it."

His road trip suddenly had a lot more noise to it.

Chapter Seven

Joe regarded the girl next to him from the corner of his eye and wondered if he was doing the right thing. He hadn't carried her over state lines, and wouldn't, even if he took her with him all the way up to the Rockies. But should he be helping her at all? What if there was an APB out on her, and the police picked him up? Would they accuse him of kidnapping? Aiding and abetting?

"So what are you running from?" he asked at last. After smiling her way into his car and taking over his CD player, the girl had clammed up, staring out the passenger's window in silence.

"Does it matter?" She looked at him with suspicion. "You don't have to care; I won't bother you. Just let me ride with you, huh?" She held her arms across her chest as if to form a protective coat.

"I think it does matter," he said. "What's up?"

"If you don't want me in your car, just say so. I'll walk."

"Whoa, whoa," Joe said, stifling a laugh. "I didn't say that. I'm just trying to figure out *why* you're in my car. Is that so strange? I mean, I pick you up in the middle of nowhere, alone and underage. Seems like I'd be an idiot if I didn't gather a little information."

She glared at him a moment, then shrugged.

"You really wanna know? I'll show you."

Alex clutched her yellow T-shirt at the waist with both hands and pulled it up, exposing the thin slit of her belly button and the clearly defined lines of her ribs. Joe could see the white of her bra strap and the bottom of a cup as she lifted the shirt up over her face.

"Hold on," he said, suddenly feeling the blood rise in his face.

"Just look," she said. "Look at what they did to me."

She twisted in her seat so that he could see her back, its creamy, freckled skin marred by long stripes of ugly maroon. There were spots between and over her shoulder blades that were a blend of scabs and angry red raw flesh; a little infected, he guessed. Lower, near her waist, the weals graduated to light pink welts, instead of swollen furrows.

"Been working on the chain gang?" he asked.

She snorted.

"Yeah. Chained by a gang at my daddy's feet," she said. Alex pulled her shirt back down and sunk into her seat, careful not to meet Joe's eye.

"So you packed up and said, 'I'm not taking this anymore'?"

"Pretty much."

"They'll be looking for you."

"I don't think so."

"Parents don't usually give up that easily," he said. "Especially if you spit in their eye when you left."

She shrugged, and Joe caught the slight grimace of pain that accompanied the motion.

"Look," he said. "If your parents put the cops on your tail, and they find you with me, who do you s'pose is going to take the heat?"

"They won't find me. They won't find you. Just don't worry about it."

With that, Alex twisted away from Joe, staring again out the window.

He decided not to press it. For now. But Denver was a couple hours away, and the Rockies an hour beyond that. If she camped with him tonight, there'd be time to find out the rest of the story.

Joe nodded and stepped on the gas a little harder. The white lines blurred to a solid dash behind him. The girl stared out the window, volunteering nothing more.

He pulled in for gas at a BP station in Loveland, and Alex finally broke the silence.

"You'll take me all the way up into the mountains, right?"

Joe nodded.

"Would you wait for me here then? I want to run over there to the drugstore. I'll be back in a minute."

"You're not going to rob it or anything, are you?"

She shot him a dirty look and said, "Just don't ditch me, okay?"

With that, she slipped out of the door and ran across the parking lot to a Walgreen's.

The credit card reader on the pump was broken, so Joe had to pay inside after filling up. He grabbed a couple bottles of cold Coke and a bag of potato chips, and was just walking back to the car when he saw Alex hurry out of the Walgreen's with a bag. She was out of breath when she slid back into the seat next to him. He could see her visibly relax.

"That was quick," he said.

"I didn't want you to leave without me."

"I wouldn't have."

"I couldn't be sure. And I don't know where we are."

"Does it matter? You're a couple hours from home, for sure." As he said that, Joe realized he really didn't know how far Alex had come from. Was she from a small farm town on the border of Nebraska, or Colorado where he'd picked her up? Or had she hitchhiked halfway across the country?

She shrugged.

"Tell me this much," he said. "How long have you been on the road? If your parents were to set the cops out looking for you, would they have gotten a call yet?"

"I left yesterday," she said. "But don't worry about it. Just get me to someplace that I can change clothes and stuff"—she held up the bag—"and you'll have nothing to worry about."

"We're not far from the base of the mountains," he said. "I

figured on finding a camp area and pitching a tent. It's not a big tent, and I've only got one sleeping bag and some blankets. Up to you if you want to keep going with me, or head out on your own. You can probably find someone else to tag along with here in town."

Alex scowled, the lines of her face twisting in obvious fear.

"Take me with you?" she pleaded.

Joe bit his lip. The kid obviously needed some help, but in just a couple hours she'd gone from belligerent self-reliant road tramp to dependent. She was obviously scared to death of being left behind. But he didn't really want a tagalong right now. Let alone a "wanted" runaway. If she'd been gone overnight, the police had to be looking for her by now. Still, it wouldn't be long before they could disappear into the deep, rolling forests of pines that hid ravines and rivers and cabins and humans, indiscriminately.

Joe turned the key and put the car in gear.

"All right," he promised. "We'll see where we end up for the night."

It was amazing how fast the Rocky Mountains switch from being hazy bumps on the horizon to looming hills of jagged rock and evergreen dead ahead. Joe had been watching them grow from fuzzy faraway ghosts to grandiose monuments for the past three hours, but now, suddenly the road was rising, and the flatlands were disappearing.

"Welcome to the mountains!" he proclaimed, and Alex gave a slight smile. She was still clutching the bag she'd bought at the Walgreen's tight in her hand.

"Coke?" he asked, offering one of the bottles he'd bought at the gas station, and she accepted with a mumbled thanks. The car filled with shadows as the trees thickened on either side of the car, and in moments they were both staring in awe at walls of rock that enveloped the road. CAREFUL, FALLING ROCK, a sign warned, and Joe wondered how you could possibly be "careful" about a falling rock. If it came down off one of these craggy boulder-strewn hills, you were either going to be crushed or lucky. Nothing you could do would make a difference. You sure couldn't hang a left or right turn to avoid it—you'd either hit a solid wall of stone or plummet off the edge of a cliff.

The engine strained a bit as the incline increased, and soon they were driving round S curves in the hills, following a stream that crashed and frothed over a long strip of boulders. "Welcome to the land of sky blue water," Joe said out loud, thinking of the friendly bear from the old TV beer ads, but Alex said nothing. He wondered if she even caught the beer commercial reference. Did they even make Hamm's anymore?

They were only a half hour or so into the mountains when Joe pulled the car off into a gravel-packed lane. A round wooden sign hung from one of the tall pines near the main road advertising: ELMA'S CAMPGROUND AND CABINS. A vacancy sign was tacked to the bottom of the main sign, and he guessed if the cabins were open, some camp space ought to still be free.

"Let's try here, huh?" he said, and Alex gave a by-now familiar shrug. He shook his head, pulled up in front of the weathered log cabin office and killed the engine.

"Wait here," he said, and slid from the car.

Elma was a rotund bear of a woman, one of those Amazons with a larger-than-life personality and a hoary mass of silver hair to match. Joe thought her steely hair looked rough enough to use as wire.

"How can I help you?" she trilled as he entered the cabin guarding the start of the campgrounds. She moved from behind the pine-log counter to extend a meaty hand.

Joe shook thick sausage fingers and asked for a spot to set up a tent.

"Oh we've got those. Plenty of those. But wouldn't you rather take one of our cabins? Only twenty dollars a night more, and I can guarantee that the mattresses will be softer than your sleeping bag."

"That's not promising much," Joe joked, but she didn't take it as humor.

"You questioning my facilities, young man?" she said,

voice raising quickly. "You think you can find a sweeter cabin in these here hills?"

"No, I only meant . . ."

Elma doubled over. "I was just kidding, boy. My cabins are crap heaps." She laughed until her breath came in wheezing gasps. Finally, she straightened up and slapped Joe on the shoulder.

"Those cabins probably got more bugs inside 'em than the ground outside," she said. "You take your tent and set up wherever you like past the sign that says 'camping'—just down the path out here."

She pointed farther down the lane that Joe had followed to get to the campground's office.

"I'll just say this," Elma said, lowering her voice and leaning conspiratorially closer.

"Your tent may be cleaner, but my cabins are safer. You watch what you do with your food tonight, or you may be sleeping with a grizzly by morning."

She slitted an eye at him and nodded. "And that's no joke, believe you me. Had a fool here just last summer who left his dinner pots out by the fire and his scraps in a bag by the back of the tent. Had a five-hundred-pound black bear sniff out those leftovers and put his claws right through the tent looking for more. Guy lost an eye before one of the other campers got wise and fired off a couple shots. Bear took off back to the woods, but that camper . . . well, I'm guessing he never looked at things quite the same again, know what I mean?"

Elma scratched the wide round shelf of her ass, tarped over in loose dungarees, and then stepped back around the stand to the cash register.

"Tent camping, then, eh?" she said and hit a couple buttons on the register. "That'll be . . ."

They drove back into the woods, following an increasingly narrowed, rutting path until the motor homes, tents and clearings that held them became few and far between.

"Far enough," he announced and pulled the car off underneath a tree. Alex helped unload the trunk without complaint, and by the time the sun was throwing deep orange shadows across the tops of the pines, they'd set up the tent, tested the large lantern and smaller flashlight, laid out the sleeping bag and a couple of blankets Joe had kept in the car just in case, and gotten a small campfire going within a ring of fist-sized rocks. Alex enjoyed tossing in the dead pine needles to see the fire flare. Her orange kinky hair glowed brighter in the flare of the fire and the deepening hue of the sun.

Joe finished pulling out canned goods and fire-scorched pots from the trunk and sat down next to her with a grunt.

"Alright," he said. "I think we can survive a night or two here, provided it doesn't get too cold. Or the bears too hungry."

She lifted an eyebrow at the latter comment. "You've got more meat on you than me, so I'm not worried."

"True," Joe nodded, stroking his chin in thought. "But younger meat is usually sweeter."

"And faster." She smiled. "They'll never catch me."

"Speaking of which," he began, but suddenly Alex shot to her feet.

"I almost forgot—I wanted to change and rinse off before dark. I'm going to run back up to that building with the showers, okay?"

"You want me to drive you up?" he volunteered, but she shook her head. "I wouldn't mind the walk. It's pretty here."

"I'll cook up some victuals while you're gone," he said, holding up a couple red and white cans. "Do you prefer beans and pork, or pork and beans?"

"You decide," she grinned, and retrieved her backpack and Walgreen's bag from the car. "I'll be back."

"Is that a promise or a threat?"

She stood in front of him and raised both of her eyebrows, flashing an evil grin. Then she turned and started walking back down the red-rutted path towards the front of the camp-grounds.

Joe used a portable can opener and emptied a tall can of pork and beans into one of his camping pots. Then he dug out a small can of corn and poured that into a second frying pan. He set both pans at the edge of the stack of burning wood that they'd scavenged from the woods around them. The small sticks and arm-sized logs wouldn't burn for long, but they'd cook the food and warn away wildlife until it was late enough to turn in.

He lay back with his hands behind his head and stared up at the sky. The smoky scent of burning pine colored the air, but still he could taste the freshness of the breeze here. It had a crisp tangy scent, flavored by the woods and the fresh water streams that ran from the peaks to the base of these mountains. He could see the white globe of the moon hanging at about 10 o'clock in the still-blue sky. He traced the dark spots and craters with his naked eyes, wondering how they'd formed. He wondered if once, the moon had held the same amazing breadth of trees and crystal clear streams around those craters as the earth held now.

He daydreamed that the moon held wicked spirits in the bottoms of those craters, spirits that just waited, in patient malevolence for men to come along and stir them up, as he'd stirred up the sadistic evil of Malachai in the base of Terrel's Peak.

None of my breed, whispered the demon in answer to Joe's silent speculation. *But perhaps the Curburide call the dimension beyond some of those dead lakes and frozen marshes of the moon home. From there they could lie in wait, peering through the shadows alert for the call. The invitation to come through to this side. From there they could launch a bloody expedition to wipe the earth clean.*

"Cut the crap," Joe growled. "If you've got something useful to tell me about the Curburide, spill it. Otherwise, shut your invisible trap."

Malachai laughed.

When Broderick Terrel made his bargain with me to keep the Curburide at bay, he had very little patience as well. He was lucky I liked him.

"And you don't like me?" Joe asked.

There was no answer. He let it lie, and sat up to stir the corn and beans. They were crusting and bubbling on the sides of the pans facing the fire, and cool on the outside. Joe knew he should hold them over the center of the fire, but had no idea how long Alex was going to be. It would only take a few minutes to thoroughly heat both in the center of the flames. He hoped she hurried; the sun was nearly set and the cerulean sky surrounding the moon had darkened to a deep ocean blue.

He laid back and watched the moon grow brighter, ignoring his demon. After a few minutes, he closed his eyes to rest.

The voice startled him out of a fuzzy half dream of Cindy, running like a young girl around the merry-go-round at the park. She was laughing at him, and daring him to jump on the moving ride. He only waited and shook his head, hands in his pockets.

"What do you think?" the voice asked, and Joe jumped a little, shaking his head awake and snapping open his eyes.

"Uh?" he said and pushed himself up on his elbows.

There was a girl in front of him, and she looked familiar. But she didn't look like Alex. The orange curls had been replaced by a mass of jet-black ringlets, and the baggy dungarees with tight brown suede pants. Instead of the yellow T-shirt, she wore a long-sleeved shirt with trailing, flouncy wristlets, and a low-buttoned front that proved the girl had breasts to bare, regardless of how young she might be.

"Uh," he said again, and she laughed.

"Better?"

"I guess," he finally said.

"If anyone's looking," she said, "they're looking for a redhead. And a redhead who always dressed in baggy clothes and baseball caps. I picked up this shirt and some dye and makeup at Walgreen's."

She twirled around, modeling for him.

"I've never looked this good!" she laughed.

"Oh come on," he grinned. "I'm sure you've dressed up before."

"Never wanted to," she shrugged, and dropped to the ground next to him. She cocked her head towards the fire and observed, "You're burning the corn."

The smell of burnt food finally registered in Joe's nostrils and he swore as he pulled the pots back from the edge of the fire and stared at the blackened mush that was caked on the far edge of each of them. "Damn."

"I've got a candy bar in my bag," she offered.

Alex took the pans down to a stream just behind their tent and rinsed them out after dinner. They had managed to salvage enough of each vegetable to stave off the worst of the day's hunger pains, though even the nonblackened corn and beans tasted burnt.

"I never burn stuff," Joe had moaned, and she just laughed.

"I'll cook tomorrow," she promised. "But we've got to pick up something besides corn and beans."

"Deal," he said.

While Alex rinsed the pots, Joe gathered some more branches for the fire, though it was slow going. The woods had been picked clean of any logs small enough for him to manhandle, and he hadn't brought a chain saw to cut up any of the fallen trees that were too big to crack a piece off of. He imagined the rangers would be out in force anyway if they heard a chain saw going near the national park.

When he'd set a store of small branches and twigs next to the tent, and stoked up the flames until they were a couple feet high again and white-hot, Alex returned to sit next to him. She looked older, now, he thought, than when he'd first seen her, in backwards cap and loose clothes. The makeup, he supposed. And maybe the hair. He liked it black—the color was a shock against her otherwise light skin, but in a good way. He didn't dare say anything though. It occurred to him that if she was found in his tent, there'd be more than just a kidnapping charge leveled against him by the likes of her parents. The thought made his stomach turn.

"What are you thinking?" she asked, after a bit. The sticks

crackled and popped in the fire, sending sparks up to disappear in the dark blue sky.

He's thinking how much he'd like to strip you naked and push those cute little shoulders to the ground, Malachai said in his head. Joe ignored the intrusion.

"I'd still like to know what happened to you," he said. "Where you're from, how you ended up on the side of the road, why you had to dye your hair . . ."

She turned away from him, and got to her feet. Sticks and dried grass crackled beneath her tennis shoes as she walked to the edge of the tent and looked out into the pitch-black shadows of the tree line just a few yards out.

"I don't think it's an unfair question," he added.

Alex didn't move for a minute. When she did, her profile seemed to glow in the flickers of the fire.

"I'll make you a deal," she said finally. "I'll tell you my story, but you've got to tell me yours. You're not out here just on a vacation or something, I can feel it."

"Deal," he said.

"One more thing," she demanded, walking back to the fire.

"What's that?"

"We make a pledge to keep each other's secrets."

"No problem."

She reached into her pants pocket, and pulled something out. A small red pocketknife. She flicked a blade open, and slid the edge across her palm before handing the knife to him.

"We pledge in blood."

Chapter Eight

The ring was growing wider now, and she could feel her strength increasing. Soon, she would be able to draw the final razor and with the blood of her final victim, close the knot to open the door.

With every kill, Ariana felt her power increase, and the gap between the worlds grew more transparent. As she stared at the walls in the hotel rooms she killed in, she could see them fade sometimes, and see the movement just beyond. Shadowy, indistinct. But growing stronger. The Curburide were out there, waiting. Their hands reached out to her, their faces begged for release, going in and out of focus like the gasp of an unborn baby in the hazy sights of an ultrasound. She could hear their whispers in her sleep.

"Soon," they promised. "We will be yours to command. You will be ours to love."

Sometimes she felt the hair at the back of her neck and the top of her forehead move, as if a cold hand had given her a glancing caress. When she closed her eyes and focused, she could see their fading hands pass across the air before her. Waves and kisses from the other side. Soon, as she drew her net wider, and dedicated more sacrifices to them, she would grow powerful enough to speak with them directly. To see and touch and hold them. To bring them through the veil at last.

After the first kill, she'd experienced an awful doubt, the kind of stifling claustrophobia that left her balled up and crying on the floor, sure that the entire world was watching, and laughing at her foolishness. She *knew* that the police would be at her door at any second, and would find the blood of the Cat Club Bondage-a-Go-Go boy under her nails.

She had trembled there on the floor, imagining how they would track her from a stray hair left on the body, and haul her into a maximum security jail for her crime. She would have gained nothing, would have lost all. And still would have no hard evidence that her beloved Curburide were any more than the figment of a medieval cult's imagination.

She imagined explaining to them that she was only following the direction of an ancient book that explained how to call the spirits of the afterworld to her command. Ariana had stayed balled up on the floor of her living room all night long that night after her first kill, imagining the laughter of the police. They would stand, a ring of fat, pasty men with facial hair and balding pates, in a circle around her in the sterile white interrogation room, trading barbs at her expense.

But on the day after her first kill, as she lay still crying and immobile in her apartment, wondering what had become of the body she'd flayed in the hotel the night before, the sun had slowly risen, and the street noise grown in its usual cadence before fading again at the end of the day. And the sun had set without any officers coming to her door.

And when she finally stood and rubbed the crusts of salt from her eyes, Ariana had stared at her television and her gut had unknotted along with her smile.

A message had been written in the dust covering the slate gray glass of the slumbering set. It was barely visible in the fading light of sunset, yet its intent was clear.

"Forge the chain," it said.

"The chain," according to the ancient text, was a string of six murders, ritually performed in six cities from one end of a nation to its other. The final victim was to be a person of some spiritual consequence, who had communion with demons, and should be sacrificed in a place of power on the highest hill or near the sea.

It hadn't been hard to plot out the six cities. Since she lived in San Francisco, her path took her across the Southwest and would end up on the East Coast at the Atlantic. The problem had been to find a "person of some spiritual consequence" who could be sacrificed on a hill.

"Thank God for the Internet," Ariana smiled, pulling on her latex gloves in preparation for a night on the town in Tallahassee.

She knew roughly where her string of murders needed to end. She kept the map with her at all times, with its red circles plotting out the locales of her past and future kills. But while her first five murders could take the blood of anonymous strangers, her last kill had to be someone special. How to find that someone special was the problem. Her coup d'état had to be a person of some power and connection.

Ariana had done searches for metaphysical phenomena centered around the East Coast and joined a dozen newsgroups and discussion groups on the Internet related to witchcraft and demonology, looking for someone of "spiritual consequence" who lived in the vicinity of that last red circle; someone who would be an appropriate victim.

In the end, she found exactly who she needed through a Yahoo chat room. A girl who had been possessed by a spirit just a few months before. Ariana hadn't actually chatted with the girl herself, but the girl's brother had proven most informative. He even bragged of having found a book about a covenant struck with that very same possessive spirit, a hundred years before. The boy's name was Ted, and he lived in a town near the Atlantic, at the foot of a seaside cliff.

A town called Terrel.

Chapter Nine

Once the sun goes down in the mountains, the glow of the stars can be almost blinding. The tongues of the fire flickered against the dull blue tarp of the tent and the windows of the car, but its light quickly died a few yards in any direction. And not far beyond its reach, the forest began, a tall stand of heavy primeval pines that reached like black pillars into the sky. Overhead, the canopy of black velvet was sprinkled with white dots and murky clouds of star clusters and galaxies a million light years away.

Joe leaned back and sighed, feeling the cold, hard bumps of the earth digging into his back and butt, though he didn't mind the inconvenience. He'd trade a comfy couch for this in a New York minute. He was out of it. Away from it all. And while he had company in his escape, and the resultant worries that brought, his heart was the calmest it had been in weeks.

Alex sat on the other side of the flames, her face shimmering orange with the reflection of their crackling tongues. She held a long stick, and poked it into the heart of the embers now and then, stirring the sticks to flare up and burn brighter. She still held a tissue to her hand where she'd slit the palm to invoke a blood promise. Now she was keeping her end of the bargain.

"I'm sensitive," she explained, raising her eyes from the fire to gauge Joe's reaction. They looked black instead of blue in the shadows. "And I don't mean, like, crybaby sensitive. When I was little, I used to always tell my mom not to step on the man, and she would freak out."

"The man?" Joe asked.

"Yeah. I could see people who weren't there. Old shadows, ghosts, I don't know. But I got nervous 'cuz my mom always seemed to be pushing them and stepping on them. They never said anything or complained, but I thought she ought to watch where she was going. At first, she thought I just had a big imagination. But she could see how I would walk down the hall or through the kitchen or wherever, and suddenly swerve to walk around something. Something she couldn't see. After awhile, it started to creep her out, and she'd spank me for lying."

" 'There's no one there,' she'd say, and paddle my butt with a wooden spoon until I agreed with her."

"Was it just in your house that you saw these people?"

"Oh no—I saw them everywhere. At church, in the store. The world I lived in seemed a lot more crowded than my parents' world! There were some that I could barely make out, and others that looked almost solid. And some I only saw once or twice, while some of them hung around all the time. There was a girl named Stacy who came around a lot in my backyard to play on the swing set with me."

"So they would talk to you?"

"Some of them. But there were others that didn't even seem to see me."

Alex stared into the flames and her voice dipped lower and lower as she talked about the ghosts.

"Do you still see them?" Joe asked.

"Yeah," she whispered. "But not unless I really try. After awhile, my mama spanked me every time I said I saw someone who 'wasn't there' and so I started trying *not* to see them."

"Do you think she believed that you saw something?" Joe asked. "Or was she just afraid of what she knew you were tapping into?"

"Oh, she knew I saw something," Alex affirmed. "She was scared to death of it, too. You have to understand, my parents were strict Baptists. It was all about work and worship with them. And they didn't want a daughter prone to flights of fancy. Mama managed to keep the whole thing a secret from my dad for a long time. He was always working in the fields during the summer, and in the winters he'd hire himself out as a handyman as often as possible. So if he wasn't caring for our own crops and animals, he was miles away, helping with someone else's. Raising the kids was woman's work, and a girl child wasn't what he was interested in anyway, so he didn't pay that much attention to me early on.

"I remember one of the first times I mentioned the others to him. I must've been about four, and he was actually sitting in the parlor, reading the newspaper. One of the house's regular ghosts, an old man named Jack, was leaning over my dad, staring at the newspaper over his shoulder. I was playing with my dolls on the floor, and I kept looking at my dad and giggling, because Jack's face was right there next to my dad's, only fuzzier, less distinct. And Jack kept reaching for the edge of the newspaper, trying to turn the pages himself. My dad was reading the news and business sections, and Jack wanted to get to the sports section."

" 'What are you laughing at,' my dad said after a while, looking at me over his bifocals. 'I'd like some peace and quiet to read the paper, young lady.'

"I wasn't afraid to tell him exactly why I'd been laughing. 'Jack is looking over your shoulder, Daddy,' I said. 'He says he wants to know how the Cardinals are doing. What are Cardinals, Daddy?'

"My dad's face got white. 'Cardinals are birds. Who's Jack?' he asked.

" 'He's a nice old man, Daddy,' I said. 'You should say hi.'

"My dad didn't think any of this was at all funny. 'Carol!' he yelled, and my mom came hustling around the corner from the kitchen. 'Your daughter seems to think there's a man named Jack living with us. Would you care to tell me what's been going on around here while I've been away?'

"My mom was pissed. She balled up the dish towel she had in her hands and pointed upstairs. 'To your room, Alexandra,' she said. 'Now.' I remember the whole thing so clearly. Because that's when the bad times really started. I grabbed my Barbies and ran up the stairs. But I could still hear my parents. I heard my mom saying something about me 'seeing ghosts' and my dad asking 'how long has this been going on' and 'when were you planning to tell me?'

"I didn't realize how much my momma had been protecting me until that day. But from that moment on, if I made any mention of the people who shared our house with us, or stepped out of the way of a ghost that no one else could see while we were out in town, at the store or whatever, my dad showed no mercy. He grabbed me by the shoulders, bent me over his knees and paddled my ass with his hand or anything else that was convenient.

"'We will have no witches under this roof, do you understand, young lady?' he'd say. My momma didn't do anything but stand there and watch. I hated her for that. But I got really good at hiding what I saw from both of them. If I said or did anything that indicated I'd been talking to or playing with the others, I got a beating. And so I only talked to them in my room after dark. Sometimes my friend Becca would come to me then, and play dolls with me. And afterwards, she'd climb in bed with me and help me go to sleep."

Alex looked off into the darkness of the woods, her eyes shimmering with tears. "I haven't seen Becca in so long. Not since the exorcism."

"Exorcism?" Joe asked. "Your parents actually brought in a priest to banish the spirits?"

"Not a priest," she said. "My dad did it himself. He was scared to death that someone else would find out about his daughter, the witch. He couldn't imagine that the ability to see ghosts could be anything but evil and the ghosts anything but demons. So he bought a book about demonology and exorcisms, and one night, when I was sitting in my room, playing dolls with Becca, he slammed open the door and stomped into the room.

"'Are you talking to one of them?' he asked, and his face was beet-red angry. 'Don't you dare lie to me,' he warned, and

I nodded. Becca started to cry next to me, and I reached out to pat her on the shoulder, even though I couldn't feel her. 'Don't you touch it, child,' he yelled, and grabbed me by my hair, yanking me to my feet. My mom appeared behind him in the doorway, but as usual, she didn't say or do a thing. My hair was really long back then, and he held it up in the air for her to see, motioning at it with his free hand. It felt like he was going to pull it all out by its roots, and I began crying and clawing at his arm to release me.

" 'This is the culprit,' he said, pointing at the orange knot of hair sticking out of his fist. 'I read it in the book. Witches can be known by the orange of their hair and their frequent conversations with the invisible. You have birthed a witch, woman.'

" 'She's just a child,' my mom finally said in my defense, and he just snarled at her. 'Get the book. We are going to rid our house of her demons right now.'

"My momma disappeared and came back a minute later with the book. My dad didn't let go of my hair the whole time, and Becca clung to my leg and kept saying, 'I'm sorry' over and over. 'Get the white candle,' he demanded, 'and the vial of holy water.' He asked for a bunch of things, and when my momma had brought them all, he shoved me down on the floor and demanded that I stay there. Then, with his foot on my chest holding me down, he began saying a bunch of funny-sounding stuff from the book, Latin I'm guessing now, and waving the lit white candle around the room. When he reached the end of the words, his face seemed to grow larger and larger to me, and his voice boomed through the room. I'll never forget what happened next.

" 'In the name of the Lord God Jesus Christ, I command all those spirits who lack the anchor of flesh to leave this place, never to return. From my house I banish thee, from my life I banish thee, from all corners of the earth I banish thee. I command thee to release your hold on this mortal coil and follow the road you've strayed from back to where you belong. By the name of the Lord Jesus Christ, I banish thee to hell.' "

"All around me I suddenly heard the most unearthly screams and screeches, and I saw Becca rise up from the floor into the air, her mouth open wide and her eyes rolling back to white. She was growing hazy and stretched, almost like a wax candle that has begun to slide and melt. Her screams filled my head and deafened me, and I screamed out myself. Then she was gone, and the rest of the house fell silent and my father slammed the book shut.

"'Are they gone?' he asked. I was crying harder and rolling up into a ball, but he yanked me off the floor by my hair again. 'Tell me the truth,' he yelled again. 'Are they gone?'

"'Yes, Daddy,' I said. 'You killed them.'

"He smiled and nodded at my mother, but now I really began to cry in earnest.

"'You killed all of my friends,' I screamed.

"He grabbed me with both hands by my waist and threw me into my bed. 'From now on you play with real friends, and not these devils,' he said. 'I find another devil in my house, and I'll do to you what I just did to them.'"

Alex stopped talking, and Joe studied her face as she wiped away tears from her eyes and looked down into the flames. It was a wild story, but given his own tale, he couldn't completely doubt her. It was also a troubling tale in a way he couldn't completely put his finger on. What were the chances that a man haunted by a demon would pick up a hitchhiker plagued by ghosts?

"So you never saw Becca again?"

She shook her head. "Nope. Or Stacy or Jack. Or any of the others that had kept me company around the house and backyard for years. My house was like a prison to me after that day. There was no one to talk to, no one to play with. I still saw ghosts when we went shopping at the supermarket, or walking along the roadways in town, but I was careful never to talk to them. I knew my dad would kill them—and me—if he saw me talking to them. So things were pretty quiet for a couple years."

"You still see them, then?" he asked.

"Sometimes," she said. "But I've learned to block them out. Lately there's only been one that I've talked to, and most of the time, until recently, I could only hear him."

"You can't see him?" Joe asked. "Isn't that a little strange?"

"I couldn't see him before, because he was far away," she said.

"But you can see him now?" Joe asked, propping himself up on an elbow.

Alex nodded. "Yeah," she said. "He's standing right behind you. His name's Malachai."

Gotcha, a voice laughed in Joe's head.

Chapter Ten

Jeremy Bruford raised his third Scotch and soda to his lips and inhaled. There was nothing on this earth as goddamn good as the smell of a Dewar's. There were finer Scotch's, to be sure, but for a daily drink—or daily double—his bet was on a Dewar's over ice, touch of tonic, and *pow,* instant hit to the brain.

And he needed the hit. Jeremy sold spark plugs for a living. Not door-to-door, obviously, but to garages and lube shops and auto parts stores. And Jeremy didn't work for Champion, so it wasn't an easy sell. Nobody wanted to stock another generic spark plug. But every new client whose arm he twisted into giving Neutron Sparks a shot earned him another dollar that Sheila could use at the mall.

And Sheila liked to shop.

They all liked to shop, he knew. But Sheila . . . geez. He'd come home and find a whole new set of dishes on the table, just because she thought they looked "neat."

"I was buying Janie some shoes," she'd say, "and I found this really neat—" fill in the blank and empty the bank. She didn't stop. His house was bulging at the seams from Sheila's purchases.

And lately, when he'd come back from the road, he'd found a new twist to the scheme. Sheila had been getting some new jewelry. Some gauzy black and red outfits. Some expensive bottles of wine that he found empty in the trash on Wednesday nights when he was home to take out the bags.

Interestingly enough, Jeremy's credit cards showed no record of Sheila's more personal shopping sprees of late.

He wanted to ask her if the guy was giving her the gifts on his own, or was she just sleeping with him on commission, and taking the cash straight to the store herself.

Instead, he was here at the bar, downing his third Scotch and betting with himself whether she'd be at home when he got there. Last night she'd still been wearing a black dress when he'd gotten in, a little early, from a road trip to Cincinnati. She'd been surprised to see him, and definitely a little nervous.

He'd been too tired to care, but in retrospect, he should have done a panty check, he realized. That would have shaken her up.

But that would also have brought it all out into the open, and Jeremy was nothing if not good at ignoring things. Like the girl wearing black latex next to him. She'd been nursing a gin and tonic for the past half hour, shiny elbow lying just centimeters from his own, and he'd not even bothered a half-hearted hello.

Maybe Sheila had let all the air out of his tires. If she was going to spread it around behind his back, he was certainly entitled to do the same. But he couldn't even bring himself to stand up at the starting gate to try.

Not that the filly sitting next to him wasn't worth the effort. She was sleek, trim, and obviously, from the toe-to-wrist covering of her shiny black skintight suit, which perfectly molded around the flattened globes of her breasts, a little wild. Her face was pale and smooth, her makeup just heavy enough to accent her features, but not enough to overpower them. Her nose was almost hawk-thin, but small, and her lashes looked long and full. Mascara works wonders, he thought, but even so . . .

She caught him staring sideways at her and the slightest of smiles took hold of her lips. Her left hand moved to touch the button on the wrist of his shirtsleeve.

"Buy a lady a drink?" she whispered.

Jeremy's heart leaped. Hadn't he just gotten through telling himself that he was too tired to even try anymore? And here was a girl who'd piqued his interest, apparently showing . . . interest?

"Name your poison," he choked out.

"Sex," she whispered, and then laughed at the look on his face.

"Oh, you meant to drink." Her voice was cool, high. Just a hint of roughness when she dropped it to a whisper. Pat Benatar meets Lindsay Lohan.

"I'll take a gin and tonic," she said.

Jeremy gave her order to the bartender the next time he came around. The woman clutched his arm and leaned to his shoulder.

"Thank you, good sir. You've saved a thirsty lady."

"Thirsty for what, though, is the question," Jeremy spit out, aghast at himself that he could even dare to play at words with a stranger like this.

"Hmmm," she said, raising a thin black eyebrow and rubbing a hand down her ribs provocatively.

"Methinks I've played my hand too early."

Jeremy thought of his wife, probably straddling her sugar daddy right now, maybe in his own bed. A cloud fell across his eyes and he shook his head and stared intently at the woman.

"I don't want to play any games," he said. "I've played enough lately. I know this is uncouth and you'll probably walk away from me as soon as I say it and I'm fine with that if you do."

She stared at him cooly, without expression.

"Tell me what you want," he continued. "If you want a free drink, fine. You're a pretty lady, and I'm happy to buy you one. If you're looking for a pickup, I might be interested. But tell me up front what you want. I don't have the patience for games right now."

The woman in black arched an eyebrow, but didn't smile. Her drink came, and she lifted it to her lips, without taking her eyes off Jeremy. She took a sip and replaced it on the bar.

"I want to take you back to my hotel and fuck you to death," she said finally. "No games."

"Finish your drink," he said. "Then we'll go."

They didn't say another word until they left the bar.

"What's your name?" he finally asked, on the way back to her hotel. She sat primly in the passenger's seat, both hands creamy white against the midnight of her thighs.

"Air," she said. "You?"

"Short for what?" he prodded.

"Ariana."

He nodded, as if that meant something.

"I'm Jeremy. I've got a wife and a kid, in case you're wondering. I'm pretty sure she's fucking around on me when I'm not home."

"So that makes it alright to pick up a woman like me in a bar."

"Not at all," he said, glancing at her as they pulled up to a stoplight.

"I just don't fucking care anymore. You look hot, you were looking for someone to get off with, and frankly, I'm intrigued. I wasn't looking, wasn't even in the mood 'til you showed up."

"Will she be hurt if she finds out?" Ariana asked.

"Not as hurt as I was," he said, and pulled into the parking lot of the Radisson.

He opened the car door for her, and held out an arm to escort her into the hotel. She smiled, a little bitterly he thought, and wrapped her hand around his thick forearm as they stepped into the bright blue-tiled lobby and walked across the thick carpet to the elevators.

"I'm on fifteen," she said, and he pressed the button, leaning back against the car directly across from her.

"I'm starting to feel fifteen," he said. "Are you sure you want to do this with a grumpy, balding auto parts salesman from Tallahassee? You could do a lot better."

"You're what I want tonight," she said, and led him from the elevator to 1511. She slipped her key card through the slot and then slipped into the bedroom, motioning him to follow.

Jeremy watched the muscles flex in her ass as she walked across the small hotel room and pulled the drapes shut. She was a piece of ass. The nicest he'd ever gotten near, truth be told. He looked down and saw the chubby links of his fingers, covered with coarse black hair. He wasn't fat, but he sure as hell wasn't in shape, and he hadn't been exaggerating in the elevator about the balding part. He didn't have to cover his dome with three strands of doubled-back greased hair yet, but the roof was getting mighty thin.

What did she see in him that she could be interested in bringing him back here? She was worth seeing naked, no question. But why would she want to see him that way?

"Why don't you take off your clothes and get comfortable," she said. "I'll just be a minute."

With that, she disappeared into the bathroom. Presently, he could hear the water running, and Jeremy stripped off his tie and shirt, tossing them by the wall on the floor. There was a ring of pebbles and small bones between the bed and the easy chair against one wall, and Jeremy bent down to pick up one of the shiny pink stones.

"Don't," a voice said from behind him.

Her fingers wrapped around his waist from behind, and he shivered at the cool touch of her latex as it slid across his skin.

"That's my prayer circle," she explained in a whisper. "Before I make love, I always say a prayer there. I find it makes the whole experience . . . so much more fulfilling. You don't mind, do you?"

Jeremy turned to face her, and shrugged. The strange part was that a sexy woman would drag him back to her hotel. The fact that she prayed in a circle of rocks, was hardly as bizarre.

"Just as long as you say a prayer or two for me," he hazarded.

"Oh, I will," she said. "I promise. In fact, why don't you strip all the way down, and I'll pray with you now."

Jeremy smiled, and undid the clasp of his belt. She was a weird little minx, no doubt. He unbuttoned his pants and let them fall to his feet in a heap. Then he stepped out of those and pulled down the elastic of his white underwear.

"That's it, baby," she encouraged. "I want you in my prayer circle with me, in the altogether. That way you can be purified before we fuck."

Flake, Jeremy thought, but what the hell. If Sheila was busy bumping some other fool's balls, he might as well enjoy this strange little piece of ass. Definitely something different.

He laid down on the floor, and Ariana stood over him, black crotch positioned over his face as she raised both her arms to the ceiling.

"I call upon all the forces of the other side," she announced. "I call upon you to witness. Curburide, I beseech thee. Taste our lust, taste our blood, taste my need for you tonight and come."

She dropped to her knees, the smooth stretch of her ass slipping along the length of Jeremy's quickly hardening cock.

"Who are you praying to?" he asked. "Doesn't exactly sound like an Our Father."

"God is passé," she grinned, and leaned down to give him a peck on the lips. She tasted warm and earthy, and smelled of gin.

"I worship the demons called Curburide, and our sacrifice here will help to bring them from their imprisonment beyond the veil of our dreams, to manifest here."

"Sacrifice?" he asked. "I thought we were going to have sex?"

"Isn't every sexual conquest also a sacrifice?" she asked. "In taking a woman, don't you also give up something of yourself?"

"Yeah, I guess so," he said. He could feel his cock deflating at the left turn this seduction had taken.

"Every time I take something from a man who has come to have sex with me, I give something of myself away, too. I give it to the Curburide, and they grow stronger."

"So, you fuck guys to strengthen some spirits?" he asked.

"Something like that," she said. "They hear my prayers and taste the blood. And soon they will be able to join me here." She reached into the small pocket sewn in the back of her catsuit.

"What blood?" he asked.

"Yours," she replied, reaching down with the razor she'd retrieved to slice Jeremy's neck.

"Fuck that!" Jeremy yelled, and punched her hard in the head as the blade bit into his neck.

Ariana fell to the side, taken by surprise, and Jeremy leapt up from the floor, holding a hand to the side of his neck. In seconds, blood was leaking out from between his fingers, but he didn't stop to assess the damage. Instead he kicked Ariana in the stomach, and then in the face, catching her full in the teeth. Pain shot through his foot, but her head snapped back on the floor and she cried out, rolling to the side as he kicked at her again, missing this time.

"You bitch," he screamed. "What kinda fucked-up freak are you?"

Ariana moaned, watching Jeremy through slitted eyes. He raised a foot to kick again and she flipped herself sideways, and continued to roll until she was on the other side of the bed from him. Then she forced herself up into a crouch, and showed him the razor.

"Fucking bitches are all the same," he said, advancing on her despite the weapon. "Take a guy for all he's worth and then bleed him dry."

"I'm not like the rest," she gasped. "I would have made it go fast."

"Not as fast as you're going to go," he said, and punched her hard in the chest.

"Ugh," she gulped, and dropped to her knees.

Jeremy kicked her in the thigh, and then punched her hard in the face. He felt a tooth through her lip, and smiled when he saw the blood running down her chin.

"Fuckin' sick of being taken," he said, and grabbed her with his free hand by the hair. She moved to bring the razor around, but he took his hand away from his neck and grabbed her by the wrist, squeezing it hard.

The blood made his grip slick, but he held on tight as she struggled.

"Drop it now," he said, and she did. The blade fell to the pink floral-patterned comforter on the bed, and Jeremy laughed.

"Cat's not so dangerous without her claws, is she?"

Rage overwhelmed him. Jeremy had locked in a lot of emotions over the years, especially over the past six months. Ariana suddenly was more than just a crazy with a razor. She was everywoman. She was his boss, who raised his quotas even though the entire market was down. She was his wife, fucking every guy in town but him.

He grabbed both of her wrists in one hand and with the other sucker-punched her in the stomach.

"I'm . . ."

He hit her again.

". . . So . . ."

He slapped her in the face, the sound echoing through the room like a whip crack.

". . . Sick . . ."

He grabbed the black length of her hair and used it to throw her against the wall like a rag doll. He could feel his cock growing erect in spite of himself.

". . . Of . . ."

He walked over to the woman, her face beet red and swelling from his blows. He put his foot on her crotch.

". . . You . . ."

And put all his weight on that foot, so that he could kick her in the ribs.

". . . Cunts . . ."

Ariana curled up in a ball, crying in horrible gasping sobs, but Jeremy didn't stop. He grabbed her again by the hair and forced her to her feet.

"Strip," he said. When she didn't move, he slapped her again in the face.

"Now!"

She wheezed in fast, sharp gasps, but tried to reach around behind her back to grab at the zipper. Her hand stopped short, and she cried out in pain.

Jeremy flipped her around by her shoulder and yanked the zipper down himself.

Tears and blood streaming down her face, Ariana peeled the vinyl from her body, at last standing hunched and naked before the man who was supposed to be her victim.

He put his hand under her chin and raised her face to look at his.

"You look as good as I thought you would," he said, admiring the pink knobs of her nipples and the tight, flat plane of her belly. With his other hand, he ran a fingernail between her breasts, and down to the short dark triangle of her sex.

"You picked the wrong guy tonight, honey," he said. "I've been pushed around one too many times. You pulled the last straw."

"It wasn't personal," she whispered.

"Neither is this," he said, equally as soft, but with a tone of steel. "But now we're gonna do what we came here to do."

Chapter Eleven

"You set me up!" Joe said out loud, as he stalked around the edge of the campsite, looking for a semihidden place to let loose. The demon answered by singing in his head:

Matchmaker, Matchmaker, make me a match . . .

"What's your deal here?" Joe railed, crying out to the still, black sky. "What is she supposed to do to me? Or make me do?"

Find me a find, catch me a catch . . .

Joe unzipped a few yards to the rear of the tent and sent a stream out to water the ferns in front of him.

"I'm serious, Malachai. Tell me why you brought us together. What's going on?"

I'm in no rush, maybe I've learned. Playing with matches, a girl can get burned . . .

"Malachai!" he hissed through his teeth.

"Please don't be mad," she said from behind him.

"Give a guy some room, huh?" he asked.

"I'm going to need to do that myself in a minute," she said. "Should we keep it in the same place? Do bears get attracted to that?"

Joe's stomach grew cold. He hadn't thought of that. Maybe he should have pissed farther from the tent.

"I'm not sure," he said. "But that's not a bad idea. Hang on."

He shook himself, adjusted his underwear and zipped up.

"Right over here," he pointed, and she stepped past him.

"Please don't go far," she said. "I . . . I'm a little afraid of the woods."

"I'll stay right here and turn my back if you want."

"Cool."

Tinkle, tinkle, little star . . .

"Malachai!"

Alex announced she was done, and the two walked back to the campfire. The flames had died down to orange embers, and they threw the remaining sticks and twigs on the center. A yellow tongue guttered to life again, and Joe rubbed his hands as close to it as he could without burning. The night was turning chilly.

"Tell me about you," Alex said, after a minute. "Tell me about the man who follows you."

"Hasn't he already told you everything?" Joe said in a tone of sour lemons.

"Please don't be that way, Joe. You're wrong about Malachai." She shook the too-black ringlets out of her eyes. "He hasn't told me anything about you. And almost nothing about him. He was there for me when I was in pain, that's all. He talked to me, helped me get through it. And when I finally escaped from my parents, he told me where to go. He said if I walked down I-80, a man would come along who would help me. A nice man. A man who would understand. As soon as you pulled over and I saw him sitting in the seat next to you, smiling, I knew I'd found you."

Joe grunted. "So you can see him, huh?"

"Sometimes," she said. "He's not always very clear. But it seems like he's been pretty near, most of the day. I didn't say anything before because I wasn't even sure you knew about him."

Joe let out a rueful laugh.

"Oh I know about him alright. We're joined at the brain."

"Tell me about it?" she begged.

"All right," he conceded. "Fair's fair. What do you want to know?"

"I don't know," she said. "Start at the beginning. Where are you from? Why are you here? What are you running away from?"

"That obvious, huh?"

She shrugged, and leaned in closer to the fire.

"Most guys aren't driving up to the mountains in the middle of the week, all alone except for an invisible passenger. They've got jobs. And families."

"Well, count me in for neither at the moment. I walked away from my job last week, not to mention two different women, either one of whom would have been happy to start a family with me. Just so happened they were mother and daughter."

Alex's eyes widened. "No way!"

" 'Fraid so. Thanks to my good friend, Malachai. A couple years ago, I had a good job in Chicago, working for the *Tribune*. I was doing a lot of exposé stuff, thought I was a real hotshot, fresh out of college and breaking page-three stories. When one of those stories ended up busting my fiancée, I kinda got sour on the big-city newspaper business, and so I hopped in my car and headed out to the East Coast. Found a little town called Terrel right on the ocean, and signed on as their one full-time reporter. It was a little boring after Chicago, but I got used to it. And then this kid committed suicide from the cliff outside of town. At least, everyone said it was a suicide. I started to wonder when the editor didn't want to report on it at all, and so I started asking around. Turned out that there had been a lot of jumpers from that cliff. I mean *a lot*. So I put on my big-city reporter hat again, and started looking through the old newspapers and stuff to find out what was up. It was really weird. Every year around Halloween, for as far back as I could go in the newspaper morgue, there was a report of someone falling to their death from the cliff."

"Spooky," Alex said.

"It got worse. Over the past few years, there had also been 'jumpers' nearly every spring. Now the Halloween deaths had usually been out-of-towners, for the most part. But the recent deaths—those had all been kids from the town. And the weirdest thing was, the mothers of these kids had all been swimming in the bay like 20 years ago, when one of their friends turned up dead."

"Whoa."

"I got to be friends with one of the mothers, a woman named Angelica, and she told me about this spirit that lived in the cliff. She said the thing wouldn't let her or any of the women leave town. Turns out, they'd all had to pledge to sacrifice their firstborn children to the spirit in exchange for their own lives. That spirit was Malachai."

A low chuckle flooded Joe's head, and Alex raised an eyebrow.

"He's laughing," she observed.

"He's got a very bad sense of humor."

"So what happened? How did he end up following you?"

"Well, it turns out, Angelica was the one woman in the circle of friends who hadn't sacrificed her child to Malachai when the kid turned eighteen, as she'd promised. Instead, she'd given the baby up for adoption to save it. And until her kid was sacrificed, the bargain Malachai had struck with the women when they were eighteen remained unfulfilled. So the other women in the group basically kidnapped Angelica and tied her up in a cave underneath the cliff, trying to torture her into telling them where to find the child. In the meantime, I'd been trying to find out the same thing through a contact I had in Chicago. It turned out that Cindy, the girlfriend of the last kid who jumped off the cliff—the one I wanted to write a newspaper article about—was actually Angelica's daughter. And the two of us had gotten pretty friendly, because she'd been helping me research the deaths and the history of the cliff and all that."

"So you got involved with this Angelica, and then with Cindy, and then found out they were mother and daughter?"

"Pretty much. Totally weird. Anyway, Cindy and I found this old entrance into the bowels of the cliff underneath what used to be the town's old lighthouse. I found this journal down there that talked about how an old lighthouse keeper had made a bargain with a demon to protect the town from an invasion by these other demons, called the Curburide. The demon—Malachai—agreed to protect the town for one-hundred years in exchange for a sacrifice. That's why the townspeople didn't want me playing up the whole suicide thing in the paper. Not that most of them knew anything about the pact, but they were used to death at the bottom of the cliff. They'd all grown up with it and didn't see anything at all abnormal in someone turning up in the bay every year."

"So, how did Malachai end up attached to you, though?"

"Well, it turns out that our friendly demon had outstayed his welcome. When I added things up, I realized that his one-hundred-year covenant was over, and the bargain he'd struck with the five girls for their firstborn was not a fair bargain at all—he coerced them into it. I found Angelica down in the caves below the cliff, along with the other women, and basically had something of a showdown with Malachai, who for a little while, even managed to possess Cindy. Since he was unbound, and I knew his true name from reading the old journal, I was able to bind him again, this time to myself, and I got him to set both Angelica and Cindy free."

"Sounds intense," Alex said. "But you won. Why did you leave them?"

Joe shrugged. "Cindy wanted me to stay. But it just didn't feel right. Every time I was with her, I could feel Malachai behind me, looking over my shoulder at her. He knew every inch of her, and I could feel how much he wanted to own her, if only for a few minutes, again. In the caves, he'd totally possessed her, and she'd been ready to kill or do . . . anything at his command. I couldn't stand it that every time I was with her, he was that close to doing the same thing to her again."

"But he's locked to you," she said. "He has to do your will, right?"

"Until he can find the right loophole, yeah."

"Why would he want to leave you if your covenant is all that lets him stay here?"

"Because he didn't get anything out of our covenant except the deal to stay. No sacrifices, no perversions, no weak-willed master who he could run like a puppet. If he can get rid of me but have someone nearby that he can cut a better deal with before he's forced to return to his own realm . . ."

Joe stood up and walked to the car to retrieve a bottle of water.

"Had enough for one night?"

"Yeah," she said, yawning and stretching. "Even the hard ground sounds comfortable right now."

"Good," he said. "Cuz I'm beat." He poured the water slowly over the glowing embers, which had long since given up the ghost of flame. The glowing hunks of wood hissed and sizzled, sending up a cloud of white-hot mist to the sky. By the time Joe had emptied the whole bottle on the coals, the fizzing and hissing had all but died out.

"It's really quiet out here," she observed. The hum of crickets buzzed all around them, but outside of the bugs, the night was still.

"I can almost hear my own heart beating," he laughed.

"Yeah."

Joe took a deep breath and stared up at the sky. Could some evil force called the Curburide really be struggling to find a way through that velvet curtain to rend and kill?

Yes.

A shiver took his spine, and Joe ducked through the tent flap to find the flashlight. His fingers found it, after fumbling in the dark for a moment, and he set it to shine at the ceiling.

"All right," he called. "Runaways get the sleeping bag."

Alex poked her head through the flap and smiled.

"So you're sharing it with me?"

"Very funny. It's yours."

She thanked him and shed shoes and socks. He did the same, and looked the other way as she unzipped her pants and shimmied them down her legs.

"I can't sleep in pants," she explained, quickly slipping her feet into the bag and pursing her lips in a raspberry "burrrrr."

"Me neither," Joe admitted, and doffed his jeans keeping his back to her, and then pulling the top blanket up and over him.

"You should sleep close to me," she said after he turned the flash out. "Body heat."

Joe grunted, feeling an uncomfortable stirring at the thought.

But after a minute or two of cold toes and teeth that were beginning to chatter, he pulled his blanket closer to the girl's heavy, down-filled bag.

He slipped his feet under the edge of her bag and his shoulder under the edge of its top. The warmth of her arm soaked through to him, and he relaxed, the uncontrollable shivering of his teeth slowly abating.

"Good night," he murmured.

But her breath had already slowed to the deep, steady rhythm of sleep.

Chapter Twelve

The book was very old. So old, in fact, that Ted was afraid to turn its pages. Every time he did, pieces of the yellowed paper would crumble and fall off on his desk. A lot of the pages were stuck together with mold and dampness, and he didn't know what to do to pry them apart—the paper was so deteriorated, he was afraid of ruining a dozen pages at a time if he tried peeling one back. Maybe, he thought, if the book sat in his room for a few days, where it had to be a lot drier than the damp cave he'd rescued it from, some of the pages would dry out fully and become easier to manage.

Regardless of the chunks of the journal he couldn't read, Ted had learned a lot from the pages that he could.

He'd learned about an old lighthouse keeper, Broderick Terrel, who wrote late at night as he watched ships steer by the light of his tower to avoid the needle-sharp fingers of rock that extended up in the shallow lengths of the bay. He'd learned that Broderick liked to spice his tea with a healthy dose of "spirits" to keep the cold of the cliff winds at bay. He'd learned that Broderick had a soft spot for one of the altos in the church choir down at St. Agnes and that Broderick fancied—just once—to turn the light in the wrong direction and guide one of the ships from Raleigh straight into a keel-shredding stand of limestone.

But most importantly, he'd learned that Broderick Terrel had a bad feeling about the things that were beginning to happen on the beach. He'd seen figures slipping up and out of the sand in the purple hours of twilight. He'd seen crabs march together in armies to set upon and disembowel a beagle that had made the unfortunate choice to go trawling the beach one night.

Broderick knew something was up, and he paid more attention than ever. Soon he was seeing ghosts pass through the upper stories of the lighthouse at dawn, and eyes staring down at him in the dusk from clouds.

He started waking in the night from the laughter.

And it wasn't just dream-laughter. There were no houses for miles down the road that led to Terrel's Peak and the lighthouse, but Broderick was soon being awakened every night by cackling, giggling, guttural laughter. And screams.

He woke every night with his heart pounding, and his forehead awash in sweat.

Broderick decided that he needed help. But when he'd gone into town to ask for help at the "house of God," the parish priest only patted his shoulder and said to lay off the sauce. And maybe come into town more often. The lighthouse was driving him batty, the minister said, nodding his head sadly.

Broderick did come into town. He took out every book in the library on spirits, witchcraft, the occult and more.

Mrs. Parkside kept looking at him over the top of her glasses as she checked each title out.

"How're you doing, Broderick?" she asked.

"Fine, just fine," he insisted and disappeared back up the road to the lighthouse with his treasure.

That night, as he poured over a volume on the five castes of demons, a cool hand passed over the pages of his book. He looked up and a figure stood next to his desk, its hair coiffed in a genteel sway that slid down its back, and its face looked as smooth as a boy's.

"What do you want?" he whispered, seeing the ripple of the fire in the fireplace through the creature's snowy white robes.

"We're coming," it said, and with a grin, it vanished.

"I did not believe that anything good could come from such a visit," Terrel wrote in his journal. "And yet, I did not know of any means at my disposal to prevent the being from tor-turing my days and nights with its obscene presence. I stood at the window after its visit, a cup of spirits in hand, and watched the white crash of the waves on the shore below. I could swear that figures walked down there in the freezing cool of the surf. But such figures as to send the chill of win-ter into a man's bones. Women that glowed and advertised their nakedness like beacons, yet the dark algae of the rocks shown through their perfect bodies. And the men. I watched them gather in circles and twirl and dance like children, only to stop, grab one thing or another from the beach and vanish.

"Every night, the procession seems to grow, until now, as I stare down at the edge of the deadly surf, I can see a village of the naked, cavorting ghosts shimmering and showing them-selves for a moment or an hour before winking back out into the glow of moonlight from which they came."

Ted kept the book hidden beneath his bed, so his parents and his sister wouldn't find it. But every night, he brought it out to the desk and teased its pages open to continue the story of the old man in the lighthouse. The man who suffered from visions of ghosts on his beach.

Tonight was no exception. Carefully he turned to where he'd left off the night before, and leaned close to the tight, faded script. The musty smell of the book sometimes made him sneeze, but that didn't keep him away.

July 8, 1893:
They mean us no good. I can see that now. In the past, I've seen them run down a dog using a pack of crabs. But tonight I saw them attack a man.

He was strolling along the beach after dark. I did not recognize him from my post at the top of the lighthouse, but I saw his form walking close to the surf. He appeared in no hurry, but neither did he stop and stand. The ghostly village was alive on the shore, dancing and darting in a cloudy cabaret. The man seemed not to notice the rest, as he blithely walked among them, stepping through their silvery forms without pause. But then something strange happened. The frolic of the beings began to wane, and soon they were all standing still, silent glowing sentinels all along the beach. As the man strode unaware into their midst, walking among and through them, they also began walking towards him.

Soon there was a bright mob of the creatures all moving up the beach, destined to meet him. It was as if the light of the stars had all gathered in a fog that walked with legs and arms down Terrel Beach.

As I watched in horror, the man's gait began to falter and he slowed. Soon a thick crowd of the ghosts surrounded him, and the man stood still, looking right and left. Still he didn't seem to see the beings that clawed at his face and chest, but he could feel something was wrong. He sniffed the air like an animal, trying to determine the cause of his malaise, and then I witnessed the strangest thing.

He began to remove his garments.

They were guiding his hands. The ghosts were so thick, I could barely see the man anymore, but I could see the dozens of hands wrapped around his own, guiding him to strip naked. He was aroused, that much I could tell even from the air, and I saw the beings kneel at his feet and wrap their arms around his chest from behind. His head lifted back, and he let out a long, loud call to the moon with his open mouth.

And then, they began to herd him towards the waves. Their hands all pushed at his back, and held his ankles, lifting and pushing, guiding him into the angry night surf. I yelled for him to stop, but it was too late. His feet were already covered in the black saltwater as I ran down the stairs to try to stop him.

When I emerged on top of the cliff, he was gone. In the moonlight I could see the pile of his clothes, and the dark shadows of his footsteps that led to the bay. And I could see the twining, dancing mob of the evil creatures twisting and cavorting at the point where he'd entered the water.

But the man was nowhere to be seen.

First they took over the sea crabs. Then they took apart a dog. Now they're taking our own. They seem to grow stronger and more dangerous by the day.

Soon they'll be coming for us all.

Part Two:
Dangerous Liaisons

The Curburide thirst for human blood, it is true. But it should never be forgotten that blood is of secondary importance to these demons. Those who have tried to invoke the Curburide by sacrifice have met savage, shocking deaths before ever leaving the circle of the Calling.

It is no accident that some early sects of Gaelic druids actually worshipped an icon of a Curburide demon named Omenad. This demon was invoked at each of their ritual ceremonies, where they sacrificed a virgin to guarantee another year of fertility in the region's crops and livestock. But the key aspect of the ritual was not, in fact, the sacrifice of the girl, but rather the sexual intercourse performed with her by all of the members of the sect, both prior to and after her disembowelment. According to some texts, the virgin had to give herself to the druids freely for the sacrifice to appease the demon. There has been some indication that both men and women belonged to this violent Curburide sect, and that a communion of sexual fluid and sacrificial blood was the ultimate consummation of the ritual.

The Curburide demon thirsts, first and foremost, for sexual perversion. The blood is the frosting, not the meat of its meal.

—Chapter Three, *The Book of the Curburide*

Chapter Thirteen

Ariana woke to pain. She was still in the hotel room, in the bed, and her jaw throbbed. It felt like when she'd had all of her wisdom teeth pulled. And her neck ached. There was a stabbing feeling when she tried to roll over. She reached down to touch her ribs, to see if anything was broken, and realized that she had no control over her arms. Ignoring the awful blinding fire in her neck, she craned her head around and stared up at where her arms disappeared over the pillow.

Her wrists had been tied above her to the headboard. A faint trace of light was trickling through the sides of the window drapes, and in the murky shadows, she could just make out the sleeping form of the man next to her. It all came back. The bar, the easy pickup and the release of an anger more violent than her own.

She had been so stupid! He was the most burly of all the men she had picked up so far, and the only one she hadn't managed to disable quickly, fatally, before he even knew what was going on. She'd gotten too confident, too careless. And now she was paying the price.

Damn. It would be too comical if it all ended like this. Her early fears that the cops would get to her before she forged the last link in the chain were bad enough, but this was worse. A killer never let her mark get the upper hand.

Jeremy stirred, his breath suddenly sputtering and uneven, and Ariana held her breath. She wasn't ready for him to wake yet. Every muscle in her body screamed for her to move, to turn, to breathe. But Ariana waited, and after moving an arm to the side and shifting his head deeper into the pillow, Jeremy stilled.

Closing her eyes, Ariana drew in a quiet breath and then willed herself to relax. Her arms threatened ice-hot pins and needles, but she focused her energy on reaching out.

Reaching out with her mind.

She had twice now seen the ghostly faces of the Curburide peering at her from the air as she completed her rituals after sacrificing her victims. The last time, in Austin, she'd felt the moist, cool brush of a silvery hand slip across her brow as she'd moved the knife from side to side and then cleaned it by swiping each side on the dead man's palm. The excess blood had sluiced off the blade and trickled down his fortune lines to pool in the well of his hand. He looked as if he'd been crucified.

They were out there. And they were watching her. Urging her on. Eager for her to reach the finish line.

She pushed with her mind, trying to see through the black sheath of her closed lids, and her internal night pulsed to flecks and clouds of red and rust and gold.

Curburide, I call you, she bellowed inside her brain. Her lips formed the name and sent its silent syllable over and over again into the gloomy shadows of the rented room. The screaming bruises and tortured muscles faded into the background as Ariana emptied her mind of everything but her Calling, her prayer.

Curburide, I need you, she begged. In the furthest corner of her mind, she felt a stirring, and she fed its interest, reliving the careful slaughter of each of her victims. Her inner eye grew bloody red and the whispers began.

Curburide, I love you, she pledged, and imagined their shadowy forms positioned above her, astride and beside her. They anointed her in the foul rot of each man she'd killed, rubbing the brown remains of crushed testes and dried mucousy sperm on her forehead. In her mind's eye she kissed the stained hand that reached for her face. A calm overcame her as she tasted its decayed offering, a communion between her and the other realm. A fleeting, disintegrating host of dead and disappearing flesh that bound her to the mortal, and promised her the future of the incorporeal.

She took its insubstantial fingers between her lips, pursing them and widening them to take the entire hand of the spirit inside her.

"I am yours," she whispered. "I serve you. Tell me what to do now."

The taste of salt and iron suddenly flooded her mouth, a warm broth that tasted both like seawater and blood that caught in her throat and warmed her belly as she gulped it down. Her limbs seemed to tingle, and she could feel a wetness growing from the valley between her legs. Her body seemed on fire, floating and burning.

Ariana opened her eyes, and gasped.

A man hovered in the air above her. Half a man. Only his face and torso were visible, and even those were faint. His shirt hung loose about his long, lanky frame, and seemed to shiver and sway in the air like a flag billowing under a moonlit storm. But his eyes were wide and black, and his silvery hair hung like the well-brushed, slightly curled mane of a horse; his insubstantial shoulders touched her chest. She could feel prickles of icy electricity spark where his ghostly hair trailed in feathery touches across her body. But the center of energy came from his skeletal fingers, which reached out and stroked their tips across her open lips. With each touch her mouth and lips felt more swollen and her throat more heated and thick.

"You came," she whispered out loud.

The creature showed a row of dangerously sharp and blinding white teeth and brought its other hand out of where it had rested—in the limbo of somewhere else—and into the room to caress and massage her hair and her forehead. She almost leapt upwards to meet its touch. Every slight connection with him was like kissing a battery. Her brain was suddenly flying, exulting in a high better than any toke she'd ever inhaled. All the pain and fear and aches of her battered body faded, replaced by a silent ecstasy.

She moaned and the creature lifted a finger to its lips.

That's when she saw the others.

She—and he—were being watched. The others were hazier, seemingly farther away, less distinct. But they were there in the room, watching. They hovered beyond his slim shoulders, most only showing a faded face or sometimes an entire head or maybe only the hint of a glowing eye in the farthest shadows of the room.

They had come for her. To nourish her. To save her from her own foolishness.

The Curburide. It was all real. Every word she'd memorized, every book she'd tracked down, they had all hinted at this. And they hadn't lied.

If she hadn't fully believed it before, the flickering wraith covering her body was the final evidence she needed. They were out there, waiting for her to bring them all the way over. It took power. That's probably why even the most visible of their number wasn't fully revealed. His legs disappeared into a line of blackness in the air above her. And the rest could barely show more than a face on this side of the veil.

"Forge the chain," the spirit demanded. From behind it, the rest of the Curburide echoed its command.

"Forge the chain," they said, in ghostly unity.

"But how?" she cried, a tear running down her cheek. "I can't move."

"Forge the chain," the creature moaned again, slow and distinct. It pulled its nourishing finger back from her mouth, and she saw its translucent white caste had deepened to a crimson stain. It leaned down out of the air and pressed lips to her forehead and her body jolted and shivered at its kiss.

"What the fuck is that?" Jeremy whispered from beside her, and like the pull of a chain, the Curburide winked out of existence.

"Ariana," he said, after a few seconds passed. "What's going on here?"

"That," she answered, with a croak that barely resembled her normally crystal pure voice, "is going to take some time to explain."

He rolled away from her and got out of bed, walking immediately to pull the shades and let the morning light flood the room. He stood there, naked, hands on his hips, seemingly unaware of the hairy paunch and shriveled equipment that he was displaying for anyone on the street to see. He turned back and looked around the room as if searching for explosives dangling in the air.

"I've got all day," he finally said. "You drink coffee?"

"With cream," she answered. "But I'll need my hands."

He picked his jeans off the floor from the crumpled pile of clothing near the wall and stuck a leg in.

"I'll be right back," he promised.

He was out the door before he had both arms through his shirtsleeves.

Chapter Fourteen

New Orleans, After Ariana

Carolyn Hayes pressed the sheets down around her daughter's shoulders, tucking them until only Hannah's dimpled chin poked out.

"Snug as a bug," she said, tapping a finger to the girl's nose. "Daddy and I are right through the door there," she pointed at the adjoining door of the room. She nodded at the empty bed next to her.

"Your sister will be back in a couple hours. You get some sleep now. Tomorrow we'll go see Aunt Linda."

Hannah smiled, and then opened her mouth wide to let a yawn escape.

"Okay, Mom, good night. Don't let the buggies bite."

"You neither." Carolyn ruffled her daughter's head and stood up. "I'll see you in the morning."

She flipped the light switch off and pulled the door shut behind her as she returned to the other side of the adjoining rooms.

"She good?" Tom asked, and she nodded. "I hate to leave her in there all alone, though."

He walked up and stood behind her, wrapping solid, strong arms around her waist and drawing his fingers slowly up the front of her thighs.

"She could stay in here with us until J.C. comes home, but then we won't have any private time."

Tom's lips were on her ear and she shivered. Her body melted when he did that, and her husband knew it well. He wasn't playing fair. She pushed his hands away and stepped to the windows to pull the blinds. The city glowed in every shade of neon below their room and she wondered how her older daughter was faring down on Bourbon.

"I know, I know," she said. "But I've got one little girl out on the sin strip all by herself and another one in a strange bed all alone next door. I feel like I've abandoned my girls."

Tom crossed to stand next to her at the window, looking down at the blinking reds and whites of the traffic. He was worried about his daughter wandering Bourbon Street after dark himself but, she was an adult now.

"J.C.'s a big girl," he said, "and she'll be fine on her own. You know she's been doing the bar strip at college for the past year. And we showed her the ropes here this afternoon."

He stroked her hair and pulled her closer.

"Hannah's growing up, too. I know you think of her as your little baby, but she's going to be eleven soon."

He turned her to face him and ran heavy hands around her back to cup her ass, pulling her closer. "Now quit worrying about your daughters. This is *our* time."

The door behind them opened, and Hannah stood behind them, rubbing her eyes.

"Mommy?" she said, sounding unsure.

Carolyn jumped away from her husband and ran to hug her. "What's a matter, baby?"

"There's a ghost in my room."

"A ghost?" Carolyn said. "What sort of ghost?"

"A man," she said. "He's all see-through and floating in the air by the window."

Tom stifled a grin. "Honey, there's no such thing as ghosts, you know that."

"He asked me to come with him," Hannah argued. "He was there, right by my bed. He said I would help him forge a chain."

Tom stepped past both of them to the adjoining room and flicked the lights on.

"Come in here, both of you," he said. Hannah poked her head back in, with Carolyn's arm on her shoulder.

"Look," he said, waving his hand in the air. The room was a mess, suitcases lay on the floor with a trail of T-shirts and socks leading away from them, and the sheets and bedspread on Hannah's bed were dangling off the mattress and touching the floor from her hasty exit. He strode across the room and bent over until his nose nearly touched the ground, making a big show of looking behind the dresser and under the bed. When he stood up finally, he clapped his hands together.

"No ghosts," he pronounced. He grabbed his daughter under the arms and hoisted her in the air.

"All clear," he said. "Ghostbusters win."

She giggled at that, but still protested as he slipped her feet back beneath the covers.

"But he was here, Daddy, I saw him."

He kissed her on the forehead, and Carolyn ran a hand through her daughter's hair.

"Well, he's gone now, baby. Get some sleep now; we've got a big day tomorrow."

Carolyn kissed her again and then Tom pulled her by the arm away from the bed. He flipped off the light.

"Night, night, sleep tight," he said.

"Don't let the buggies bite," came the ritual response from Hannah.

He pulled the door shut behind them and pulled his wife back into an embrace.

"Don't Tom, not now."

"She's fine," he promised. "Just scared of being in a new place."

"We should let her sleep in here."

He went for her ear again, and this time, she relaxed a little into his arms.

"This vacation is for us, too," he reminded her. Carolyn's hands stroked his back and slipped lower, in answer.

"Tell me again what you want to do to me?" she whispered in a girlish voice.

Tom smiled and led her to the bed.

* * *

Carolyn pulled the curtains open to let the morning sunshine fill the room. It was after eight o'clock, but Tom was still out like a light, his lips slack and open against the pillow. Her face beamed as she looked at him; it had been a good night and he had fulfilled just what he'd promised. She went to the bathroom and brushed her teeth, then pulled on one of the big white terrycloth robes from the hotel. If she had one of these at home, she might never get dressed in the morning.

She knocked lightly on the door to her daughters' room, and then opened the door.

J.C. was still in bed, but half awake. She lifted a thin hand to scratch her head through the mess of auburn hair that covered her pillow and mumbled a "g'morning."

"How was your night?" Carolyn asked.

J.C. smiled, and then frowned and lifted the other hand to hold her head.

"Ow. Um, it was good. I ended up at Pat O'Brien's though."

Carolyn laughed. "Hurricanes?"

J.C. nodded.

"You'll learn. Rum is the devil."

Carolyn nodded at Hannah's empty bed. "Is the princess in the bathroom?"

J.C. frowned. "No. I thought she slept with you guys?"

"What do you mean?" Carolyn asked, alarm creeping into her voice.

"She wasn't here when I got home, so I figured she'd crawled into bed with you and Dad."

"Oh my God," Carolyn said, turning back to her room and staring at the single king-size bed, where her husband still lay sleeping. Alone.

"Tom," she said. "Tom!"

He jerked awake and looked up, squinting at her.

"What's a matter, hon?"

"We've lost Hannah."

Chapter Fifteen

The tent glowed with the morning sun when Joe finally admitted defeat, and opened his eyes. He'd been lying there, unwilling to move and start the day, but unable to fall back to sleep either.

The sun was a hazy ball of light that turned the blue fabric of the tent almost colorless where it hit, just to the side of the door flap. He rubbed his eyes and yawned, then turned to see if Alex was awake yet.

Her sleeping bag was empty.

Joe sat upright. Could she have suckered him? Told him ghost stories, waited 'til he went to sleep and then taken off in his car?

He threw off the blanket and shivered at the chill of the morning air. Grabbing his jeans from the floor, he quickly slipped in a leg, and then the next, walking hunched over to the doorway before he'd even zipped up.

The car was still there beneath the overhang of a low evergreen branch.

Alex was sitting beside a small fire, drinking from a tin cup.

"Morning, sleepyhead," she said cheerfully. "I found the coffee and canteen set, so I boiled us up a pot." She held up a glass container half full of dark black liquid.

"It's not Starbucks, but it's got caffeine."

"That's the important thing," he agreed, and moved to sit beside her.

"We don't really have anything for breakfast," she said, "unless you want beans."

He shook his head. "I'll pass. Sorry about that though—I really didn't pack for two. And I figured I'd stop someplace pretty quick for extra supplies once I got up here."

"I usually just have a bowl of cereal in the morning," she said, brushing a stray lock of raven hair away from her eyes. "But I also usually shower before I let anyone see me, so I'm breaking all the rules today."

He laughed. "Tell you what. How about I drop you at the showers while I head into town and do some shopping? Then you can come back here and keep an eye on the tent and stuff."

"Works for me," she said, draining her cup. She held it and the pot out to him. "Care for some mountain brew?"

He stared at it suspiciously.

"It's awfully thick, isn't it?"

"Call it espresso," she said. "Trust me, you'll love it."

Joe poured himself a small cup, and set the pot back by the fire. He put the rim to his lips and blew for a moment, and then tilted the cup up a hair, sipping carefully. A spoonful slurped into his mouth, and involuntarily, his eyes and lips wrinkled into a twisted grimace.

"That's . . ."

". . . awful," Alex finished. She stood and curtsied in mock formality to him. "Wait 'til you taste my cooking."

He held the cup behind his back, and turned it upside down. "Have I mentioned how much I enjoy cooking?"

Joe dropped Alex and her backpack at the shower building at the front of the campsite, and then continued down the road back down the mountain into town. He had a list of items to look for, including another pillow and blanket, or cheap sleeping bag. The blankets he'd slept under last night were intended as pads for his trunk, not sleeping aids.

The mountain road wound down and around, snaking through ravines that rose around the car like a rock-hewn tunnel, and then opening out to precarious strips of asphalt overlooking valleys of rustic-looking hotels and cottages. It seemed like it was taking even longer to get down the mountain than it had to go up, when Joe saw a cutoff leading to a generically marked General Store.

He'd been worried he'd have to drive all the way back to Loveland for supplies, and while this place would probably be more expensive than a convenience or grocery store a few miles farther down the road, he pulled in and parked. They didn't need that much stuff, and he didn't want to be away for too long.

His feet crunched on whitened chunks of limestone gravel as he walked across the unpaved lot to the store, a dilapidated red-painted building with a front door that swung closed on a giant spring. It squeaked like a bird having its tail feathers pulled as he yanked it open and let it slam closed behind.

"Mornin'," an old man called from behind a formica counter cluttered with trinket stands and candy bar racks. "Help you with somethin'?"

"Sure," Joe said, pulling out his list and walking to the counter. The man's face was as weathered as the mountain, covered in a fine brush of white beard pierced only by the red tip of his nose and two gleaming blue eyes. His blue-and-white-checked flannel shirt was stained with orange spots and his overalls looked as old as he did.

"I need a cooler, some groceries for dinner, one package of"—his face wrinkled—"Tampax maxi pads, and do you carry any cheap sleeping bags?" Joe asked.

"You going up to the national park?"

"Does anyone come in here who isn't?"

The old man's beard twitched, and he nodded sagely.

"Have I got a deal for you. One instant campsite kit coming up."

Fifteen minutes and $50 later, and Joe was loading a bag of food, a cooler of ice and a sleeping bag into the trunk. He went back inside to retrieve the 12-pack that he couldn't carry the first trip and grabbed a copy of the *Loveland Daily Reporter-Herald* from a rack near the front door. The old man put up a hand when Joe went for his wallet to pay for the paper.

"On the house," he said. "Enjoy your stay in the hills."

"I will," Joe promised.

He set the pack of Coors in the back, slid behind the wheel, and tossed the newspaper to the passenger's seat. It landed with the lower half of the front-page fold facing up, and as he turned the key in the ignition, a headline caught his eye:

NEBRASKA COUPLE VICTIMS OF BRUTAL SLAYING; TEENAGE DAUGHTER MISSING

Beneath the headline, was a picture of an unsmiling girl with long curly carrot-colored hair.

A picture of the same girl Joe had picked up yesterday along the highway.

He swore under his breath, and pulled the paper to his lap. The article was short, eclipsed by a piece about the Denver sanitation department scandal.

Bruce and Selma Collins, both 38, were found dead in their Okawa, Nebraska home on Thursday. Police report that the couple had been beaten severely, before their bodies were chopped into pieces by an axe.

The bodies were discovered by a neighbor, who noticed that while their cars were in the driveway, their mail had not been taken in from the previous day.

Police have no suspects as of yet, however, they are looking for the couple's 17-year-old daughter, Alexandra, who was not found in the house and has been missing from school for a week.

Arthur Hale High School Principal Anthony Linelle said that the school called the Collinses on Tuesday to find out why Alexandra had not been in class for several days.

"I spoke with Mrs. Collins on the phone on Tuesday and she seemed fine then," Linelle said. "She told me that Alexandra had been sick, but would hopefully be back in school soon."

Okawa Police Chief William Rees said that the investigation is still in the early stages, and they are ruling nothing out yet.

"We've gone over the house with a fine-tooth comb,

and sent a lot of things out to a state lab for investigating. We'll know more in 24 hours."

Police are not yet saying if they believe that Alexandra could be behind the murders, or if she might have been kidnapped by the killer.

"She was a very good student," Linelle said of the girl. "Her grades were always good, though she was very quiet. She didn't socialize with the other kids very much. She preferred reading to group activities."

Rees said he believes this is the first double murder in Okawa history.

"It's very sad," he said. "The Collinses were respected members of this community. Whoever did this has a sick, sadistic mind. The violence here was unimaginable."

If anyone has any information that could help this investigation, they are urged to contact the Okawa Police Department.

Joe leaned his head back against the seat cushion and let out a long, slow breath. Malachai had set him up. He knew better. Should have known better. The demon had never tried to help him, had only sent him Trojan horses. And this one took the cake. An innocent-looking, luscious little teen, who knew her way around an axe murder.

Mentally he went over the list of what he'd left up on the mountain. Tent, pots, a suitcase of clothes . . . was there really any reason to head back there at all?

He started the engine and pulled out of the lot, turning in the direction of Loveland.

Cold feet, little man? Malachai's voice taunted in his head. *Can't take her heat?*

Joe ignored the demon, and kept driving. In minutes, the road had leveled off and he was headed back across the flatlands, retracing his miles of the day before.

You're making a big mistake.

He pulled up to a stoplight.

"Why?" Joe said out loud. "Because I'm walking away from a murderer who will probably slit my throat and toss my arms and legs down a ravine by the weekend?"

The woman in the Honda next to him was staring at him, and Joe realized he probably looked pretty strange, sitting in his car yelling at no one. He clamped his mouth shut and mumbled quietly.

"How did you find her? And why did you send her to me?"

Ahhh, the demon croaked. *At last he asks the right questions. Weren't you a reporter once?*

The light changed, and Joe pulled away from the staring woman and headed towards the business district of town.

"Yes," Joe said. "And a damn good one. Now tell me what's going on?"

Is that how you coerced all of your sources? No wonder you're out of a job.

"Malachai!"

You need her, the demon said. *I could hear her voice through the ether. She's strong. More than she knows. And she did what she had to do. But if you were a real reporter, you'd get the story from the prime source, not a questionable third party.*

"Been taking some college journalism courses yourself lately?" Joe asked.

Just telling you what you already know.

"What do I need her for?" Joe said after a moment. "I'm out. You might have noticed I've set up camp in the mountains. Away from everybody. And everything."

You can run, but you can't hide, Malachai whispered. *The Curburide are coming. And it's up to you to stop them.*

"You make me sound like some kind of fuckin' superhero!" Joe laughed out loud, then looked to see if any other drivers were staring. They weren't. "I can't do anything to stop them. I'm not psychic or super. I'm just a washed-up, broke ex-journalist saddled with a sadistic demon who's always looking over my shoulder."

You are the only one who knows about them, Malachai said. *You are the only one with the tools to stop them.*

"And if I don't?"

Your soul will be sucked dry and your body will rot on the ground unburied. If the horde comes through, all the way this time, every person you have ever known will be seduced and sucked dry of energy. They will feed. On you and Alex and Cindy and everyone. They are legion. The cracks between you and them are few. But they are growing.

"How do I know this isn't just an elaborate story you're telling, so that I go back to Alex, end up as her next victim and you are set free?"

You can keep watching the news. There will be more sacrifices. But by then, it may be too late to stop them.

Joe pulled into a gas station on the corner and stopped the car. He watched a woman in a black skirt and white blouse hurry down the sidewalk, clutching a purse. Late for work? he wondered, watching her cross the street and hurry into a small office building. Across the lot, a tired-looking man in blue jeans and a Harley T-shirt pumped gas into a rusting Buick. Was there really a scourge waiting to lash out and knock these people down? A force that would flatten them in their tracks, and make all their mundane problems and victories meaningless. And so what if there was . . . what did a little teenage axe murderer have to do with it?

A real reporter would talk to the source, not run from her.

Joe sighed. What did he really have to lose? He put the car back into gear and turned out of the parking lot.

Back the way he'd come.

Chapter Sixteen

As soon as Jeremy left the room, Ariana flipped over on her belly and examined the knot around her wrists. The last thing she remembered from the night before was Jeremy violently thrusting between her legs. He had thrown her on the bed and pushed himself inside her, taking all of his pain and anger out on her bleeding body as she'd writhed and kicked beneath him. His own blood had dripped on her breasts as he held her hands and then her mouth to silence her cries as he took what pleasure he could from the act. But when she'd bit him on the palm, he'd hauled off and slugged her with a fist to the jaw. There were stars of pain, and a moment of blurriness, as she tried to keep her eyes open to see the man on top of her, to at least stay aware of how badly he was violating her, and then it all went gray.

The elastic band that strangled her wrists looked to be a tie-rope that he must have gotten from his trunk after knocking her out. It was yellow with blue twinings and it was wound tightly around both of her wrists and then tied again around the mattress frame below the headboard. She wasn't getting out of it on her own.

Ariana rolled onto her back, and cried out loud at the sudden return of sensation to her arms from her brief change of position. The blood was returning, and it hurt like hell.

She tried to focus on the ceiling, and the window, but her entire existence seemed to be pain right now. Her jaw was swollen and throbbing, her neck was a flaming brand, her stomach and ribs felt as if she'd been run down by a truck. And to top it off, there was a dull ache between her thighs, from the rough, fighting-for-dominance treatment he'd given her just a few hours before.

Ariana did not feel very well. She almost wished that he would come back with the coffee and slit her throat and be done with it. Hell, she deserved it from his point of view— that's exactly what he'd stopped her from doing to him!

The bed bore testament to that. The crumpled white sheets had smears of dull red-brown blood all over them, and the pillow covers were ruined with streaks and splashes of blood as well. The maids were going to shit when they came to clean this place.

The door opened and shut and a moment later Jeremy stalked into view, two Styrofoam cups in hand.

"Coffee with cream, lady witch," he said, setting the cup down on a nightstand.

He placed his on the desk behind him, and then came to stand over the bed and her.

"I can't drink like this," she pointed out.

"I could pour it down your throat. Of course, the contents might be hot and you might be burned. But why would I care?"

"What are you planning to do with me?" she asked. "If you're going to take me out, just do it and get it over with. Otherwise, let me out of these ropes. I can't feel my arms."

Jeremy walked to the window and looked out at the parking lot below. He said nothing. He turned to look at her, stretched out, bound and naked on the bed, and then bent down to pick something off the floor. When he stood up, a silver square glinted in his hand.

"Your weapon of choice," he noted, staring at the edge of the blade and then pantomiming the use of it, slicing with quick, downward slices through the air.

"I wonder how long you'd feel the pain," he said idly.

She didn't say anything. What was there left to say?

Jeremy tossed the blade at the windowsill and walked to the head of the bed.

"I'll release you on one condition," he said.

She cocked an eyebrow and listened.

"You do exactly as I say, and don't try any cute escape or attack tricks. You try to take me out, or run out the door, and I swear I will kill you if it's the last thing I do."

Ariana nodded, grimacing at the pain the motion brought her.

"I'll be good," she promised.

"Hope so," he said under his breath, and reached behind the headboard to undo the fastenings that held her to the bed.

In a minute, she was free, and rubbing the circulation back into her wrists. It returned in a fire of pins and needles, and Ariana doubled over on the bed, laying her hands below her feet as she cried out at the discomfort. "Shit, shit, shit," she moaned.

Jeremy did nothing, only sat down at the desk and sipped his coffee, keeping a close eye on her.

When she stopped complaining, and sat up to gingerly lift her coffee cup from the nightstand, he spoke.

"Better?"

"I've been," she said.

"Yeah, well, me too," he said, pointing at the angry red scab across his neck. "I never had a scar here before."

"Most guys don't have the chance to scar," she warned.

"Most girls don't get a second chance after they try shit like that," he answered. "Now, do you want to spar, or are you going to tell me what the fuck's going on?"

"You want the CliffsNotes, or the whole story?" she said.

Jeremy looked at his watch. "Hmmm. Let's see, it's after nine A.M. I haven't been home all night and haven't shown up to the office today. I guess I'm in for the duration. Give me the whole story. I want to know why a girl tried to kill me, and then had a freakin' ghost brigade show up after I fucked her. I'm guessing there's a story there that's worth hearing all the way through."

Ariana brought the coffee to her lips, cringing as she lifted her arm and sloshing some of the brown liquid onto her calf and the sheets.

"Better leave the maid a big tip," she said and took a loud, tentative slurp.

"Don't worry about the maid," he warned. "Just worry about convincing me that I shouldn't be using those sheets to transport your body to my trunk."

She looked at him over the edge of her cup, showing him the most innocent, wide brown eyes she could muster. But he didn't bite.

"I'm waiting," was all he said.

"Okay," she said, nodding quickly. Ariana took another slurp of the coffee, and then pushed herself back to lean against the headboard. She shoved a pillow behind the small of her back and took a deep breath.

"It all started when I was going to divinity school at the monastery."

"You're a fuckin' nun?" he asked, jaw dropping.

"Almost," she grinned, spreading her legs for him to see the pink, noncloistered flesh between. "But not quite. Does it look like I'm a nun?"

"Not exactly," he admitted, leering up the expanse unveiled by her legs. "So what happened?"

"You know what you saw in the room this morning?"

He nodded.

"That happened. I discovered that there really was something beyond kneeling at a dead statue and saying endless rituals of prayer that didn't reach anyone. Something that's kept hidden from us behind all the Ten Commandments and eight Beatitudes bullshit."

"You became a devil worshipper."

"No," she said. "When I was studying to join the convent, I discovered that there was more to the other side than just God and the devil. I discovered the Curburide."

Chapter Seventeen

Once he'd made up his mind, Joe pressed the pedal to the floor and, despite the incline and twisting road, raced up the mountain to return to the campgrounds. He had too many questions. Too many things he had to know. He couldn't leave with that much unanswered. It was against his nature.

When the turnoff for the campground came up, he almost passed it by. He turned the wheel hard to the left and felt the car skid on the gravel as he slipped off the asphalt and onto the mountain path that served as a road for the campground.

The shower building passed in a blur, and then one by one he sailed past the campers and tents at the front of the campground, kicking up a cloud of dust behind him to hide his trail into the depths of the park.

Finally the blue tent came into view, along with the tiny stream of smoke that still rose from the anemic campfire they had built together.

Alex sat next to the fire, wearing a faded blue T-shirt and old blue jeans. She looked relaxed, but as soon as Joe pulled into the grassy area beneath the tree where he'd parked the night before, she jumped up and ran to the car.

"I thought you'd ditched me," she said, as soon as she put her face to the window.

Joe motioned her away from the door, and then opened it and stepped out. He popped the trunk, and grabbed a bag to carry, leaving one for her. She picked it up and followed him to the tent.

"I thought about it," he said finally. "It would have been nice if you'd given me the whole story."

He stalked back to the car, and pulled out the 12-pack from behind the driver's seat. Then he grabbed the newspaper from the front and slammed the door behind him.

"What do you mean?" Her voice trembled, just a bit, and he nodded at the fire. She took a seat next to it, and he dropped the paper beside her, bottom half up to reveal her incriminating pre-dye-job picture.

"Well, for starters, you might consider telling me why you knocked off your parents."

Alex picked the paper up gingerly, as if it might carry poison ivy. She skimmed the article for a moment without answering.

"Damn," she said. "Principal Linelle said this? About me?"

"I was a little more concerned about the brutal slaying part myself," Joe said, voice oozing sarcasm.

"Yeah," she said, absentmindedly, still scanning the paper. "You're a guy, you would be."

Joe stepped over to her and grabbed her by the shoulders. She looked up in surprise, eyes wide.

"I'm serious," he said, squatting down next to her. "I really almost didn't come back. But something made me give you a second chance."

"Something named Malachai?" she said, a small smile slipping over her lips.

"Maybe," he admitted, letting her go. "But that won't keep me here. You spun a nice little story last night. I want to hear an even better one now."

Alex's face grew dark, and her gaze dropped to her lap.

"I didn't tell you a story last night," she said. "That was the truth."

"Okay, fine." Joe put his finger under her chin and pressed upwards until her eyes stared directly into his own.

"Then tell me the rest of the truth. What happened with you and your parents?"

She pulled away from him.

"They hurt me," she said. "So I hurt them back. That's all you need to know."

"Bullshit," Joe said. "Give me the story, or hitch yourself another ride off this mountain, 'cuz you ain't going with me."

Alex said nothing for a moment, and then sighed.

"Get comfy," she said, "This is going to take awhile."

She eased over to lie on her side, head on her elbow, facing Joe and the fire. "It really all started when my dad found out that I saw things. He started surprising me, you know, bursting into my room to see if I was talking to the air. Sometimes he'd listen at the door, and if he heard me say anything, he'd slam it open and crack me across the face."

"I thought he exorcised all the ghosts?"

"He did, but over time, some new ones turned up. And as the years went by, he got more and more weird about it. He was convinced I was some kind of witch, and it was his God-given mission to beat the crap out of me until I gave up my 'evil ways.' As I got older, he wouldn't just spank me or send me to bed. He had a special room for me. He called it the Cleansing Room. And last week . . ."

Joe shifted position, and lay down on the ground next to her, settling in for the story.

"So what happened?"

"This has been coming for years," she said. "But last week, it finally got completely out of control . . ."

Alex tossed her book bag on the bed and flopped down on her beanbag. The day had totally sucked. After getting back her history test with a weak C- (she thought she'd scored at least a B), she'd had a run-in with Jason, who backed out of their date on Saturday claiming that his parents weren't going to let him have the car. She knew better though, because Jen had already told her that some of the guys from the football team were putting together a kegger at one of the guys' houses, since his parents were away for a few days.

"Has Jason asked you to go yet?" Jen had said. "I know he's one of the guys putting it together. If he takes you, can you get me in too?"

"Sure," Alex had promised, a little apprehensive about the idea. She didn't need to get caught at a house party. Her dad was already enough of a nutjob with her.

But those worries were all for naught anyway, because when she saw Jason after sixth period, he bailed out of their previously planned date on Saturday. She didn't even confront him with the house party information. If he didn't want her there, he didn't want her. And it saved her from coming up with an excuse to get out of the house Saturday anyway. She hadn't cleared the date yet with her parents.

Still, the deceit weighed heavily on her. She'd thought he really liked her. She settled into the beanbag and pulled her arms tight around her shoulders in a self-hug. Pulling her knees up in the fetal position, she let a tear slip down her cheek.

"It'll get better, child," a voice said.

Alex raised her reddening eyes to see the hazy shape of an old woman in front of her. The woman looked like a film projected on smoke; her face and figure were clear, yet, transparent and wavery.

"Who are you?" Alex sniffled. She didn't jump or cry out at the intrusion, she was used to ghostly beings walking in and out of her life.

"I'm Gertrude," the aged ghost said. "Now I want you to save your tears for someone who deserves them."

"How do you know I'm crying about a boy?" Alex asked.

"Is there anything else that a girl cries for?" Gertrude said, cocking her head and raising a vaporous eyebrow.

"Sometimes I cry because my dad hits me," Alex admitted.

"Again, because of a boy," the ghost said. "A big boy, admittedly, a bad boy surely, but just a boy."

"I guess," Alex said. "Why are you here?"

"Well, because you called me, girl, why do you think?"

"I didn't call you."

"Like a policeman on a bullhorn, you did. Your cries were

playing and crackling like a bad skip in a record. I thought I should stop by and see what was going on here."

"I'm sorry," Alex said, hanging her head. "I didn't mean to be so loud."

Gertrude placed a see-through hand on the top of the girl's head. Then she knelt down to be at eye level with the teen.

"It's alright," she said. "I don't really mind. Though you're gonna have to learn how to control yourself in that regard. Most of the living can't reach the dead the way you can. You keep up that noise, and who knows what kind of miscreants you'll call over."

"How do I keep quiet?" Alex asked, rubbing her eyes and nose dry with a quick swipe of her hand. "I don't even know that I'm doing it."

"Maybe that's something I can help you with," Gertrude said. "Stand up a minute. I want you to put your hands out and close your eyes. Like you are flying blind."

Alex stood and did as she suggested.

"What am I supposed to be feeling?" she said.

"Don't feel anything. Focus on hearing," Gertrude said. "When you think everything is quiet, I want you to think hello to me. Don't open your mouth, just think it at me."

Alex kept her eyes closed and thought *hello* over and over, pushing the word with her mind. She tried to picture Gertrude in her head, and see herself speaking the word to the spirit.

Hello yourself, came a loud voice in her head. *Think about how this voice sounds, here in your head. It's different than when you speak and hear with your tongue and ear. You need to feel the difference; talking—and learning to keep quiet—on the spiritual plane will be like learning a whole new way to talk.*

Like this? Alex said, projecting herself through her mind.

Quieter, child, you're screaming.

Alex laughed out loud.

And that's when he backhanded her in the face.

She stumbled backwards, opening her own eyes to see the fury in her father's.

"Dad," she gasped, grabbing the edge of her dresser to

stop her fall. "What's the matter? I didn't know you were here."

"Witch," he accused, advancing on her. "I have put up with it for long enough. You have brought wickedness into this house again and again. The Lord will not forgive you for consorting with the damned. And he won't forgive me for allowing it to go on. You have put all of our souls in danger."

"Dad, I've done nothing wrong. Sometimes ghosts come by and I talk to them, that's all . . ."

He slapped her across the face.

"You'll speak not another word to me of *ghosts*. You are through with summoning demons under my roof. Come with me."

He grabbed a handful of hair and dragged the girl after him down the hallway to the kitchen. There, he opened the door leading into the cellar and pulled her after him down the steep flight of wooden stairs.

"Dad, no, what are you doing?" she begged, but he didn't answer.

He pulled her past the laundry table, covered in piles of clothes that her mother had left fresh from the dryer in piles for folding and putting away. He pulled her past the washer and dryer and the shelves of canned goods.

He pulled her to a dark corner of the cellar near his workbench, and then lifted one of her arms into the air. With a metallic click, Alex felt something close over her wrist. Then he repeated the same step with her other arm. He stepped away and Alex looked up to see the chains leading from the cuffs on her wrists to the wooden beams above. He had planned for this. But what had he planned to *do*, exactly?

"In the Bible, it talks of wearing sackcloth and self-flagellation to make restitution for our sins," her father said from somewhere in the depths of the cellar behind her.

"I'm sure that you will not do either of these penances yourself," he said again, this time at her shoulder. His hands began to unbutton her school blouse. She tried to move away from him, but could only step a couple feet in either direction before the chains restrained her. It didn't stop her father, whose fingers fumbled and yanked at her buttons, at last ripping the shirt open to uncover the white cups of her bra. He held up a pair of long shining pruning shears, and slit the shirt in half from the neck down. Then he put its cold metal blades against her sternum and forced it to slide up, underneath her bra until a sharp and deadly tip poked just beneath her throat.

"No daughter of mine will consort with demons," he promised. His eyes frightened Alex more than his actions. She'd never seen him so angry. The brown pools of his pupils seemed rimmed in red, and his forehead maintained a constant ripple of wrinkles. The side of his mouth twitched, and he put a hand on her bare shoulder to hold her still.

"You are my daughter, and I love you," he said. "But I have to do this for your own good."

He brought the teeth of the shears together and clipped through the front of the bra, each half of which fell down to hang at the side of her ribs from her shoulders. Her breasts were exposed to her father, and her normally pale pink nipples were erect with the chill of the basement and the adrenaline of fear.

"Daddy," she pleaded, tears running down her face.

With the shears, he walked around her, cutting off the remains of her shirt and bra, and then sliding a blade down the crack of her ass.

"Daddy no!" she screamed, and he slapped her again in the back the head.

"Shut up," he growled, forcing the shears together with both hands to open the waistband of her pants. They slid down to her feet, exposing her sky blue bikini briefs. The pair she'd hoped Jason at school would have gotten to see on Saturday. The cold touch of the blade against the inner cleft of her buttocks made her clench, but her father only shoved the shears down harder, yanking the elastic of the panties down before he closed the blade to loosen and cast off her underwear. Now she stood naked and chained before her father, goose bumps covering her body.

Her face flushed red as he walked around her, examining her exposed body with a fierce gaze. Alex closed her eyes and whispered, "This isn't happening. This cannot be."

"It is happening," her father snapped, cracking her in the mouth with the back of his hand. "It's time you paid attention to the real world, instead of talking with ghosts and spirits. You will give up your witchcraft, girl. Or I will do to you what must be done."

"What?" she asked.

"Witches are burnt," he said, walking away from her again. But his voice came back from the far reaches of the cellar.

"At the stake. Alive."

Alex shivered at the image of her father tying her arms to the wooden post of the clothesline in their backyard and piling cords of firewood around her feet. Would he actually burn her alive because she saw ghosts?

"You must repent and do penance," he said. "It pains me to have to do this, but your mother agrees that it must be done."

Alex jumped as a white-hot crack slapped against her back. She turned to see what he had hit her with and saw his arm in motion, bringing down the long brown rope of a whip. The second stroke caught her across the ribs and she shrieked.

"Stand still or it will hurt worse," he promised, and brought the whip down again on her back, lighting the skin from her left shoulder blade to the tender top of her ass on fire.

"Dad, please, stop!" she cried.

"Punishment is never easy," he answered, and brought the whip down again. It cracked like the slap of a ruler against a wooden table, and Alex screamed.

He cuffed her across the mouth.

"Make that noise again, and I'll gag you," he said, stepping back to deliver the fifth stroke. Her skin was already red and welted in crisscrosses up and down her back, but her father brought the whip up and down five more times, until thin trails of bloody perspiration striped her back. Alex had choked back her screams, but not her sobs. Her face was wet and her breath came in loud, choked gasps.

When the beating stopped, her father stepped away to the fruit cellar and returned to drape the rough, scratchy burlap of a potato sack around her. He pinned the ends together so that it would stay on, covering her nakedness, but providing little warmth or comfort.

"Ouch!" she complained. "It hurts my back, Dad."

"Good," he said. "Think about that for now. Focus on the pain. On how awful it feels. Think about how Jesus suffered worse than this, for your sins."

Alex listened to her father's footsteps echo on the concrete floor as he walked away. The wooden plank stairs creaked as he mounted the first two steps, and then the sound stopped.

"I want you to repent, Alexandra," he said. "I want you to think about God."

The stairs creaked again, and she heard the door shut.

She cried until her eyes were almost swollen shut. Gradually, she lost the energy to cry, and began to consider her situation, testing the strength of her chains (they wouldn't budge) and speculating about how she might slip her wrists out of the cuffs snapped to them (she couldn't). She had never really paid much attention to the cellar before. As a child, she'd been afraid to come down here at all, and later, the only time she did was to help her mom retrieve the laundry. Looking around, it almost felt like a foreign prison. The washer and dryer were familiar, but everything else seemed different, surreal.

After awhile, Alex simply stood and stared at the pockmarks in the concrete foundation walls in front of her. The only light in the cellar came from the small two-foot-tall windows that were at the bottom of window wells outside, but it was enough that she could read the Idaho Potatoes stamp across the brown scratchy cloth that hid her nakedness, and she could trace the black cracks and holes in the concrete wall. She wished Gertrude or someone was there to talk to.

Isn't that how you got into this mess in the first place? a low masculine voice whispered in her ear.

Alex jerked around, gasping at the pain from one of the whip cuts as she did so. There didn't seem to be anyone around.

Don't look, listen, he said. *It's time you started to learn to use your gift. And what better time than when you're all tied up with nowhere to go but the cellar?*

"Who are you?" she whispered.

Have you learned nothing after all this time? His voice sounded vexed. *Talk with your inner mouth. Stop announcing your vision to the world. They don't understand. They will only hurt you for it. Look at what your own father has done to you.*

Her eyes welled up instantly at the reminder.

Talk to me in your mind. In silence.

Who are you? she thought, without speaking. *Can you really hear my thoughts? Why can't I see you?*

I can hear your thoughts if you want me to, he said. *You can't see me because I'm far away now. But we'll meet soon. Especially if you keep your mouth shut and practice talking with me.*

The pain in her back seemed to roll over her in a wave all of a sudden, and her breath caught fast in her throat.

It hurts, she complained.

It's going to get worse before it gets better, he promised. *But how long you put up with it is up to you. I would suggest that you don't for too long. This sort of thing can be dangerous to your health.*

What can I do? she asked. *I'm tied up. I can't get out of this on my own.*

There is more to you than arms and legs, he said. *You should know that by now.*

She didn't answer, and he could feel her puzzlement through the ether.

Think about it for tonight. Call me, if you need to talk.

"Wait a minute," she whispered, but he didn't answer. A smile crossed her face and she formed the words again, only this time not aloud but within her mind.

Wait a minute.

I'm here.

I don't know your name to call you.

Malachai, he said. *If you need anything, just call for Malachai.*

★ ★ ★

The light slowly faded in the cellar, and Alex could hear her mom in the kitchen, moving about and clanking pots and glassware as she prepared dinner.

Would they feed her? she wondered. Or would they make her fast, as well as suffer beatings?

After awhile, she dozed on her feet, the darkness providing a cool, velvet black blanket to warm her. It was soothing, a respite from the stinging, throbbing ache of her back. She let the darkness cover the pain in waves, and slipped away inside it. There were no fathers in her darkness, no mothers, no whips and no ghosts.

And then she jerked to full consciousness with a start. Something was touching her.

"It's me, honey," her mom's voice said. "Daddy said I could give you a little bread to chew and water to drink."

With that, the crust of a roll slipped past her lips and Alex bit into it greedily, nearly pulling it out of her mother's hand.

"I told you to stop playing with those spirits, honey," her mom said as Alex chewed. She nearly choked the bread back up.

"Mom, it's not my fault they come around. And they're not evil. They're just people, like you and Dad."

"They're dead," her mom pronounced. "And if they're not in heaven, then they're evil."

Alex drank from the offered cup and then looked hard at her mother. The woman was aging poorly, lines creased her forehead and the corners of her eyes, and her short black hair was run through with strands of silver and white. Her eyes refused to meet her daughter's.

"I have to pee," Alex announced. "Can you let me down to go to the bathroom?"

Her mother shook her head, no. "Go where you stand, child. There's a drain right over there. Your father says you must marinade in your sin and blood and filth, and only then can you cast it off and be cleansed of evil."

"So you agree with what Daddy is doing?" Alex asked, her

voice getting higher and louder. "You think it's just fine that he stripped me naked and whipped me? You think it's just fine that my father looked at me *naked*, Mother? Isn't *that* sinful?"

Her mother didn't answer, but instead backed away from her, shaking her head.

As the older woman hurried back up the creaking wooden stairs, Alex's voice trailed her.

"So you think it's just fine that he looks at my boobs and whips my back 'til I bleed and then dresses me in a potato sack, *Mother*?"

In her heart, Alex felt the fire of her anger grow with every word. How dare he do this to her? How dare he treat her like some kind of criminal? In that moment, any love that was left for her parents fled, and Alex swore that she would have her vengeance. Not just on her pigheaded, self-righteous, sadistic father, but on her meek mother, who allowed this not only to happen, but to continue. She would escape from these bindings. And they would pay.

Gertrude shimmered into being before her.

Anger, child. It's a magnet. And you're turning the juice on strong. I could hear you from miles away. You've got to learn some control.

"Well damnit, I'm angry," Alex hissed out loud.

In your mind, Gertrude reminded.

I'm angry. And I have a right to be! My back is killing me, I can't even feel my arms, and I'm chained up in a basement just because I see things that other people don't see.

You do have a right to be angry. But you have to learn to channel it. You have to learn not to broadcast it to the world. There is a time and a place for that—someday you may want to call on the spirit realm for help. But there's no need to advertise yourself to the cosmos every hour of every day.

Gertrude pressed a ghostly finger to Alex's wet cheek and shook her head sadly.

Oh child. If I had only discovered you earlier, perhaps you could have avoided all of this. If you'd been trained when you were young, you could have learned control. And learned that most people are not

*ready to hear that you can see us. Your father is not the only man who
would hurt you for what you see.*

So how can I hide my anger? Alex asked, forcing herself to
calm down.

You just did it, to some extent, the ghost said. *You are angry, but
you pulled back from letting your mind rant and rave and scream
about it. You put the anger on your mental shelf. It's there, but it's not
sending out fireworks. There is a difference in the way you think. If
you are just thinking, I cannot necessarily hear you. But when you try
to send your thoughts out, or when you just let them stream out like a
firehose, that's when the dead can hear you. It's like the difference between thinking a thought and opening your mouth and speaking it
out loud. Your inner mouth is always open—everything you think is
just streaming out for anyone to hear. You need to learn to close it a bit.
Let's try this. Think about something you love, but try to think "quietly." Then try to talk to me about it with your mind.*

Alex thought about her dog, Prudence, a brown Lab who'd
been hit by a car back when she was in eighth grade. She
thought about playing Frisbee in the backyard with Prudence
as a pup, the two of them running and stumbling and rolling
down the long sloping hill of grass that led from their back
door to the start of the cornfields.

Then she "spoke" in her mind to Gertrude, describing the
memory.

Good, Gertrude said, nodding. *I really couldn't hear much of
what you were thinking until you intentionally framed it, and tried
to tell it to me. Could you feel the difference in your head between
those two states of thinking?*

Alex nodded, a small glimmer of warmth gathering again
in her heart. She could do this!

Let's try again with something else, Gertrude said. *Think about
something for a bit, and then address me with your mind and tell me
about it. I want you to feel the gap between the two states. I want
you to understand the difference implicitly.*

For the next hour, Alex and Gertrude practiced, sending
thoughts and then intentionally trying to hide thoughts from
whoever might be out there, listening. The aches and pains in

Alex's wounded body faded as she focused her attention on learning this new skill. Then she yawned, and Gertrude called a halt.

Time for sleep, she pronounced.

Okay, Alex agreed, yawning again, even wider. *But, all this practice—am I going to have to be aware of my thoughts all the time? It'll be like, I'm always on guard or something.*

It will get to be second nature, Gertrude promised. *You have a sense that most people don't have. After you learn how to use and control it better, you won't even know that you're doing it after awhile. It will be as natural as the difference between thinking and speaking out loud.*

Thanks, Gertrude, Alex said, and the ghost leaned forward to plant a silvery kiss on her cheek.

Get some sleep, child.

And she was gone.

Alex's bladder was now screaming about its discomfort up her spine, and with a sigh of resignation, Alex spread her feet apart as far as she could and released it, feeling the warm stream spray against her inner thighs and spatter warmly on her feet. She watched the yellow pool collect beneath her, and then begin to run forward, following the subtle slant of the concrete toward the drain by the washer and dryer. She cringed when she brought her feet back together, and felt the cooling wetness under her feet and dripping from her legs.

All the aches and stings and pain filtered back and Alex let a tear or two trickle down her cheek. Why her? All her life, she'd been different, and everyone let her know about it. Her parents punished her, the kids at school shunned her. Maybe she should just let her father burn her at the stake. She imagined the scene in her head, her father, eyes still smoldering with anger, piling log after log of firewood up around her feet. He'd complain about how this was going to cost him precious wood for the fireplace this winter, making her feel guilty even for the effort it took him to kill her. Then he would sprinkle gasoline across the logs and strike a match.

He'd hold it in front of his face and shake his head at her. "If only you would have learned from your mother," he would say. Then he'd toss the match on the pile, standing there with arms crossed, as the flames licked their way up the wood, ascending in a blistering blaze to burn her potato sack clothes away and melt her flesh like soft wax from her bones. Her mother would be there, standing behind her father, weeping, but saying nothing. Alex could almost taste the charcoal in her mouth as she imagined the skin on her face blistering and bubbling and then, at long last, blackening as her mouth stretched open in a perpetual scream.

It would hurt, for awhile, but then it would be over, and she could roam free like Gertrude, and all the other spirits she'd spoken with over the years. She hung her head and let the feeling wash over her. *Just burn me,* she thought. *Burn me and get it over with.*

Self-pity is a wonderful thing, isn't it? a male voice whispered. *Wouldn't you love to just hang there forever and let your father have his way with you each and every night? Don't you deserve that?*

The voice was cold, serpentine. He was disgusted with her. *Malachai?* she asked.

Pull yourself together, child. Or all that you fear most will come to pass.

She said nothing.

Tomorrow you will need all of your strength, he said. *Rest now. As best you can.*

The night passed slowly, but Alex tried to sleep. Pins and needles came and went in her arms, which shifted from numb to hot pain and back to numb without warning or provocation.

In the morning, as the sun warmed the far side of the room with lemony rays, Alex lost her temper again and began to scream. She'd been awake for at least an hour, moving from one foot to the other, trying to take some of the pressure off her arms, but no matter how she stood—or let herself hang from the chains—she was in awful discomfort. Finally, she just let her anger go in a long, ululating screech that echoed throughout the cellar. She knew they heard her upstairs.

"Let me out of here," she yelled through the ceiling. "Let me down."

She yelled the same thing, over and over and over again, to no avail. Her arms were on fire, and her cheeks felt crusty with tears. Her back burned with every twist and movement.

"God damn it, let me go, you fuckin' bastard," she screamed.

That did it. There was a thump upstairs and quick stomp of footsteps. The cellar door opened, and the faint light in the basement grew brighter as the wooden stairs creaked and her father appeared at the base of the stairs.

"Don't you ever take the name of the Lord in vain in this house again," he bellowed. "It's bad enough that you use your mouth to speak other filth, but you will not swear by the Lord's name."

"Then let me go," she said.

"You will stay there for as long as necessary," he said. "You will stay there until you are cleansed. You will stay there until I can be proud to call you my daughter again."

"I'll do whatever you want," she promised, "but let me down. I can't feel my arms."

"The kind of change I'm talking about cannot happen overnight," he said. "You're going to have to do your penance here for some time."

"What about school?" she asked, panic rising in her chest. He actually intended to keep her chained up for days!

"Your mother will say you are sick. And she will not be lying. You are sick in the soul, Alexandra."

"God damn you," she spit. "You are the sick one."

"I warned you," he said and began to walk towards her.

"God damn you, goddamn you, goddamn you," she said. "You're the bastard who's going to burn in hell."

He ripped the potato sack from her body, opening the scabs that had set around its fibers the night before, and Alex shrieked, pulling away from him only to lose her balance and find herself hanging from her wrists for a moment. And then the whip cracked and snapped, and all of her old sores were new again.

"God Damn You!" she screamed, and the room was suddenly full of people. Ghostly, silvery people staring and pointing at her. They were faint at first, but grew more and more solid as Alex hurled curses at her father, who continued to whip her until her back became a bloody mess.

Gertrude broke through the crowd and stood before her, a finger over her lips.

Child, they are coming because of you. Think about what you are doing now. Think hard. Is this what you want?

"No!" Alex screamed, and then released her anger entirely. It flew from her like a bird, and all she was left with was pain and exhaustion. Her bladder cried out its discomfort and she released it again, this time not even caring that it wet her legs and feet. She hung her head and cried. Twice more the whip kissed her skin. At last, her father quit raising the leather strip aloft, and walked back to the stairs.

"This hurts me to do this," he announced. "But you'll thank me someday."

The stairs creaked as his weight ascended, and Alex stared down at the pool of urine on the floor.

"I'll kill you someday," she whispered.

Hours later, it seemed, her mother came down to offer bread and water. She hesitated when she reached the bottom of the stairs, and saw Alex.

"What's the matter, Mom?" Alex sneered, watching her mother's slow progress across the cellar. "Not used to seeing your daughter naked and bloody and hanging from the ceiling? Dad loves me this way."

"Stop it," her mother said in a low voice. "Your father is doing what he has to do. He hates it as much as I do."

"I don't think so, Momma. The Lord never said anything in the Bible about stripping your daughter naked. And I don't recall anything in there about whips and chains either."

"Shut your mouth if you want anything to eat today," her mother hissed.

"It will be hard to eat with my mouth shut," Alex laughed. Her brain was reeling now, reveling in the edge. Her body keened with pain but somehow she felt freed.

Her mother set the bread and water down on the floor a few feet away from Alex and then stood up.

"If you continue to speak like that about your father, I will not feed you."

With that, Alex's mother turned and walked back up the stairs, as fast as she could go. As the door closed upstairs, and the light from the kitchen faded, so did Alex's bravado. Her stomach rumbled, and the pins and needles in her arms came back. She let out one loud cry, and then hung her head, the tears falling like rain to dot the top of her breasts. The salty water pooled at the ends of her nipples 'til she dripped like a statuary fountain from tit to floor.

The hours passed and her hunger grew. She tried to take her mind off of it by connecting the black pits in the concrete wall before her in an intricate game of connect the dots. She crafted detailed mental pictures of her father being flogged and her mother fucked by a horde of giant demons—*irony*, she thought—but tired of the game quickly, as her stomach began a continuous loud churning.

Malachai, she called finally.

He answered almost instantly.

Yes, child.

I need help.

You need only ask, he said.

I'm starving, she said. *I'll die here if they keep this up.*

Eventually, yes, he agreed. *But you are in no danger now.*

She stared at the bread on the floor, tantalizingly close, but out of reach. *Can you lift the bread for me?*

Call for your friends, Malachai advised. *Working together, they might manage it.*

She thought a moment. Since the exorcism, she had not spoken with many of the dead on a regular basis. It was as if they knew being near her could cause them harm. Banishment. But there were a few. She pictured them in her mind.

Matthew, the Puerto Rican punk teen from Brooklyn; Candace, the mousy housewife from Denver; Rick, the tall, thin accountant from Milwaukee; and of course Gertrude. She called them all by name, and begged for their help.

One by one, they popped into being beside her, each of them (except Gertrude), opening their mouths in horror when they saw her state.

Please, can you help me? she asked. *Just lift the bread over there for me. If you all work together . . . ?*

Gertrude smiled at her thinly, but said nothing.

Matthew raised an eyebrow though, and complained. *You think we don't got our own problems, we gotta come serve you breakfast?*

"Please," she whispered.

Rick cuffed the ghostly punk and the four ghosts all reached down to the hunk of bread. Where their hands all met and merged beneath it, the air glowed white-blue; the communal hand looked almost solid and opaque as they pushed the bread up into the air, and brought it to Alex's lips. She bit into it and chewed greedily, her taste buds singing in ecstasy at the simple yeasty flavor. Her cheeks tingled as she chewed, and the ghosts held the piece for her until it was gone.

Then Gertrude led them back and they brought her the glass of water, tilting it so that she could drink. She downed the contents in four gulps.

"Thank you so much," she whispered.

Gertrude put a finger in front of her lips and pointed to her head.

Thank you, Alex said again, through her mind only.

Don't get used to it, Matthew warned, following the chains up from her wrists to the ceiling beams with his ethereal eyes. *You better get yourself out of this soon.* With that observance, he winked out of sight.

Candace leaned forward and kissed her on the cheek and disappeared as well. And then Rick put his hands on her face, and kissed her forehead. *Be strong,* he said, and faded.

Only Gertrude remained.

You did what you had to do, the old woman said. *But be careful. Once you begin calling on the dead, it is only a matter of time.*

What's only a matter of time? Alex asked.

The old woman was already fading, but her voice trailed behind her. *With power comes responsibility,* she said.

Her mother screamed when she saw the empty glass, and missing bread. She backed away from Alex, tripping and falling backwards over an old paint can in her retreat. She caught the railing to the stairs with her right arm and pulled herself back up, raising a finger at Alex, who only stared silently at her mother's flight.

"You *are* a witch," her mother proclaimed. "Your father has been right all this time. I hoped, I prayed you would grow out of all this but . . . Oh Lord have mercy," her mother cried and ran up the stairs, slamming the kitchen door behind her.

Alex laughed. How the hell had she been born to this insane couple of losers? She used to respect her parents, as a child, but the older she'd gotten, and the more she'd seen how other parents were with their kids—the few friends Alex had managed to meet and hang out with on occasion—the more she'd realized how freaky her own parents were. Other parents didn't force their kids to kneel with them in front of a back bedroom shrine every night to recite a litany of prayers. Other parents actually allowed their kids to date when they were 16 or 17. And other parents, she was quite sure, didn't chain their children up in the basement and whip them like it was the Middle Ages.

Her father came in from the fields, and even before he changed and washed up, he came downstairs.

"Your mother tells me you've shown your true colors," he said. "I was hoping that this would go easier, that you'd repent and realize the error of your ways. I was hoping you could deny the witchery in your blood. But apparently evil is steeped in you. I had hoped to spare you the fire, but you have had your chance. The Lord demands that we be stern and follow the law. And the law says that we shall not tolerate witches among us. I hope that you enjoyed that crust of bread. It will be your last."

With that, he turned away, but Alex called him.

"Dad, this is ridiculous. Let me down from here. This is not the 1500s, people don't act like this anymore. I can see ghosts, that's all. I'm not a witch. There's no such thing."

"This is not the 1500s," he agreed, "but God and the devil are eternal. And a witch by any other name is still a whore of the devil. You must burn, my child. And maybe the fire will cleanse your soul so that you may still know heaven. I will give you the night to make your amends."

His feet were heavy on the stairs. When she heard the door upstairs close, Alex started to laugh. She couldn't control herself. The situation was absolutely ludicrous. She hadn't been in school for the past two days because her father had chained her up in the basement and whipped her until the blood dripped on the floor tiles. And now, he was apparently going to burn her in their backyard at the stake.

Alex's laughter turned to tears, until her chest was heaving in desperate need of air.

Malachai, she said. *Malachai, he's going to kill me.*

The spirit's voice spoke in her mind almost instantly.

He'll only do what you let him do, child.

What can I do about it? she asked. *I'm chained to the ceiling.*

Did you let your mother starve you? Malachai responded.

That was different, she insisted.

Was it? Listen to me, child. Your father was right about one thing. You are a witch.

"I'm not," Alex said out loud.

What do you think a witch is? the spirit asked. *A witch is just a woman who can speak to the dead, and sometimes, convince them to help her in a task. When you called upon the spirits of the dead to help you today, to bring you food, you acted a witch. Don't fall into the same trap as your father. Witches are not inherently evil. They are just different than the average plow pusher or shopkeep. They have a power, vision. How they use it is the question. But the power isn't evil, any more than holding a gun is evil. The gun can be used to kill innocents or murderers. How will you use your power, Alex?*

I don't have any power.

That's where you're wrong. And you've only got a few hours to realize it.

In the morning, Alex listened as the floorboards creaked overhead. Her throat was dry with thirst, and her stomach burning with emptiness. Her entire body was burning for one reason or another. Her back itched and cracked with painful scabs, her arms were deathly pale from lack of blood, and her legs ached from standing for three straight days. Upstairs, her parents moved about from room to room, and she heard the outside door open and close several times.

Finally, the kitchen door opened, and the stairs creaked under her father's step, slow and deliberate. Behind him, the quieter creaks of her mother followed.

"It's time," he announced, when he reached the bottom of the stairs.

Alex said nothing, only stared hard with bloodshot eyes at the two of them, her father in his stained overalls and wild gray hair, and her mother, wearing a flowery housedress that would have been old-fashioned 30 years ago.

Her father walked to her, and reached up to unlock her left cuff with a small silver key. "Hold her arm," he told his wife, and Alex's mother grabbed her forearm with a pinching grip. When he set the first arm loose, it drooped against her mother's body, and when he released her other wrist, he let the arm fall to her side. Released from the support of the chains, Alex felt her legs begin to wobble, but just as she began to sag and fall against her mother, he put a solid arm around her back and held her upright, pressing the scabs of her back painfully against his chest.

His hand slid around her ribs and as she slumped back against him, his hand ended up cupping her right breast.

"Look, Mother," Alex said, a hint of laughter in her voice. "He's not so holy. He stripped me so that he could look at me. And touch me."

Her father grabbed her hair and pulled her upright with it, slapping her in the face with his other hand.

"Serpent," he spit. "Sowing the seeds of evil even as you are led to your punishment. I feel no remorse at this, now. You are not my child. You are a witch."

"And you are a self-righteous asshole pig," she answered, only to catch another crack to the mouth. She could taste the iron in her mouth and feel the lips begin to swell, but she didn't care.

"Can't handle the truth to be spoken out loud?" she asked, and this time he didn't answer, only dragged her by hair and arm to the stairs. There, he grabbed her around the waist and lifted her up as he mounted the stairs. Alex's mother followed behind.

"Proud of the man you married?" Alex called down to her mother. "A Bible-thumping man who can touch his daughter's breasts and then burn her alive. He's a real catch, Mom."

"You will burn," he said, gritting his teeth as he shoved her through the doorway and into the kitchen. "You will burn to ash here in our backyard, and then you will burn in hell forever."

He pulled her through the kitchen, and Alex tried to struggle, but couldn't move either of her arms, and her legs were so weak she could barely stand on them, let alone try to kick or resist with them. She saw a cleaver lying on the counter near the old wooden cutting board and tried to throw her body in that direction, but her father only yanked her by the hair and dragged her through the screen door and into the backyard.

Half walking, half dragged, he brought her to the clothesline post, where a pile of freshly cut logs lay scattered. An axe extended from a cutting stump, where its blade had embedded an inch into the wood.

"Let me go," she said.

"And let you spread more evil in the world?" he said. "You are our responsibility, and I am going to take care of it."

"Let me go now," Alex insisted, the anger burning visibly in her eyes. "You have whipped me, and chained me like an

THOMPSON - NICOLA REGIONAL DISTRICT LIBRARY SYSTEM

animal. Now you have brought me naked outside, in front of you and my mother. You have done your best to humiliate and hurt me. Your job is done. Let me go. I won't be any trouble again."

"Damn right," he said, and dragged her to the post.

Michael, Sarah, Gertrude, she cried. *Agnes, Bill, Charles and Chad. Bertha and Madge and Eileen. Arnold, Terry and Betty-Sue. Help me now! I beg you and any friends you may have in this world. Please.*

Gertrude shimmered into wavery form before her, the sunlight making it difficult to see her clearly.

Be careful, child. Watch what you do.

Help me now! Alex screamed in her mind. *I have played with some of you and talked with you and traded secrets with you. We have passed the long nights together. And I need you now. Please help me!*

The air seemed to gust, and Alex's father pulled her hands around the post until her back was touching the weathered wood and her wrists were tight together. He called for the rope, and Alex's mother walked to him with a ball of brown twine, her hair lifting and covering her eyes in the breeze.

The backyard was suddenly alive with smoky faces, and the murmuring awareness of the dead.

Malachai? Alex called, not having heard his voice yet amid the growing clamor. Her parents didn't seem to notice the crackling sparks of blue fire, or the unseasonal whip of the wind.

What would you have us do? Gertrude asked.

A tall man in a black, old-fashioned suit with dark, deep-set eyes and brows, separated from the mass of spirits gathering around the stake and stood before Alex and next to Gertrude as the rope began to wind around Alex's wrists.

What would you have me do? he asked.

Malachai? Alex said, instantly recognizing his voice. He bowed, and Gertrude eyed him with distrust.

Watch your alliances, the old woman warned.

Make them stop tying me, Alex begged.

How? Gertrude asked. *You must direct us if you would have us do your will.*

Can you push or blow them backwards or something? she asked. The old woman nodded, and stepped back to call the other spirits to action. In seconds, the air around them became a blur of blue-white spirits, racing faster and faster around the post. They drew the wind in a growing hurricane with them.

"The wind is really picking up!" Alex heard her mother complain. Her father was nonplussed.

"It's her," he said. "We have been harboring a powerful witch under our roof all this time."

The wind gusted and grew, the old elm near the house beginning to twist and creak in the howl of the wind.

"What's happening?" her mother asked, holding on to the post to keep from blowing away.

"Stop this now!" he demanded, abandoning his efforts to tie Alex's wrists behind the post and stepping in front of her. "You are only delaying the inevitable," he screamed through the wind. "You will suffer the penalty for this witchcraft."

I can't move my arms, Alex told Malachai. *Can you help me move them?*

Would you have me inside your body? he asked. *I can take over your body, for a moment, if you would have me do so.*

Yes, she said.

They will say you are possessed, he warned.

It's that or be dead, she responded, and then called out to the horde of spirits.

"Gertrude, everyone, help untie my ropes," Alex cried out loud, forgetting herself. "Malachai, possess me!"

Her father's eyes opened wide at her command, and the wind swirled sharply around his legs, making him stumble as he turned to see his wife fall to the ground from the same gust.

"Devil child," he cried out. "Serpent in girl's flesh!"

The half knot of twine around Alex's wrists suddenly undid itself and her arms fell to her sides, just as a voice slipped into her brain closer than any voice had ever been before.

What would you like to do? Malachai asked. At the closeness of his touch, Alex felt something inside her shift. Her soul grew hard and sharp, deadly as a razor. The last dregs of unconditional love she'd once felt for her parents dissolved like fog in the desert. They had treated her worse than a dog, and tortured her without cause for most of her life. And she had sat still for it. As Malachai's serpentine spirit slipped into her bones and helped her find new strength, Alex became something more than human. And something less.

Fury filled her steely heart as she looked with pure hatred on her parents.

I want the axe, she said.

Hold them to the ground if you can, she asked of the screaming blue film of spirits that clouded the air, and her father suddenly fell to his knees. With Malachai's control, she walked to the stump, reached out and rocked the axe free.

Then she walked to her father, still twitching and struggling against the arms of a hundred ghosts all pushing with eternal strength at his chest to hold him pinned to the earth.

"The Bible talks about things other than punishment, Daddy," she said, standing over him with the axe held high. "It talks about mercy. But you don't understand that, so I guess I won't give you any more than you planned to give me."

With that, she swung the blade down, catching his forearm just below the elbow.

The stroke cut clean, and her father screamed an awful cry of terror as his hand gripped and released air, while the biceps that once drove it twitched. Blood sprayed from the arm and dripped down Alex's shins, but she did not stop.

"I'll tell you where the evil is in this house, Daddy," she said, bringing the axe down again, this time against his shin. The bone cracked, white splinters sticking up and out of the gore as she wiggled the axe back out. This time it hadn't cut clean through.

"The evil is in your head," she concluded, and brought the axe down again, severing his other leg.

His screams had turned to hissing gasps, as his eyes bugged out and he hyperventilated, unable to move anything but his head as his daughter dismembered him, one limb at a time.

"Honey, God no," her mother screamed nearby, her cries growing in volume as her husband died.

Alex brought the axe down on his other arm, and then stood over him as his heart pumped spurts of life out onto the grass and his eyes began to roll back in his head.

"You were an asshole, Dad," she said, and brought the axe down on his chest, crushing his ribs and sending a fountain of blood into the air to speckle her face. She brought the axe down again and again, hacking off pieces of his chest and freeing his intestines to slide like gory snakes to the ground. At last, when his eyes shone white against the blood that ran like grape juice tears down his cheeks, Alex walked to her mother, who still screamed in short, hard squeaks.

"Thanks a lot, Mom," Alex said. "You never even tried to stop him."

She killed her mother with one blow, severing her head with a solid stroke. She raised the axe once more, and brought it down to lodge in between the dead woman's ribs.

Enough? a voice whispered inside her mind.

Yeah, Alex said, and she fell to the ground as the spirit released his hold on her.

The buzz of spirits around them was already decreasing, as the dead saw that the crisis was over. Some slipped across the ground to stop briefly in front of Alex, nodding or smiling sadly before winking out of sight. Alex looked for Gertrude, but couldn't find her in the dwindling mob of blue-smoke forms.

She lay on the ground, staring back and forth from the clothesline pole to the mangled bodies of her parents, blood still spreading in pools around the remains of their bodies. From far away, she felt a cold scratching against her skull, as if someone was tickling her with a thorn-tipped feather.

They felt the focus, Malachai said. *Get your things. You can't stay here anymore.*

Who's they? she asked, and he gave a mental shrug.

Later, he said. *Clean yourself up and gather a few things. There isn't much time. You need to hit the highway.*

And do what? she asked, the enormity of her actions settling in. Her stomach felt sick, and she coughed. Bile rose in her throat.

Not now, he insisted. *I'm not far away now. If you hurry, a man will stop to pick you up on the highway. I'll be there. This is your time,* he said.

It's begun.

Chapter Eighteen

"So you were going to be a nun?" Jeremy said again in disbelief. "What could possibly have turned you from a Bible thumper to a killer? What was this Curburide?"

"You want me to tell you that my father raped me from the time I was five," she said, staring without blinking at his confused look. "You want me to tell you that he brought his friends over to gangbang on me when I was twelve, and that he made me go down on my uncle when he lost a bet in a game of poker? You want me to tell you I grew up in a crack house and worked the streets until I hated every living soul?"

Jeremy shrugged.

"Well, I'm not going to tell you that. My parents were jerks, but they had a lot of money. So I got what I wanted. But I was kind of a fat kid, and used to get picked on a lot. It wasn't until I was in high school that I started to fill out into a decent shape, and suddenly the boys all wanted to go out with me. Especially when I tried on makeup and hip-huggers. Pissed me off. Guys who'd pulled my hair and called me all kinds of names suddenly slip their grimy hands into my panties. For awhile I had fun teasing them . . . but, I don't know. It disgusted me to let them touch my body after what they'd done all through grammar school. Sex felt good, but afterwards, I used to fantasize about cutting their dicks off and giving a little back, ya know?"

Jeremy nodded, but said nothing.

"So I was eighteen, and pretty much fed up with people in general. They were all shallow and . . . users. They only wanted one thing, and only if you looked good," Ariana said, rubbing the side of her jaw as she spoke. The damage of Jeremy's beating a few hours before was really revealing itself the more she talked. "I'd gone to Catholic high school and it seemed to me like the nuns had the right deal—they got a decent house, they had built-in jobs and they didn't have to worry about dating these pathetic losers. And I really thought I believed in God and the importance of someone carrying on the work. Maybe some people could be saved, I told myself. Though I'm not sure when I really think about it, that I ever totally believed it. When I looked at the other kids in my class, I imagined them all naked, and burning in a pit of fire. Sometimes I'd daydream about the cheerleaders and the jocks during class and laugh out loud. The teachers would ask me what was so funny, but I never told them I'd just imagined Bobby and Buffy bent over the mouth of a smoking Weber grill, being sodomized by ten-foot-tall red demons with giant schlongs!"

Jeremy laughed. "Some imagination."

"It passed the time. Anyway, in my senior year, I started to talk to one of the sisters who taught my religion class about entering the convent. She coached me, and helped me get in. She never realized that I was more interested in seeing my fellow man burn in hell, than finding the kingdom of heaven. I didn't really want to save mankind, I thought it should be punished."

"Tell me about it," Jeremy said, pulling a pack of Camels from his jacket and lighting up. He leaned the chair back on two legs and rested his feet on the bed as he smoked. Over the next hour, her story slowly unfolded . . .

Ariana tried to walk quieter, but it was no use. Her steps, even in soft street shoes, echoed through the massive marble halls of the Lady of the Angels monastery. She'd been here a month now, and still hadn't gotten used to its immensity. The sisters all seemed nice, if sometimes stern. Every morning they woke to the sound of church bells, ringing low and sonorous throughout the giant enclave, and assembled in the dining room for breakfast. She ate with the two other initiates, Carla and Anne, but she didn't feel any connection to them. They were just like the girls in high school, concerned with looks and whispering back and forth about George Clooney and Brad Pitt and their favorite lipsticks. Ariana cared about none of that. She wondered how they could be set on joining the order if they were so concerned with such worldly, shallow things.

If she hadn't yet gotten used to living in a building that felt like a museum, Ariana had instantly adapted to the lifestyle. She appreciated the quiet meditation hours and the prayer times. She folded her hands and earnestly called upon God to save her soul and the souls of countless millions outside these doors. She devoured the books they were given to read, and spent her nights writing reports on those volumes, determined to fully understand and appreciate all of the subtleties of Thomas Aquinas and Coran, Pope Pius X and Father Ramone.

And now, she was walking through the guest foyer between the rooms (barracks, she thought of them) and the schooling section of the convent. Here there were classrooms (mostly unused, as girls just weren't entering the order these days like they used to) and a vast library of religious texts. It was late. The sound of snoring initiates echoed like distant foghorns through the halls. Ariana was restless. She'd finished a slim volume on the *Ethics of Corporeal Punishment*, and it had left her uncomfortable, and filled with dreams of men jerking and gasping in the electric chair, and dangling with bugged eyes and purple tongues from the noose. It filled her with a strange excitement.

The library was dark, but Ariana eased open the door and flipped on the lights. She stared across the rows and rows of shelves. Her heart leapt. It was all hers. She could spend her entire life here, reading and learning, studying the follies and furies of man in his pursuit of God. She'd given up on man and his pursuit of women. Well . . . not women per se. More his pursuit of pussy. He didn't care what the warm, pink hole was attached to as long as he could get his dick into it. She walked down a row of theological tomes, bound in red and burgundy leather, all of them worn and old, their pages yellowing.

The next bookcase was packed with biographies, lives of the saints. She pulled out a volume about Joan of Arc, then replaced it. There would be plenty of time to read about martyrs, but not tonight.

She wound her way through the already familiar room, making mental notes on books and sections she wanted to look at further. The library wound around corners in a U shape, and where the bookshelves ended, a pile of boxes began. The nuns had turned the hidden corner of the library into a storage area for old papers and equipment. A transparency projector stood forgotten to one side, the pole of its light source bent and flecked with rust. A clock radio with giant plastic dials lay upside down on the floor, its brown cord wrapped around it like a strangling rope.

Ariana wound her way through the piles of boxes and forgotten appliances until she came to the back wall of the library. The light barely reached back here; the fluorescent bulbs hadn't been replaced when they'd burnt out in the farthest couple of fixtures, and there were no windows in this part of the building. There *was* a door. A heavy, mahogany-stained wooden door hid behind the detritus of a century of prayer and missionary spirit. Curious, she stepped over a box of brochures about Catholicism and birth control and tried the knob.

Locked.

Figures, she thought, looking around the door for some indication of where it might lead. But like most things in the convent, it didn't advertise its use. Nuns, she had found, dealt with things on a need-to-know basis, and if you didn't know, well, that meant you didn't need to. It was all about faith, after all. Knowledge wasn't really important.

Shrugging, Ariana threaded her way back through the library, stopping in the Philosophical Discussions section to snag an old, frayed copy of *The Myth of Grace*, and then turned the lights out and headed back to her room.

Back in bed, with the musty smell of her latest find tickling her nose, Ariana couldn't shake the thought of the locked door. It was probably just another storage closet, she told herself, imagining shelves of yellowing paper and boxes of old rubber-banded piles of index cards inside. After trying unsuccessfully to delve into *The Myth of Grace*, she put the book down and turned her reading light off for the night. It was long after midnight, and the prayer bells would start ringing in just a few hours. She beat an indentation in her pillow and settled her head there, willing her mind to settle, to sleep.

But she kept seeing the door . . .

The next day, Ariana found herself wandering through the library again. Mother Martha was in the aisle of the saints, and Ariana smiled and nodded as she sidled by. A moment later, Mother Martha stuck her head out into the aisle.

"How are you, child?" she asked. "Enjoying Our Lady of the Angels so far?"

"Yes, Sister," Ariana replied. "I especially love this library. I just love books."

The older nun nodded and smiled, a stray wisp of white hair peeking from beneath her black veil.

"That's good to hear," she said. "So few new initiates want to read and study. But you know what they say, if you don't learn from the past . . ."

". . . you'll be doomed to repeat it," Ariana finished. The old woman walked to Ariana's side, and the two moved down the center aisle.

"Here's one of my favorite sections," Mother Martha said, pointing to an aisle marked "Sisters in Stories."

"What's in there?" Ariana asked.

"A guilty pleasure," the older nun said. "Books and stories that have nuns as characters. One needs to read something other than theological discussions and histories sometimes, so one of the sisters a long time ago began collecting books that featured nuns as protagonists, or even minor characters. It was a study, of sorts, on how the regular world sees us, but it also meant a little 'dessert' reading, too."

"This library just seems to go on and on," Ariana noted, pointing at the shelves that curved around the wall and opened into a whole other section.

The older woman laughed.

"Well, when you don't get out much, you tend to read a lot!"

"What's all the stuff back here?" the girl asked, as they rounded the last bend and the boxes and abandoned equipment came into view.

"Just what it looks like," the old woman said. "All of the things that we should have thrown away but couldn't quite bring ourselves to. Sisters are packrats! So instead they pile up back here. One of these days we'll have to back a truck up and dump it all."

Ariana stepped into the maze of precariously stacked boxes and lifted an old, black manual Corona typewriter. The keys were black with white inlaid lettering, and one metal spoke stuck out from the lower left without a letter. It was missing the Z. She pushed the handle of the carriage return and turned to the older sister.

"I haven't seen one of these since I was a kid!"

Mother Martha laughed. "Child, I was still using that typewriter a couple years ago!"

"What's back there?" Ariana finally braved, pointing at the wooden door in the back wall.

"The door?" Mother Martha asked. "That's our rare books room. Lots of old texts that some of the sisters brought over from trips to Europe and the Vatican and such. Many of them are irreplaceable, so we keep them locked up back there. Wouldn't want one of the older sisters tucking one under the mattress and forgetting about it, now would we?"

"Can you show me?" Ariana asked.

The older woman reached into the creases and folds of her

habit and came out with a gold key on a chain. She raised an eyebrow and revealed a mouthful of yellowed and graying teeth.

"Ask and you shall receive," she said, and led the way through the boxes to the door. She unlocked and pulled it open, ushering Ariana inside after flipping a light switch just inside the door. A bare bulb glowed yellow-white in the center of the ceiling.

This "mini-library" was much smaller, just three bookcases tucked inside a room not much bigger than a closet. *That was probably its original intent when it was built,* Ariana thought.

"Some of these are in Latin," Mother Martha explained, "which most of our initiates don't read anymore. These over here," she said, pointing at a row of faded green leather tomes, "are a collection of the lives of the saints that Padre Pio once had in his own collection."

She moved to the second bookcase and pointed at the top shelf. "This was Sister Augustina's collection. She studied a lot of obscure religions and ancient cults, and some of these books come from as far away as Africa. Others are nearly as old as the Church itself. We really should donate them to a special library, now that she's gone."

"What happened to her?"

"Same as will happen to all of us." Mother Martha shook her head. "Old age. She passed last year. She was ninety-one. She was still teaching world religions down at the university until she was in her eighties. Nothing ever slowed her down. She brought most of these books back herself from Belgium and Saudi Arabia and Turkey and Italy and the like. She was an amazing sister."

"Would it be okay if I looked at some of her collection?" Ariana asked.

Mother Martha nodded, her eyes visibly glossy. Her voice cracked a little when she spoke.

"I think Sister Augustina would be honored to have another student take an interest," she said. "But you must promise to be careful with these texts. Many of them are irreplaceable, I'm sure."

"I will," Ariana promised. "I'll return whatever I take directly to you, if you want."

"Yes," the older nun said. "I think that would be a good idea. Some of the other sisters might be a little apprehensive about letting a new initiate take things from this room. But I think Augustina would have wanted you to see these books. She was always, always teaching and encouraging students."

Ariana stepped up to the bookcase and began to peruse the titles.

"I'll be out in the general stacks," Mother Martha said, turning the inner lock on the door. She dabbed a tear from her cheek with the edge of her veil. "Just pull the door shut behind you when you're done browsing."

Ariana thanked the older woman and pulled out a dusty black volume with Greek lettering on the spine. When she leafed through its pages, she found the whole book was in foreign text, but it also included a series of inserts—colored artists' renderings. One depicted demons rising from the earth, and angels descending from heaven with glowing gold spears in hand.

She picked through texts that were both foreign and ancient—page edges crumbling to dust when she opened them—to fairly new, American-published softcovers. From what she could tell, they all had a similar theme: the literal struggle between good and evil. They all featured stories, art and discussions of angels battling demons on the battlefield of earth.

Ariana pulled a thin, black cloth-bound volume from the second shelf. In gold leaf, on the cover, it said simply: *The Book of the Curburide.*

She turned to the inside, and smiled at the frontispiece, a black and white sketch of a sleeping man in his bed, stocking cap twisted against his pillow. In the air above him, two figures emerged from nowhere. Their faces were long and pointed, they seemed engaged in some otherworldly conversation; one of them was looking at the other, his mouth open in speech to display equally long and wicked-looking teeth as he pointed at the sleeping form below. They both seemed to be hanging or emerging from some other realm; only their torsos and heads were visible. The artist had cut them off abruptly at the waist. The caption beneath it read:

Curburide are drawn through the cracks by vicious dreams and evil deeds.

The next page said the book had been published by the Edinborough Abbey Press in 1827. The author was listed as Msr. Patrick O'Connor.

She flipped the page and began to read:

CHAPTER ONE

Throughout human history, there have been numerous reports of demons and spirits breaking through the barriers of hell to cavort and cause havoc, with the voluntary assistance of men and women here on earth. Over the ages, witches have been known to take demons as familiars, using the otherworldly talents of the spirit to gain power and wealth in this realm, as the demon feeds off of their lusts and desires. But demons, just as humans, come in all shapes and sizes. The more powerful the demon, the more difficult it is to unlock the bindings that hold it in hell, safely removed from contact with mankind. There are Hymantic demons, dull-witted and slow-moving creatures which exist in the Ninth Circle and possess relatively few powers. These, not surprisingly, are the easiest demons to call and capture. Many a witch throughout time has found the way to ensnare a demon, only to find herself with a useless Hymantic devil as her familiar. Since the spells of binding, once performed, generally lock the witch to the demon for life in a symbiotic relationship, this is an especially disconcerting discovery for a witch to make.

Also, there are the Syphitic demons, sometimes known as Succubi and Incubi. These spirits gain power by assuming human form and seducing men and women as they sleep. While these creatures have been known to feed on unknowing men and women, most often they are called to our plane by one skilled in the demonic arts. Succubi and Incubi have been used by witches as an invisible poison sent to their enemies. The demons gain power from their sexual intercourse with humans while the victim is slowly drained of life—often with the victim's consent, as the experience is reportedly pleasurable beyond the scope of human-to-human relations.

There are many other forms and manifestations of demons on earth, but the most powerful and dangerous are the Curburide. These are creatures that feed on the most evil of human acts. Vicious torture, sadistic and deadly sexual relations and mass murder serve as the sustenance for these demons. Not surprisingly, witches throughout the ages have performed ritual killings to attract the attention and servitude of these creatures, who, when manifesting in the earthly realm, possess astounding and devastating power. Not surprisingly, in the architecture of the afterworld, the Curburide are the most closely guarded of demons and have great difficulty slipping through their bonds to appear on earth. It takes a long period of dedicated ritual and Calling for a witch to bring the Curburide through to the earthly realm. And once manifested, the demons are rarely bound to the will of the witch; they are extraordinarily powerful and independent, and many a witch has met her just and painful end at the hands of a Curburide spirit that has been brought through to the earthly realm without adequate binding spells.

In this volume, I will document the most infamous Curburide apparitions that have been recorded. No doubt there are hundreds of incidents that have gone unreported over human history. But from the documented instances of Curburide appearances, it is clear that this is the most deadly and difficult of the demons of hell to control. The Curburide are seductive, sinister creatures whose sole mission is to violate and eviscerate humankind.

The hairs on the back of Ariana's neck raised as she read the text recorded nearly 200 years before on these yellowed, flaking pages. She had heard the legend of the succubus before, but never of the Curburide. She decided to take that, and a more recent volume titled *Demonic Possessions Through the Ages* back to her room to study further.

Ariana turned off the light in the tiny, hidden library and pulled the door shut behind her, checking the knob afterwards to make sure it had locked. Mother Martha was back in the Lives of the Saints aisle, and smiled at the girl as she showed the old woman her choices.

"She studied a lot about demons and angels, didn't she?" Ariana asked, holding the book on *Demonic Possessions* out for the nun to see.

Mother Martha nodded. "It was a favorite subject of hers."

She leafed through the book's pages, and then looked Ariana sternly in the eye. "Just remember as you read these, that the Church frowns these days on stories of possession and demons. It is the belief now that heaven and hell are separate realms that living men cannot interact with. So most of Sister Augustina's collection would be dismissed by our cardinals and theologians today."

"I understand," Ariana said. "I won't bring these up in class!"

The older sister put her hand on Ariana's shoulder. "The world is wider than we will ever know, child. There are things that we cannot see, and forces at work that are best for us not to know about. Be mindful of that as you read; and don't be afraid to put some knowledge back on the shelf, unread and unlearned. There are some things it is best not to know."

"Thanks, Mother Martha," Ariana said. "I'm just curious, that's all. I won't keep reading if anything bothers me."

The older nun pursed her lips in thought.

"If you have questions, come to me, and I'll answer what I can. Now run along; you're going to be late for morning prayer."

Ariana hurried back to the "dorm" side of the convent and hid the books in her dresser drawer beneath her underwear. Then she went to morning prayer, but instead of focusing on the Hail Mary's and Our Father's, her mind kept slipping back to the books she knew awaited her at the end of the day. She wanted to know more. Her stomach tingled when she thought of the words she had read. She rolled the word around in her mind, wondering if such a being could really exist. *Curburide,* she thought. *Curburide.*

"So, my guess is you never returned that book to the old nun's library," Jeremy said, stubbing out his fourth cigarette of the morning. He stretched, groaning at the aches and pains from last night's violence, and stood, walking across the room to the hotel window.

"No," Ariana said. "I returned the other book to Mother Martha the next week, and gave her an old theology textbook I'd picked up at a used bookstore in place of *The Book of the Curburide.* She didn't notice the difference. She probably would never have known the difference if I'd given her back a couple of cookbooks. She was pretty old, and not very sharp."

"So, does the book say that you have to sacrifice a man?" Jeremy asked, looking back at her from the window. Ariana shook her head, grimacing at the pain the motion brought.

"No," she said. "Just that it has to be a person primed for sex. And after they are sacrificed, the rituals must be observed."

Jeremy came and sat on the edge of the bed next to her.

"You'd like to stay alive to finish calling these demons, wouldn't you?" he asked rhetorically. She nodded.

"I'd like to stay alive and not become one of your sacrifices," he said. "I think we can make a deal here and both leave this room alive. But you have to agree to do one thing."

The corners of Ariana's lips twisted up higher and higher

as Jeremy unveiled his plan. When he was finished, he folded his arms across his chest and set his chin to granite, awaiting her reaction. It was not long in coming.

"I think we're going to make a great team," she pronounced.

Chapter Nineteen

Terrel Beach was not dotted with umbrellas or covered with a patchwork quilt of garish towels and oily, sweating bodies. That didn't stop Cindy from setting up an electric yellow towel, stripping off the white T-shirt (it read *What are YOU lookin' at?*) and shimmying out of her denim shorts. It was like her own private beach, and Cindy had always felt free and safe here. Even when she hadn't been.

Too many bodies had washed up on shore here after taking that oddly frequent fall from the cliff for most people to feel comfortable swimming here. But Cindy knew all that was over now. The spirit, Malachai, had left its residence in the cliff which loomed over the bay, and would no longer be accepting sacrifices from the mothers of Terrel.

Feet sinking in the soft, hot sand, Cindy looked at the black crag and felt a cloud of remorse smother the day's sunshine. The last time she'd been here, wearing this very same Day-Glo bikini, Joe had been with her. He'd complimented her on her tan and her sexy suit and the way her long blonde hair accented the brown of her skin. They had made love that night at his apartment. And not long after that, she had gone into the bowels of Terrel Cliff with him and Malachai had taken possession of her body, using her as a lure for Joe, almost getting him killed.

He had forgiven her that, but once Joe had struck a new covenant with the demon and Malachai had become his constant companion, things hadn't been the same between them.

They had dated awhile, but slowly he drew back from her, and then one day he had called and said he'd quit his job at the paper and was leaving town.

Her eyes misted up thinking of that last conversation. What if she'd begged him harder to stay? What if she'd driven to his apartment and planted herself in front of the door? Could he have really run from her if she'd forced him to say good-bye to her face?

It didn't matter. She'd lost the two most important guys in her life to the cliff. The first, James, had jumped from it to his death, to fulfill the promise that his mother had made to Malachai. And then she had met Joe—serious, shy Joe—who had healed her still-bleeding heart from aching at the loss of James. Joe had romanced her with his adorable clumsiness, and drawn her into his investigation of the deaths that seemed to circle the cliff like a flock of buzzards. But his curiosity had nearly killed them both, and his solution had been to take Malachai into his head when they arrived at an impasse in the caves deep inside the cliff. She had lost him then, she knew it now. At first she'd kissed and hugged him, her savior. But the troubled looks had started at that moment, and by the time he had called her to say good-bye, it was no surprise to her. He was haunted by Malachai, and couldn't stay in Terrel anymore. Never mind that Malachai was going to be with him wherever he ran.

Maybe that's what she needed to do, too, Cindy thought, walking alone towards the edge of the cool blue-green water. Now that Terrel had no hold over her, spiritual or romantic, maybe it was time to leave.

She walked out into the waves, bracing herself against the crash of the water as it sucked outwards towards the ocean, and then rolled back in, slapping her thighs like an icy board. When its level ranged from thigh-high to belly-deep, Cindy stopped and waited for a wave to come in. Just before the next one hit, she leapt into the air and arced into the oncoming wave, cutting into the sea with her hands full-forward, and disappearing below the white foam of the crest.

There was nothing left for her here but the ocean, she thought, and kicked her way down to slip along the smooth sea fronds below.

Chapter Twenty

"So now what?" Alex asked.

"You actually chopped up your parents with an axe?" Joe stared at the innocent-looking teen lying next to him.

"They kept me chained in the basement, naked, without food, and were about to burn me at the stake for being a witch," Alex said, punching him in the shoulder. "What would you have done, kissed them on the cheek and said thanks?"

Joe laughed. "No, I s'pose not. I guess I'll try not to do anything to piss you off too badly as long as you're riding with me, though."

She propped herself up on her elbow, her freckles spreading as her lips opened to a grin. "You mean I can stay? You're not going to ditch me?"

"As long as you promise not to hack me into bits, or carve me up with a pocketknife or something, no. You've been messed up by demons just like I have, and one demon in particular has brought us together. It's about time we found out exactly why."

"You think he wants something from us?"

"Malachai doesn't do anything out of the goodness of his heart. He doesn't have one. Either he led you to me so that you would slice me up and set him free, or he needs you for something else."

"I'm not going to hurt you, Joe," she promised.

"Heard that before."

"I mean it," she insisted, crawling over to lean on his chest.

"I like you. I wouldn't do anything to hurt you. You've been really good to me."

Joe looked into her eyes and saw truth pooled there. Something familiar stirred in his heart, and he put his hands on her shoulders. They were small but strong, and he longed to run his hands along her arms, and down her ribs to her waist . . .

"Malachai," he called out loud, breaking this unwanted train of thought. He looked away from her, out into the dark stand of ancient pines. "Malachai, it's time for some answers."

The campfire flared, sparks spitting up into the air as a log settled and waves of heat shimmered above the tongues of fire. The air rippled and curved as the fire died back down, and an almost invisible figure rose from the center of the fire and stepped back to the opposite side of the flames from where Joe and Alex lay. The air seemed to fold around the figure giving it shape where the light refracted at its edges, as it stepped across the brown, matted grass and then sat its shimmering haunches on a log.

The eyes glowed electric blue from the shadowed face, and Alex grabbed Joe's arm as the spirit lifted an arm and pointed at them.

"Ask the right questions if you want the answers you seek," it said out loud, and Joe recognized its voice as Malachai's. It was deeper, more foreboding when not lodged inside his head, but it was definitely the demon.

"Why did you bring Alex to me?" Joe asked.

"She was a friend of mine," the demon replied. "And she needed my help."

"Why did you seek out her friendship?" Joe countered.

"Am I only to be friends with you, then, master?" the demon asked, drawing out and exaggerating the word *master*.

"Enough games, Malachai," Joe said. "There is a reason that you want Alex and me together, and I demand that you tell us what it is."

"I thought you'd make a cute couple," the demon jeered, standing and walking towards them. It put a ghostly hand on Alex's shoulder, and gestured with his free hand.

"And I was right," Malachai finished.

Alex drew back, scooting away from Joe and the demon, and Joe raised a finger at the hazy figure.

"Does this have to do with the Curburide?" Joe asked.

"Perhaps," Malachai said. "You're getting warm."

"Jesus," Joe swore.

"No, Malachai," the demon answered. "Though I can see how you'd be confused."

"Malachai, please," Alex said, finally entering the fray. "You helped me. You saved me. But why? What do you want from me?"

The demon shimmered, as if he were a pool of water that a rock had skipped across. Then his image seemed to strengthen, and Joe and Alex could see his features clearly. His eyes still shone bright, but now his craggy cheeks and dense, dark beard became visible, as well as the long black cloak that covered most of his body.

"I am not allowed to want," he announced, bending closer to Joe's face. "I am but a servant to my master."

Joe laughed.

"Oh yeah," he said. "I can always count on you. To get me killed."

"By the terms of our covenant," Malachai announced, suddenly sounding strained and formal, "I am yours to command. Mine is not to act independently or to guide you in matters of church and state. I do your bidding, master."

"What the hell, Malachai?" Joe asked. He opened his mouth to say more, but then saw the look in the demon's eyes. The spirit itself looked haunted.

"Okay," Joe said. "You are not the mastermind behind bringing Alex to me. It just happened. But now that she's here, I'm guessing there's a use for her spirit sight. She could probably help me against the Curburide somehow, right?"

"If you were to choose to stop them from breaking through the barriers into this world and destroying all of your kind, yes," Malachai said. "She could be very helpful if you were to embark on such a quest."

"I see," Joe said, looking at Alex to gauge her reaction. The girl raised an eyebrow, but said nothing.

"And if we were to begin such a foolhardy quest, where would we go?"

The demon grinned, pleased that Joe was playing along.

"Well, you're the reporter," the demon said, "but, I imagine you would go back to the beginning."

"And where was the beginning?" Joe asked.

"The first sacrifice occurred in San Francisco, as you know," Malachai said. "It was only a couple weeks ago, so the trail should still be warm." The demon leaned forward to stare at Alex. "And if any of the Curburide are lingering there, waiting for the chain to be forged, *she* should be able to see them."

"Sounds like a witch hunt," Joe said.

The demon grinned and began to fade.

"And if we find one?" Joe called after him.

"Run," Malachai advised, and disappeared.

"Well, that was helpful," Joe said, turning to Alex. "He's difficult to deal with normally, but, talk about pulling teeth!"

"It seemed like he was forbidden to talk about it," she said.

"Maybe," he admitted. "Though I can't think by who."

"How did you bind him to you in the first place?" she asked. "Could it be the terms you placed on him somehow?"

Joe shook his head. "No, all I did was call him by name and demand that he pledge himself and his power to me."

"Maybe it has something to do with his being allowed to stay on earth," she suggested.

He shrugged.

"Whatever it is, we now know he wants us to go to San Francisco. I've got a car, a couple of grand and no job. You've got no parents, no car and are wanted for questioning in a brutal double-murder case. Feel like a road trip?"

Alex beamed.

"Sure."

* * *

Joe cooked a pork roast over the fire for dinner, since he'd loaded the car with supplies, and afterwards they lay back on the ground and stared up at the stars. After a while, Alex scooted closer and rested her head on his chest. He stifled the urge to pull her even closer.

"Have you ever really looked at how many stars there are?" he said instead, and she drew in a long, slow breath.

"It's amazing," she said, drawing invisible lines in the air between the lights. "Millions and millions of them, and all of them billions of miles away."

"Think there are demons on other planets?" he asked.

"Yeah," she said. "I think there are demons everywhere."

"Nice attitude," he laughed.

"Evil seems to be stronger than good," she said.

"Your parents didn't win, did they?"

"No," she said rolling across his chest to straddle him, "but I had the help of an evil spirit. Maybe they *were* the good guys."

"Hmmm."

Joe put his arms around her and gave her a hug, pulling her close.

"I still think good won over evil," he whispered in her ear. "Whaddya say about catching some sleep. We've got a long drive tomorrow."

She pushed back from him and nodded, picking up pots and dishes and keeping her eyes from meeting his. He'd embarrassed her. Good. It should keep them apart for at least another night. Joe bit his lip and rolled to his feet.

Dangerous waters here, indeed.

Alex was quiet the next morning, and Joe didn't push the issue. He wound the car back down the mountain and headed north to merge back on I-80 West, towards Salt Lake City. It would take at least a day of nonstop driving to get to California, and he hoped the girl could spell him a couple hours if he got tired. Of course, if the cops pulled them over . . .

The morning passed uneventfully, and Joe pulled off around 1 P.M. to find lunch in a small town. Just off the highway, he pulled into a truck stop and filled the car with gas. They walked into the diner section of the truck stop after, and sat down on some art deco—era stools across the counter from the grill.

"I'll have the cheeseburger and fries, everything on it," Joe told the pinstripe uniformed waitress after scanning the plastic-coated one-page menu. Alex followed suit. The waitress—a portly middle-aged woman with dirty blonde, tightly kinked curls peeking out from beneath her pink and white cap—disappeared with their order through hanging silver doors to the kitchen.

The place was modeled after a '50s drive-in, with red vinyl booths and formica counters. An old jukebox separated the men's and women's bathrooms, and Alex excused herself to use the latter. There was only one other person in the place with them, an old man in a faded blue jacket at the far end of the counter. Joe noticed him, but didn't think more about him until Alex came back.

"Everything come out alright?" he asked idly, and she snorted.

"Like a thunderstorm," she said. "Thunder and lightning and everything."

"You playing with Malachai again, or taking a leak?" he countered, but she didn't answer. Instead, she elbowed him and nodded in the direction of the old man, leaning back to put Joe's body in between them so that he couldn't see her.

"What's up with him?" she asked. "He won't stop looking at us."

Joe looked at the man again, and noticed the bright gleam of the eyes that did seem to be awfully focused in his direction.

"Can I help you?" Joe asked. He'd found it never hurt to be bold.

The man grinned.

"They're coming," the man said, and began to laugh out loud. "They're coming."

"Who?" Joe said as Alex's grip tightened on his arm, but just then the swinging doors crashed open and the waitress bustled through, a plate in each hand.

"They're hot, so watch yourselves," she warned, slapping the heavy white ceramic plates down in front of them, fries rolling off onto the counter.

"Ketchup for your fries?" she asked, and Alex said sure. The woman leaned to her right, reached under the counter and came back with an unmarked plastic container with a thin funnel at its end.

When she stepped back toward the kitchen, Joe looked at the other end of the counter. The old man had vanished.

"Malachai," he hissed under his breath.

It wasn't me, a voice said in his mind. *There are others who are concerned about current events as well.*

Why are they talking to me about it?

They know you are on the trail. They hope you will hurry.

"What did he say?" Alex asked.

"He said we'd better eat fast and get back on the road," Joe growled, lifting his burger. "Apparently we're the only game in town, and we have a cheerleading squad."

Chapter Twenty-one

The house was dark, except for the light of the television in the back bedroom. Sheila's station wagon was parked, as usual, in the driveway, but a Sonata was parked next to it. And the Sonata was not Jeremy's.

"You didn't come home last night," Ariana whispered as they tiptoed up the front lawn. "Maybe she had a friend come over to keep her company."

"Yeah, and I know exactly what kind of company she's keeping with him," Jeremy said and hopped the fence to the side yard. Ariana followed, her latex catsuit creaking as she threw a leg over the top of the fence, and Jeremy put a finger to his lips.

"Shhh."

They crept between the fence and the air conditioner and in seconds were in the backyard next to the window projecting the flickering blue light of a TV.

Ariana put her hand on his arm, holding him back from looking.

"Does it matter what she's doing in there?" she asked. "If she's not making time, are you going to back out on me?"

"No," he promised. "She's yours, no matter what, just like we agreed."

She nodded, and released her grip. Jeremy stood next to the window and slowly moved his eyes to the right until he could see inside. The network news was on, a talking head anchorman sat behind a nondescript desk as a small window of live footage played next to his head. The blue and red light of the tube reflected off the small of Sheila's sweat-slicked back, which writhed sinuously up and down, back and forth. Her hair was matted and stuck to her shoulders, and she leaned down to rest herself with her hands on a man's chest for a second, before sitting straight upright again and wiggling back and forth against the stranger's groin. He couldn't see the man's face, but Jeremy could see his hairy legs sticking out from beneath his wife's white ass, and the man's big, thick-fingered hands clenching his wife's waist. She was giving her lover a full show, tilting her head back and massaging her own breasts for him, rubbing them up tight to her body and then letting them free to flop and shake as she bounced and moved in a passion dance across her lover's groin.

Jeremy held up two fingers to Ariana, and she nodded. He dropped away from the window to a crouch and let her check out the scene so she was aware of what they were walking into.

She pressed her body to the brick and slid her face across the lower section of the window until one eye connected with the scene in the room. She grinned silently as she watched the woman wantonly fuck the man in her bed. She could see why Jeremy had put up with being cuckolded for so long; Sheila was a knockout. Long, kinky hair the color of apple juice, full, rolling breasts with wide brown nipples, a waist that tapered to a tightness most women would kill for, and a round bottom that had, so far, escaped the tracks of cellulite. Ariana couldn't see her face clearly, but she had the impression of an aquiline nose and aristocratic good looks.

Sheila reminded her of the socialite cheerleaders who had snubbed her all through high school. She was going to enjoy killing this one.

Ariana pulled herself away from the erotic scene inside and crouched next to Jeremy.

"Ready to have some fun?"

He nodded.

"You've got the rope?"

"Yeah."

"The gun?"

"Check."

"The key?"

"Unless she's changed the lock."

"Lead on Mercutio!"

Jeremy led her to the basement stairwell, and fumbled the key into the lock. He turned the knob slowly, and then cushioned the door with his shoulder as he pushed it open, trying to make as little sound as possible. Taking her hand, he guided Ariana around a laundry basket to the slatted door that led from the utility room they'd entered by, into the downstairs rec room.

They stopped for a minute there, to let their eyes adjust, and then Ariana put two fingers to his back and pushed.

He moved on, towards the stairs leading up into the kitchen, and then stumbled, his foot slipping off the head of a doll. The toy squeaked, just a bit, and skidded to the side as Jeremy began to fall. But Ariana grabbed him at the waist and held him until he recovered his balance, breathing heavy and listening hard. There were no sounds from upstairs, beyond the faint cadence of a newscaster.

He started up the stairs, rounding the corner of the kitchen and then stopping at the hallway that led to the master bedroom. He put a hand up to Ariana and held his head out into the hall, listening. The TV was louder, and now he could hear the muffled sound of other voices, and his wife's unmistakable moan of pleasure.

He waved two fingers and started down the hall, stopping at his daughter's bedroom to peer inside. The door was open, and the bed still made. Good. As he'd suspected when he saw the car parked outside, Sheila had sent their daughter to her mother's, or a friend's for the night so she could have her fun undisturbed by conscience. Or interruption.

They tiptoed down the hallway, stopping just before the half-open door of the bedroom. Ariana motioned for Jeremy to take a breath, and he took a deep one. Then he reached into his pocket, pulled out the toy gun, and nodded. She held up three fingers, dropped one, then another, and then the third. They pushed through the door together.

Sheila was on her hands and knees now, taking it from behind, and the two adulterers looked up as one at the intrusion.

"Aw, shit," the man said. Sheila didn't say a thing, only rolled her eyes.

"Don't mind me," Jeremy said, crossing his arms. "Go about your business. I can wait for a few minutes until you're ready to tell me why you're fucking *my* wife in *my* bed."

"Who's the catwoman, Jer?" Sheila said with feigned disinterest from her ungraceful position on the bed.

"Oh no," Jeremy answered. "I think you should introduce your boyfriend first."

Sheila slid her haunches to the bed and lay on her side, exposing her all to Jeremy and Ariana. The tight line of her pubic hair glistened with moisture; they'd been at this for awhile.

"Whatever you like, dear. Jeremy, this is Paul. Paul, Jeremy. And . . . um . . . Catwoman. Been out for Halloween, Jer? I missed you last night. Figured you'd given up the spark."

Paul had stepped off the bed and was looking bemused. He was a big man, at least six foot, dark-haired and well-muscled. His cock dangled at half erection, and he tried surreptitiously to hold his hands together to shield it from view. But it wasn't working; a pale pink blob of flesh peeked out from beneath his fingers, like a fat worm inching towards the wet earth.

"I haven't given up, Sheila," Jeremy answered. "But I have a new game to play. A spectator sport."

Ariana pulled the rope out from the bag Jeremy carried and tossed it on the bed.

"Tie his hands behind his back," she said cooly.

"Do it yourself, catgirl," Sheila said, stretching out lazily on the bed.

Jeremy took his cue and raised the gun. It all depended on this moment. He didn't think he could take Paul in a fair fight. He was built, but Paul looked pumped.

"Do what I say for once, Sheila," he said. "Tie your boyfriend's hands behind his back if you want the two of you to stay alive. We're going to have a little fun tonight. And then I'm going to get out of your hair and you never have to see me again. If you're up for it, you can fuck whoever you want, whenever you want. But right now, you're mine for one last time."

Sheila saw the look in his eye, and sat up. She glanced back at Paul, looking for advice, or permission. His cock had shriveled to hide fully, finally, behind his hands, and he nodded.

Sheila took the rope and slipped off the bed to start tying it around her boyfriend's wrists.

"Behind his back," Jeremy reminded, motioning with his gun.

Paul moved his arms to grip his hands together behind his back, and Sheila knelt behind him, face level with the tan line of his ass to tie his wrists together with the heavy twine Ariana and Jeremy had bought that afternoon, at the hardware store just blocks away.

Ariana stepped forward and reached into the hidden back pocket of her suit. Something clicked, and when Sheila looked up, it was to stare at the four-inch business end of a switchblade.

"Tie them tight," Ariana demanded. "I'm going to test them and if they're not Houdini-safe, I'm going to carve my name in your back. That way, you'll never forget it."

Jeremy moved closer, still threatening with the fake pistol, and Ariana held the very real knife to Sheila's back.

The naked woman wound the rope tight around her lover's wrists, and at Ariana's direction, crisscrossed the strands and drew the noose tight. When she was done with his hands, Ariana directed her to tie his ankles together as well.

"That hurts," Paul complained at one point, and Ariana answered, brandishing the knife at his face.

"Better that than this."

He shut up.

When Paul was sufficiently hog-tied, Ariana cut the end of the rope with her knife and told him to lie down on the bed.

"You just watch now, baby," she cooed. "Jeremy," she said, voice dripping all honey, "tie up your little slut here."

He crossed the room and handed Ariana the gun. She stepped back and watched as Jeremy pulled the rope tight around Sheila's wrists, and then did the same to her ankles.

When he was done, he pushed her down face-first on the bed. She rolled to her back and wrinkled her nose at him in disgust.

"Don't fucking make faces at me, you whore," he said. "You smell like the cum bucket you are."

"No different than I smelled from yours, dickhead," she spit.

"All right," Ariana said. "Let's not get ugly. We're here to have fun, right Jeremy?"

"Exactly," he agreed. "Good, clean, fuck-everyone-in-sight fun."

"I'm glad you still agree," she said. "Because I think I'd like a taste of your wife's beefcake here. If he can get that thing up again, it looked like a rod worth a ride."

She unzipped the side of her black latex suit and let a tit hang out for him to see.

"Whaddya say, Paul?" she urged. "Think you can do the job for me? I know I don't have jugs like your squeeze over there," she nodded at Sheila, who was starting to finally scowl in anger on the bed next to him.

"Whatever you say," he answered, and Ariana laughed.

"That's the spirit," she said, stripping the suit down to her boots.

Paul obviously admired the tight line of her belly and thighs as she walked to the bed, still wearing the long black boots and elbow-length gloves. The catsuit trailed behind her on the floor, and her otherwise pale, flawless skin showed yellow and purpled around her ribs from Jeremy's kicks the night before . . .

"Guard your whore, Jeremy," she advised, and knelt on the bed to straddle Paul's already admirable erection.

"Just a little lesson in how it feels to have something of yours taken right out from under you," she said to Sheila, retracting the blade of her knife.

She put the haft against Paul's chest.

"My finger's on the trigger," she warned. "I hope you're not a shaker. Make one false move, and I won't wait to see if it's because you're cumming or trying to escape. I'll release the blade into your heart."

She could feel his cock tremble and grow harder against her thigh at the threat, and she grinned. Amazing what turned some people on, she thought, and lowered herself onto him.

"Yesss," she grinned as he entered her, and she began to repeat the motions that Sheila had been making, not long before. Only Sheila had taken her time—she hadn't been holding a knife to his chest, so Sheila hadn't fucked fast and dry and hard. Ariana grunted and sighed, as much from pain as pleasure. Paul lay wide-eyed and silent beneath her, aroused by the violation, but aware of the hands tied behind his back and the knife at his heart. Despite the fear—or perhaps because of it—he found himself cumming as soon as Ariana announced her orgasm. She closed her eyes and rode him even faster, squeaking in short bursts of pleasure as the orgasm flowered from her groin to her thighs and belly in a wave of heat and pleasure. She raised herself off of him just as his own last jet of sperm dribbled from his cock to slide like extra hand lotion down his shaft.

"Jealous, bitch?" Ariana asked Sheila, pulling her catsuit back up and rezipping the zippers until once again, she was a vision in black.

"Bite me," Sheila snapped.

"Oh no," Ariana said, tugging the last zipper down her arm. "You're getting ahead of me now. I had something else in mind."

She pointed at Paul's now-flagging, glistening cock.

"Bite him," she demanded.

When Sheila didn't move, Jeremy grabbed her hair with his free hand and pushed her head to Paul's crotch.

"Suck it like you do when you're alone," Ariana demanded. "See what it's like to taste someone else's juice on your lover."

"Fuck you," Sheila said and rolled back.

Jeremy slapped her on the side of the head with his hand.

"Get busy," he said. "For once in your life, you'll do as you're told."

Sheila looked up at him, hatred in her eyes, and then took Paul's dick in her mouth, sliding it in and grimacing.

"You love it and you know it," Ariana laughed, and then said sweetly, "Jeremy, cover Paul, would you?"

Jeremy walked around the bed, and shoved the gun barrel up under Paul's throat, where he couldn't get a good close-up look at the weapon. For a few more minutes, the ruse had to work.

Ariana hit the button and let the switchblade out again. She held it to the muscle popping and retracting in Sheila's neck.

"You might want to sit on him," Ariana suggested, and Paul went bug-eyed, as Jeremy threw his leg over the man's bare chest and rested his full weight against him, crotch to sternum.

"Keep sucking," Ariana advised Sheila. "You're really good at this. Jeremy, did she ever do this for you? If so, you were a pretty lucky boy."

Jeremy looked over his shoulder and shook his head.

"No, she claimed she hated it after the first couple times. She never did it once we were married."

"Ah," Ariana said. "Just goes to prove, some things are best left for affairs."

She pressed the knife against Sheila's throat, so the woman could feel the pinch of the blade. Her skin turned white around the edge of the blade and a drop of blood slid along the edge, as if the knife were a new capillary to guide it somewhere else.

"Sheila," Ariana said, bringing her face down close to the woman's cheek, still sucking and releasing the persistent erection of Paul. "I want you to listen to me. I know you're enjoying that lovely piece of meat there; it's really a sweet piece.

But Jeremy and I have discussed this already, and what I'm about to say is what you're going to do. If you try to get out of this without doing it, I'm going to slit your throat. And believe me, I don't have a problem with that. But I don't think you want me to do that."

Sheila shook her head as Paul's cock bobbed against the side of her cheek.

"Sheila," Ariana said. "I want you to bite Paul's cock off."

The woman's eyes went wide, and Paul began to struggle beneath Jeremy when he heard the direction.

Jeremy pushed the barrel of the gun harder against the soft skin beneath Paul's chin and cautioned, "That will hurt a lot less than this."

"Be quick and bite hard," Ariana suggested. "It will hurt you both less."

Sheila began to pull back from holding Paul's dick in her mouth and Ariana pressed the knife against her throat. Blood began to flow freely against the blade, dripping on Paul's thigh.

"Do it now," she said, and her voice didn't leave room for argument. "I'm not fuckin' joking."

Sheila looked wildly from Ariana's cold eyes to Jeremy's back.

"Now, Sheila," Ariana demanded. Her voice was steely as a bear trap.

Sheila closed her eyes, and brought her jaws together as hard as she could. There was resistance, but not as much as she feared. And then her mouth was flooded with the warm taste of iron and she drew back, spitting and gagging at the giant disengaged dick stuck between her teeth and her epiglottis.

Paul screamed, and Jeremy fell on him, holding him down, covering his cries with his chest.

"Nice," Ariana praised, as a jet of blood spurted from the man's crotch to dot both hers and Sheila's faces. The other woman opened her eyes wide at the sight of her bloodied boyfriend and gagged, spitting out both the rubbery shaft of his dick and a burst of vomit on the bed.

"A gag would be good," Ariana advised, and Jeremy hopped off the bed to pull a pair of nylons from his wife's dresser. He wrapped them around Paul's face until the man's cries had subsided to low gasps. Despite his height and girth, without his penis, Paul shrank to the size of a large child, curling into a wounded fetal position and crying softly to himself.

"Jeremy," Ariana said. "You were right. Your wife really is a cock eater. You wanna last taste of her before we go?"

Jeremy smiled.

"I think maybe I will. It's been awhile, after all."

"Think you can handle it, with her legs tied together and all?"

"She's wide as a train tunnel, obviously," Jeremy said, leaving his guard of Paul and unhitching his belt. "Shouldn't be a problem."

"Want me to hold her down for you?" Ariana asked, and Jeremy nodded. "Thanks, that'd be nice."

Ariana dragged Sheila by her hair away from the pile of vomit and bleeding cock on the bedspread, and then pushed her down on the bed with a hand on her forehead. Then she sat on the woman's neck.

"Enjoy it if you can," she advised, and then Jeremy was forming a fleshy human triangle with her, holding Ariana's shoulders as he thrust himself between the tight thighs of his wife and into her hidden caverns, still slippery with her previous exertions.

"It might be awhile before you feel anything like this again," he said, hugging Ariana's latex tighter and tighter with his increasing rhythm, until with a gasp, he came inside his wife, one last time.

Ariana slid off the woman and stood beside the bed. "Care for a souvenir?"

Sheila looked dazed and unmoving, while Paul was rocking slowly, curled in a pathetic C at the far edge of the king-size mattress.

"Yes," Jeremy agreed. "Something to remember her by."

Ariana reached out and tweaked one of Sheila's broad nipples between a black-clad thumb and forefinger.

"You liked these, right?"

He nodded. "Definitely suckable."

She flicked her arm around and with a lightning flash of silver, severed the stretched nipple with her knife, tossing the rubbery, bloodied pink tip to him.

"Enjoy," she said. Sheila screamed and thrashed on the bed.

"Try the other one yourself," Jeremy advised, holding his wife by the hair. "They're probably better when attached."

"I've never sucked tit before," Ariana said, raising an eyebrow at him.

"Never a better time than the present . . ."

"True," she agreed, and lowered her face to Sheila's bounteous still-whole left breast, getting her cheek smeared with blood in the process from the woman's bloodied right.

Ariana sucked at the nipple, marveling at how it grew harder and more defined in her mouth. And when it got to the point where it felt almost solid—gummy chewy between her teeth— she bit down. Hard.

Ariana pulled back from the woman flopping up and down against the mattress and spit the rosy nipple out onto Sheila's spastically bucking belly.

"Yeah," she said, "they're better attached. You wanna shut her up?"

Jeremy retrieved another set of nylons and gagged his wife, who bit and thrashed as he tied the material around her neck.

"I never used to be mean," he whispered in her ear, "before I met you."

"Okay, enough fun. I need to say the words," Ariana said, leaving the bed. "Cover them."

Jeremy held the gun on the two, but the threat wasn't needed. Hog-tied and bleeding from their most private places, neither Paul nor Sheila were trying to escape. Instead, they each had curled into balls and seemed to be hiding their faces, hoping their captors would just go away.

Ariana reached into the pack she'd carried and extracted 16 bones and 21 pebbles and placed them in a circle. Then she knelt in the middle of the floor by the bed and murmured something that sounded to Jeremy like church. Latin maybe. Every now and then he thought he heard her say "Curburide."

When she rose, the blade glinted evilly.

"It's time," she announced. She walked to the side of the bed, and put the blade against Paul's throat. He looked up finally, eyes stretching to leave his face, disbelief coloring the wrinkles around the nylon that stuffed his mouth.

"You should have stuck to women who were really available," she said, and slid the blade along the side of his throat. The skin was white as the knife slid away from it, and then it changed to a thin red line.

And then it was an angry, weeping red line.

And then she slid the blade like a credit card across the front of his neck and blood began to fountain across the bed.

Even through the gag, Sheila's screams of rage were very audible, and Ariana turned to the struggling woman and grinned.

"Oh, don't worry," she said. "I'll get to you next."

Paul began to shiver and tried to roll off the bed, but Ariana stopped him, plunging the blade straight into his chest.

"Sometimes the way to a man's heart is through his ribs," she advised the observing Sheila, who cried even louder.

"And sometimes," she continued, moving the knife to a point just above the hair of his groin, "it's through his stomach."

Ariana pushed the knife in deep, and drew it upwards, following the line of oily black hair from his crotch to his sternum. When she was finished, she dropped the blade to the ground and reached into Paul's opened gut with both hands, and withdrew the pink and crimson rope of his intestines for Sheila to see.

Her fingers and wrists were slicked with gore, and Jeremy looked away.

"It all comes down to this," Ariana warned. She pulled the intestines out of his body, one curl at a time, giving a hard yank when the last bit remained stubbornly connected.

When she had it all out, Ariana draped his guts around his head in a halo, and then reached up inside him, through the rib cage, to yank down his heart using only her fingers and nails.

She came back with a bloody organ, and held it out for Sheila to see.

"Care for a kiss?" she asked. "His heart is yours if you want it."

Sheila screamed again, and tears flooded her face like a rainstorm. Ariana placed the organ between the fresh corpse's legs, and then went back to pull out more bits and pieces. She arranged each organ in a circle around Paul's dead body.

At last, Ariana reached into the pile of red and yellow vomit on the bed, and fished out the white slug of Paul's penis. Removing his gag and prying open his mouth, she looked into his unblinking blue eyes and cautioned, "This isn't going to taste good."

Then she pushed his severed cock into his mouth.

"Curburide," she intoned, "I call thee. Take this sacrifice to your beds and soil him as you wish. This is my offering. This is my gift."

She slid away from the body, bent down to pick something off the floor and walked around to the other side of the bed where Jeremy still waited, guarding Sheila. Once there, she handed Jeremy the knife. He discarded the toy gun without blinking.

"Your turn," she announced. "Your beautiful wife needs some attention."

Jeremy fingered the blade and held it close to his wife's face. Blood oozed down from the haft across his fingers, and he smeared it across her cheek and forehead, in a cruel pantomime of cleaning the blade. Her eyes grew so wide, they looked ready to pop. "You treated me like shit for way too long, baby," he announced. The tip of the steel slid to her throat.

Sheila begged for mercy through the thin restraint of the gag. He couldn't quite understand anything except the word "please."

"You made your bed," he declared, holding the knife to her throat, and brushing the coppery hair away with his hand, delicately, like a lover.

"Now die in it," he said through gritted teeth, and jabbed the knife in a hard, vicious thrust.

Her screams broke through the gag, but quickly died in a gagging bubble of air.

"That's it," Ariana coached.

Jeremy's hands were buried in his wife's belly, and he pulled foot by foot of knobby, gnarly strands of fist-thick intestine out of her. His hands slipped on the grisly rope, but he pulled it out anyway, hand over hand, until the last piece clung stubbornly to her insides.

"Here," Ariana said, and flicked the knife across the last stubborn bit of gut.

"Now arrange them in a circle around her head. And then the heart between her legs, and the other organs around her arms. It's the pneumatic circle; a powerful statement of intent. When you're done, we'll kneel and say the words together."

Jeremy felt his stomach go queasy as the stench of blood and feces filled the room, and he saw his wife's blood coating his arms. She'd been a bitch, but he'd never in his wildest dreams thought of reaching up through her still-warm ribs to pull out her heart.

"Fuck," he said under his breath.

"Later," Ariana answered. "I promise."

At last, the circles were complete. Both bodies, side by side, lay disemboweled, their organs decorating the bed like crimson stars. His wife and her lover were surrounded by the bloody constellations of their past.

"Repeat after me," Ariana insisted, and he knelt at the foot of the bed, side by side with her.

"I have tasted the sweetness of the vine," she said.

"I have tasted the sweetness of the vine," he answered.

"I have severed its sugar with my bile."

"I have severed its sugar with my bile."

"I have pledged my love to you, Curburide," she said.

"I have pledged my love to you, Curburide," he echoed.

"And my body is yours to ride."

"And my body is yours to ride."

The prayer went on, offering service and bloodshed for the demonic spirits, if they would only manifest and aid the Callers in their daily quests. Jeremy felt a strange lassitude come over him as they spoke the words, and the blood and gore receded until he felt only the urgent pressure of his engorged cock. It was as if they had slipped into a pornographic dreamworld where the slaughterhouse was erotic, and consummation the prize for perversion. Jeremy felt strangely distant . . . possessed. The room seemed to whisper around them with sibilant calls to rut.

At the end of the ritual, Ariana bowed her head, and looked up with wickedness in her eye.

"Are you horny?" she asked.

"Um, I'm covered in my wife's blood, and the room stinks like a slaughterhouse," he answered. "But I want to fuck."

"Exactly," she said, standing up and stripping off the rest of the catsuit. She grimaced in pain as she bent to peel off the long black boots.

"I've never had a partner, so I've never gotten to fuck right after. But it always makes me so wet. It's like . . . I've done a good job, ridding the world of another idiot, and orgasm is my reward. Can you feel them?"

"Feel who?"

"The Curburide. They're all around us. I can feel them."

She rubbed a hand across her groin, and then pinched a nipple between thumb and forefinger. "I can almost taste them," she whispered. "They accept our sacrifice."

She lay down between the two bodies, her back crushing the flesh of two human kidneys and a liver.

"Mmmm," she said. "A bed of true love."

Jeremy shook his head and pulled his shirt off. The room pulsed warm and cold, and a breeze seemed to slip between his legs, urging him forward to take the woman covered in the blood of his wife. The Curburide *were* here. He could feel it. He understood now why she wanted them to come through the door. All the way through. God would they fuck.

"You're a sick bitch, you know that?"

"Yeah," she grinned, holding her arms out to him. "Fuck me in the same bed as your wife and her dead lover. And do it good."

Jeremy released his belt and slipped off his underwear, surprised at how hard his cock was. He looked at the raw and bleeding breasts and opened bloody belly of his wife, and the even more gore-streaked remains of Paul. Perversely, his desire rose. Stroking his cock with a blood-slicked hand, he put a knee up on the bed, and crawled forward to meet his new love.

"Whatever you command, mistress," he said, and pushed his cock into the hot wetness of her. She was excited. More than excited. She was oozing as if she'd already been used.

Ariana moaned and scratched at his back, and the bed rocked with his efforts. Blood mixed with the sweat of their lust, and soon they slid in a pink sheen of desire that lubricated their movement like oil. Ariana reached up and gripped something from the bed beside them. And then she slipped it around his neck. A strand of meaty, slippery intestine. She pulled it back and forth like a noose, drawing him near and then letting him back off. She lost herself in the abomination, and shrieked in an ascending o-o-o-O-O-Oh of orgasm.

He kissed her iron-tinged lips and sighed. Something

invisible rushed across the skin of his ass, and Jeremy looked up into the shadows of the room which seemed to shift and pulse with unnatural movement.

"Curburide," he whispered. "I love you."

Chapter Twenty-two

"If we drive all afternoon, we should hit Salt Lake City for dinner," Joe announced as they pulled onto I-80 West.

Alex reached into her backpack.

"And we're not going to listen to Blink-182 the whole time."

Her face fell.

"Okay, once," he relented.

She grinned and flipped the case open to extract the CD. "What are we going to do when we get there?"

"Good question," Joe nodded. "I have no fuckin' idea. Malachai?"

Yes, master.

"You want to tell us what the hell we're doing?"

You're going back to the beginning.

Joe shook his head and rolled his eyes at Alex. "Can you hear him?"

She nodded.

"Why, Malachai? What will we find there? And how do we even find the beginning?"

And you were a reporter once?

"This is maddening," Joe shrugged. "I should know better than to expect help from a demon."

Alex said nothing.

"I guess when we get there tomorrow, we should dig up some old newspapers and try to track down the hotel where the first murder took place. Maybe you'll be able to feel or see something there with your second sight. I don't know."

On the stereo, the guitars crashed in a manic three-chord punk-rap fest. Joe focused on the thin line of the endless horizon and Alex settled back and closed her eyes. Lunch had settled heavy in her stomach, and she felt like dozing. In her ear, Malachai whispered only to her: *Don't waste this time, child. Practice your control. You're going to need it.*

The afternoon slipped by in a blur of geometric fields of grain and long barren flows of rocky earth dotted with dying patches of scrub grass. Alex was quiet, and Joe replaced her punk CD with an old ambient techno Delerium disc long before they passed Green River. Occasionally he snuck looks at her, but she didn't seem in the mood to talk. If she wasn't dozing, she was staring vacantly out the passenger window.

He let her be. He couldn't imagine the horrible images that must be still fresh in her mind, haunting her. It had only been a couple days since she'd axe murdered her parents, for God's sake. And this was really the first extended time she'd had to think about it. First she'd had to gather her things and run, then she'd hooked up with him and was nervous about being abandoned, or caught. But now . . . it seemed they were really beyond the law, with nothing but time on their hands. She had time to think. Time to ache.

"You okay?" he said at one point, and she jumped.

"Huh?" Her eyes looked wild, caught.

"I asked if you were okay."

"Oh, yeah," she said. "Just thinking."

"Wanna talk?"

She shook her head and looked back out the window. He let it be for now. The kid needed to come to terms with what she'd done. With what she *was*.

"Oh my God, I feel sick," Jeremy whispered. Ariana stirred next to him. Her eyes flickered open in the gray light of dawn.

Jeremy looked around the shadowed room. Pieces of his wife and her lover were all around them. On the floor, on the bed with them. He grimaced as he moved a leg and felt something cold and sticky. Heavy.

"I'm gonna throw up, I think."

Ariana ran a bloodstained hand through his hair. "I know baby," she whispered. "The first time is hard. It'll pass."

Jeremy pulled away from her and lurched out of the bed towards the bathroom. His left foot touched something wet and cool, and then he slipped as his right foot came down on something that squished. A heart? Entrails? He fell to his knees, and found himself staring at the open eyes of his wife's lover. The severed tip of the man's own penis was still lodged in his pale lips, a gruesome lollipop.

"Oh God, what have we done?" Jeremy gasped again, and ran headlong into the master bath. His painful, wracking coughs filled the house for several minutes.

Ariana lay in bed listening, and let him get it out. She stretched, and moved herself, as the bruises from Jeremy's rampage in the hotel Sunday night made themselves felt even more than yesterday. She caught her breath as she yawned; her chest felt like a knife was lodged in her side.

Damn. What if a rib was cracked? She couldn't exactly check in to a hospital right now. She ran her hands over her chest and winced at the tender spots. Then a horrible thought struck her. What if last night's sacrifice hadn't even counted? *The Book of the Curburide* never specified that the murders should be on a Sunday, or a week apart. That was her little touch. It seemed to add a more ritual element to the murder. The book only demanded that the sacrifices be made in connection with sexual advance, and that they occur in a string of different cities. Each city a link in the chain she forged. The chain that, when complete, would flog the genitals of all mankind.

Still, Ariana worried about breaking her own chain of similarity. She had missed her Sunday night deadline, and then when she had killed, she had fucked the victim first. In her previous sacrifices, she had never fucked the victim before killing him; mainly because she thought that the closeness would make her lose her resolve. But what if it tainted the Calling?

She replayed the scene in her mind, and remembered clearly chanting the prayer, as Jeremy kept watch over the wounded couple, and then dragging the man to her circle and slitting his throat. It should have counted. It followed the loose guidelines of the book, and she had taken not one, but two sacrifices this time. She was in the right locale, and had taken her sexually charged victim ruthlessly. She had then emptied his body of its organs as well as its life and arranged them in the ceremonial way, heart to kidneys, a clockwise testament of death. An ordered celebration of entropy. She hadn't been the one to do the woman, but Jeremy had followed her direction for the ritual exactly. Two sacrifices, in the same place, should strengthen the Calling, no?

She *had* felt the hands of the Curburide reach out to her last night, as she had after the other killings, and they seemed stronger than ever. She thought they had influenced Jeremy, given him the strength to complete the atrocity. She smiled at the memory of Jeremy's sacrilegious sex with her. God, he'd been an animal! Face speckled with the blood of his wife, eyes burning with the fire of the kill and the still-potent rage at his cuckolding. The pain from the beating he'd given her had been, temporarily, overshadowed by his biting and kissing and fast, furious fucking.

Water was running in the bathroom now. Ariana shook away her doubts about the sacrifices. She had nearly completed the cycle. San Francisco, Phoenix, Austin, New Orleans, Tallahassee. Just one last stop.

Terrel.

Chapter Twenty-three

Joe pulled a *Salt Lake Tribune* from the metal box, while Alex grabbed the city's tabloid *Weekly.* Tucking it under his arm, he led her into a Greek diner, and in moments they were settled in a cracked red vinyl booth. The formica tabletop was yellowed and spiderwebbed with age. They pored over the sticky, plastic-coated menu that seemed to have more food choices than a grocery store. The place looked as if it had been in business without an update since long before Jerry Lee Lewis thought about "Great Balls of Fire" or taking his second cousin to the backseat. The metal backsplash behind the grill was painted in thick coats of yellow, orange and black baked grease, and the speckle-patterned floor tile, while clean, had clearly seen decades of traffic; its surface was dull and uneven. Joe guessed it once had been mainly white, but not in a generation or two.

"Take your order?" the waitress said, slopping two glasses of water on the table. She looked old, overweight and terminally bored.

"Patty melt," Joe shrugged. Alex ordered a gyro.

"You're gonna brush your teeth after you eat that, right?" he asked.

"You don't like the smell of onions?"

"In a frying pan maybe. Not in my car!"

She smiled, and flipped open the *Weekly.* Joe began scanning the *Tribune.* They were looking for anything to do with murders; Alex's or the serial killer's.

Alex leafed quickly through the *Weekly*, frowning slightly as she turned the pages. Then her face lit up.

"If we stick around town, we can see a Blink-182 cover band tomorrow night."

"Nixed."

"Spoilsport," she said, and flipped back to the beginning of the paper to scan more closely.

"Got it," he said presently.

On page 15, the paper detailed the latest killing by the woman they'd dubbed "The Sunday Slasher." She had now killed on four successive Sundays in four widely separated cities.

New Orleans Police Chief Douglas Chandler reported that there is little doubt that Sunday's brutal murder in the Sheraton is the work of a serial killer; the latest in a murder spree that stretches cross country from here to San Francisco.

"We cannot release full details," Chandler said. "The victim's throat, like the other Sunday Slasher killings, was cut by a razor blade. We know that this is not a copycat murder, however, because other details of the scene, which I can't release to you, match those first three murders in San Francisco, Phoenix and Austin."

The first murder—or at least the first one connected to the Sunday Slasher—occurred overnight on October 17 in the Marriott Hotel, in downtown San Francisco. A maid discovered the dismembered body of Ted Slater, a 34-year-old computer salesman, on Monday morning. According to the victim's friends, Slater had last been seen the night before at the Cat Club.

On the night of October 24, exactly one week later, the second murder occurred, this time at a Ramada Inn in Phoenix. A maid found the body of Jack Sketz, 33, bound and dismembered during her cleaning rounds late in the morning of October 25. Sketz had reportedly been at a Phoenix club called The Nile the night before. Police reports indicated that there was evidence that the crime had been committed by a woman, and was sexually related.

The third murder, and the one which confirmed for authorities that this was indeed the work of a serial killer, and again, pointed to a female perpetrator, occurred on Halloween night, October 31, in Austin, Texas. The body of Ryan Nelson, 27, an insurance agent, was found in the Marriott near the capitol the following morning by the maid. Authorities estimated that he had been killed sometime between 10 P.M. and 2 A.M., but, just as in the other cases, occupants of the adjoining rooms in the hotel reported no disturbances or odd noises.

"We've seen several patterns at work in these crimes," Chandler said. "We believe, based in part on the sexual element of the crimes, as well as other evidence, that the killer is female. Aside from the specific nature of the murder method, obviously, they've all occurred on Sunday nights. And they've been successive Sundays. What concerns us the most, however, is that each murder has been several hundred miles away from the last, which makes it difficult for us to set a trap. We do know that she has, so far, been headed almost due east after each event."

"She's on her way somewhere," Joe said, after reading the clip to Alex.

"Yeah, but where?"

The waitress slid a plate of fat golden fries and a thick charred burger across the table to Joe, and slapped down a platter of pungent gyro meat, onions and a side plate of pitas in front of Alex.

"Getcha anything else?" she asked, already looking down the aisle to the next table.

"Sunday Slasher?" Joe smiled.

The waitress looked at him crossly, then shook her head, clearly confused. "You want ketchup?"

He grinned. "No thanks."

The waitress moved to the next table, but not without looking back over her shoulder at them twice more.

"Think you spooked her," Alex said.

"I think we need to get to San Francisco and find us some real spooks."

They pulled into The Night's Inn, a cheap one-story motel off the interstate just outside of Salt Lake City around 8 P.M.

"I'm not hot about the idea of heading through mountains in the middle of the night," Joe said.

Alex stifled a yawn. "Fine with me. I haven't slept in a bed in, like, a week. Literally."

"God, I'd forgotten about that. It actually has been a week, hasn't it?" Joe whistled. "Holding up pretty good."

"Well," she corrected. "I'm holding up pretty well."

"Ah, now the runaway's an English major?"

She gave him a queen's dismissive wave. "Just book us a room, driver."

"Of course, your majesty." He stepped out of the car and bowed as he went.

Alex followed him. "I need to stretch my legs," she announced. "And see if they've got a pop machine."

The motel office was tiny; just a foyer with a desk, a phone and a filing cabinet. A tiny TV sat on one side of the desk, and the balding clerk looked annoyed that he had to pull his glance away from a noisy rerun of *The Untouchables*.

"Help ya?"

Joe nodded. "Need a room for one night for my daughter and me."

Alex kicked him in the shin. He ignored her.

"You got one with twin beds?"

The clerk stared at the two of them over the rim of his glasses for a moment. In a seedy little "just outside of town" joint like this, he probably heard the daughter line all the time, but rarely got a request for separate beds.

"Cash or credit?"

"Credit," Joe said, and dropped a Visa on the counter.

The man palmed it, swiveled his chair and pulled off a set of keys from a hook on the wall behind. It looked as though the VACANCY sign out front hadn't lied; most of the hooks had occupants. He passed the keys, attached to a large green plastic number 9 across the counter to Joe, along with a half sheet of paper.

"Fill this out," he said. "License?"

Joe handed over his driver's license and filled out the form as the clerk ran a copy of his plastic.

"Room's right down there," he pointed left of the office door. "Phone's free if it's local. Dial zero if you need something."

Alex elbowed him as soon as they stepped outside.

"Daughter, my ass! No way you look old enough to be my father. You're what, twenty-five?"

"Twenty-eight," he shrugged.

"Oooh, you had me at age ten, huh?"

"And without your makeup, the first time I saw you, I thought you were fourteen or fifteen."

That earned him another punch.

"Look, I can't afford to get us separate rooms if we're going to be traveling awhile, and some places are weird about who they give rooms to, so, for the duration, you're my daughter."

"Green shag," Joe announced as he flipped the light switch. "Wow. I haven't seen green shag since . . ."

"Since you saw bedspreads with deer on them?" Alex plopped herself down on the bed nearest the door. She pretended to pet the large 12-point buck that adorned its center.

"Pretty much."

Joe kicked off his shoes and threw a suitcase on his bed. She yawned again and laid back. "Oh my God, am I going to sleep. I don't even care if this room is full of cockroaches."

He looked at the matted green yarn between his feet. "Thanks for bringing that up."

She popped up then and grabbed her backpack. "First dibs on the shower." The words were barely out of her mouth before the door to the tiny bathroom shut behind her.

"I'm going snack hunting then," he called, and palmed the keys.

The sound of the highway offered a steady whoosh of background noise, as Joe took a walk around the almost abandoned motel. Only one other car was in the lot, parked three doors down from #9. He went the opposite direction, away from the front office. There hadn't been a vending machine there, and he had a sudden craving for a bag of Fritos. But when he reached the end of the long building and walked around towards the back, there was no snack machine to be found.

Joe leaned back against the brick face of the building and sighed. "What the hell am I doing?"

He looked out over the open scrubland, which dead-ended into an embankment that led up to the highway. The stars were out, and somehow the rush of the cars in the distance made him feel even more lonely than when he'd been truly removed from civilization, when they'd been camped up in the Rockies.

What *was* he doing? He'd run away from Chicago, and now he'd run away from Cindy. And somehow, Malachai had him on the trail of . . . what? A serial killer? With a fledgling witch in tow? What did the demon expect of him? Was he supposed to simply be a bodyguard? Was he supposed to actually do something to stop these "Curburide"? Was this all a wild-goose chase to amuse the spirit and ultimately land him in jail for harboring a runaway? Would he be implicated in the murders she'd committed, however justified they may have been?

"Cool night, eh?"

Joe jumped at the voice.

A match flicked in the darkness just to his left, illuminating the craggy face of an old man. A priest, by the look of him. The cigarette glowed to life and the man took a deep pull before releasing a cloud of smoke into the night air. Joe thought it looked incongruous with the black shirt and white collar. But why couldn't a priest hold onto that particular vice? he asked himself. After all, they certainly indulged in worse ones on occasion.

"Yeah," Joe finally answered. "Didn't hear you come up."

The older man nodded, a tuft of thick white hair bobbing in the light wind. "Move like the spirit, sink like the stone," he said. "Only the quiet will find their way home."

What the hell? Joe thought, but didn't answer.

"She'll need your help," the priest said after a moment.

"Who?"

"Your girl. She can't do this alone."

Joe smiled. The guy must think he'd gotten her pregnant. The priest's eyes reflected the ember of the cigarette. The old man was staring hard at him.

"Look, you don't understand," he said. "It's not like that. She's my daughter, and we're on our way . . ."

The priest laughed. "To grandmother's house?"

Joe took a deep breath and looked away. He didn't want to lie to a priest, but he wasn't about to try to explain why they were here or where they were going.

"Remember what I said," the priest whispered. He blew a puff of smoke past Joe's ear.

"They're coming."

Joe's eyes shot wider and he turned to face the priest. But the priest was gone.

His cigarette lay abandoned on the sidewalk, a tight curl of tobacco smoke unraveling from it to slip away in the night air. Joe ground out the ember with his shoe, and soon the only evidence of the priest's passage was dissipating quickly under the empty sky.

In a moment, it too was gone.

Alex was already in bed when Joe let himself back into the room. His heart was still beating hard. He'd called for Malachai after the apparition, but the demon had told him nothing. "I told you, more than I are watching this unravel," was all the stubborn creature would say.

Joe brushed his teeth, pulled on a pair of shorts and slipped into the bed. Alex's eyes were closed when he turned out the light.

"You asleep?" he whispered.

"Not quite," came the blurry reply.

"Can I ask you something?"

"Mmmm-hmm."

"Have you seen any ghosts since you've been with me?"

"Some," she admitted. "If I don't talk to them though, they don't usually bother with me. In fact, I barely even notice them anymore unless I really make an effort to. It's like, they're there the same as air, ya know? Do you ever think about seeing air?"

"Makes sense."

"Why. Did you see a ghost?"

Joe was silent. Was the priest a ghost? Had the man in Ogalala been a spectre? "How would I know?"

Alex laughed. "You could see through them, silly."

"All of them? Didn't you ever meet a ghost who, what's the word . . ."

"Manifested?"

"Yeah. Haven't you ever met a ghost who manifested so strongly he appeared solid?"

"A couple. Not often. Usually only ones that I talked to a lot. Like, our friendship gave them power or substance or something. Genna was like that. Sometimes I forgot she was dead."

"Could she lift something physical?"

"I don't remember her ever trying. But, when I was tied up in the basement, and I called on her and some of my other friends for help . . . they lifted my bread and water to me. It took all their effort though, I think."

"Mmmm."

"What's up, Joe?"

"I just saw a priest outside smoking."

"Yeah, so? Jesus never said, 'Thou shalt not smoke'!"

"He told me 'they're coming,' like that guy at the diner. Then it was like he disappeared into thin air."

"You saw him disappear?"

"Not exactly. He was right behind me, and then when I turned around, he was gone."

"So he walks fast."

"No way," Joe insisted. "No way he could have gotten out of sight that fast. He said something, I turned around, and he was gone."

"Did you ask Malachai about it?"

"Yeah. He gave me the usual Malachai dodge. Maybe tomorrow, you can keep your ghost eyes open?"

"'K," she agreed. Her voice was slurred with sleepiness. "I'll keep my eyes peeled for cigarette-smoking priests."

Joe didn't answer, and in seconds he heard the deep sighs of sleep in her breath. He rolled over and stared at the dark wall beyond the bed. What was beyond that darkness? he wondered.

What would come through if the Sunday Slasher completed her call?

From the far side of the room, his fears were answered by a snore.

Chapter Twenty-four

"Whoa," Alex exclaimed. "That's it, isn't it? The bridge. It's huge!"

"That's it," Joe said, eyes on the toll sign. "And they're going to rape us to cross over."

The Golden Gate Bridge stretched out ahead of them, a monstrous span of reddened steel crossing from the north stretch of Route 1 into the legendary city by the bay. They'd been driving for hours, taking turns at the wheel after each rest stop. Joe could feel the heat from the engine seeping through the floorboards. It made his feet sweat. But now the breeze from the San Francisco Bay slipped in through the windows and he felt a chill.

Alex straightened in her seat and peered out the window.

"I can see a sailboat," she announced.

"I imagine you'll see more than one."

"Is the prison on that island out there?"

"No," he said, handing over five dollars to the toll-booth attendant. He dropped the change in a cup holder and eased forward to cross the long bridge into the city. "Alcatraz is on my side, I believe."

"The Sean Connery movie was filmed there, wasn't it?"

"I think so."

"Can we go?"

"On one condition."

She gave him a cross look and folded her arms. For a moment, despite the fake black hair, she was the "15-year-old" hitchhiker as Joe had first seen her just a few days before.

"What?"

"Find us some ghosts today who are willing to talk. We need some info."

"Deal."

"And until then . . ." He broke off as the road shifted and wound down a steep drop and reemerged from beneath a viaduct to a blur of trees and tall gabled houses.

"What?"

"Get your eyes on that map! How do we get downtown?"

After missing a turn and ending up near the wildly diverse tie-dye district of Haight-Ashbury, Alex and Joe finally negotiated the up-and-down streets of San Francisco to arrive on Market Street.

"There's a cable car!" Alex enthused, and Joe smiled.

"We'll take one to the dock when we do the boat ride to Alcatraz," he promised. "Now . . . about the Marriott?"

"Dead ahead!" she said. "Should be on the right. Is that it, up there?"

She pointed, and Joe looked up to catch a glimpse of the familiar tripod architecture of the art deco spire that demarked Marriott's across the country. Moments later he'd taken a right, slipped around the block and into the parking garage of the mammoth structure.

"Let's hope they've got a room for us," Alex said, mouth agape at the line of cars awaiting the valets to park them.

Joe pulled as far up the curved entry road as he could and put the car in park.

"Let's hope I can afford a room for us here," he said.

After taking a receipt from the uniformed valet, they entered the lobby and started towards the long check-in counter. Alex grabbed Joe's arm.

"Can I be your sister this time?"

He grinned. "What's the matter? I'm a lousy dad?"

She made a face.

"Okay, okay. Here you can be my sister. But if we have to go to Arkansas, the only safe thing is for you to be my daughter. Course, on second thought, even that might not be . . ."

She punched him. "Just go."

"Room 1104," Joe announced, stepping away from the counter. "That okay with you, sis?"

"Only if it's got two beds."

"Nope, just one cozy king. We're family, remember?"

"Then you're in the bathtub," she said, shifting her backpack up higher on her shoulder.

Joe shook his head and smiled. Then the smile slipped away and he leaned closer to her ear.

"See any ghosts?"

"You want me to do this now?"

"No, we can dump our stuff first," he said. "But do you see any?"

Alex looked hard at the spaces between the milling, noisy mix of walking, talking, sitting and cell-phoning people in the lobby. Milky shapes twisted and wound in between the chairs and sofas and milling people. As she stared, those steamy blurs became more distinct, and some turned to look back to meet her gaze. She shivered.

"Yeah, they're here. Plenty of them."

"Good. Then let's freshen up and then come back here and make some friends!"

One of the silvery forms separated from a crowd at the Fourth Street door and faded in and out as it crossed the lobby towards them. They stepped into the elevator, and the long-eyed form slithered through the closing doors like a puff of shimmering smoke.

"Joe?"

"Yeah?" he said absently, punching the 11th floor button.

"We've got company."

The elevator shivered and then rumbled upwards, as Alex stared at the ghost who'd shot through the lobby to follow them.

"Hi," she whispered.

The ghost flickered at the sound of her voice, like an electrical current with a bad connection. Its eyes were the deepest ebon, and Alex could see the outline of a tie around its ephemeral neck. Its body was a charcoal blur, but as she stared into its eyes, its face grew more distinct. A caterpillar puff rose from above both of its abysmal eye sockets, and the smoky fuzz of a white beard faded into nothing from its chin. When its lips opened to speak, she saw the buttons of the elevator wall in the space between.

"They're coming!" it said faintly.

"Who?" she said. "Who is coming?"

"The evil ones," it hissed, and then faded, like a smoke ring in a spring breeze.

Alex put a hand on her chest to still the pounding in her heart. "Shit," she murmured as the elevator rattled to a halt and the doors opened.

Joe put a hand on her shoulder. "C'mon," he urged, pushing her out onto the carpet. "Let's find our room, and you can tell me what just happened. But don't faint on me first. You look white as a ghost."

"That's because I just saw one," she breathed, willing her eyes to stop bulging. She could feel her whole body pounding with blood. "And I've never seen one like that before."

Joe pulled open the dresser drawer and dropped his underwear in.

"Which drawer you want?" he asked.

"Whatever one you're not using," she called out from the bathroom, where she'd begun disassembling makeup and other sundries from her backpack. "Wouldn't want you seeing your sister's underwear now, would we?"

"Still wearing Care Bears?" he taunted.

"Ha," she called. "Thongs, baby, thongs."

"You get the top drawer," he called back. "You're right. I don't want to see those."

" 'Fraid of cooties?"

"And butt cracks," he agreed.

"Chicken."

"Born and bred. Now can we get a move on before we lose the light? I'd like to see some of this city before the day is over."

The door to the bathroom closed as Alex yelled. "Be out in a minute."

"Or an hour," Joe murmured, and stood at the window looking out at the city. He could see the sprawling convention center to one side, and the brilliant blue of the bay in the distance. A freighter, probably inbound from the Orient, bobbed on the horizon. "Now that's a view."

They stepped out onto Fourth Street and turned right to head to Market. People slammed past them in a continual rush of heedless pedestrians.

"Stay close," Joe warned, and Alex grabbed his shirtsleeve to keep from being separated.

"Ever been to a big city before?" he asked, as they stood at the corner of Market, waiting for the light to change. Alex's fingers were sharp around his arm.

"No," she said quietly. An old bum wearing a stained green winter coat brushed past them, and she wrinkled her nose. "Are they all like this?"

"In some ways," he admitted, and stepped out onto the street to cross with the traffic.

"Wow," was all she said.

At Alex's request, they stopped in a Tower Records and Joe agreed to pick up the latest Green Day CD for her. Then they walked up to Union Square Park and sat on a bench as the sun's rays began to turn from gold to bronze. Pigeons stepped proudly across the sidewalk, daring the darting pedestrians to step on them. The stupid birds almost never flew, only bobbed their heads and hurried forward or sideways to keep from being stepped on.

"See any ghosts?" Joe said when they'd been settled a minute.

"Maybe," she said. "But I'd rather look at the palm trees."

"Ghosts," he insisted. "We're here for a reason."

"What if someone sees me talking to it?"

"In this town, you'll blend right in," he promised. "In case you haven't already noticed, there's a crazy person babbling to himself on almost every corner here. And anyway, aren't you supposed to be able to talk just with your mind?"

"Yeah," she admitted. "But sometimes I forget."

Alex looked over her shoulder, across the green square of the small park. The telltale sparkle of spirits flickered on the next park bench, and across the square. But one flicker was even closer. She stared at it, and like a blooming rose its form opened to her inner eye.

The ghost nodded politely at her, whitened hair adrift in a breeze of supernatural direction. "Hi," Alex murmured, struggling to keep her lips shut and to speak with her mind only.

The spirit did not smile, but still acknowledged her greeting with a bowed head. He seemed to be wearing a long black coat that hid any details of his form. Only the thin, drawn lines of his long face were at all clear to her.

The spirit crossed the walk and stood before her. "You can see me," it said. Its voice was like chocolate and vinegar; sweet and pungent at the same time.

"Yes," Alex said. "Have you waited here long?"

"A week or a year," it said. "What's it to me?"

"So you know you're a ghost?"

"Of course," it said, its voice sharp now in her ears. "Do I look like a twit?"

"No, no," she insisted. "But . . . many ghosts don't even know."

"I know I'm dead," it said. "And I know I haven't been called. And I know that you are here looking for a murderess."

"You're not going to say 'they're coming' and disappear on me, are you?"

The spirit smiled, its mouth a pink line of amusement against the darkening twilight of the busy street behind it. "No," it promised. "I've been waiting for you."

"See something?" Joe asked, oblivious to her conversation.

"Shhhhh," she insisted and turned her attention back to the ghost. "Waiting?"

The faint form nodded. "I heard his cries that night when she took him. And I heard her prayer. I knew that if the evil ones were called, someone else would hear, too. I hoped that it would be sooner."

"We came as fast as we could."

"She's long gone now," the spirit said. "But her evil lives on."

"How?"

"The rift," the spirit said. Its head nodded slowly, a blurring mix of the shadows of moving cars, tourists and hustling businessmen eager to get home after a long day at work.

Alex struggled to keep her lips closed, as she mouthed, "The rift?"

"She killed to open a rift for them. And they found it."

"Where?" she breathed. "How?"

"Room 255," it said. "You have to close the door before they come through."

"How can we close the door?"

"Stop her before she makes the final sacrifice. If she succeeds . . . nothing you or anyone can do will send them back. If all the doors are open, all the Curburide can come through."

"Should we close the door somehow at the hotel?" Alex asked.

The ghost shook its head. "Stay away from the door or your very soul will be in danger. She is the key."

"Who?"

"The nun."

Part Three:
They're Coming

The ritual of the Calling has three aspects. Early sects of Curburide worshippers performed sexually charged sacrifices in prayer circles comprised of 16 human bones (representing the 16 aspects of hedonistic perversion that are most appealing to the demon) and 21 stones (representing the 21 levels of hell beneath the earth to which the worshippers may be damned if their sacrifice was found unworthy). These rituals were designed to garner specific favors from a Curburide demon (such as the fertility rite performed by the early Gaelic druid sect).

Individuals also may perform a joining rite which could allow a Curburide demon to temporarily come through to this realm by cooperative possession of the Caller. A successful union between priest and demon can bring the priest great power and the demon the freedom to ravage this plane—something for which all Curburide inherently yearn. The violence and unpredictability of the Curburide makes such Callings extremely risky for the Caller, however.

There is a third type of Calling, and it is the most dangerous of the three. This Calling is the hardest path, but provides the Caller with the ultimate power, and revenge. It was attempted unsuccessfully by Helladius in the 3rd century, to punish the Roman emperor for his banishment. This Calling involves "dedicating" one's homeland to the whim of the demons, by performing five ritual sacrifices across the breadth of the land. Helladius followed a very specific mapping and timing ritual for his sacrificial path, but it is unclear whether this has a true impact on its success. Because the key part of the ritual involves opening a doorway to this realm for many demons, the final sacrifice must be of someone who has already experienced possession. This preconditioned vessel . . .

—Chapter Seven, *The Book of the Curburide*

Chapter Twenty-five

"It's my wife," Jeremy explained to the white-smocked nurse behind the counter. "She fell the other day and it's been hurting her ever since. I think she might have busted a rib."

The nurse barely looked up from her computer screen. "Got insurance?"

"Yeah," he said. "Blue Cross."

"I'll need to make a copy of your card, and your driver's license."

As he pulled both from his wallet, she reached down and retrieved a clipboard, already preloaded with a patient information form.

"Fill this out and bring it back up when you're done." She couldn't have sounded more bored. Jeremy thanked her and took the board back to where Ariana sat on one of the orange vinyl waiting room chairs. There were a couple dozen of them spaced around the carpeted area beyond the white tile hall that led from the nurse's station into the heart of the hospital. About half the chairs were filled with crying children or desperate adults. He handed the clipboard to her.

"Are you sure this is going to work?" she whispered.

"Should," he said. "Not like they keep pictures on file. And by the time the claim gets into the system . . . we'll be a hundred miles away."

"Shhhh," she said, looking around nervously. A black woman in a blue floral housedress sat across from them, stroking the head of a child. Her girth seemed to extend beneath the armrests of the chair to serve as a cushion for the boy, who looked about eight or nine, and had been coughing since they'd walked into the ER waiting room. Jeremy found himself wishing they'd sat somewhere else. He didn't need fuckin' pneumonia on top of everything else.

Two chairs down, an older man sat stiffly and watched the nurse's station. He held a washcloth over one eye. Jeremy didn't know what color it once had been, but it was now a rich shade of saturated crimson. He wondered how long the man had been bleeding here. And if they weren't immediately taking him . . .

"Bernard James?" the nurse called, and the old man staggered to his feet.

"Thank God," Jeremy mumbled as the man teetered to the nurse's station where a blue-coated man waited.

"Hmmm?" Ariana looked up from filling out the form.

"Thought they were going to let him bleed to death out here."

"What's my birthday?" Ariana asked quietly.

"April 26, 1969."

"Maiden name?"

"Secks."

She laughed. "You're kidding, right? Your wife's name was S-E-X?"

"No, S-E-C-K-S. Might as well have been sex though. Sheila Secks—S.S. First Mate of the *S.S. Whore*." His voice began to rise. "Good old fuck-every-dick-on-deck Sheila Secks."

Ariana elbowed him, and Jeremy saw the black woman was watching them.

"How do you feel?" he asked, changing the subject.

"Hurts like hell." Her breath caught just a bit as she said "hell."

"I don't know if there's anything to do for it," he said. "But I know we need to make sure it hasn't punctured a lung or something."

★　★　★

"You can wait here, Mr. Bruford." The nurse pointed to the chairs on the wall in the hallway. "We're going to take her in for an X-ray now."

Jeremy leaned forward and kissed Ariana on the cheek. "Good luck, honey," he said.

The corner of Ariana's mouth crinkled, and she raised an eyebrow at him, but said nothing. The nurse led her through the double doors into the radiology lab and Jeremy sat down to wait. His stomach was starting to knot up. Maybe this ruse wasn't such a great idea. After spending an hour in the outer waiting room, they'd been brought in to see a doctor. Jeremy guessed him to be about 45 or 50; there were wrinkles at the corners of his eyes when he smiled, and though he still sported a thick mustache and a full head of black hair, both were generously sprinkled with silver. He wore bifocals, and as Ariana/Sheila told him of how she'd been carrying a big load of laundry, and then missed the top step of the stairs, he kept peering at Jeremy over the top of the frames. With the flat of a thumb, the doctor traced the purpled and yellowing line around her left cheekbone that no amount of makeup covered.

"And you hit this—" he looked over at Jeremy for an instant, his eyes stern—"on the stair? On the rail?"

Ariana had shrugged, and then winced from the movement. "I don't know. It was all so fast."

The doctor had nodded. His voice remained very quiet. "Well, we'll just take an X-ray of those ribs and see what's going on there."

Jeremy could imagine the conversation going on between the doctor and his nurse. "He beat the crap out of her," the doc probably said. "How many times do these women have to 'fall down the stairs' before they march out the front door?"

He wondered if they would call the police. His stomach churned, and Jeremy bent forward to still the acid. Damn . . . maybe this little charade had been a bad idea. He had worried mainly about the identity theft aspect of slipping Ariana through the X-ray machine under the guise of his wife. But if the hospital reported it as a domestic abuse situation . . . it could be the end for both of them. He didn't know if the law now called for them to do that, if there was any suspicion. On the other hand, if she really was hurt . . . he knew she could be bleeding inside. She needed someone to look at her.

The speakers overhead demanded that a Dr. Aruba report to room 343, and the traffic of nurses and carts through the hallway in front of him seemed constant. A technician wearing a white hospital smock—at least he assumed that's what the guy was—pushed through the double doors where the doctor had led Ariana.

All he could do was sit here and wait. And think about the morning. And last night. And the night before.

The whole situation was surreal. Just a couple days ago, he was an ordinary, miserable working stiff sitting at a bar, hoping to drown out the unavoidable knowledge of his wife's cheating with an unhealthy dose of alcohol. An image of Ariana, accepting a drink from him came to mind. It seemed so long ago. He had never before picked up a woman at a bar while married to Sheila. And God, what a price he was now paying for the transgression. Not that Sheila had gotten away scot-free with her adultery. He remembered her body as it lay there this morning, cold and gutted. Purple and red gobs of flesh arranged around her head in a hellish halo of grue. Her once pink, perfect nipples replaced by ghastly red slashes. Her eyes staring blankly at the ceiling in frozen agony, her face spattered and smeared with her own blood.

She had paid. And strangely, Jeremy found that he felt no remorse. The beating he'd given Ariana had opened the floodgates of hate and resentment he'd built up over the past few years. He'd tried for so long to repress it, giving her excuses. He'd told himself that she still loved him, but needed more. The humiliation that he was apparently a lousy lover had kept him in a pit of depression that grew deeper with every night that she announced she was "going out with the girls" or "working late and leaving the kid to stay over at Ma's."

And then, when the anger surged, he'd remind himself of his daughter. He didn't want her growing up in a broken home.

Jeremy laughed out loud at the thought, and then looked up to see if anyone had heard. The nurse at the oval-walled station just down the hall continued her typing.

How was his daughter going to cope now? Her mother had been brutally murdered, and her father was about to become number one on Florida's Most Wanted List. Fuck.

He'd called Sheila's mother and asked her to pick up his daughter after school again today, because they were both working late. Doris had agreed, and then handed the phone over.

"Hi, Daddy," Amy Lynn's tiny voice came on the line. "We had ice cream last night. Did you have ice cream?"

"No, sweetie," he'd said and was instantly overcome with the memory of the last thing he'd tasted the night before; the iron of his wife's blood warm and thick on his lips as he pumped his cock between the gore-smeared thighs of Ariana. "No ice cream for Daddy."

"Maybe Mommy will let you have ice cream tonight?" little Amy Lynn asked, genuine concern in her voice.

"Maybe, honey, maybe. You be good for Grandma, okay?"

Tears welled in his eyes as he remembered her last words to him.

"I love you, Daddy."

"I love you too, pumpkin," Jeremy whispered to the empty air in the hospital corridor. He knew he would never see his daughter again. And someday, when she was old enough to understand, she would be glad of that, and would despise him.

When the doctor finally reappeared, holding the door open for Ariana to walk slowly through ahead of him, Jeremy was quietly crying.

"Jeremy," Ariana called to him, and he quickly brushed both hands across his cheeks. He held up a finger and feigned a sneeze, and then dug quickly into his pocket for a tissue as he stood. Pressing it against the corners of his eyes to blot the water, Jeremy blew his nose, and struggled to clear his face of emotion.

"What's the good word?" he finally asked.

"Rest," the doctor said. "She's pretty beaten up, lots of bruising, and a hairline fracture on the lower left rib. There's nothing we can do for that; it just needs to heal. I'd like her to stay off her feet the rest of this week. She'll have some problems lying down, so she may need to sit a lot. Do you have a recliner?"

Jeremy lied.

"Good. Set her up in that with a good book or two. She's going to spend a lot of time there the next week or two."

"Should we wrap it or something?" Jeremy asked.

The doctor shook his head and led them to the nurse's station. "I'm giving her some codeine for the pain. As long as she keeps from any strenuous exercise, it should heal naturally, without causing any further damage."

The doctor wrote out a script and handed it to Ariana. "Stay off the stairs," he said pointedly, and then looked at Jeremy. "You were lucky. The next time, it could be a lot more serious."

Chapter Twenty-six

It was still almost 75 degrees in San Francisco, warm for November, but Alex shivered, despite the unseasonable heat. She was leaning forward on the park bench, staring at a spot a couple feet in front of them. No one was there. But as Joe watched her silent exchange, he noted that none of the hurried pedestrian traffic in front of them ever physically crossed that spot. Maybe because Alex was acting like a street freak. Or maybe because innately, they could sense something occupied that space, however ghostly and unseen. Where the spirit stood was a dead zone. Invisible but potent. Gently, Joe put a supportive hand on her back. "What do you see?" he whispered.

Alex didn't answer immediately. Then she shook her head, and leaned back on the bench to press tight into his shoulder. "I've talked to ghosts all my life and never been afraid," she said. Her eyes were wide as she looked up at him. "That was fuckin' freaky."

Joe squeezed her arm and pulled her closer. "What happened?"

Quickly Alex related how the ghost had told her it had been "waiting" for them, and that it wanted them to "close the door."

"Did it say what room she killed in?"

She nodded. "255. But it said to stay away, or my soul would be in danger."

Joe frowned. He looked around at the march of people, a hustling melting pot of pin-striped suits, high-heeled business women, tourists in baseball caps, college kids in khakis and jeans, and the occasional unkempt bum. They jostled elbows as they moved down the street, mixing races and missions and perfume (Joe had smelled everything from the background scent of a eucalyptus tree to overpowering, cloying perfume to urine in the ten minutes he'd sat on the bench). All were probably oblivious to the spirits in their midst. "Then how are we supposed to close this door?"

"It said 'she is the key.'"

"Yeah, well, we don't know who she is! Did it offer a picture or some insight on how we're supposed to find her?"

Alex shrugged. "No. But it did say one thing I thought was weird."

"What's that?"

"It called her a nun."

After Joe and Alex left the park, they walked some more through the crowded downtown streets of San Francisco. At the corner of Hyde and Market, they found the line for the cable car that would take them up Nob Hill out of downtown and into the wharf district on the far side of the Embarcadero.

"You up for it?" Joe asked.

Alex looked at the long line of people waiting to hop a short ride on the historic tourist trap that was the San Francisco trolley, and shook her head. "I'm starved, actually. Can we get something to eat first?"

Joe grinned. "You like Chinese?"

"Sure, why not?"

He wrapped an arm around her and turned them towards the ascent of the hill. "Then you, my dear little witch, are about to visit one of my favorite places on earth."

"What's that?"

"Chinatown."

Stockton Street was just as Joe remembered it.

"I came here for a job interview when I was in college," he explained, pointing out the pink temple peak of an upscale restaurant a block away. "I stayed over a couple days and beat around the city. It was great—they have absolutely everything here. Beaches, beautiful parks, great food. I think the best place I ate was at a cheap little dive here in Chinatown though."

"Can you find the place?"

"No way," he grinned. "I was just out wandering one night, and stopped at this little hole-in-the-wall place. No idea where it was or what it was called. But I never forgot the food!"

They walked up the hill, stopping at every storefront to peer in at the mélange of touristy postcard racks, Oriental statuary and colorful sarongs and other clothing. It seemed almost every storefront included many, many racks of T-shirts, all displaying some emblem denoting the landmarks of the city, from pictures of the trolley to the Golden Gate.

Finally they came to a corner, where a dim sum restaurant provided a long backlit sign with photos of its many dinner offerings. Joe's stomach rumbled at the sight.

"How about here?" Alex asked, and it took no prodding.

"Works for me."

A golden Buddha larger than any living man welcomed them inside the doorway. The restaurant was dimly lit, and Alex marveled at the rich red tapestries that covered the walls as a man the very opposite of the Buddha led them to a table. He was so thin you could almost see through him, and shorter than Joe or Alex. His hair was shock white; it seemed to almost glow against his black suit collar. He bowed as he gestured to the table.

"Is okay?"

Joe smiled and said yes, and in seconds they were both poring over the menu, as a waifish girl in a red and gold dress poured them each a cup of green tea. The restaurant was quiet, the few scattered white table-clothed tables of patrons separated by as many empty ones. Joe picked up a set of chopsticks and tried to fit them correctly between his fingers. He clicked them like pincers, and reached out to use them on the container of sugar and Sweet 'N Low. After fiddling with the sticks for a moment, at last he pried up a white packet of sugar and clumsily unseated it from the holder. It fell to the table before reaching his empty plate.

"You're gonna starve if you try to use those," Alex warned.

Joe grinned. "Do you like spicy, or no?"

"Spicy, yes," she returned mimicking a Chinese accent.

"How about a curry, then?"

"Never had one. Will I like it?"

"You never know 'til you try. Let's find out!"

When the young Oriental girl in red returned, they ordered a red pot curry and some ginger chicken and when the food arrived, they dove in hungrily, loading their plates with rice from a large ceramic bowl and dowsing it alternately with hot curry and colorful spoonfuls of chicken surrounded with spikes of ginger and red and green shards of pepper. With her mouth still full, Alex declared it the best thing she'd ever had.

"Told you," Joe smiled. "Course, it could have something to do with surviving for the past week on my camp cooking and diner food. We haven't exactly lived well the past few days! But this is good."

When they had both stuffed themselves to the point of pain, Joe leaned back and sighed. The owner or manager stood silently across the room near the cash register.

"I wish we could stay here," he said. A cool breeze rippled the hair on the back of his neck. He reached around and scratched at his hairline. The good feeling was instantly replaced by something tenser, colder.

"Have you seen any ghosts in here?"

Alex frowned. "Yeah, they're always around. Why?"

"Not sure," he said, looking at the other tables, where both Chinese and Caucasians chattered and lifted chunks of noodles, rice and chicken to their mouths with sticks that Joe had long since decided were ill-designed to carry a mouthful of anything.

"Just a weird feeling."

A busboy who looked as if he'd just gotten off the boat from the Orient quietly slipped their plates out from beneath their arms, and as he disappeared through the drapes into the kitchen, the old man appeared once more at their table.

"Food is acceptable?" he asked.

"Very good," Joe and Alex said together.

"Dessert now?"

Joe put a hand to his belly. Alex laughed.

"No, just the check I think," he said.

The older man returned with the bill and two fortune cookies. Despite being full almost to bursting, they both grabbed for the cookies. Joe pulled the plastic off with his teeth and cracked open the thin cookie to get at the white paper slip with his fortune inside.

"I love these," he grinned.

"Me, too!" Alex said. "Although we didn't eat at these kinds of restaurants much when I was growing up."

"Your parents probably didn't like the whole Buddha thing."

Alex nodded. "We wouldn't have gotten through the door if a restaurant had had a statue like that one. Or that one," she pointed to the back wall of the restaurant where there was what looked like a shrine to the statue of a half-nude woman with six arms fanned above her head. Alex opened the paper to read her fortune. Her smile clouded.

"What's your fortune say?" she asked softly.

Joe opened his, and the hair on the back of his neck stood straight up. "Ah shit," he whispered. He held it out for her to see as he mouthed what it said: "They're coming."

She held hers out to him to read and Joe saw the same two words:

They're coming.

Chapter Twenty-seven

Alex didn't talk much on the way back to the hotel. Before dinner, the bay breeze that slipped between the buildings and ruffled her hair had made the city feel vibrant, alive, exciting. Now the air just put a chill in her bones. She had never been afraid of ghosts before, but now . . . she wasn't so sure. They were manifesting in ways that were unlike any she'd experienced before. How had they altered the fortunes in the cookies? Certainly the Chinaman running the restaurant couldn't have done it . . . he couldn't have known about them or their quest. And what about the ghosts who'd spoken to her on the elevator, and in the park? They'd instantly known who she was, and what they were about. There were a lot of players in this game, Alex realized, and she and Joe hadn't begun to meet them all.

You've got that right, a familiar voice whispered in her brain.

Malachai! She spoke with her inner lips. *Where have you been? What's going on?*

There are those who'd like the Curburide to come through, and those who would do anything to stop them. The former will coalesce around the Caller as if she's a lightning rod. And the latter . . . will look for you.

But why me? she asked. *What makes me so special?*

You can speak with the dead. And you've broadcast your interest. When you agreed to become involved, you became the focal point. The witch who would stand against the incursion, who would lead the opposition.

Alex shook her head visibly, and Joe watched her from the

corner of his eye. She was speaking silently to someone, he could tell. But he said nothing.

I'm just a girl, she insisted. *I don't know shit about evil spirits or Curburide demons or whatever the hell they are. And I certainly don't know how to fight them. You dragged me into this.*

You came willingly, Malachai said, his voice a silky sonorous whisper.

Well then I can go willingly.

I don't think so.

Why not?

Look around you.

Alex stopped focusing internally and looked at where they'd been walking. They were nearly back to the hotel, walking along the red brick sidewalk. It was dark on Market Street, but the streetlights and the solid row of storefront building lights, neon signs and even the occasional adult theatre marquee kept most of the shadows at bay on the red bricked walkway.

But at the edge of the shadows, Alex could see a disturbance. The air shimmered like a strip of tarmac at high noon in the desert. Normally when she hadn't completely focused on a ghost, that was the isolated effect. The world often looked a little shivery to her. But this was different than that. This wasn't a pocket of potential here or there on the street awaiting her concentration to bring it to focus . . . this was all around them.

"What's going on?" she whispered out loud.

"What do you mean?" Joe asked.

She could see faces now, and outstretched arms through the spiritual fog. The shimmering dissolved before her eyes into a host of translucent, but distinct silvery forms. Men in torn shirts, children trailing rags, women clutching scraps of worm-eaten dresses to their bosoms as they moved steadily forward. A jogger in a striped running outfit leapt ahead of the wall of souls and ran straight at Alex. They were coming from all sides, from in between the adult theatre and the run-down hotel. They stepped into the street from the secondhand clothing store, and cars ran through their foggy forms without impact. They slipped into view from between the closed doors and the locked bars that protected the closed storefronts from entry at night. They materialized in the bus shelter in the center of the busy thoroughfare.

And they were all converging fast on her and Joe.

"They really are coming," she answered him aloud.

They won't let you give up now, Malachai said. *I think you'll find them, um, very persuasive.*

"Who's coming?" Joe asked, still oblivious to the mob of souls about to catch up with them.

"Ghosts," Alex said, clutching his arm and stopping in the middle of the sidewalk. "They're everywhere."

Joe peered up and down the street, trying to see the spirits that Alex said were all around them, but to no avail. An electric bus slipped with a screech to a stop at the glass enclosure a few yards away, and a stream of people got off and filed across the street to disappear in opposite directions down Market. Stragglers—all men—sauntered back and forth near the adult theatre just down the block, and Joe avoided making eye contact with any of them. An old woman pushing a small personal grocery cart passed them by.

The street was alive with walkers, but none of them looked see-through to Joe.

But next to him, Alex shook in visible fear, and clutched his arm.

"No," she whispered. And then, louder, "NO!"

Her eyes grew wide and Joe reached an arm out to cut the air in front of her. It met no resistance, but suddenly Alex screamed.

"What is it . . ." he began, but then her grip on his sleeve loosened, and the green of her eyes rolled back in her head until all he could see were the whites. "Alex," he cried, and grabbed her as her knees gave way, pulling them both to the ground.

"Malachai!" he yelled, oblivious to the stares from people all around.

Yes, master. The spirit cawed. *How can I be of service?*

"What's going on? What did she see?"

She saw what would happen if she doesn't stop the Curburide from coming through the rift between the worlds.

"God damnit!" Joe yelled, gently slapping Alex's face in an attempt to bring her around. When that didn't work, he held her by her shoulders and shook her. Her head lolled back, jet-black hair swimming on the bricked pavement. "Why did you show her that?"

I didn't show her anything, the demon said. *I told you that there are many who are watching your progress very closely. I wouldn't procrastinate, if I were you.*

Alex opened her eyes, but she didn't seem to see Joe's face in front of her. Her face was blank for a second. Then she opened her mouth to scream again. Joe covered it with his hand. "Alex, honey, it's me!" he said, shaking her a little. "It's Joe."

The glazed look slipped away. Her eyelids fluttered three, then four times. "Joe," she said softly. "Oh God, it was awful. It's going to be awful."

"Shhh," he said, helping her up from the street. "Let's get back to our room and then you can tell me."

She nodded, but kept shooting glances all around them as they started to walk again. The ghosts had disappeared as completely as they had overwhelmed her, but not everyone had left the street. As they walked past the porno theatre, one of the dreadlocked, tattooed men leaning against the wall let out a whistle. And it wasn't at the photo of a bronze-skinned nude woman perched on a motorcycle flaunting her enormous breasts next to him. Someone else started clapping, and Joe put his arm around Alex and urged their steps faster.

She's popular with the living and the dead, Malachai jibed in his head.

"Whose side are you on, anyway?" Joe hissed.

The winning one.

Back in their room, Alex kicked off her shoes and sat on the edge of her bed. She hugged herself and closed her eyes. Joe stood by, not sure what to do. He wanted to hold her, to kiss her and let her know it was all okay, but . . . no. That wasn't right. She was just a kid. He was supposed to be supportive, but not fatherly . . . he felt something stir inside him as he looked at her, and clenched his jaw in argument. She was just a kid, for Christsake.

An image of Cindy passed through his mind. She'd been too young for him, too, but not this much. And look how that had turned out.

He blanked the thoughts from his head and denied the desire to take her into his arms. Instead, he paced in front of the bed.

"What happened back there?"

Her voice sounded small when she answered. "The ghosts," she said. "They . . . they came from everywhere. It was like a stampede of the dead. They were all pointing at me, and saying things. And then they just closed all around until I couldn't breathe. I know, you couldn't even see them, but I was drowning. They kept saying 'they're coming' over and over and then all of a sudden I was falling. It was like . . . I was in a cloud of something bad. Everything was red and black and the air smelled like rotten eggs and sewer and someone was screaming."

"I think that was you," Joe suggested.

"Maybe. It was just . . . horrible."

"It's alright now," he said, trying to sound strong. But inside, he could feel it all slipping away. Malachai had dragged him into this to help her, but there was nothing he could do. Hell, he couldn't even see the ghosts that she was going to have to fight. All he could do was drive her around and pat her shoulder.

Maybe that's all you need to do, his inner voice said.

"When I lifted the axe to kill my father, I knew there was no going back," Alex was saying. "When I let the blade down to chop off his head, I felt a lot of my friends slip away, as if they were ashamed to be near me. And when I killed my mom, I knew it was a horrible, horrible thing. Something you will go to hell for, no matter how much you're sorry later."

She sniffed, and Joe reached over to wipe a single tear from her cheek.

"But Joe, I wasn't sorry then. And I'm not sorry now. I'm a terrible person. My father was right. All of those ghosts wanted me to do something to save them. But I can't save anyone. I'm not a good person. I'm going to hell."

Joe brushed the hair from her face, and tilted her head up to look into his eyes. Her gaze was eerily bright, electric, as tears pooled at the edge of her lashes. "You're a good person who did what she had to do," he said. "You're not going to hell."

"I'm scared," she whispered.

"Me, too."

And then she put her arms around him and pulled him tight. She hugged him so close he could feel her heart beating through their clothes.

"Hold me," she pleaded. "Just stay here and hold me?"

"I will," he promised.

Alex looked up at him then, and suddenly Joe didn't think she looked 15 or 17 or any age at all. She just looked beautiful. He bent to kiss her on the cheek, but she turned in his arms and met his lips hard. She was warm and wet, and pulled him into her mouth with her eyes and tongue. They kissed for a long time, and then Alex pushed him away.

"Wait," she whispered, and pulled down the sheets on the bed. The maid had already taken off the bedspread for the night.

Alex slipped off her jeans and socks, and climbed into the bed in her T-shirt and panties. Then she patted the empty space next to her.

"Stay with me tonight?" she begged. "I need you to be close."

Joe didn't say a thing, but mimicked her preparation and kicked aside his jeans and socks. He worried about what she would say when she felt the bulge of his erection against her through his underwear. But he turned out the light and slipped in to bed beside her. She pressed her back against his chest and he put his arm around her, covering the soft swell of her chest with his forearm. She didn't seem to mind the hard-on that snuggled into the cleft of her ass. She only shimmied her hips until there was no air between them at all.

In a faraway place, Joe heard a low, familiar chuckle.

Legend has it, that the strongest witches are virgins, Malachai said. *Of course, the bitch who's calling the Curburide clearly isn't. So maybe that's just an old hard-up witch's tale. Care to test the theory? Looks like she's willing.*

Shut up, Joe said silently.

Mmmm. You think you can keep your wick from her wax for awhile? I'm betting not.

The demon laughed again, and Joe felt the girl in his arms begin to breathe deeper as sleep took hold. He was painfully aware of the faint smell of her sweat from their walk through the city, mixed with a flowery scent of shampoo. His cock begged to be set free on her, *in her,* and he closed his eyes hard, struggling to picture something nonsexual. But whenever he tried to imagine her as a child who needed him to protect her, the child in his mind opened her piercing green eyes, pulled her shirt over her head to expose her naked breasts. They were small, as he liked them, and flawlessly creamy. Her nipples were pink and wide, and they stood erect as she grew from child to woman before his eyes and stepped forward to slip her pale, pink tongue between his lips.

It was a long time before Joe fell asleep.

Chapter Twenty-eight

Alex woke up before Joe. She felt a twinge of panic at first, when she realized there was an arm locked around her, but then the memory of last night came back, and she relaxed, tracing the dark hair on the slumbering arm with her fingers.

He had stayed with her all night. He really did care. Unlike that asshole at school who stood her up. For a moment, her heart felt full, and she pressed herself against the heat of him, relishing the closeness.

But then the memory of the ghosts intervened. This was not the time to get all girly. She knew that Malachai had guided Joe to her so that Joe could take her to wherever it was they needed to go to fight the Curburide. For *her* to fight the Curburide, she corrected herself. And to do that, she needed to learn a lot more about them, about her abilities . . . everything. Without delay. *It may already be too late,* she thought.

Easing Joe's arm over her head, Alex slipped out of his protection and the bed, and closed the door of the bathroom quietly behind her.

After brushing her teeth and taking care of other business, she poked her head back out into the room. Joe was still sleeping.

Alex pulled on her jeans, and slipped her feet into her sneakers. She pocketed the room key, and let herself out into the hallway. She knew he would kill her for this, but she also knew that she alone could get away with what she planned. For once, youth—and being a girl—were on her side. She was smiling as she stepped on to the elevator and pressed the button for the second floor.

There were voices in the breeze. Moaning, sybaritic voices. "Ohhhh, mmmm," sighed one, with a tone thick as melted caramel. "Yes, like that," came a male answer, along with the slap of leather on skin. Someone choked, a rasping, coughing, wet gurgle.

"In the mouth," the woman insisted, and the gravelly answer came instantly. "Yes, just like that," he said. Again came the slap of skin and a cry of pain. But with the pain, a moan of excitement. "Deeper," she insisted. Something howled then in agony, followed by the rapid squealing barks of the woman, "oh-oh-oh." She was orgasming to the sounds of pain.

Joe felt his penis rise with the lure of whatever hellish ecstasy they were indulging in. He tiptoed through the dark hallway towards the sounds of sex. He didn't know where he was, or why he was naked. He didn't care. The lure of the voyeur was too much, and he throttled the head of his cock to relieve the strain of its need. The tip was wet, and he prayed that there would be something for him when he found the source of the voices. Someone for him.

"Now-now-now," the man barked and then howled himself, a low, guttural release of pleasure. The voice came from just beyond a closed door at the end of the hall.

Joe took his hand off himself, and twisted the knob slowly. It opened without protest, and he peered into a darkened bedroom. A woman's dresser with a tall mirror was just to the right of the door. And in front of the dresser, a rumpled pile of tangled sheets and a royal blue comforter hung half on and half off the edge of a king-size bed.

In the center of the bed lay a spread-eagle, blood-streaked woman. She was thin, bone-thin. The slats of her ribs showed through her pale skin, and her breasts barely poked out from the flat slope of a chest striped angry red with the marks of a strap.

The nipples on those breasts were thick and engorged, blood-filled brown mushrooms that thirsted for biting and kissing. From the ugly weal that striped across her belly and left breast, oozing a tiny glisten of crimson, clearly she, and her breasts, enjoyed abuse. Her nipples looked bigger than the mound of her breasts, Joe thought.

She hadn't noticed the newcomer to the room yet. Her attention was on her partner, a broad-shouldered man kneeling next to her on the bed, his hair and naked ass facing Joe. The man's left hand held the black rubber handle of a whip.

"In the mouth," she begged again, and the hand lifted and fell, bringing the crack of the leather again across her unprotected skin. It caught her across the chin and right tit and her entire body convulsed at the sting.

"Ahhhhooow."

Joe felt his erection turn to steel at the perversity of her begging to be whipped in the mouth. He reached down absently to stroke himself when the man on the bed shifted position, moaning and throwing his head back as he moved to show the woman his cock.

But it wasn't a cock that Joe saw when the man turned.

It was a head.

The man held a woman's head by a knotted curl of dark hair. He slipped his long, glistening penis in and out of the dead mouth. One open green eye stared sightlessly at Joe, and he felt his own erection wither as the man on the bed reached down to cradle the head by its bloody stump of neck as he pressed himself faster and faster between its unprotesting teeth.

"Yeah-yeah-yeah!" he growled. "This bitch always did give the best head."

It was then that Joe finally noticed the gutted body on the floor next to the bed. It had to be the woman's, though there was too much blood to be sure. Its chest and crotch had been sawn open and scraped clean of internal organs. But they weren't missing. They were arranged in a bloody halo around the place where the head would have been, if the man on the bed hadn't been fucking it.

"Damn," the man sighed, and dropped the decapitated woman's head on the bed next to the bloody woman. A thread of creamy handsoap-thick drool leaked from the side of the dead woman's lips to pool on the bedsheets. The live woman stroked the hair of the dead head as if it were a kitten by her side, and stuck her tongue out until the man bent to kiss her.

"I have nothing to compare it to, but let's see just how good she still is," the woman said. Joe's eyes widened as she wound her fingers into its hair, lifted the head with both hands from next to her thigh, and positioned it between her thighs.

"You broke her in," the woman said, groaning slightly as she ground the dead face against her pubic bone. "She's . . . good . . . and . . . wet."

"Well, bloody, anyway," the man said bending to bite on a mushroom nipple.

"Yessss," she moaned, and then suddenly sat up. She turned to stare at Joe. That's when he saw that her eye sockets were pits of shriveled black flesh. Empty. "Seen enough yet, pervert? This is what we'll do to your girlfriend when they come through."

That's when it registered to Joe that the frozen eyes in the broken head had been green.

Joe jumped, and opened his eyes. Light was streaming through the windows to light the room, and he realized that he was in the bed in the hotel. It was morning. The slaughterhouse room disappeared, and he took a deep breath to clear the images from his head. Then he remembered falling asleep the night before, his guilty groin rubbing against Alex, and he rolled over, looking for her. The sheets next to him were empty. And cold. *Maybe she's in the shower,* he reasoned. That idea satisfied him for a second, until he saw that the bathroom door was open, and the light off.

"Ah, shit," he complained, and levered himself with a groan out of bed. "What now?"

You might want to get dressed. The demon's mental voice sounded concerned, none of the usual taunt in its manner. *Alex needs you. Now.*

Chapter Twenty-nine

Alex raised her hand to knock on the door of room 255. Before her knuckles connected with the wood, someone screamed inside.

"Oh shit." She gulped, but raised her hand to knock again. Now she could hear laughter from within. Refusing to let her resolve down, she forced herself to continue with the plan. But when she touched the door, a static shock jolted her back a step. She was still staring at her tingling hand when the door opened and a middle-aged man in a T-shirt and sweatpants looked out at her. There was still a splat of shaving foam on the side of his cheek. "Can I help you?" he asked.

Alex forced herself back into character, dropping her hand to her side. "I hope so," she said, offering a lopsided grin. "I stayed in this room a few days ago, and when I got home, I realized that I'd lost my charm bracelet. I think it fell behind the dresser. Would you mind if I took a look? The hotel said they didn't have it in lost and found."

The man thought about it a moment. He opened his mouth to say something, but then thought better of it and shrugged. "I guess that'd be okay."

She walked past him into a room very much like the one she and Joe had slept in last night. By the time she had reached the center of the room, she was shivering.

"You really keep it cold in here, huh?" she asked.

He looked at the thermostat on the wall by the door. "It's sixty-eight," he said. "Not so cold."

"Hrumph, must be me," she said, rubbing her arms to

warm away the goose bumps. She made a show of bending over to peer behind the dresser. With an audible grunt, she got down on her knees, and peered closer around her at the floor. The neutral beige carpet was older, worn. Behind her, just beneath the lip of the bed, she saw a dark stain. Blood? she wondered.

"See it?" the man asked, still waiting by the door. He'd retrieved a towel from the bathroom and wiped his face with it.

"Naw," she said, and turned on her hands and knees to crawl to the foot of the bed. "Maybe it's under here."

"Careful," he warned. "Never know what might jump out to bite you from under a hotel bed."

"I'm not worried," she laughed, and poked her head between the mattress and the floor. Something twitched in the darkness and she pulled her face back. But it surged forward in a flash, and something frozen grabbed her wrist.

"You should be worried," cackled an ancient voice. The gnarled face of an old crone shot out from the shadows to press against her own. Its rheumy eyes were streaked with threads of red, and its hand wielded a rusted straight razor, the kind they used in old-time barbershops.

Alex shrieked and fell back, and the man hurried over.

"What happened?" he asked, voice filled with concern. "I was only kidding."

Alex put her hand to her heart and looked at the empty space beneath the bed again. Something shivered in the dark air, but the hag was gone as fast as she'd come. "Thought I saw a rat," she lied.

"Jesus I hope not," the man said, and held out a hand to help her up. Alex accepted. As she straightened and brushed off her jeans, someone laughed behind her. Goose bumps again raised on her skin as the room temperature dropped and a cold wind tickled the hair on the back of her neck. It felt like a freezer door had opened. She turned around to look at the empty corner of the room, and saw the reason.

The crone was there. Behind her, a ragged tear stitched back and forth across the 90-degree angle where the walls joined.

The tear shimmered and quivered as she watched, and a black-gloved hand suddenly pushed through one section of the thin divide. Another hand followed, this one naked and ugly, its knuckles surrounded by a crooked forest of purple veins. Both hands reached out from the silver-black fissure that stretched nearly to the ceiling, and held the shoulders of the hag.

"We've been waiting for you," the crone grinned. Her teeth were yellowed and sharp, and, as she laughed, Alex could see the black scars of her gums.

"Come closer," the wrinkled hag said, and the two bodiless hands both curled their fingers at her, urging her forward.

Without thinking about it, Alex took a step towards the wall. And then another.

"What are you looking at?" the man asked her, a puzzled look on his face. The girl was moving in slow motion, it seemed, towards a bare corner of the room. But she didn't answer.

"That's it," the creature smiled, its lips curving in a purpled sneer. "Come to mama, that's it. We need you, oh yes. Nobody needs you like us."

Alex felt the fear drain away from her bones. Joe had made her feel warm, loved, last night. But now, as the chill fumed through the crack behind the hag and swirled out into the room, lassoing her and dragging her forward, Alex felt a call in her heart that she couldn't deny. Within the cold, there was a heat that she thirsted for. With each word from the old woman, she could almost taste it. She felt terribly tired too; her muscles wanted to relax. She could barely stand anymore. But she had to touch that feeling . . .

"One more step, my sweet, one more step. You know your mama loves you, don't you?"

Alex held out a hand to the woman as her eyelids closed of their own accord. She couldn't keep them open anymore. In her mind, she could still see a snow-covered cottage just ahead, with smoke swirling from the chimney and a warm light of hearth and food beaming from within.

"Your mama loves your bones, yes," the crone cackled and

reached out to embrace the girl, who felt her very life pulled from her by the hungry flicker of cold.

Alex fell forward towards the wall, and the man grabbed her beneath the arms to keep her upright. But as he pulled her up, the girl clumsily swatted him back.

"Don't touch me, I'm going home," Alex mumbled dumbly, and turned back towards the wall and the old woman and the cottage that smelled of frozen blood and boiling stew.

Joe pushed through the doors of the elevator as soon as they opened on the 2nd floor, and frantically looked for the signs on the wall noting how the rooms were numbered.

"200–288" read one, with an arrow pointing left.

"255, right Malachai?" he breathed, but didn't wait for a response.

Better hurry, the demon whispered.

Joe ran down the hotel hallway, the tangled design of the mauve and royal blue carpeting passing beneath his feet in a dizzying blur. He counted the numbers as he went, "201, 209, 213 . . ."

Finally he got to 255 and stopped. He raised his hand to knock, but saw that the door hadn't closed all the way. "No time for polite," he said, and pushed it open. For a split second, he couldn't understand what he saw.

A man stood next to the bed in the middle of the room watching Alex, his jaw dropped wide. The girl had stepped into the corner of the room next to the dresser, and reached out to touch the wall . . . only her arm passed right through it.

Joe shot into the room and saw that most of Alex's right arm was . . . gone. Before he could take another step, her face leaned into the strangely shimmering wall and started to pass through as well.

"Alex!" he yelled, and shot forward. He pushed past the man, and grabbed for Alex's left hand. Her whole upper torso was submerged in the wall now. She looked the reverse of a deer head mounted on a bar wall . . . only it was her body sticking out without a head, not the other way around.

Joe pulled her arm with all his strength, but only an inch of Alex reappeared in the room.

"Help me," he cried. "Pull her back." The other man reached forward and grabbed her by the belt. "Pull!" Joe shouted, and together, they struggled to pull the girl back.

"aaaaahaaaaAAAHAHHHH," they cried in unison, straining against an inhuman force to bring her back to the hotel room, to the plane on which she belonged.

Alex screamed. A piercing, horrible cry of agony, as, with a silent pop, she plunged backwards into room 255 and tumbled on top of the two sweating, straining men. Joe hit his head on the bed frame, and saw stars.

For a minute, all that could be heard in the room was the rasp of heavy breathing, as they all tried to come to grips with what had just happened. Then Alex shook her head, as if to clear away cobwebs, and pushed herself off of Joe's stomach. She sat up, and Joe saw the tears streaming down her face. She looked absolutely lost; wounded to the core.

"Mama," she cried. Her eyes were still someplace else.

Chapter Thirty

"Where did you get that?" Cindy demanded, hands on her hips and fire in her eyes.

"I did a little spee-lunking," Ted grinned, giving her his best aww-shucks look. He pushed the book to the side of the desk. "I wanted to see where you'd gone, you know, when Joe saved you."

"You little shit," she breathed, and stalked through the door. She grabbed the ancient book from her little brother's desk and shook her head as she flipped through the molded, dusty pages. *The Journal Of Broderick Terrel,* read the cover.

"Don't you get it? I almost died down there. It's dangerous!"

"But Joe saved you," Ted nodded. "And he exorcised the demon Malachai. There's nothing there now."

"He didn't exorcise the demon," Cindy said. "He took it inside himself. And that took him away from me. I don't know if there's anything in those caves now or not. But you shouldn't have gone down there. You should know better."

"Sorry," he said, hanging his head. "It was really cool though. That one cave with all the blue crystals—that was something else."

Cindy remembered when Malachai had possessed her, and stripped her naked. He'd made her lie on the pedestal in the center of the glittering chamber of blue crystal, and had intended on having either a hippie cave explorer—or Joe—impregnate her, so that the demon could have a new child pledged for sacrifice. If she had had Malachai's child, the demon would have forged a new covenant, and thus gained license to stay on this plane unfettered for years to come. But instead, Joe had put himself in between; the invisible bullet that was Malachai had become pledged to him . . .

Cindy thought of her little brother walking around that haunted cavern, where she had been raped and almost killed, and shivered. What would he think if he knew the whole truth of what had happened beneath the lighthouse on Terrel's cliff?

"Stay out of there," she insisted.

Ted shrugged. "Okay," he said. "But can I read the book? It's just an old journal. And it's kinda cool, the way this guy called all these spirits and stuff. Like he was a warlock."

Cindy considered. With Malachai gone from Terrel along with Joe, it probably wouldn't hurt if Ted read what was, basically, a 100-year-old diary.

"Okay," she agreed. "But promise me you won't go back down there without me?"

"Deal."

"And take care of the book? It's probably valuable. It's really old."

"I will," he insisted.

She dropped the book back on his desk and turned to leave the room. She hesitated at the door.

"Do you miss Joe?" Ted asked.

She felt the tears start as she nodded. Then she hurried from the room before he could see her cry.

After Cindy left, Ted turned to the computer on his desk, and brought up his e-mail. He started drafting a letter:

> To: curburide@aol.com
> Fr: TedIsTooCool
> Hi Ariana,
> When are you going to get here? I know my sister will be excited to meet you. I can't really tell her about you, but I think I've found a way that I can get her to

take me out to the cliff when you come, so that we can all talk and won't be bothered by anyone. We could talk all about what she did with the demon that possessed her a few weeks ago. She won't really tell me everything about it. But I bet you guys will get along. She really could use someone who understands about demons and stuff I think.

I went to the cliff the other day and found this old journal down in the caves where she was possessed, like I wrote about to you before. It's really old—some of the pages fall apart when you turn them. But this guy wrote all about these demons and he mentions the Curburide and stuff, just like you wrote me.

I'd do anything to help you help them come through, if they'll give me the power you said they have. I want to be able to fly. Like Superman or something. And you said they were really into sex. Would they help me find a girlfriend?

Can't wait to meet you,
Ted

Chapter Thirty-one

"Yeah, it fuckin' hurts," Ariana growled as Jeremy ran his hand down her side. "How'd you like me to kick your ribs in so you could know what it feels like?"

Jeremy took his hand from her side and ran it through his thinning hair. "Look," he said. "You were trying to kill me. What did you expect?"

"I expected you to fuckin' lie down already. Just die."

"Better to have me around though, isn't it?"

She grimaced. "Sure," she said, not sounding sure at all. She eased herself onto the chair near the window in the motel room and pressed the curtains aside to stare out into the half-empty parking lot. They'd driven a couple hundred miles after leaving the hospital, and pulled off after dark to the first exit they found that boasted lodging. "Now I've got a chauffeur," she said. "Never mind that I didn't need one to get from San Francisco to Phoenix to Austin to New Orleans to Tallahassee."

"Maybe it's time you had some help."

"Well." She closed her eyes and shifted positions. "Thanks to you, yeah, now I need some."

Jeremy knelt at her feet and stroked her hair. "I'm sorry I hurt you," he said. "I'm not sorry I hurt my wife. Does that make any sense?"

Ariana's eyes flickered open, and she forced a weakened smile.

"Yeah," she said. She undid the button on her jeans. "Your

bitch didn't take care of you, and for better or worse, you're my lapdog now."

She grimaced, and forced her jeans down her thighs until they fell at her ankles. Then she slipped a finger beneath her pink thong, and slipped the tiny cotton brief down as well.

"So lap," she demanded.

Jeremy nosed between her thighs and shivered at the earthy scent of her. Could he have really fallen from father and husband to this? And when was the last time he had felt so needed? He didn't fight it. Pressing his head down, he began to trace the moist flesh of her desire with his tongue.

"Lap, yes," she moaned. "That makes it all better."

Chapter Thirty-two

Sometimes there's a silence between two people that's best not broken. After the events of the past 48 hours, Joe took comfort in the fact that Alex was saying nothing.

They had left San Francisco as soon as possible after rescuing Alex from the clutches of the Curburide. She hadn't said much about what she had seen, but she had agreed when he suggested that they skip their trip to Alcatraz and head towards the next stop of the Sunday Slasher.

They had stopped at a couple of roadside diners for food and a break, but Joe had driven all afternoon and all night. Dawn had broken a couple hours before, and Alex had woken, but said little. And he himself had nothing to say. He knew she was scared. He suspected that she wanted to turn back. But what could he do? What could either of them do? She had made a gesture of giving up in San Francisco and had been lynched by spirits. He didn't know what Malachai would try if he simply stopped the car and refused to go on. He didn't want to know. And so the highway passed in a brown blur behind them and Alex stared out the passenger window at the desert wastelands.

They'd be in Phoenix soon, and he'd be asking her to talk to ghosts again. To play detective. Or reporter. Wasn't that his role?

Joe shook his head and reached forward to turn up the radio. Sound to blot out the silence.

When they finally reached the city limits of Phoenix, Alex reached into her backpack and pulled out the battered copy of the *Salt Lake City Tribune*. "Jack Sketz," she said. "Killed at a Ramada Inn."

"Any ghosts around that you can ask to tell us how to get there?"

"Guys really will try anything to keep from stopping to ask directions, won't you?"

"Depends," he said. "Who's giving the directions?"

She whacked him on the head with the paper. "The devil."

"Then let's keep driving," he suggested.

It only took one gas station stop to track down the Ramada. There were a handful in the area, but Joe simply had to mention that they were supposed to be staying in the one where that murder took place a couple weeks ago, and the station attendant was pointing to a map in seconds. A little blood always makes the memory stay keen.

The sun was blazing overhead as they walked from the car towards the double doors of the Ramada Inn lobby.

"Far cry from San Francisco, eh?" Joe said, wiping the instant beads of sweat from his forehead.

"Feels good," she said. "Maybe it will burn away the bad ghosts."

"Don't bet on it."

They were still blinking to adjust their eyes from the brightness outside to the dim coziness of the lobby when the first one came.

Alex grabbed Joe's forearm and whispered, "Wait."

He nudged her out of the line of traffic towards the lobby sitting area, where a couple businessmen waited with suitcases and cell phones in hand, and a woman in ASU shorts laid back against a sofa armrest and read a paperback novel.

"Can we sit?" Joe asked, and when Alex nodded, he ushered her to a sofa that faced away from the reception desk and the others waiting in the lobby. She sat slowly, as if in a daze, and stared at the space between their feet and the outer wall of the hotel.

"What is it?" Joe asked finally.

"He says we need to keep moving," Alex whispered.

"Who says?"

"He says they're getting close to the final sacrifice."

"Who is it?" Joe insisted. He could see nothing but empty air in front of them.

Alex didn't answer immediately. Joe could see the blood draining from her face.

"He says his name is Jack," she breathed. "Jack Sketz."

The man was blond, and tan. He was also semitransparent. He stood a little taller than Joe, and had one of those lopsided grins that made you just want to believe whatever he said, without question. The kind that made a great salesman.

I know why you're here, he said to Alex. He reached out a large, manly hand to pat her shoulder, but as she involuntarily braced for his touch, his fingers—one with a large golden college fraternity ring—slipped right through her skin. Her skin prickled with icy chills.

You are tracking her now, and that's good, he said. *You need to understand where she's been, what she's done. But you need to hurry. The door is only a crack here, but with every sacrifice, the opening grows deeper, wider. When she completes the chain, all of the links she's forged will join. The evil ones she prays to will come through here, and in all of the other places she's killed. In the end, it won't matter where they come through from . . . they'll overrun the entire world.*

"Is there . . ." Alex spoke out loud, and then remembered to still her tongue. *Is there an old woman now in the room you were killed in?*

I've seen a crowd of devils in there, he said. *I try to stay as far away from that place as I can, but something keeps pulling me back.*

Can you show us? she asked.

The man nodded. *Yes. But you shouldn't go too close.* He eyed Joe up and down. Joe meanwhile, was crinkling his eyebrows and looking right through the space the ghost stood in. *Tell him that he should hold you when we get up there.*

"Come on, Joe," she said, and stood. "We're going upstairs.

"Where?" he asked.

She flipped her hair and nodded to the right. "Follow that ghost."

"How did she do it?" Joe asked Alex in the elevator. "How did she kill him? And what did she do with the body after? The newspapers keep hinting that there's something particular about how she's murdering."

"Why don't you ask him yourself?" she said.

"Because I can't see or hear him. Apparently I failed witch school."

A heavy frown crossed Jack Sketz's ethereal face. *I don't like to think about it,* he said. *But it's all I can think about anymore.*

"I'm sorry," Alex whispered. "If it hurts too much . . ."

No. You should understand.

The elevator doors slid open and they stepped into a small waiting area with two chairs and a mirror.

The ghost stepped out and immediately took the hallway to the right. Alex and Joe followed.

She's evil, he continued. *Pure evil. She showed up at the bar, all decked out in black latex . . . totally a hot little kitten looking for some action. She latched onto me, and I couldn't believe it. I'm never that lucky, I mean, she was one prime piece of . . .* He looked over his shoulder and realized who he was telling the story to again. *Um . . . sorry. Anyway, so she brings me back here and tells me to strip. She's got this circle of small bones and rocks on the floor and she says sex is kind of a ritual with her, and she wants to do it in the middle of those. I think, well, that's a little weird, but to get close to the skin beneath that catsuit is going to be worth it. So I drop trou, and sit down naked in the circle. She's in the bathroom, I figure changing, but when she comes out, she's still in the catsuit. She makes me lie down, and then turns her back to me and at the time, I wondered why she was mumbling some kind of nonsense. I realize now, she was praying to them. Then she straddled me, and when she bent down to kiss me, she slit my throat with a razor blade.*

"God," Alex said aloud.

That's the nice part, he continued. *After I was dead, she took off that catsuit finally, and was totally naked with my dead body. I could see her; it was weird. Like I was floating there and spying on myself with this beautiful woman and . . . um . . . she touched my dead . . . um wood, and . . .*

"She fucked you?" Alex said, without qualm.

Joe looked at her sharply. "Careful," he warned. But there was nobody in the hallway.

The ghost nodded. *Best time of my life probably, and I missed it. Well. I didn't miss it exactly, but I couldn't feel it. And when she was done, she took out her razor again. Damn, it gives me the willies just to think about it.*

He stopped in front of a door and turned to Alex.

She took that razor, cut off my penis, and stuffed it in my mouth.

Alex made a face and shivered. *I'm sorry you had to see that.*

That's not the half of it. Then she slit open my chest and belly, and spent the next hour pulling out all of my insides. It was horrible. Her arms and body were covered in my blood, but she didn't seem to mind. She just kept reaching in and coming back out with another wet piece of my liver or my heart or whatever. She took each piece, kissed it, and set it in a circle around my body, but inside the circle of rocks and bones.

He pointed to the door. *And she did it in there.*

"This is the place," Alex said.

"How do we get in?"

"Haven't gotten that far yet."

There's nobody inside right now.

"That doesn't really help us though," she pointed out. "If someone was in there, I could get them to open the door for us, make up some excuse."

You still don't get it, do you? Malachai whispered in her ear.

Alex smiled at his voice. "There you are," she whispered, looking up towards the ceiling. "Been wondering why you were so quiet."

Switzerland is rarely heard from, do you understand?

"Yeah, well, I'd say you're as neutral as a vegetarian at a ribfest."

Joe looked askance. He could only hear half of the conversation. "What's up . . . more company?"

"Malachai has decided to join us."

"Great . . . then we're doomed. What does he want?"

The demon ignored its "master" and spoke directly to Alex. *You're a witch,* Malachai said. *You need to discover yourself before you can hope to confront the murderess. Or the Curburide. There is power in you, but if you do not learn to use it . . .*

"So I'm supposed to think my way through the door?" she whispered.

Use your head, Malachai snapped. *When you were starving in your basement, and you couldn't reach the bread, what did you do?*

But I don't know any ghosts here, except Jack, she said silently. Then she looked at Jack. *Can you turn the lock?*

The ghost shrugged and reached an ephemeral hand to twist and jiggle the doorknob. *Guess not.*

You don't need to know anyone, Malachai continued. She could hear the patience in his voice slipping. *It's not about asking, it's not about knowing ghosts, and it's not about friends. It's about power and will. You have within you the power to call upon the spiritual realm to bend the physical to your will. Use that power. Insist that the lock be tripped.*

Alex stared at the lock and wished for it to open. Then she put her hand on the knob and tried to turn it. It wouldn't budge.

This isn't working, she complained.

You're not using the power, the demon said. *Will is different than wish.*

"We can't stay here much longer," Joe warned. "There's a maid coming."

Alex closed her eyes and reached deeper inside herself, searching for a familiar place. It wasn't an emotion, it wasn't a muscle . . . but it was something palpable that she knew. There was a feeling she had whenever she called out to ghosts. More than a feeling . . . a power. When she used it, she could feel adrenaline in her body, like an electric charge. Maybe if she could make herself feel that feeling about the lock . . .

Alex put her hands on the knob, focused on the lock and searched for the power. "Like calling a ghost," she murmured,

and in her mind, she pictured the bolt she knew was on the inside of the door turning. She felt invisible arms reaching out,
dowsing for energy, and when she found it, her brain felt aglow
in warmth . . .

"Can I help you?" The maid had reached them, and was no
doubt wondering why the two were standing there in front
of a door, without going in.

Hey, Jack complained.

Something audibly clicked and Alex opened her eyes to see
a wisp of Jack slipping like smoke from the slot of the door
lock above her hand. She turned the knob on the door. This
time it opened.

"No, we're good," Joe answered the maid, and pushed the
door open for Alex and him to step inside. When the door
closed, he grinned. "Cutting it a little close there," he said.
"How'd you do that?"

"I think I made Jack do it," she said.

The ghost was staring at his right hand, which seemed to
fade and then pulse with light. *That tingled,* it said.

*The only way you can win this war is to use their power against
them,* Malachai warned. *Do you understand?*

I think so, she said, before turning to Jack. *Did that hurt?*

The ghost shook its head. *Not hurt. But I can't say that I
liked it.*

We've been waiting for you, another voice announced. The
room suddenly filled with an icy wind and Alex grabbed
Joe's arm.

In the far corner of the room, a spectral shape floated just
above the floor. Alex couldn't tell its sex; the face was a writhing
mass of blinking eyeballs and clacking teeth. It seemed to have
three or more mouths . . . the more she stared, the more they
slipped in and out of each other, like a collage of overlapping
transparencies that were always in motion. But while the face
never seemed to gel into something understandable, the arms
were clearly human, and were now moving forward, faster
across the room towards them.

We should leave, Jack suggested.

"What is it?" Joe asked. "I can't see anything."

And then he yelped. "But I can feel something." His arm was suddenly gripped in a cold vise, and he stepped forward, away from Alex.

"Alex, what's going on?"

"It's a Curburide, I think," Alex said. The spirit emanated from a dark crack in the corner of the room, and had stretched itself in a tangle of shimmering, shifting clouds of darkness across the room to fasten its hands on Joe's left arm. Alex pulled on the right, holding him back. But the demon turned a myriad of jostling eyes at her and laughed with all of its intermingled mouths.

He's mine now, it said. *And you're next.*

I don't think so, she said, and pulled harder. But it was no use. Joe's feet were creeping forward across the carpet.

"Alex," he whispered. "Something has me. I can't see it but it won't let go."

"I see it," she said. "It's coming from a crack in the wall. That must be the doorway that she opened here when she killed Jack."

He stepped forward involuntarily again, and now they were halfway across the room, standing in front of the bed.

She killed me right here, Jack announced. He stood at Alex's side, and shook his head sadly at the monster in front of them. *It's hideous. And there are millions of them.*

You wanna help me here? Alex said to the ghost. She had dug her feet in and was playing a game of tug-of-war with Joe. The demon's body grew thicker and more forceful with every step they got closer to where its smoky feet were anchored in the wall.

Jack tried to take hold of Joe's sleeve, but his fingers slipped right through. *I don't think I can,* he said.

Another step forward, and now the demon was cackling mercilessly. *The chain is almost forged,* it said. *And your devil friend has provided us with the final key.*

"Malachai?" Alex asked, and loosened her grip momentarily. Joe stumbled forward, and in a heartbeat his arm was disappearing into the wall.

"No," Alex screamed, as Joe's head slipped out of sight. "Let him go, you bitch!"

Now or never, Malachai offered.

"You fucker," she breathed, and then remembered what he'd said in the hallway. Joe's chest slipped out of the room and his arm had disappeared past the elbow. Alex let go of his hand, grabbing him instead around the legs as, inexorably, his body pulled away from the room to someplace else.

Closing her eyes, she focused again on finding that place inside. That feeling. She tried to imagine a chain around Joe's waist that held him here, and in her anger, she wished—no demanded—that the creature release him.

"Let him go!" she screamed, her anger releasing whatever walls she kept up normally between herself and her inner secret power that she didn't understand. She felt the fire race through her fingers to cascade along Joe's body. When it met the blackened crack in reality where his form disappeared, the smoke of the Curburide seemed to glow bright with tension. "Now!" she insisted and pulled with every secret muscle that she'd ever used to talk to a ghost.

And then Joe was tumbling backwards, knocking her to the floor as he was set free. Alex heard a deafening shriek in her mind, a scream that was answered by distant howls of contempt.

"Holy shit." Joe gasped, and shook his head, choking as he rolled off her. He didn't pause to regain his bearings or discuss what had just happened. He only grabbed Alex's hand and pulled her to her feet. "Let's get the fuck out of here!"

She was dizzy, and could hear the screams gaining in the distance. They were growing louder fast. Like a train that was approaching a station.

"I think we had better do that right now," she agreed, and staggered ahead of him to throw open the hotel room door.

Chapter Thirty-three

"What was it like?" Joe asked, turning his eyes away from the gray ribbon of asphalt. It stretched out in front of them like eternity; the way to Austin would take them that long driving, it seemed. It was more than a thousand miles. He hoped they would make it by Tuesday. After four days of long drives, they were going to need to hole up and rest somewhere soon.

"What was *what* like?" Alex asked.

"Growing up in Nebraska. Kind of out in the middle of nowhere, like this." He pointed at the clear blue sky, and the red-rutted gullies beside the road. The land on either side of the highway stretched lifeless and unused as far as the eye could see.

"Well, it wasn't this bad," she said. "We had fields for corn, and there were some people about. Not like this. I only lived in purgatory. This is hell."

You have not a clue, Malachai offered. *But you will know soon.* She ignored him.

"I grew up praying every night for the day when I could be old enough to get away. I used to construct these amazing fantasy escapes, where I stole a car and drove to Las Vegas and became one of those dancers with all the glitzy outfits and feather headdresses until I could make enough money to go to L.A."

"What did you want to do in L.A.?"

"Work at Disneyland? Be in a movie? Hang out at the beach all day and work as a lifeguard?" She shrugged. "Anything, really. It didn't matter. All I knew was that I had to get away from home, and the longer I stayed, the more I knew that if I didn't do it soon, I was going to die. Literally."

"From what, boredom?"

She laughed. "Hardly. Though I *was* pretty bored—my parents didn't even allow me to watch TV or listen to the radio. Claimed they were the devil's tools."

"So . . . from what?"

Alex was quiet for a moment, alone with a thought she didn't know how to phrase.

"That time I told you about, where my dad whipped me in the basement . . . that wasn't the first time he did something like that."

"Kinda figured," Joe said. "It sounded pretty bad, but, I thought maybe there was more to make you go so . . ."

"Psycho?"

"Maybe a little."

"More than a little," she said, and looked back out the car window. "Most kids don't take a hatchet to their parents. But most kids don't spend half of their childhood being locked in a closet, with nothing to play with but the ghosts and the attic mice."

"He used to lock you in a closet?"

"It was supposed to be a pantry, between the kitchen and the front room.

"It was kind of a weird space right under the stairs. But my parents didn't keep food in it. Oh no . . . that would be too normal for them. Instead, they made this . . . chapel. They put in a statue of Jesus, with a kneeler in front of it, and on the shelves where you were supposed to put cereal or flour or sugar or whatever . . . they put candles. When my father found out that I talked with the dead, he made me kneel in that little room and pray to Jesus for, what he called, my 'wicked fraternizing with demons.' "

"I'd think a religious person would have been excited about his little girl seeing spirits," Joe said. "Kinda like, it proves that there's an afterlife and all. Maybe that you're a girl God had given special gifts to, as well."

"Yeah, well, my daddy didn't see it that way. I think it scared the hell out of him that I could see ghosts, and the way he saw it, if they were really dead people who were still here on earth, then they hadn't lived their lives right or they'd be up in the light, having dinner with the Father, Son and Holy Ghost. So if they were here still, they were either the spirits of the damned or demons themselves. He wasn't too keen on the idea of me talking with either.

"Anyway, he used to make me go in there and kneel for hours. Every now and then, he'd open the door really fast, to see if he could catch me off my kneeler, or talking with someone invisible. After I got caught doing that a couple times, and had the switch spanked across my bare ass for it, I wised up, and kept my knees to the kneeler. The more he put me in there though, the less I prayed. Sometimes he'd open the door and see my lips moving and holler 'Who're ya talking to, young lady?' and I always said 'Jesus.' But it wasn't Jesus, and I think he knew that. But what could he do about it? Usually it was Genna I was talking with, telling her about how mean he was being to me, and when my dad poked his head in and I told him I was talking to Jesus, she'd laugh like crazy. It would be all I could do to keep the smile from creeping across my face as she was doubled over next to me, whispering things like 'Can you see my halo?' and 'Never mind my breasts, I'm the king of heaven!'"

"Sounds like a character."

"She was. I really miss her. She's the one who helped me make friends with the attic mice."

"What do you mean?"

"Well, sometimes my dad would lock me in the room overnight. I used to wonder if he would just forget about me and leave me in there for a week to starve. Genna told me to hide some food in there when things were okay, so that it would be there for me when things got bad . . . which they did every couple weeks.

"So I tucked a couple candy bars behind the candles on one of the shelves. One night, I had been locked in the room for hours. It was stifling in there, with the candles going. The smell made me dizzy, like being locked in church with incense under your nose. Sweat was dripping off my forehead. A drop actually ran down my nose, I remember, and dripped on my hand. I was so tired, I didn't even wipe it off. I just laid my head down on my arm, stretching my hand forward until it rested on the little altar shelf that Jesus was on. I started slipping into sleep.

"But something tickled my hand. I don't know how long I was out; probably not too long or I wouldn't have woken up from such a small touch. But I felt the tickle, and struggled to push open an eyelid to see what it was. For a second I thought that it was a hairy spider, and a chill went down my back. When my eyes finally opened though, I saw it wasn't a spider at all. It was a mouse. Its little pink nose was puffing in and out, and it looked all jittery. Its head twisted back and forth and then it pushed its little mouth up to my hand and I saw a pink tongue flick across my skin to lap up the bead of sweat there."

"Cool."

Alex nodded. "It was. That night, when I moved my hand, it skittered away. But later, I started leaving little crumbs around the statue, and I would kneel there and wait. Sure enough, if I was patient for an hour or two, the mouse would come, and chow down on whatever I'd left for it. Genna would help me sometimes, letting me know that the mouse was near so I would be still. It took a long time, but eventually it got so used to me, that it would eat right out of my hand."

"So you made it a pet."

"For awhile. Until my dad found out."

"How'd he do that?"

"One night, it was really late; and I'd been in there for hours. I figured my parents were asleep, so I was laying there on the kneeler, petting the mouse with one finger, and feeding it little bits of this granola bar with my other hand. I don't know how long he had been watching me, but he saw enough. He must have had the door cracked; I never heard it open. But then there he was, yanking me by my hair off the kneeler and dragging me out into the kitchen.

" 'No matter what we try to teach you about goodness and purity, you have to do the opposite, don't you?' he said to me. 'I try to protect you from cavorting with demons and so you take the next dirtiest thing and befriend the rats. You're a dirty, scandalous child, Alexandra,' he said and shoved me face-first up the stairs. But not before he said the words that I've never, ever forgotten."

"What's that?" Joe asked, though he was afraid to hear the answer.

" 'I wish you'd never been born,' he said. And the next night, when he got home from work and shoved me into the closet, I wished I'd never been born, too."

Alex squeezed her eyes shut, holding back a tear.

"What happened?" Joe asked.

"That night, when he pushed me in the closet, well right there in front of Jesus, next to a sprinkle of granola crumbs, was a little spot of blood. The blood had dripped from the mouth of my mouse. His little neck was twisted and broken from where my dad's mousetrap had snapped it. The poor thing was still there, dead and mangled in the trap, next to Jesus' feet. I cried a long time that night, and petted the soft fur of the poor thing. It was my fault that this had happened, and I couldn't bear to see that accusation written there in its glassy eyes. It had come to the trap lured by the granola I had fed it. Granola I had taught it to think of as safe. That was probably the first time I wished my father dead. But it wasn't the last. Not by a long shot."

"Man," was all Joe could think to say. The car was silent for the next hundred miles. Joe was afraid to ask any more questions. Instead, he just started looking for a likely town to find a place to get a couple good meals and spend the night in.

"So, what do you wanna do in Austin?" Joe asked, when a road sign finally announced the town was just over a hundred miles away. They'd spent the night in a tiny town just shy of the halfway point, and gotten an early start the next morning. Now the afternoon sun was slanting into Joe's eyes.

"What do you mean?"

"Well . . . in San Francisco, we didn't get a chance to check out Alcatraz. Didn't know if you'd ever wanted to see Austin."

"Don't know anything about it," she said. "Bunch of country boys there, isn't there?"

"Actually, no. Austin's like the only place in Texas I'd recommend going. It's totally a Mecca for music and stuff. They call it the Live Music Capital of the World."

"In Texas?"

"Yep. It's a college town and the state capital, and there's even a lake there up in the hills. It's different than the rest of the state. There's a really famous nude beach there by the lake—Hippie Hollow. We could go up there if you're curious."

Alex punched him in the shoulder. "You wish. If you wanted to see me naked, why didn't you just say so? You've had enough opportunity this week, sharing a room and all."

Joe took his hands off the wheel and raised them above his head.

"Me? I'd never take advantage of a lady."

"Naw, you'd just take her up to a nude beach and make her show everyone what she's got."

Joe laughed, and flicked a strand of coal black hair from her cheek. "Yeah, you'd be showing them pretty clearly that the carpet doesn't match the drapes!"

She rolled her eyes. "Let's just find the hotel and see if there are any ghosts still hanging around that know any more about this slasher chick."

"Suit yourself," Joe said. "But don't underestimate the attraction of fat naked guys lolling around a lake in the sun."

"I'll pass. You go. I'm sure they'd be interested in seeing your white ass walking around. Maybe you'll find yourself with some new admirers." She gave him a long look up and down and grinned. "Make sure you take some soap to drop."

"You've been watching too many prison movies."

Alex put a hand over her heart. "*Moi?* I don't know what you mean. I'm an innocent girl from Nebraska remember?"

"Innocent, my ass."

The Marriott was just off the highway, a few blocks from the convention center and the city's famous Sixth Street club district. Joe got directions at a gas station, and moments later pulled off I-35 and found the hotel.

"Why here?" Alex mused, as they walked into the black marble lobby. Someone was playing a piano near the bar. "I thought she killed a guy here on Halloween . . . someone who was all dressed like Beetlejuice and walking in some parade."

"Not a parade," Joe said. "A few blocks from here though, they close off the whole street for Halloween and a lot of other festivals. It's like a big party district."

"Okay . . . well . . . skip the hippie nudies and take me there."

"Got a fake ID?"

"Naw. But I'm sure you can get me in. You're a big, strong older man and all."

"Flattery will get you drunk. Now shoosh while I get you a bathtub to sleep in."

Joe got a room with twin beds and pointed the way towards the elevators. When they were out of earshot of the front desk, he asked, "So . . . any ghosts lurking about?"

Alex nodded. "Some. None have really paid attention to us though, so I haven't encouraged them. I'd kinda like to take a nap first."

"Wimp."

"Nudist."

"Only in the shower."

"Thank God."

"You're feeling pretty feisty for a girl who wants a nap."

"I'm mouthy when I'm tired."

"Hate to see you when you're awake then."

They stepped off the elevator on the fifth floor, and found their room. Joe waved a hand at the beds and proclaimed, "Your boudoir, mistress."

"I'm no mistress," Alex announced, bouncing up and down a few times on her butt on the nearest mattress. "I'm a dangerous murderer who talks with ghosts and is on a top secret mission to save the world from demons."

"Mistress is easier to say."

"Keep dreaming," she said, and laid her head back on the pillow, closing her eyes. "That's what I'm going to do."

In seconds, Alex was sleeping. Joe looked out the window at the city and decided to do the same. His back was sore from driving, and he found himself stifling a heavy yawn. In moments, both of them were lying on their beds on top of the comforters, mouths open, eyes shut. Alex began to snore.

"This looks like a good spot," Joe said. They had both awoken and showered, before taking a walk to the downtown hub for dinner. After passing about 20 bars, ranging from the blatantly titled Chugging Monkey and the clear utility of Buffalo Billiards to the testosterone whimsy of Jackalope and the more ethereal Eternal, they had stopped in front of an Irish Pub, B.D. O'Rileys. The 10-foot-tall front windows were open, and people sat at square wooden tables drinking beer and eating sandwiches while looking out at the street. It was dusk, and the neon lights of the bar district had just started to glow.

"Think they have burgers?" Alex asked.

"I'm sure."

"Think they'll serve minors?"

"Never hurts to try."

They took a booth along the south wall, and sat at a high table barricaded from its neighbors by a tall dark-wood panel inset with frosted glass.

"This is kind of like what Bennigan's wants to be," Joe said, admiring the weathered but elegant wood, bent glowing wall sconces and wide plank floors which looked several years removed from their last coat of urethane.

"What's Bennigan's?" Alex asked.

"Never mind. It's a chain of restaurants that wants to be a real Irish bar. Any invisible people to talk with here? The place looks like it could be haunted."

Alex nodded. "Just because it's old doesn't mean it's haunted," she said. "But yeah, there are some here."

"See if anyone knows anything? Maybe it's safer to ask questions here than at the hotel."

"You mean, like, they won't attack us and try to pull us into the fifth dimension here?"

"Something like that."

"Wait 'til we get dinner," she said. "I'm starving."

"I think you're stalling. First you want a nap, now you want food . . ."

Alex bristled. "Look. I didn't ask to get sucked into this little joyride with you. If I don't want to talk to fuckin' ghosts, than I'm not going to talk to fuckin' ghosts, okay?"

Her eyes were wide and her nostrils flaring. Joe held up his palms.

"Whoa, girl," he said. "I was just kidding. I didn't ask to be part of this thing any more than you did. But here we are. Don't turn on me, okay?"

Alex hung her head and stared at the table. "I'm sorry. I just . . . I'm nervous about all this, okay? I mean . . . somehow Malachai and all of these others think that I'm supposed to do something about this killer woman. And the Curburide things. And—" she looked up at Joe, and he saw her eyes shimmered with tears—"I don't know what the fuck I'm supposed to do."

Joe took her hands across the table and squeezed.

"I know," he whispered. "I don't know what I'm supposed to do, either. But that's okay. We'll figure it out." He squeezed again. "Together, alright?"

Alex nodded.

When the waitress came back to take their order, Joe ordered a bean queso dip for both of them for an appetizer. Then he asked for a burger and a Newcastle.

"I'll have the same," Alex nodded, as if she ordered with him all the time.

The waitress had a slight brogue and black hair cut as tight as a pixie.

"You got it," she said, and slipped back to the bar.

Alex's eyes lit up and she whispered, "We did it! She didn't ask me for ID!" Then she frowned a little and said, "What's a Newcastle?"

Joe laughed. "I guess you'll be finding out shortly."

Alex's eyebrows crossed when she took her first sip of the dark amber ale, but that didn't stop her from finishing the glass. Or saying "Sure!" when the waitress asked later, "Another round?"

She was giddy as they stepped back out on the street after dinner. The air was alive with guitar solos and the echo of pounding kick drums. "Let's see a band," she said.

Joe laughed, but led her to the doorway of the closest bar that had live music. They stepped up to the doorway, but a hefty bald bouncer stopped them.

"No cover," he said. "But I'll need to see ID."

Alex's face fell.

"I'm old enough to"—she hiccoughed—"drink."

The bouncer said nothing and Joe pulled her back to the street. "C'mon," he said. "Let's take a walk."

They passed a couple more places with prominent door bouncers, and then a tattoo parlor.

"I want a tattoo of a ghost!" Alex proclaimed, peering in at the parlors brightly lit walls, all of them covered by samples of designs, a myriad of garishly colored roses, skeletons, skulls and butterflies. A girl with electric blue hair sat in a chair at the back of the room, while an artist bent over her back, marking out whatever pattern she was about to have etched indelibly in her shoulder.

"Tomorrow, maybe," Joe grinned and dragged her on.

A few steps farther on and they joined a crowd on the sidewalk to watch a street painter. Kneeling on the asphalt of a small open lot between buildings, the man wore a gas mask to protect him from the cloud of paint that he kept in the air at all times. A boom box vibrated out ambient dance music behind as he grabbed spray paint can after spray paint can, blasting a heavy paper canvas on the street with a mix of yellows, blues, reds and blacks. His hands never slowed; he'd point and shoot with one can, and immediately set it down and grab another, squirting a blast of white or blue across the wet sheet at his knees.

In moments, the mess of color began to take shape, as the man lifted a coffee can lid from where it was protecting a part of the canvas and began to use crumpled newspapers to smudge and shape the paint into a startling array of spiky mountains—an alien landscape that lived in silhouette against a glowing moon.

At the end, he lit the spume of an aerosol can and waved the flames over the finished painting to seal the paint. The crowd clapped, and someone stepped forward instantly, pulling out his wallet to buy the piece as Joe and Alex slipped back to the street.

"Wow," she enthused. "That was like magic. I wish I had a talent like that. He's incredible."

She stumbled against him and Joe put his arm around her and turned the corner back towards the hotel. "You do have a talent like that," he said, hugging her shoulder tightly. "You can do real magic. Don't ever forget that."

" 's not magic," she argued, eyelids at half-mast. "I just talk to people that . . . some people can't see." She waved a hand in the air. "No big deal."

"Yes, big deal," he said steering her across a crosswalk. "You're going to save the world."

She put a hand to her mouth. "Not before I get some sleep."

Chapter Thirty-four

"Next time you decide to kick me in the ribs, take your fuckin' boots off." Ariana held a hand to her side as she slowly rolled off the bed.

Jeremy stood in the bathroom doorway, looking sheepish with a towel around his waist. "Well, keep your claws to yourself then. Is it any better?"

"Gets worse every day. I don't know how we did that shit on Monday. I couldn't fuck now if my life depended on it."

"Didn't stop you from enjoying my tongue last night." He shrugged. "You were still in shock the day after. But all those endorphins wore off yesterday." He leaned back out of sight, and then returned with a pill bottle in his hand. He tossed it on the bed. "Take another. We hit the road and you can crash for a couple hours."

Ariana palmed the bottle and nodded. "I want to be awake when we get there."

"I'll wake you. But first we need to find some breakfast. And coffee."

Ariana yawned, and then slipped past Jeremy into the bathroom. She snaked an arm around him to take a nipple between her fingers. And twisted.

"Hey!"

She giggled evilly. With a swipe, she ripped the towel from his waist and pushed him, naked, into the room.

"Bring me back a hash brown?" she asked sweetly. She twirled the towel into a knot, and then flung it at him, whip-style. The crack of its end against his bare ass echoed through the room.

"You bitch!" he yelled, but jumped out of range.

"Orange juice, too," she sang, and closed the door.

He managed to find a Burger King and some hash browns, and Ariana walked straight from the shower to the greasy bag, water still dripping down her plastic-smooth back. He watched her pop about five orange-brown nuggets into her mouth before asking, "Hungry?"

She eased herself onto the bed and spread her still-glistening legs for him to admire, all the while still chewing greasy fried bits of potatoes. "Behave, and you can have dessert before we hit the road."

He'd had his dessert, and been eaten too, and now they were on the expressway again, headed east and into the glare of the sun.

Now Ariana was stretched out with the seat tilted back, black shades hiding her eyes. The reflection of cottony clouds moved across the mirror of their lenses, and Jeremy kept sneaking peeks at her, still not sated. The woman was phenomenal. A taut, curved bundle of dangerous, electric sex. Even now, bruised and in pain, she looked hot. She'd worn a pair of black stretch pants for the car ride that showed the swell of her ass when she moved, and a plain white T-shirt that didn't bother to hide the shape of her nipples through its pores. Not surprising, since she hadn't bothered to pull on a bra when they'd packed up and left. "Pulling this over my head hurts enough," she'd said.

"So what happens when we find this backwater town?" Jeremy finally asked. It was pathetic, but he realized he was just looking for something to say so that he could hear her voice again.

"We find a place to crash, and hopefully an Internet café. Or maybe the hotel will have a connection. I need to e-mail a friend there and let him know we've arrived. He'll set up the meeting with our sacrifice."

"So you've got a whole network now, huh?"

She laughed, and then grimaced, holding her side. "Oh yeah. You, me and the twerpy Internet nerd . . . we're a regular Interpol."

"When we kill this guy, that will be it?" Jeremy asked. "The spirits will be able to come through and help you then?"

"When we kill *her*," Ariana corrected. "This one's a girl. So I may really need your help this time."

"I don't hurt girls," Jeremy mumbled.

"Fuck that." She groaned as she rolled towards the window. "You got plenty of hurt in you. I just need you to help me get close to her, gain her trust. One quick flick of my claws and she won't be fighting for long."

"Gonna wear your catsuit again?"

"I don't think I could if I wanted to. But no. This one's *au natural,* for all of us. We need to bathe in her life, to call forth death."

"You're a poet and I didn't know it."

"Shut up and drive, lapdog."

"Your pussy is my whip."

She snorted.

Chapter Thirty-five

Captain David Carroll stepped through the line of squads and walked towards the lawn. The red and blue lights flickered eerily across the dirty white siding of the otherwise nondescript split-level house. Two paramedics were feeding the back of an ambulance with a body bag.

Dave had known before he reached the house that this scene was locked up. But he'd felt the need to come anyway. It had happened in his jurisdiction, damn it, and he wasn't going to sit it out. Nevertheless, he knew his presence here was perfunctory. Frank Alton, the man who'd introduced him to his wife, as well as his best poker buddy, stepped out of the front door, and took off his cap to scratch a balding head.

"Looking grim?"

Frank's face lit up at Dave's voice, but then instantly fell. "It's a damned abattoir in there, Captain."

Dave knew it had to be badder than bad if Frank was calling him captain. The man was rattled. Heavily.

"Two bodies?"

Frank nodded. "But it looked like five. She painted the walls with them."

"You really think it's the Slasher?"

"It's brutal in there, man. All the organs were pulled out. Took them a couple hours to connect all the pieces to the bodies."

"But the others were all in hotels. And all men."

Frank shrugged. "Slightly different, yeah. But it's all a razor job. And who would know to cut off their genitalia and feed it to them? Who would know to put the liver at eleven o'clock around the head, and the heart at one? It can't be a copycat, unless the killer has been following the Slasher around."

"Sounds tight. Number five, huh? And still no idea who the hell she is."

"No idea who *she* is," Frank agreed. "But she may have a new traveling companion."

"Meaning?"

"The man we took out of that bedroom was not her husband. 99 percent sure on that, based on photos and the wallet. And the vehicle in the driveway that's not registered to Jeremy or Sheila Bruford. If the rituals weren't so methodically exact, I'd say this was a crime of passion. Sheila was flogging someone else's pony."

"And Jeremy?"

"Gave the grandmother a call this morning and asked her to hang onto the kids for the night; he and his wife were supposedly busy. He's in on this one, Dave. And while we may not know who she is . . ."

Dave grinned. "That's the break they've been looking for in San Fran, Phoenix, Austin, New Orleans . . . we'll take it."

"APB on Jeremy went out a few minutes ago."

"Good. Anything left inside to see?"

Frank laughed. "Lots of stains. They've marked and photographed the site, so don't worry about it. Take a look. I just hope you haven't eaten lately. You'll forgive me if I don't give you the guided tour."

Dave slapped him on the shoulder. "Get out of here. I'm just gonna take a peek to say I was here and then I'm heading home myself."

The house was creepy.

Dave stepped inside, and instantly the noise of chatter and squawking radios dropped off, and the oscillating lights of the emergency vehicles faded to some long colored shadows on the far wall of the living room. He stepped through the darkened foyer and into a hallway which he guessed led to the back bedroom where the murders had happened. A call had come through before he'd come on duty about the discovery; an old woman, the mother of one of the deceased, had come by to pick up some clothes for the grandchild who was staying with her. She let herself in with her own key, and according to the call log, practically had a stroke before she managed to call 911 to report the grisly murders.

But that was hours ago now. Tuesday night was coming on with a long shadow, and the house was still after the crime units had made their critical passes. The pictures taken, the hairs collected, the body parts removed. A forensics tech bustled past him and slammed the front door, and Dave knew he was alone in the house.

The slaughterhouse.

He could smell the blood. It wasn't like some scenes, where the bodies had fruited and rotted for days until the stench was rich with the perfume of maggots and sewer. No. This was fresh. He could still taste the faint scent of iron in the air.

There was no question about what room it had all happened in. At the end of the hallway, in the fading light he could see the dull glow of light blue walls. And the blotches of bloody spurts and handprints marring the robin's egg purity of the walls.

He stepped into the room and saw what Frank had referred to. On the wall above the queen-size bed, someone had written in smeared, drippy blood. They'd written the same thing that had appeared in the carefully guarded reports he'd pulled from out-of-state precincts on all the other scenes of the Sunday Slasher. Who for some reason, in Tallahassee, had decided to kill on the day after the Lord's day. Maybe she got her calendar mixed up, he thought.

Come Curburide

Set Us Free.

Dave shook his head at the scrawl. What the fuck was a Curburide? And free from what? Then he looked at the rest of the room and his stomach turned.

The carpet he stood on was saturated in the blood of the victims. His feet stuck to the fibers when he lifted them. The bodies were gone now, but it was clear where they'd lain. Deep red stains circled those areas, though the room had been stripped of virtually everything else. Evidence.

He pivoted and studied the room, looking for more writing or blood spray. But the other walls were clean. Except . . .

He noticed a crack in the wall the bed butted, a crack that ran floor to ceiling near the corner of the room, where the back wall joined the wall of the window. Guy wasn't much of a fix-it man, Dave mused.

He stepped closer, and then closer. It was a crack all right, but not really a normal one. It seemed to be . . . bleeding black. Not just a simple fissure in the paint and drywall, but a seepage of something from behind the wall.

"What the fuck is that shit?" he whispered, and stepped around the bed and nightstand to peer closer at the flaw.

The squad lights set up a kaleidoscope behind him that he tried to ignore as Dave leaned closer to the crack in the wall. He felt a chill in his neck, and turned around to see if someone was at the door.

The doorway was empty. But when he looked back at the wall, someone was looking back at him.

Someone with an eyeball missing, and a jowl-hung face that looked a thousand years old. Someone who grinned with blackened teeth and whispered, "We've been waiting for a little peace and quiet."

"Huh?" was all Dave could say before two bony hands reached out from the seeping black crack and grabbed him by the wrists.

"We're not coming," the gnarled ghostly face hissed, locking the police captain's hands in a vice grip both icy and unbendable. "We're here."

With that, David Carroll's salt-and-pepper hair suddenly

smacked hard against the wall. But the room wasn't filled with the snap of cracking vertebrae, or the thud of a skull cracking. Rather than breaking or thumping, Dave's forehead—and then his head and neck—passed *through* the wall, and two more ghostly arms reached out to grab the captain by his belt loops.

In a moment, without a single cry, the bedroom was empty once again.

Part Four:
Sacrifices

There has been some speculation that if the Curburide were to be given access to a country by way of the third and most dangerous type of Calling, that their reign would not end at those sovereign borders. Such a Calling, it is said, could bring upon the earth an age of degradation so vile, so laved in blood, that all of humanity's corpses would, at its end, lie naked and unburied for the wolves to feast upon.

Nevertheless, the ritual has been constructed and attempted, albeit unsuccessfully. The cornerstone of the ritual, which is preceded by five degradations, is the final sacrifice. This should occur in a place of spiritual power, and should involve a sacrificial victim who has already been used in the throes of possession. But the sacrifice must also involve another, who willingly engages in the mutilation and sexual conquest of the flesh . . .

—Chapter Nine, *The Book of the Curburide*

Chapter Thirty-six

Alex woke up with a headache. The room was still dark, but something had awoken her. Her heart pounded double time. When she rolled over to look at Joe's bed, she felt a dull ache at the back of her skull. She laughed inwardly and cursed herself. *Lightweight.*

But the hangover ache wasn't what woke her, she knew it. Holding her breath, she squinted into the darkness. She'd been sleeping deeply, couldn't even remember dreaming. It would have taken a good noise to wake her, and Joe was still wrapped up in blankets in the other bed. His breath came in long, slow rhythms. It hadn't been him.

Something moved by the short hallway to the door. She tried to call out to Joe, to alert him, but her voice wouldn't come.

In a heartbeat it was there, next to her bed.

A man. Or, at least, some *thing* that looked like a man. An old, old man. A wizened, well-lined face bent over her bed, and Alex could see the hair growing out of the moles on his forehead and cheeks. Age did not become him.

He raised a pale, gnarled finger to his lips. "Shhhhh."

Don't listen to him, Alex.

Malachai. He'd been strangely silent for most of the past couple days.

Who is it? she asked in her mind.

Nobody you want to know. Or trust. You should send him away.

The old man bent to brush cool, dry lips against her forehead. With a cold hand he began to stroke her hair against the pillow. Again Alex tried to call out to Joe, but her throat seemed locked. No sound would come out.

"Who . . ." she finally gasped.

"Shhhhh." The old man slid from sight, and Alex was afraid to turn, afraid to see where he'd gone. But then she felt the covers move, and she knew right where he'd gone. His hairy naked legs suddenly entwined with hers, and his liver-spotted arm slipped around her middle familiarly.

His voice rasped now in her ear. "Shhhh, my sweet. Wouldn't want to wake the boy when a man's here to do what a man's gotta do."

Alex's eyes shot wide, and she felt something hard poking against her butt. Something cold and hard. His chest hair grated against her T-shirt, and she elbowed him, sharp, hard, in the gut.

But her elbow felt as if it had sunk in a winter pond.

Malachai! she screamed inside.

Meet a real, dead Curburide, the spirit whispered. *Consider it your first test.*

The old man's bony palm was now kneading her chest, slipping up and down the slope of her breasts and cupping her nipples as he rolled first one and then the other between his icy finger and thumb. While her mind screamed and cried for her body to move, her flesh would not respond. A strange blanket of lethargy weighed her into the mattress like bags of flour, and instead of screaming and throttling the old lech, she only lay there as his fingers probed her tits and then slipped beneath the waistband of her underwear to scratch and rub at the curly hair hidden there.

Help me, she screamed, but nothing came out of her mouth.

The waistband of her panties was slipping down her thigh, and then his sour breath raised the hair in her nose. "So pretty, pretty," the creature breathed across her cheek. His cool, dead flesh pressed down against her face, and she gagged on his smell. His face felt like a bowl of sticky rice that had sat out on the counter for hours. It was bumpy and wet and cold. And his fingers were touching her, touching her there and it felt good but she didn't want to respond to it, no. It was wrong;

she couldn't let this *thing* take the only thing she had that was truly hers to give. The thing she had started to think about giving to Joe . . .

Help yourself, Malachai answered. *Or turn around and go home.*

Fucker, she hissed.

Whiny, insolent brat. Are you going to just lie there and let this beast inseminate you?

Even as he said it, she could feel the prod of the old man's penis pressing between the back of her thighs. She clenched them tight, and tried again to roll back against the thing. But its body seemed spongelike; her shoulder arched into something cold and amorphous, and for just a second she thought she felt the soft but solid touch of the mattress before the cool pocket of Curburide expanded again and gently pressed her back to her side. Then his sharp bony hands were on her shoulders, rolling her facedown on the mattress, and his legs were scissoring between hers, spreading her for him to take from behind, like an animal.

His weight eased upon her, and his hands slipped across her breasts again as he pulled himself tight to her, slipping easily now with his cock between her virginal lips, teasing at the entry she'd only plumbed up to now with her fingers.

As he kissed and licked her earlobe, he whispered, "You are mine now. I will keep you safe. From the rest."

There was a tornado in Alex's chest as she felt the coldness entering her and with a flash of pure, unflinching fury, she wrenched herself free from torpor.

"You . . . will . . . *not.*" She screamed. It came out as a whisper . . . but it came out. She closed her eyes and remembered the feeling when she had turned the lock on the door in the hotel in Phoenix. She understood now. It seemed like it was a physical thing, but this was a Curburide. A spirit. You couldn't fight a spirit with elbows and knees. You could only fight it with soul.

Alex gathered her hate in a tight, hard ball and threw it from her heart like a steel punch. The coldness between her legs jerked back, and she felt her limbs loosen. Not missing a beat, she flung herself out of its grasp and off the bed, landing with a thud on the carpet. The floor slammed against her, jarring her tailbone like a hammer. But the pain helped; it drove the torpid spell of the Curburide from her. As the evil, hoary man reached for her from the edge of the bed, she imagined him, not in her room, but in a fiery pit of searing, burning logs. An inferno that would take that creature's coldness and turn it inside out. For a second, the room seemed to glow with the illusion of fire, and the Curburide shrunk back to the bed. The demon shrieked.

"Get the fuck out of my room, you asshole," she hissed.

The man slipped off the bed and backed away from her, shaking his head.

"I'm not so bad," he said. "I would protect you. When they have their way with you . . ."

"Go," she demanded, and sent another heartfelt jet of flame at his face. She wanted his white, kinked hair to burn until it was black ash on his bubbled, blistered forehead. Again he screamed, raising an arm to ward off her spectral fire. He cursed her, and in a flash, was gone from the room.

As she sat there, sweat running down the sides of her forehead, trying to catch her breath, Joe finally woke up.

"Whaddya doing down there?" he mumbled sleepily, peering over the edge of his mattress. "You fall out of bed?"

"Sort of."

Alex thought of the unnatural cold thing that had pressed between her legs and shuddered. The rumpled covers hung half off of her empty bed. Her stomach turned over, a little late to the emotional party. She couldn't go back to that bed, not tonight.

Alex turned back to Joe and straightened her T-shirt to cover her panties. Then she pushed a hand on his chest.

"Move over," she said. "I'm coming in."

"All hands on deck," Joe laughed, and scooched himself backwards to accommodate her. She pushed up against him and curled into a ball, hogging his pillow, and breathing in the warm smell of him on it.

"Bad dream?" he asked, stroking the hair away from her ear.

"The worst," she whispered. And in her mind, added, *because it was real.*

He reached around her, to hug her close, and Alex smiled as he struggled to keep his arm from brushing her nipples. His arm felt right wrapped around her. She slipped a hand around his wrist and pushed his arm up, so he couldn't help but crush her breasts against his forearm as he hugged her.

She sighed and pressed his hand to her breast, enjoying the reaction she felt from behind. He struggled to shift his erection and it slipped against the thin panties like a warm sausage. He was exactly opposite of the Curburide; warm where it was cold, young where it was old.

"Sleep," Joe whispered in her ear. His breath smelled rich, like life. Life with a touch of onions. Alex craned her head around just in time to plant a kiss on his lips. His eyes widened, but he returned the gesture, and then gently pressed her back to the pillow.

"It's not the time," he said. "Not now." He leaned in and kissed her cheek and then slid back to the pillow, whispering again, "Sleep."

Alex realized at that moment that she was in love with Joe Kieran.

This time, when Joe woke the next morning, Alex was still in bed with him. And still sleeping. He pressed his raging morning erection against her and buried his face in her hair.

God, did he want to fuck her. How he had ever managed to say "not now" to her last night, he didn't know. But something had made him hold back. And he remembered Malachai's warning about witches and power and virginity. Sounded like an old wives' tale, but he wasn't taking chances at this stage in the game.

Still . . . he could have had her. He closed his eyes at the subtle jasmine scent of her hair and imagined her naked beneath him, eyes trained on his as he moved, gently but firmly between her legs. God, God, God. What if they didn't make it out of this? What if he'd passed up his one chance to be with Alex?

"Is that a baseball bat on my ass, or are you happy to see me?"

Joe opened his eyes and laughed, rolling back from her, a little embarrassed. He hadn't intended for her to feel him touching her that way, just for a moment.

She rolled over to face him, sleep still clouding her eyes. "It's okay," she said. "I hear all guys get that in the morning."

"No, I really am happy to see you," he ventured.

Her lips spread into a pale grin, and she gave him a dry peck, and then poured herself over him, in a full body hug.

"No real kisses 'til I brush my grody teeth," she whispered in his ear.

"No real kisses 'til we get rid of the freakin' psycho and her army of ghosts," Joe answered.

"That's how it is, huh?" She pulled back and raised one coy eyebrow.

"That's how it is."

She rolled off the bed. "Then we better get moving and get this little war over with."

He did the same. "Dibs on the bathroom," he called, and darted around the bed past her.

"Uncool," she pouted.

"Only cuz you lost."

When the door closed, Alex sat down on the bed, and waited for the sound of the water. Then she buried her face in his pillow. And breathed him in, one slow breath at a time.

Chapter Thirty-seven

The road twisted and turned through a maze of thick emerald forest. They had been climbing slowly for the past half hour, and Jeremy's ears popped with the gain of altitude. According to the directions Ariana had from her e-mail, they should be coming to the old port town any minute now. All he could see were trees.

They were close though, he could taste it. Literally. The air had grown tart with the flavor of the salty ocean breeze. Ariana had popped the pain pills at the hotel, and five minutes after they got on the road, she was out cold.

He passed a rusted mailbox beside a gravel driveway that led off to the left from the road, and then shortly thereafter, a sign, half obscured by a wide weedy frond the size of an elephant ear.

TERREL 5 MILES

"At last," he sighed. Jeremy had begun to get claustrophobic in the midst of all this dark foliage. It was as if they were driving down a one-way road to a green hell. He hadn't seen another car in fifteen minutes.

The road took a new curve, hard to the right, and then snaked left. Jeremy realized he could see glimpses of brightness through the thick bush and tree cover on the passenger side of the car. Then he saw a longer streak of bright blue. The road cut again toward the right and suddenly the trees disappeared altogether and Jeremy found himself with an unobstructed view looking out off a high ridge over an expanse of deep blue water that stretched out in a long shadow to the pale, blue sky.

The road appeared to wind down into a valley where the spires of a church, and some other, smaller buildings poked out from between the trees. And farther down the line of the bay, the road obviously climbed out of the valley and up again. He could see the unusually high promontory of a cliff on the far side of town. *That's gotta be the place,* he thought. *Terrel's Peak. The place where the girl they were here to find was first possessed.*

And the place where, in just four more days, she'd be sacrificed.

Chapter Thirty-eight

"We need to find the room," Alex announced, sitting on the floor and pulling her shoes on. She hadn't yet told Joe about the reason she'd climbed into bed with him. She wasn't sure she was going to. It made her feel slimy and dirty just to think of it.

"Can we get breakfast first?" Joe asked. "I need coffee."

"We can do both. I want to stay in the hotel and try to talk to some ghosts here."

She stood up. "We've had good luck so far in the hotels."

"Hmmm . . . you define luck differently than I do," he grinned. "When I'm talking about getting lucky . . ."

". . . stow it, mister. You had your chance at about two or three o'clock this morning. Luck is what you make of it."

Joe shook his head and followed her out the door. He really *had* thought she was fifteen the first time he saw her. He sure didn't anymore, as he watched her ass moving tightly against the pockets of her jeans down the hallway. He kicked himself, mentally, again and again. What had he been thinking then? What had he been thinking last night?

He pulled the door shut until he heard the lock catch. "Damn," he mumbled and hurried to catch up to her.

Joe grabbed a newspaper from the lobby, and then they went downstairs to the hotel's restaurant, Red Rojo, for breakfast.

"What's a Rojo?" Alex asked as they stepped past the hostess podium and into a bright atrium filled with square tables.

They were seated at a table near the windows, looking down at the pool, and the flagstone path along Waller Creek.

"Isn't it a chocolate and caramel candy?"

"That's Rolo, stupid."

Joe flipped open the paper, and skimmed the headlines. He'd only flipped the front page when he suddenly said, "Uh-oh."

"What's the matter?"

"Something's changed."

"What do you mean?"

"Hang on," he said, and then, after reading a moment, passed her the paper. He pointed to a box on the bottom of page 4.

SUNDAY SLASHER STRIKES AGAIN

A double homicide committed in a residential neighborhood in Tallahassee, Florida has been linked to the Sunday Slasher, despite the fact that the killing apparently occurred on a Monday, rather than a Sunday.

Coroner's reports confirm that the bodies of two victims, a male and a female, were removed from a residential section of Tallahassee late on Tuesday, after being murdered late the night before.

Austin police confirm that while this killing does not exactly match the pattern of the previous four murders linked to the elusive Sunday Slasher, the "design" of the killings has the indisputable signature of the killer who took the life of a man in the Austin Marriott Capitol two weeks ago on Halloween. The same killer is also linked to murders in Phoenix, San Francisco and New Orleans. Police sources speculate that, given the pattern of these killings, the next attempt will likely occur in an eastern seaboard city; each killing has been several hundred miles almost due east of the last. After Tallahassee, the next most likely urban areas are Jacksonville, Fla., Orlando, or Savannah, Ga.

There remain no suspects in the bizarre string of murders that began in San Francisco a month ago. For purposes of confidentiality, police remain silent on the evidence that they maintain ties each of these cases together.

"She missed a day and took two to make up for it," Joe said when Alex laid the paper back on the table. "What do you make of that?"

"She's getting sloppy?"

"No," Joe shook his head. "There's something different about this one. I wonder what's up. And where she's going."

Just then, a waitress stopped and offered them menus, while pointing out the ease of the buffet. As soon as she left, Joe looked over his shoulder at the long table of eggs, bacon, oatmeal and potatoes, and said, "No."

When Alex made a face, he explained. "I've never been to a hotel where any of the food on the buffet was actually 'hot,' except for the omelets. You do what you like, but I'm ordering off the menu."

"Whatever you say, old man," she said, picking up the menu.

"Take my word for it, jailbait. Or take your chances."

Alex took his word for it, and a half hour later, sated with toast, Denver omelet, pancakes, coffee and orange juice, they waddled into the lobby.

"I don't know what the buffet was like," Alex said, patting a still-taut-looking tummy beneath a loose white T-shirt. "But Mom never cooked like that."

"Hmmm," Joe said. "It was good. But you need to eat at my place sometime."

"I'll bet you say that to all the girls," she laughed, and skipped ahead.

"No," he said, not sure if she could hear. "Just the ones I love." She didn't answer, but hopped down two stairs to the bar area.

"I want to just sit here," Alex said, pointing at the maroon padded chairs near the registration desk and untenanted bar.

"I'd feel better if we can find someone to talk to in the open, you know? Like in Phoenix. He was nice."

"Wherever," Joe agreed, flopping into a sofa chair next to hers. "I can barely move."

Alex settled into the chair and stared around the lobby. It was quiet this morning; not surprising since it was a weekday and anyone here on business had probably already left. A hotel in the midst of the city like this had to be geared towards business travelers. Nevertheless, a couple people slipped back and forth through the lobby as she watched, and she could see the bellman escort one of them out the door and poise a whistle to his mouth to call a cab.

The lobby was strangely clear of ghostly presence, though she had noticed the hazy shadow of one over near the elevators, and another in the entryway to the registration desk area. They were so indistinct, that she didn't even try to call them; such vague energy wouldn't likely be connected to what was happening here, now.

Looking for someone?

The voice came from behind her, and Alex jumped. She turned around and he was there. Clearly. Almost physically.

Are you real? she asked, but not out loud.

No, he said. *Just angry.*

Angry?

That you're sitting around here. The bitch has gone. Days and days ago. Why are you here? Get on her trail and stop her before it's too late.

Who are you? Alex asked.

Just another dead person who doesn't want the Curburide to suck my little slice of heaven dry. What do you care? Get out of here and stop her.

Alex looked up at him, amazed at the anger that emanated. His face was drawn, shaven jaw set in a block of tension. His eyes seemed blue in the hazy fading light he drew around himself, and his hair was tight; salt-and-pepper gray and black. He wore glasses, too; little round sit-on-the-edge-of-the-nose specs that almost seemed an affectation.

Why are you mad at me? she asked in her mind. *We're just here trying to find out something about her so that we CAN stop her. Give me something to go on. At least tell me where she killed here, so I can see the doorway. That might help.*

The ghost looked up at the ceiling of the bar. *Can't you feel it?* he asked.

No, Alex admitted. *I don't feel anything but a bit of a hangover from the beer I drank last night. Are you going to help me, or not?*

Room 618, he said. *But if you don't know that already . . . maybe there's no point in telling you.*

Fuck you, asshole, Alex said. *I don't have to take that kind of shit from a dead guy. You want to help me find her, great. You want to dis me . . . fuck off.*

The spirit reached out a hand to her, but it passed through her shoulder. *I'm sorry,* he said. *I just want to . . .* He chuckled . . . *rest in peace. And currently . . . let's just say there's no rest for anyone still in this realm.*

So how am I supposed to stop her? Alex asked.

The being shook its head sadly. *I'm sorry,* it said. *But if you can't feel the pull of room 618 in this hotel, and you don't know how to stop her . . . you're not the one to do it. You should go home.*

With that, the spirit faded from view, and Alex threw her hands up.

"What?" Joe asked.

"First my fuckin' father says I'm damned for talking with the dead, and then the dead tell me I don't do it good enough to earn the freakin' witch scout merit badge."

"What the hell are you talking about?"

She related the conversation with the ghost, and Joe shook his head.

"They want it all," he said. "Salvation, heaven, justification. He had issues. Let's just check out the info he gave us. Room 618. We can go there. It doesn't matter if you can feel it or not, you're still learning."

"Yeah, but if I'm still learning, what's going to happen when we actually come face-to-face with the masters?"

"You're gonna surprise the shit out of them."

"Why, because I can see them?"

"No, because they will fear you, knowing that you're a redhead, even though your hair appears strangely black," he grinned. "Chill."

"Easy for you to say." She pointed at an empty spot near the manager's station. "You don't have ghosts coming up to you to tell you that you're not worth shit."

"Naw," Joe said. "I had parents for that."

He stood up, and motioned her to precede him.

"Let's see what's on the sixth floor, so maybe we can get outta here."

"You don't like Austin?" she asked.

"I love Austin. I just know I'm not gonna get any until we stop a psycho killer. And I want some. So let's hit the road, Jack. I mean Jill."

Alex flashed him a thousand-dollar smile. "You're a lot nicer than the ghosts around here."

"You don't even know," he said. "Just you wait."

"Just get me through this little war of the worlds," she said. "And I promise, you'll be very, very happy."

They stepped into an open elevator and Joe punched the button that said 6.

"Happy is as happy does," he proclaimed.

"What does that mean?"

"I was hoping you knew," he said. "I don't have a fucking clue. But it sounds good."

Room 618 was closed. Not surprising . . . all of the rooms on the sixth floor were closed. But when Alex knocked, no answer was forthcoming.

"Can you throw the lock again?" Joe asked.

"I don't know. There's nothing to pull from," she said. "In Phoenix, I had Jack's energy to draw on."

Have you ever been anywhere that you haven't seen a ghost nearby? Malachai asked.

And there you are again, Alex said in her mind.

Malachai's voice sounded strained. *You are so close,* he said. *And so far.*

"What's the matter?" Joe asked, noticing her pause.

"Malachai's making fun of me."

"He likes you."

"Got a strange way of showing it."

"Well," Joe said. "He barely ever talks to me anymore, and I'm the one he's married to."

Alex grinned. "Good point, I guess." She pointed to the door. "He seems to think I can open this with just the random ghost energy that's always around us."

"Can you?"

Alex shrugged. Then closed her eyes and focused on the lock. She tried to remember the way it felt when she'd "found her center" in Phoenix. It had been a desperate bid, but she'd somehow found that special place between her head and stomach that had been able to turn the trick. And now she needed to again. Maybe in a more difficult way, since she didn't have a ghost at her shoulder to draw power from.

She closed her eyes for a couple minutes, and imagined the lock opening. But when she put her hand on it, the knob didn't budge.

"Shit."

"Relax," he said. "You're trying too hard. You have to feel it."

"Now you're a psychic expert, too?"

He took the hint and shut up.

Alex stared hard at the knob and pulled from that place. She imagined she was talking to Genna and sent her desire from the place that she used to talk to ghosts with. It was like a small, warm circle in her chest, a place that was always there. She drew from it, somehow, and willed it to enter the doorknob and throw the lock.

It did just that.

Alex reached out and twisted the handle. "Here we are," she said. Joe pushed the door and led her inside. The room was cold; someone had turned the thermostat all the way down, because the fan was humming even now in the background.

"Looks like all the others," he said.

"Yeah, kinda," Alex said, walking past the bathroom to the double beds. Then she pointed. "But this one has a custom-made doorway to hell in the corner. And it's wider than the others we've seen."

It was true. In the past two hotel rooms they'd seen, the fissure between here and the realm of the Curburide was thin; a faint black line like a crack in the paint. Here, it was as if someone had pulled back the wall with a crowbar. Instead of a spider-thin fissure in the drywall at the corner of the room, there was an inch-wide gap.

"Can you feel them?" His voice was low.

"Sort of," she whispered. "I can't really tell if the cold is because of the air conditioner, or them. But there's a feeling of . . . something bad here."

"Um, like her?"

Alex followed the point of his finger, which indicated the faint, ghostly refraction of an old crone gripping and pulling desperately to free herself from the crack in the drywall of the room.

"You can see her?"

"Yeah," Joe said. "And call me conservative, but it seems kinda weird that she's trying to crawl out of a wall."

The wretched creature slipped with audible pain through the crack and then stood in the center of the room, a slow wicked grin growing on her face. "You," she said, pointing at Alex. "Would you like to come with me now? We can save you from the others."

"Not if I can blow them up first," Joe mumbled.

"Why are you here?" Alex asked.

The creature laughed. "Why, to suck you, my dear," she said, opening her mouth to expose a dazzling array of fangs. "You'll be delicious, I'm sure."

"Who called you?"

"I don't answer to anyone," the Curburide hissed. "Who called you?"

"I came because I heard leeches like you were being let out of their bottle," Alex retorted.

The old woman grinned. "Indeed. And I came because creatures like this"—she reached into the wall and pulled a dark mass of hair out; then she dragged the head it belonged to into the room—"needed to be shown the way. With teeth and claws."

She bent over the head to clamp those ancient teeth on its neck, and Joe shivered as the head shuddered, blue eyes snapping open to stare hard at him, as if somehow he was the reason it suffered such indignity.

"You're not going to eat me, are you?" the head asked feebly.

"No," Alex agreed.

The hag pulled the head out farther, so that she could see the blood dripping from a crosshatch of gashes in his forehead and cheeks.

"Who are you?" Alex asked.

"My name is Jamie Gartside," he said, his breath coming in wheezing gasps. "I was just staying here in this room on business one night. I heard a noise . . . thought it was a bat or something at the window. And when I tried to kill it, this . . . this . . . thing pulled me out of my room. Now I can't get back. They're holding me hostage! And not just me, there's a kid here, too."

Jamie reached a hand over the hag's shoulder and struggled to gain a purchase on the wall.

"Help me come home?" he begged, and the demon cackled. Her laughter was like a motorcycle engine mixed with the hiss of an angry squirrel.

"Tell me where the killer is now," Alex said, "and I'll do my best."

The hag laughed. "You'll never find her. She's gone to where no one has ever gone before."

The man looked up and licked the blood from his lips.

"Bullshit," he said. A smile crossed his face. "I know where she's gone," he said. "I've heard them talk."

The hag spit on the man's face and her hands began to push Jamie's head back through the crack. But he struggled against her, grabbing her hair and pushing forward, then gripping her neck with both of his hands and holding on. He struggled to stay partially visible for a few more seconds in this realm. He met Alex's eyes, and in that moment, he looked completely alive and alert.

"They're just waiting for her to make that final kill. The kill that will let them come all the way through the doors. The doors like this one. The next time she sacrifices, it will be the one that throws it all open to them. They'll kill every human being on the planet. Slowly."

The hag screamed and beat a fist down on his half-visible back. But he didn't shut up.

"She's on her way to do it right now."

"Where?" Alex said. "Where will it happen? When?"

"This weekend," he gasped, as the hag turned on him and began to shove him back, inch by inch through the glowing gap of crimson light that lit the room.

The warted spirit laughed, and with both hands grabbed onto Jamie's ears and twisted. She brought a bony knee up to pound his face with, but still he barked his story to them.

"She'll set them all free this weekend when she kills," he yelled, and then screamed as the hag thrust two fingers into his eye sockets, pushing his neck and most of his head back through the crack.

Still he didn't give up.

"She's there now," he said. "You have to go there and stop her."

"Go where?" Alex yelled, frantic.

"To the coast," he screamed, the last strands of his hair disappearing back into the wall.

"To Terrel."

Chapter Thirty-nine

Jeremy found a hotel in the center of town, right smack in the middle of Main Street. Terrel was one of those classic Norman Rockwell kind of towns, with fake gas lamps and barrels of flowering plants on every corner, cobblestone sidewalks and kitschy, quaint little stores. A pipe shop was just across the street from the hotel, which, to Jeremy's eye, looked to have once been a mansion; probably the home of some early shipyard magnate or town elder. Now it was diced up into a bunch of bedrooms for out-of-towners.

He carted their bags past a sitting room with rocking chairs and a small, quiet fire in the hearth, and got a key from the front desk that, he noted, was actually still a *key*, not a plastic swipe card.

Ariana yawned and followed, happy to let him do the registering and carting. When they reached the room, however, she grinned.

"Oh lapdog," she laughed, hurrying to press her hands against the thick mattress of the four-poster mahogany-framed bed. "We're going to have some fun here."

She pulled off her T-shirt, dropped it to the floor, and carefully climbed up onto the royal blue comforter. With a slight gasp of pain from her ribs, she lay back against a tower of pillows and moved her arms up and down on the silky covering. "Mmmm, heavenly," she moaned, closing her eyes.

"Okay," he agreed, and tossed their suitcases to the floor. He kicked off his jeans and pulled himself up on the bed with her, kissing her hard on the mouth. "But this time I'm not doing all the work."

"Oh please," she laughed, nipping his ear while reaching between his legs to squeeze. "I didn't hear you complaining back in Tallahassee."

She pulled his shirt over his head, and then drew him to her breast. He took one rosy nipple between his lips, and didn't complain anymore in Terrel either.

When Jeremy awoke a little later, Ariana was sitting at the dressing table, her toes pressed against the edge of its dark wooden top. Jeremy's T-shirt hung loosely over her shoulders, but its end had ridden up to expose the round of her ass against the chair, as well as the close-cropped thatch between her thighs. Jeremy slipped out of bed and was at her shoulder before she stirred from reading the book in her hands. She gave him a raised eyebrow, but said nothing.

"What's that?" he asked, running his hand along the back of her neck before slipping it inside the front of the shirt.

She brushed him away. "Don't," she said. "I'm concentrating."

He drew a line from the ball of her foot, hanging off into space from the dressing table up the sleek creamy skin of her calf, over the inverted V of her knee and back down her thigh to slip underneath and cup her most satiny skin. "It's hard to concentrate when you look like this."

"Then go back to sleep."

"C'mon, give," he said, reaching for the book. "What is it?"

She shut it, and handed the book over to him. Jeremy whistled as he turned it over and over in his hands. "This is it, huh?"

She nodded.

"This is what started it all. Damn." He opened it to a random page, and put his nose to the paper, inhaling deeply. "Even smells old," he said before closing it, and looking once again at the title, in simple gilt lettering: THE BOOK OF THE CURBURIDE

He handed it back. "I didn't know you still had this. Stole it from the old nun, huh?"

Ariana tilted her head to look up at him. "You didn't think I was going to let them lock this back up behind a bunch of broken-down desks and kneelers did you? Besides, that old nun didn't have a clue. I gave her back two books to put away . . . it's just that one of them wasn't one that I'd taken out of the room."

"So what do you need it for now?"

"You want to have ultimate power?" she asked. "Or do you want to accidentally blow up the world?"

"Gimme a break. I haven't seen any magic out of you yet. I don't think you're going to say the wrong words and blow up the freakin' planet."

"*I* won't blow it up," she agreed. "But if I do the Calling wrong, and the Curburide aren't bound to me . . . we're all dead."

Jeremy held up his hands in surrender. "But you've been doing this over and over, with the stones and the sticks and the words. You're a pro at this point. You didn't need the book at my house."

"The final Calling is different," she said. "There's more to it."

"Got it. Study." He stepped back and picked his jeans off the floor.

"I'm going to take a walk and see where we might find some dinner. Study. Study."

Downtown Terrel was not exactly littered with haute cuisine opportunities. Jeremy peered into a diner with plaid curtains, and stopped inside the pipe store to buy a cigar for later. As soon as he'd seen the sign, he'd had a horrible craving for a thick drag of tobacco. Then he stopped in at McColvin's Tavern, a hole-in-the-wall narrow bar with about 6 stools and three tiny round tables. He pulled up to the bar next to a burly man in a black leather jacket, and ordered a Killian's from the bartender. She was a slip of a woman, barely five feet tall he guessed. But as soon as he heard the tone of her voice when she pushed the glass at him and said, "Three dollars," and saw the way she looked at him with those steely blue eyes, he knew that this was a woman who took no shit.

"Thanks Jill," he said, reading her name tag. "Get busy in here on weekends?" he asked.

"Depends," she said, and went back to cleaning glasses in the sink at the far end of the bar.

"On?"

"On what you consider busy."

Jeremy took the hint, and concentrated on his beer. When he finished, he slipped back out without a word. He left a dollar tip, despite the coolness of the service. Given the paucity of potential places to hang out on Main Street, he guessed he'd need to stop back here a couple nights.

Chapter Forty

"So what's Terrel like?" Alex said. Her feet were bare and she pressed them against the dashboard in what looked like an uncomfortable position to Joe. Then again, every position in this car had become uncomfortable after almost a week of solid driving. He was starting to worry that the engine was going to act up out here in the middle of nowhere. They had driven from Austin to Tallahassee the day before, and now were only about a half hour out of Terrel.

"What's Okawa, Nebraska, like?"

"Small, dull, endlessly boring." She said it without hesitation.

"Much like Terrel. Don't expect this to be like Spring Break. It's more like . . . Senior Break."

"Sounds mah-vel-ous, dahling." She twisted a curl of black hair between her fingers and stuck her tongue out.

"With behavior like that, I'll be looking for a babysitter for you," he pronounced.

"Okay, grandpa," she said, and pulled out a vial of nail polish from her purse.

"What are you doing?"

"Figured I might as well make my feet pretty for you, for when you kiss them later," she said, pressing a brush of electric red paint to her big toe.

"Get that on my dashboard, and you'll be kissing *my* feet later."

Alex snorted. "I'll kiss a lot of your things, but none of 'em are on your feet."

"Promises, promises."

She winked, but didn't reply.

Joe turned the key in the lock and pushed the door open. The air inside was stale, and all the window shades pulled. He flipped on the dining room and kitchen lights and led her inside.

"Welcome to the palace. Guess I haven't been gone long enough for them to kick my stuff to the curb."

"You just left without paying your rent?" she said, stepping into the small apartment and closing the door behind her.

"I just left. Didn't know if I was coming back. Didn't tell anybody. I paid November's rent though, so we're good for a couple weeks."

She walked into the living room and plopped down on the couch. "I feel like I could sleep for a week," she announced.

"Well, you can sleep for a couple days, I guess."

"I don't even know what day it is anymore. It's like, everything's running together."

"It's Thursday," he said. "We've got basically forty-eight hours to figure out where our Sunday Slasher is hiding out. Sometime after midnight on Saturday night, she'll be slicing someone here up into hamburger meat."

"How do we know it will be early Sunday morning again, like the others? I mean . . . the last one was on a Monday."

"You're supposed to be the witch," he retorted. "I just think . . . something happened in Tallahassee. If she can, she'll do it here the same as all the others. She'll lure her victim to some private place, and sacrifice them to the Curburide. And somehow, according to your pal, this is the one that will open the gates wide for them."

"So how do we even look for her? We don't even know if she's here yet," Alex said.

She's here, Malachai announced for them both to hear.

"Where?" Joe asked. "Help us out here for God's sake."

I can't tell yet, the spirit responded. *But I can feel the disturbance her presence is causing. The Curburide are pressing hard against the membrane of the world to come through. They know she's here. They're waiting.*

"Find her," Joe said.

At that moment, Ariana and Jeremy were walking down the center of Main Street. They'd walked all the way to the edge of town, passing a fortune teller's house ("Readings By Angelica") as well as a bakery ("Bread 'n' Butter") and a mom-and-pop bookstore. "If it was any cuter, I'd have to be sick," she said, pointing out the flower-inscribed awning of the "Baubles and Beads" store.

"Well, we didn't come here for the scenery," he said. "What do we need to do today? Are you going to meet the kid?"

"Not yet," she said. "First we need to find an Internet connection, so I can e-mail him and set things up for Saturday. Then I want to take a ride out to this Terrel's Peak and see if we can't find the place where the kid's sister was possessed. From the way he described it, it should be pretty easy—he said there's a stairway beneath the wreck of an old lighthouse that leads to some underground caves. He found it himself a couple weeks ago and picked up some old book that was down there."

"A book of the Curburide?"

"Ha! Hardly. I may have the only copy of that one. No. He found some old lighthouse keeper's journal. The guy apparently called a demon to try to stop the Curburide from taking over this town a hundred years ago. And that demon is the one that possessed the girl a few weeks ago."

"So do we need to worry about it trying to stop us now?"

"I don't think so. The kid said after the possession was exorcised, the man who did it left town . . . and supposedly took the spirit with him."

Jeremy kicked a stone off the cobbled sidewalk and watched it skip into the street. "So why do we need a formerly possessed person anyway?"

Ariana shrugged, and then grimaced at the twinge in her ribs. "Beats me. I think it's because they've already been a portal to the spiritual realm or something like that. So they're kind of a . . . weak link between us and them."

"So they need a vehicle to come through?"

She nodded. "And a long, strong Calling from this side. For some reason the sacrifices have to be long distances apart from each other, stretching from one side of the land to the opposite. Sort of like an arrow, I guess."

"Murder beacons, leading the way to the door?"

"Yeah." She stopped in front of a storefront. It was framed in white wood and a pink awning. The gold letters on the window pronounced CHOCOHOLICS R US.

"Want some fudge?"

He pulled open the door, and she darted inside like an eager child, as if they hadn't just been talking about ritual murder and the calling of a race of demons from some other plane to take over and fuck the earth to death.

Or something like that. Jeremy smiled, and followed her in. He thought about how Sheila had used and abused him, and then about how Ariana was using him. The image of Sheila, lying beneath him on the bed, gutted and very, very dead, didn't faze him anymore in the slightest. She'd fucked around on him without remorse, and he had killed her with the same consideration. As he stepped behind Ariana at the glass window filled with creamy and mocha confections, he heard the tiny music of her voice calling him a "lapdog." He guessed, considering how long he'd put up with Sheila, that he actually kind of liked the position, so long as the leash-holder treated him good.

"Taste," Ariana said, and turned to press a thick hunk of chocolate between his lips.

Ariana treated him very good.

Chapter Forty-one

To: TedIsTooCool
Fr: curburide@aol.com
Thursday, 3:05 P.M.

Hi sweetie! Just wanted to let you know that I've managed to find my way through 100 miles of winding back roads and *voila* . . . here I am! I got a room in town, and am looking forward to meeting you and your sister. I've got a very old book on demons that I think you'll be really interested to see. I know how you've enjoyed that old journal you found beneath the lighthouse.

Speaking of the lighthouse, it seemed to me that the place you described with the blue crystals in the wall, where you found the journal, would be the perfect place for us to hold the ritual. That's the same place where the demon possessed your sister a few weeks ago, isn't it? I'm going to try to swing by there sometime tomorrow so that I can check it out.

How about if you meet me there with her on Saturday night? Just tell me what time, and I'll be waiting! Bloody Kisses, Baby!
Yours in Dark Arts,
Ariana

To: curburide@aol.com
Fr: TedIsTooCool

Friday, 8:15 A.M.

Hi Ariana!

Just wanted to let you know that I got your message. I'm so happy that you've finally gotten to Terrel. I can't wait to meet you! The blue crystal room is a perfect idea for the ritual. It also gives me a great excuse for dragging Cindy to meet you. I'll just tell her that I'm going to the caves to return the book, because it's like, a historical treasure or something and should stay where it was. She won't want me to go alone, so she'll come with.

How about you meet us there around 7 P.M.? Mom always has dinner on the weekends around 5:30 or 6, and I'll tell Cindy right before dinner that I'm going up there afterwards.

And if she doesn't want to come, I'll just knock her over the head and drag her ROTFLMAO!

See you Saturday!
Dreaming of Naked Curburide!
Ted

To: TedIsTooCool
Fr: curburide@aol.com
Friday, 11:05 A.M.

Hi Sweetie!

Can't wait to see you tomorrow. And if you have to knock Cindy over the head to bring her to the caves, make sure you don't hurt her too bad. She's useless to the ritual if she's already dead, you know! LOL

Bloody Kisses, Baby!
Yours in Dark Arts,
Ariana

Chapter Forty-two

Friday

It was strange to drive down Main Street again. Everything seemed smaller than it had before . . . and yet he'd only been gone a couple of weeks. It seemed like a lifetime. Joe had left Terrel after his relationship with Cindy had soured; she didn't trust him somehow, once Joe had forbidden Malachai from talking with her privately. The demon was dangerous, and God knew what the creature would have whispered in her ear if he'd allowed it.

Likewise, Angelica had grown more withdrawn as the weeks passed after Joe rescued her from the bowels of Terrel's Peak. Malachai had raped her by possessing an ambitious spelunker, and then had tried to force first the caver, and then Joe to rape Cindy, so that a child could be conceived to forge a "new covenant" and thus give the demon a human foothold to stay in this realm.

Instead, Joe had "called" the demon by its true name, and bonded it to himself. While this gave the creature its foothold, it did not give it the upper hand it would have had with a child. Joe thought Malachai was simply biding his time, waiting for a way to turn the tables on Joe so that the demon could get what it wanted, while technically abiding by the covenant. The demon's pretension of neutrality was easily seen through by Joe, but he still wasn't sure what to make of the demon's poorly hidden interest in stopping the Curburide from gaining access to the earth again. Perhaps the demon feared his old enemies. The whole reason Broderick Terrel had called the creature to this realm in the first place was to stop the Curburide. Joe laughed to himself. Maybe Malachai was scared shitless that the Curburide would kick his ethereal ass if they were allowed some power in this realm.

He'd stopped at the newspaper yesterday and rifled through recent issues to see if the paper had covered any strange events over the past week, that might give him a clue as to the Sunday Slasher's whereabouts.

Randy, the editor, had been shocked to see him at first, and then smug, assuming he wanted his old job back. But when Joe told him he just wanted to catch up, Randy had pointed to the morgue and given him free reign. "Read up," he'd said. Joe had hit up the vending machine for his usual fix of Fritos, but hadn't found a thing in the papers unusual. A high school performance of *Hamlet*, a Woman's Club bake sale, some library board assessment news and a two-car accident on the corner of Main and Second were the stories of the week.

So today he was pulling into the driveway of a house he'd been sure he'd never see again. READINGS BY ANGELICA, the sign out front read. He took a deep breath when he got out of the car, and walked up the weedy path to the front door. It opened as he raised a hand to knock.

"I was wondering when you'd get here," Angelica Napalona said. She wore a purple cape today, covered with sigils of moon and stars and skulls.

"Nice trick," Joe laughed, stepping inside. "Did you have a motion sensor installed to let you know when someone's in the driveway?"

Angelica crossed her arms and looked hurt. "No hug, no kiss, no 'How have you been Angie, I've missed you,'" she said, turning up her bottom lip.

He held out his arms for a hug, and she bent forward to "allow" him to give her one. She didn't squeeze back.

"Oh c'mon," he said, "I have missed you."

With that she gave him a squeeze, and led him into the sitting room.

"You haven't missed me or Cindy too bad," she said pointedly. "Who's the redhead?"

Joe opened his mouth to say something smart, and then thought better of it. "She doesn't have red hair."

"Sure she does," Angelica said, setting up her crystal ball in the center of the table and placing it directly between them. "She's just dyed it black."

A quiver went through Joe's stomach. Malachai had given Angelica the gift of sight when she was 18, as part of his covenant with her and her friends. In return, she had pledged to give up her firstborn, Cindy, at 18. Her refusal to sacrifice Cindy had led to Joe's involvement in stopping the demon from killing them both. But Angelica had never flaunted the full measure of her gift to him before. Or perhaps she had never used it as much before.

"Been practicing your art lately?" he asked.

She didn't smile. "Been waking up every night at three A.M. Sometimes I've seen you, and your little punk friend, wandering around in the mountains, or in San Francisco, or some other city."

"And other times?"

"Other times I've seen a skinny girl in a black latex suit carving up innocent guys with razors, and then fucking their corpses on the floor. I'm not really sure which is the more frustrating thing to see."

"You saying you miss me?"

She got up from the table and crossed to the window. Pulled the shade. "This is big, Joe. Something really awful is coming, I can feel it. Has Malachai told you anything? Who is this pretty little witch girl you're road-tripping with? Where is she now?"

"Hmmm . . . so the crystal ball and dreams don't tell you everything, huh?"

"Joe, I'm serious. Why are you back here?"

"Alex, my little witch girl as you so perfectly call her, is back at my apartment. And you're right, something big is coming. Malachai managed to sucker me into helping Alex when she was in trouble, so that both of us could end up helping Malachai."

"Why would you want to help Malachai do anything?"

Joe laughed. "Exactly. But here's the rub. He wants us to stop the Sunday Slasher from performing another sacrifice. Have you heard of her?"

"The serial killer?"

Joe nodded. "The whole point of the Sunday slashings is to offer sacrifices to open the door for the Curburide to come through to our realm. If she performs enough of them, the Curburide will be free to fuck with us all."

Angelica put a hand to her mouth. "I knew it," she whispered. "I knew it would never be over."

She walked across the room, turning her back to him. "Why are you here?" she asked finally.

"Because according to a dead guy I met in an Austin hotel room, the final sacrifice is going to take place in Terrel, tomorrow night. I was hoping, with that sixth sense Malachai gave you, that you might have felt something that would help us track down the killer, before she strikes."

Angelica's head nodded slowly. When she turned, her eyes glistened with brimming tears.

"It's the cliff again, Joe," she whispered, eyes growing weepy and wide. "I've seen you there, in the blue room. With blood on your face."

"Am I alive or . . . never mind," he said. "I don't want to know."

"Is this Alex strong? Will she be able to stop them from coming through?"

"I don't know," he said. "But now I know where to go. I had a feeling anyway. How could this not end up being connected to the old lighthouse, and that damned cliff?"

Joe stopped in at McColvin's Tavern on the way home. If there was one thing about Terrel he missed, it was the homeyness of the old Irish bar. As soon as he walked through the door, he got a loud, "Hey stranger!"

He grinned and pulled a stool up to the bar next to a burly guy nursing a Killian's.

"Hey Jill," he said to the 'keep. "How's tricks?"

A pixie of a woman pulled herself up from behind the bar and planted a kiss on his mouth before slapping him on the head.

"Where you been, ya doofus?" Jill said. "We've missed you around here."

"Had to take a little trip," he said. "Just had to get away."

"Where'd you go?" she asked, automatically pulling him a Newcastle from the tap.

Joe laughed. "Where didn't I go? Been up to the Rocky Mountains, down to San Francisco, Austin, Texas . . ."

"Collecting bumper stickers for your camper or something?"

"Don't have a camper. So I just stick 'em on my ass."

"Nice." She slid the beer across the bar to him. "I heard you quit the paper. Are you back here for good?"

Joe took a long pull on the mug, draining half the cool ale before wiping his mouth to answer her. "Don't know. Haven't decided yet. Anything been going on around here?"

"Naw," she said. "Since you left and took all the ghosts with you . . ."

"Cool it."

She flashed him a grin. "Hey, what other story is going to top yours? I guess you had to leave town. They're never going to stop talking about you."

"Well in that case, I'm definitely not sticking around," he said, and stood to leave. "Just wanted to check in, see if anything was up."

"You want another?" she offered, as he stood and chugged three more gulps of beer.

"Not now. Got some stuff to do today. But I'll be back."

"I'll be here!"

Joe admired her tight, lithe form and frowned inwardly as he waved good-bye. *Not if the Curburide come you won't,* he said silently.

Jeremy Bruford looked up from his Killian's and watched the bar door close.

"Popular guy," he observed aloud. "Who is he?"

"Oh that's Joe Kieran," Jill said. "He used to be a reporter here for the *Times*. Over the summer he covered a story about suicides up on the haunted cliff. He ended up working some kind of spell and . . . what do they call it . . . he *exorcised* the demon or something like that."

"Did he now?" Jeremy said, scratching the stubble on his chin. "And he's just back in town?"

"Yeah," she said. "Sounds like he's been getting around. I mean, from the mountains to San Francisco to Austin. He's been gone close to a month, I think."

Jeremy nodded, and sipped his beer in silence. But inside, his stomach turned cold.

Chapter Forty-three

Saturday

"So this is the place huh?" Alex picked her way carefully around the broken rubble that was all that remained of the ancient lighthouse.

"This is it. Could use a coat of paint, huh?"

"That and four walls, and you'd really have something."

"Hmm. Stairway's over here."

He led her between the boulders and broken beams to a half-obscured pit. Without hesitation, he stepped backwards into the darkness, and found a step. Then his body disappeared another foot, and he pulled the flashlight from his backpack. Suddenly Alex could see the narrow steps, disappearing beyond the reach of the light.

"Lead on," she said, and stepped in to join him.

Joe waved the light back and forth as they descended the stairs and then walked down a long, narrow corridor. The terrain was continually descending, and in moments the tiny light behind them from the opening above disappeared from view.

"Why is this here?" Alex whispered.

"It's a natural series of caves," he said. They built a lighthouse above them, probably in the late 1800s, and the stairs gave the lighthouse keeper a safe escape during a bad storm. He could slip into the solid stone beneath the tower and hide. Probably stored spare supplies and stuff down here, too."

"Hell of a basement," she murmured, pushing a spiderweb out of her face in disgust.

"Feel at home, Malachai?" Joe said aloud.

It's nothing I ever wanted to see again, the demon said.

"The last lighthouse keeper basically imprisoned Malachai here, is that it?" Alex asked.

Like a genie in a bottle.

"Very big bottle though," Joe added.

Still a prison.

"Ahhh," Joe said, as they walked towards an opening in the corridor. "Here's the real deal."

They stepped out into an open chamber, and Joe kept the flashlight pointed at the floor. "Are you ready for some fireworks?"

"Always."

"Watch this."

He moved the flashlight up to catch the nearest wall, which shimmered and sparkled aqua blue in the dull light. Then he moved the flashlight all around them in a circle, and it was like an explosion of blue fairy dust. Everywhere the flash hit, the light prismed in a rainbow of icy color that almost hurt the eyes to look at.

Alex gasped. "It's beautiful."

Then he pointed the flash at the oblong slab of rock in the center of the room. Its base was also covered in blue crystals.

"Beautiful and deadly," he said. "That's where Cindy almost died. And where Malachai became my best friend."

I'm forever in your debt, master. The demon didn't say *master* very convincingly.

"What's through those?" Alex asked, pointing to a couple open doorways leading out of the chamber.

He led them to the one closest. "This one is kind of a writing nook. I think the old lighthouse keeper used to come down here at night to put his thoughts down. Maybe so the spirits above couldn't see?"

Joe pointed at a small ledge inset in a tight alcove of gray limestone. "But someone's been here since the last time I was here."

"How do you know?"

"The old man's book is gone. I left it right there, where I found it."

They stepped back out of the room and into the chamber.

"And that one?" Alex pointed to another dark exit.

"That leads to a river that flows through the cliff, and to another cave that opens out onto the beach you saw when we drove up."

"Cool!" she said. "Shall we go skinny dipping?"

He laughed. "Not here. Too many dead bodies have been floating in that water for my taste. Anyway, you had your chance in Austin."

"Yeah well, so did you and you said no then, too. And you still want to do it, don't you?" She put her arms around him and looked up into his eyes. His face was all in shadow, but she could see the tension there as he leaned down to kiss her, quickly, on the mouth.

"Yeah," he said. "I still want to. And hopefully after whatever happens tonight, you'll still want me, too."

"I'll always want you, Joe."

"Hope so," he said, as his heart skipped a beat. "Let's get out of here for now. This place gives me the creeps."

Jeremy hit the gas as they rounded the turn that would take them out of town and up to the top of the cliff. They'd scouted the area the day before, and now planned to hole up in the cave below until Ted and Cindy showed up later this evening.

"So what do we do if the kid doesn't show?" he asked.

"He'll show," she said. "He's a hard-up, perverted little punk. We'll do him first. I need two sacrifices tonight to complete the ritual."

"Okay, but seriously. What if he chickens out?"

"Then it's going to get a lot messier. We'll have to make a house call."

"You know where he lives?"

"Let's just say that in his past e-mails, he hasn't exactly been circumspect about himself. And this ain't exactly the big city. We'll find him."

A police siren sounded behind them.

"Oh shit," Jeremy said, seeing the red and blue lights in his rearview mirror.

"You speeding?"

"A little. What do we do?"

"They've already run the plates," she said. "Pull over and see where it goes."

Jeremy edged the car off onto the gravel and the squad pulled up behind them. A big Southern-looking cop—complete with silver hair and matching shades—walked up to the driver side window. His name tag read SWARTZKY.

"You wanna be careful on these roads," the officer said in a voice soft as a whisper, but still heavy as lead. "Dangerous curves to be speeding on. License?"

Jeremy looked at Ariana, who shrugged. He pulled out his wallet and handed the card over.

When the cop walked back to his car, Jeremy clenched his hands on the wheel. "What do we do?" he hissed. "By now they're looking for me. If he runs that number . . ."

Ariana frowned. "I didn't think of that. What'd you give it to him for then? Shit."

She opened her door and stepped out onto the gravel. "Officer?" she called. The cop was just easing his bulk into his squad and reaching for his radio. He stopped, and stood up, hands on the car door.

She started walking towards him with her hands out. "Officer, I think there's been a mistake." She shimmied as much as she could, trying to draw his eye so that he didn't think about the fact that a routine traffic stop was growing into more.

"I was pushing Jer to go faster . . . my mama's real sick and I want to get home to take care of her. I'm so afraid she's gonna pass before we make it. Please don't give him a ticket, it's really not his fault."

She'd gotten to the grill of his car.

"Where's your mama live?" the cop asked, suspicious, but drawn into her story.

"She's outside of Savannah," she said, stepping right up to

the door to face him. "I know we were going a little fast, but it's really not Jer's fault. He agreed to drive me all this way and I've been pushing him to get us there faster. I just can't let him get a ticket. He's had a bad time of it and . . . well . . . he just can't afford this ticket on his record. He's cleaned up his act over the past few months. But this would kill him."

She made a show of wringing her hands, and then stuffed them both in her back jeans pockets to lean forward, making sure he saw the shift of cleavage in the V of her T-shirt. Swartzky nodded, and held the license up. "I tell you what," he said. "I'll write you up a warning, not a ticket. Now you go back to your car, ma'am, and I'll be right there. I still will have to run this license."

It wasn't the best of possible positions to be in, but Ariana knew she had no choice. She threw herself forward pushing the door against him to pin him between the window frame and the car roof, and pulled a razor from her back pocket. In a heartbeat she held the blade at his throat, cutting in enough that he could feel the pain. Blood welled up instantly as she hissed, "I'd prefer it if you'd just let us be on our way now."

He pushed back, using the door to punch her aside, but she stabbed with the blade as she fell away, opening a three-inch gash from his throat to his chin. Swartzky bellowed at the pain, and clapped a hand to the wound as Ariana hit the ground on her ass, and used the fall to reposition herself. She rolled to the right and came around the squad door, gasping as her ribs made contact with the hard ground. The cop was coming around the door to meet her. He pulled his gun, but she slashed at his leg with the razor, shredding the blue uniform trousers and digging deep into the flesh of his calf.

Ariana leapt to her feet and came up on his side, wrapping an arm around his neck even as he began to crumple from the pain in his leg. He'd gotten the gun out, but didn't have a shot as she danced behind him, once again connecting the cool edge of the razor to the soft skin of his neck.

"Drop it now," she said. "Or I'll open you up all the way." He did.

Jeremy had seen what was going on from inside the car and ran to Ariana's aid.

"Get the gun," she said, as he arrived. Jeremy trained the barrel on the cop as soon as it was in his hand.

"We're in the open," Jeremy said.

"I know. Let's fix that. Take him to the other side of the car and make him lie down. On his belly."

"Do it," Jeremy commanded, and the cop began to hobble around the front hood. The back of his pant leg was already drenched and dark.

"You would have gotten a warning," Swartzky said. "Now you're going to jail."

"We're not going to get anything, old man. Lay down and shut up. Hands on your back where I can see 'em."

Ariana came back from their car with a roll of wire. She knelt at the cop's side and wound the wire tightly around his wrists. Then she snaked the ends up his arm, away from his fingers, and twisted them together round and round and round again.

"Get up," she demanded. She took the gun from Jeremy and pointed towards their car. "Backseat. Now." Then to Jeremy she said, "Find a way to turn those damn bubblegum lights off, put the car in gear, and send it downhill into the trees here. Make sure it's out of sight from the road."

"This is not starting out well," he murmured. Ariana and the cop walked away and Jeremy slid into the driver seat of the Terrel police car. When he flipped the sun visor down to block the glare, a piece of paper caught his eye. It had the number of the squad, and a name on it. "Police Chief Harry Swartzky."

His stomach churned. "And it just gets better," he said, and drove the car off the road.

Chapter Forty-four

Cindy was helping her mom clear the table when Ted pulled her aside.

"I'm going to ride my bike up to Terrel's Peak right now. I'm putting the book back."

"Now?" Cindy's mouth twisted in surprise. "Why now? It'll be dark by the time you get up there."

"I don't want the book in the house anymore," he lied. "It's been giving me the creeps."

"Well, give it to me for tonight," she said. "I'll keep it in my room."

He shook his head. "I can't sleep knowing it's in the house. I just want to get rid of it."

"Well toss it in the garbage then."

Now it was Ted's turn to feign shock. "We can't do that! It's like a piece of history. It belongs down there in that little room. I just need to get it back there."

Cindy took a deep breath and held up a hand. "Just wait," she said. "I promised I'd help with the dishes. But then I'll drive you."

"You won't tell Mom where we're going, will you?"

"Are you insane?"

Ted smiled. He knew his dorky sister like the back of his deceitful hand.

"Good," he said. "I'll go get my backpack."

"God this place gives me the creeps," Cindy said, as they stepped slowly down the stairs beneath the rubble of the old lighthouse. Even though she'd driven them there, it was still almost dark out by the time they had parked the car and walked up the trail to the top of the cliff. Now as they descended into the caves, the blackness around them seemed absolute, except for the thin beam of Ted's flashlight.

"I don't know why this couldn't have waited," she said, rubbing her arms. Goose bumps had sprung up as soon as they'd started on the path towards the blue room. She could only think of the last time she had been down here, and the horror of the bloody cave freak lying there, dead on the stone ground with a knife in his back. A knife that she had put there. He had tried to rape her, and she had made him a sacrifice to Malachai.

"Let's get this over with," she breathed as the cave around them suddenly lit up with shimmers of electric blue. She saw the dais where Malachai had possessed her just a few weeks before. He'd forced her to lie on her back, nude and open for the taking of the hippie caver.

A hand came out of nowhere to cover her eyes; the dais disappeared.

"Not so fast," a deep male voice said. Someone grabbed her around the waist and pulled her hands together behind her back. "We're going to take our time, tonight."

"She's a nice one." Jeremy stroked the stubble on his chin and circled the dais where they'd hog-tied Cindy. Ariana had stripped her as Jeremy held her, and then she had tied the girl's hands and wrists together. Jeremy used the pink thong she wore to gag her.

"Thank God for elastic," he'd said. All the while Ted had stood to the side, sometimes walking towards the exit, other times sneaking obvious peeks at his well-built sister.

"She *is* a real blonde," Ariana remarked, dragging the edge of the razor from the girl's belly button to her pubes just heavy enough that it drew blood. "I think you're going to enjoy this."

"I didn't know you were bringing someone with you," Ted finally said from the shadows.

"I'm sorry," Ariana said, stepping away from Cindy's crotch. "You boys haven't been properly introduced. Ted, this is Jeremy. Jeremy, Ted."

She walked across the dark cavern to put her arm around Ted. With one hand, she pushed the glasses up his nose for him, and then she bent to give him a warm, long kiss on his pale lips.

"Thanks for bringing her, love. I didn't tell you about Jeremy, because he just joined me a few days ago. But he's been a big help. And I'll need him for the sacrifice part anyway. I was going to have you fuck your sister, but I always thought that might get a bit dicey."

Ted's eyes grew wide. "Um . . ." was all he got out.

"Don't worry about it," Ariana said. "I'll take care of you."

She put a hand on his belt buckle and let her fingers dangle lower as she leaned in to whisper hotly in his ear. "You and I are going to have a good time tonight."

Ted's face grew red, and he visibly shivered.

"Can you do me a favor?"

He nodded, mute.

"We need to work on your sister a little, before she'll be ready for the sacrifice. And I get the feeling you probably don't really want to watch."

He nodded agreement.

"I was going to have Jeremy do it for me, but if you could stand lookout for a couple hours for us, that would be great. If anyone shows up and looks like they're headed this way, just come down the stairs and let us know, okay?"

"Sure." Ted shifted his hips and looked uncomfortable. "But . . . what about . . ."

"You and me?"

He nodded vigorously.

"I'll call you down when it's time. You won't miss the big moment, I promise." She pulled him clumsily into an embrace, and then kissed him again, this time with tongue. "Don't disappoint me."

He gulped, and half ran back down the corridor and up the stairs.

Ariana turned back to the dais, where Jeremy was tracing his fingers around and around the wide, pale pink circles of Cindy's half-erect nipples. The girl's eyes looked ready to bug out of her skull; their natural color reflected the blue of the cavern like a mirror.

Ariana reached into her back pockets and held two short-handled razors up in the air. "Enjoy them now," she told Jeremy as he bent to run his tongue across one of the girl's pale buds. "Cuz they're coming off tonight."

"It's almost nine o'clock," Alex said. "Do you know where your serial killer is?"

Joe killed the lights and pulled the car off the road just around the curve from the path up to the lighthouse.

"I'd bet a lot of money that she's a couple hundred yards away."

He pulled a backpack from the rear seat, and retrieved two flashlights from the pouch. "Walk softly," he said, handing one aluminum-handled light to her. "And carry a big flashlight."

They closed the car doors with a soft nudge, and started up the road. In minutes, they saw the regular pull-off for the cliff path. A car was parked there, lights off.

"They're downstairs," he whispered.

Not all of them.

Joe put out his arm and crouched down. Alex followed suit. "What do you mean?" he whispered to Malachai.

Take a look at the boulders by the entry. A good look.

Joe squinted at where he knew the entry to the caves below was. The moon was rising, and the rocks shone bright as bleached cotton in its rays. Then he saw the dark shape ahead, weaving in and out of the boulders. As he watched, the figure traced a circular path, moving around the hole three times before hopping up on one of the larger boulders to rest awhile.

"Do you see him?" he whispered at Alex. She nodded.

"Malachai, what about the beach?"

It appears unguarded.

"C'mon," Joe whispered, and crab-walked backwards a few yards before rising fully. He led Alex back to the car and then backed out onto the road and flipped around before turning the headlights back on.

"Where are we going?"

"I know another way in. But we're going to have to hike it."

Joe pulled off the road a little ways down the hill. Then they slogged down the sandy embankment until they reached the rocky beach. "This way," he said, and began jogging along the farthest point of the beach from the water. The cliff grew closer and higher, and the sand turned dirty, until they were running across jagged rocks. The moon was blocked behind the cliff, and in the shadow, Joe risked pulling his flash and aimed it first at the ground. Then, he shone it slowly around them, until a dark opening was visible in the gray and green algae-splotched rock.

"That's it."

They ducked beneath the low overhang, and stepped into a small cave. Joe didn't linger, just waved Alex on to a wider room, and then a corridor.

"It's been awhile," he said, "but I think the blue room is to the right here. Keep your flash off, I'll shield mine with my hand like this until we are almost there."

Slowly, almost blindly, they walked. And then suddenly, Joe doused his light. He said nothing, only pointed.

Just ahead, Alex could make out a faint, bluish light.

Something moved along the corridor, right in front of them. Alex grabbed Joe's arm as the shape turned and ran the few steps between them. Before they could react, it stopped, and began laughing. Joe could just make out the features of a small child; pug nose, cupid lips, and eyes that glowed with the life of a transistor radio.

"They're coming," the child cawed. It pulled a long silver

blade out from what looked like a bathrobe. Pointing it at Alex, the thing charged. Alex stumbled backwards, trying to escape the deadly tip, but the child came on fast. Feral eyes glinted hotly at her own as he caught her, and plunged the blade upwards and into her chest.

Alex screamed as the blade caught her shirt and then passed through, and into her. There was no pain. And then she realized, finally, that it wasn't a real knife. It wasn't a real boy.

"Run," Joe hissed, grabbing her hand.

They turned and started back the way they'd come. Joe rounded the corner that led back to the beach caves, but Alex's hand suddenly slipped from his.

"Alex?" he hissed, and turned back. Almost immediately, something slammed hard against the side of his head. He staggered, and looked up just in time to see a thick, balding man lifting a steel rod above his head. Distantly, he heard a *smack* and then he was kissing the cold ground.

"So much for sentries," Ariana said, as Jeremy dragged first Joe and then Alex into the blue cave.

"Rope," he demanded, and she quickly bound both of them, hand and foot. By the time she'd finished, Joe's eyes were fluttering open.

"Welcome home, Mr. Exorcist," Jeremy laughed, and pulled him up against a wall. "I hear you had a good time down here before, center stage."

"Ugh," Joe said. He couldn't seem to control his tongue.

"Well, this time around, you get to be in the audience." Jeremy kicked him in the belly and Joe coughed, doubling over to spit a hot stream of bile. "Shit, man, you're front row for the big night. The ultimate performance."

Joe spit, trying to clear the acid from his mouth. He looked at Alex, who lay silent on the ground nearby. A thick stream of blood ran down the center of her forehead. "Alex," he wheezed. "Alex, baby, wake up."

Ariana stepped into view, and bent over the girl, running a

hand through her shock black hair. It came up crimson red. "How hard did you hit her?" she asked.

Jeremy shrugged. "Hard enough, I guess. Never hit anyone with a pipe before."

Ariana shook her head and stood up. "We don't need her anyway. We've got our sacrifice. In another hour, none of this will matter."

Joe looked finally at the dais, and saw the pale naked foot there, and the sleek thigh, and the overflow of blonde hair that, for a while anyway, he'd known so well. Cindy turned her head and met his eyes, then shook her head slightly.

"Cindy," he gasped. "Not again."

"Déjà vu?" Ariana grinned. "I heard you saved her once before from a demon possession. Funny how you decided to turn up again. You and your little sister should have stayed away."

"She's not my sister," Joe growled.

Ariana shrugged. "Whatever. You and your jailbait. I'm not sure she's going to wake up again. And if she does, it won't make any difference. The Curburide will have a party with you two. I imagine they'll be pretty hungry for sex and blood those first few minutes when they hit our world. From what I can tell, it's been centuries since they got some."

She bent over and pulled a handful of bones out of a backpack, and then carefully placed them equally apart, all around the stone dais and Cindy. When she was done, she interwove a handful of rocks from her backpack in between the bones.

"We've got the makings of a powerful Calling," she said to Jeremy. "If you've ever had a perverted bone in your body, now's the time to let it out. The nastier we get with our sacrifices . . . the better we'll be when the Curburide are here. They respect only perversion."

"I can think of a thing or two."

"Good," Ariana said, and started to strip off her clothes. Naked, she stepped to the corridor leading up to the steps and called for Ted. "Let's begin."

It didn't take the teen any time at all to shuck off his jeans and shirt. Not with Ariana standing cool and utterly nude in front of him. She embraced him, and felt his little pecker pop up against her thigh.

"I want you to perform the first cut," she said, and pushed him back. "I've told you that we are here to sacrifice your sister to the Curburide."

He nodded.

"And you are alright with delivering your sister to her killers."

"She's a bitch," he shrugged. "And you said I could have the sex of my dreams if the Curburide come through, right?"

Ariana smiled, and rubbed a finger still sticky with Alex's blood across the boy's lips. "You'll do," she said. "Choose now," she said. "Your sister will die by the ritual of twenty-one cuts. Before she goes, she will be defiled by Jeremy. But you will start." She handed him one of the straight razors. "Make your mark on her. But not too deep yet."

Ted's hand shook a little, as he accepted the razor. "Anywhere?" he asked.

Ariana grinned. "Wherever you like. Just don't stab. Cut."

Then he didn't hesitate to walk up to his naked sister. He placed the edge of the blade just above the jut of her pubic bone and smiled, just a little. "This is for all the times you wouldn't take me to the beach with you," he announced, and pulled the blade towards him in a flash. A line of blood instantly welled up in its wake, beads of it slipping down as she exhaled, to pool in her belly button.

"And this cut begins
our Calling with blood
Come to me, Curburide
Taste the fruit of our body," Ariana chanted.

Ted was staring at the blood slowly washing across his sister's belly, and then at the blade he'd used. His face grew white. "I don't feel so good," he whispered.

Ariana laughed. "You get used to it. Come here."

She drew the boy down on top of her on the ground.

"You've earned your reward." She reached down and stroked his flanks until his erection bobbed to life again. Ariana whispered in his ear. "I promised you the ride of your life, and I'm going to keep my promise," she said. Then she reached between their legs to position him, and pulled him close. The teen's eyes lit, and he moaned slightly.

"That a boy," she said, removing his glasses, and then drawing a tongue across his lips. "Move with me, yes. You've got it. You've got it," she squeaked, her own passion drawing his out. His hips bucked against her as he gave in to what felt natural, and she held his ass hard, not letting him slip away.

"Oh my God," Ted groaned, spit drooling from his lip. "Ohhhh . . ."

Ariana smiled, and for a second, a look of sad tenderness crossed her cheeks. But then she brought her hand up from the floor.

"Ahhhhh . . ." Ted said, his orgasm changing tone to a moan of pain. When Ariana's hand came away from his neck, the blood spilled in a fountain across her breasts. "Ahhghh," Ted gurgled, and rolled off of her clutching the new lips of ragged flesh in his neck.

Ariana stood, and traced a finger through the blood on her chest, making a curlicue of crimson that looped around the pucker of her belly and back up to shellac the point of her left nipple with nature's precious milk. She pointed at the boy and nodded at Jeremy.

"Let him ride our sacrifice for a bit," she said. "Blood to blood, as it were."

The boy kicked as Jeremy picked him off the floor, but already his strength was gone, and his breath came in gasps. He screamed in short, sharp bursts. Jeremy ignored it, and positioned the boy between his sister's legs, though the kid's face only reached her neck. Ted's blood quickly painted Cindy's shoulder, and she shook and bucked, trying to move him off of her, but to no avail. The boy's eyes fluttered, even as Ariana raised the book from the floor and read:

"And the sister shall lie with the brother
and the mother shall lie with the son
and the father shall rut with his girls
and their children shall feast on them all."

Cindy's tears ran almost as heavy as her brother's blood, but all that could be heard through the gag of cotton were faint yelps and squeals. Jeremy held the boy's face up by a hank of hair, and brought Ted's slack lips down to touch Cindy's, before he threw the boy to the ground.

"Can you feel it?" Ariana asked.

"What?"

"They're here," she said. "They're listening. Waiting."

On the floor, Joe could make out the faint outline of a child standing near the dais. The boy's eyes were glowing. And he smiled.

"Alex," Joe hissed. "Wake up, please."

"Place the blade here," Ariana said, pointing at a spot between her own breasts. "Not too hard, but enough to break the skin. The blood of our sacrifices must mingle with our own."

Jeremy traced the razor down Ariana's perfect body, cleaving her skin from chest to pubes. Ariana shivered as the blade bit at the top of her sex.

"Now you," she said, and opened a crimson line from Jeremy's neck to the tip of his penis.

"Ow," he complained, and she pulled him close. "Blood brothers of the darkest kind," she proclaimed. Then she pulled him to the ground where she'd just entertained, and slaughtered, Ted. "I'll make it up to you now though," she whispered.

The blood served well as lubricant for his quick entry.

As the murderers fucked, Joe worked to shimmy his body across the floor, drawing closer to where Alex lay, still unmoving. There was blood on the ground near her head now. With every move of his muscles, his head shot through with pain. He could see that her chest still moved, but for how long?

"Malachai," he whispered.

Not an impressive start, the demon taunted.

"How bad is Alex? Can you wake her?"

I've been trying to talk to her, but she's not responding. She's still there, but gone deep.

"Keep trying," Joe said. "Can you set Cindy free?"

I can't make the ropes fall off, no. I can't force either of them to release her either . . . they're too committed to what they're doing to sway their wills, and there is a Curburide here, even now, guarding them.

"That's who made Alex scream," Joe said.

Yes. And more are coming. With every deception and twist of her blade. They are responding to her Calling.

"Great." Joe shifted his butt slowly on the floor, inching closer to Alex. Across the room, Jeremy grunted like a pig as Ariana encouraged him with wet, erotic slaps.

Joe levered his body so that he fell to the ground on his side, staring inches away from the side of Alex's face. The skin was purpling already. A heavy drip of blood crossed her cheek like a vampire tear.

"Alex," Joe whispered. He blew into her ear but the blank expression on her face didn't change. "Alex, I'm so sorry. Please wake up. We need you."

"And I need you to stow it," Jeremy said. A rough hand grabbed Joe by the hair, and yanked him back up from the ground. The bigger man pulled Joe's face up to meet his, and grinned. Blood was smeared like a kid's watercolor painting across the hair and white skin of his chest. His engorged penis glistened with blood as it bobbed against his thigh when Jeremy shook Joe against the wall. There was even blood smeared across his balding scalp and ruddy cheeks.

"Stay away from her," Jeremy warned. "Or we'll have you join in the fun by dicing her up, one piece at a time."

Jeremy cracked Joe's head against the wall, and a stab of

white-hot pain shot through Joe's skull as one of the blue geodelike crystals that made up the wall penetrated the flesh.

"Fuck!" Joe cried, but then the stars behind his eyes took over, and Jeremy threw him like a rag doll to the ground. For awhile, nothing was very clear.

Chapter Forty-five

When Joe's head finally cleared, the room was alive with ghosts. Skeletal bodies danced in the low gleam of candles that had been lit to surround the sacrificial pedestal. Old hags massaged long, dangling, naked dugs with bony, sharp-nailed fingers, and spectral men stroked and groaned as their erections spewed bloody sperm to wet the rocky ground. A couple dozen of the ghastly spirits walked and fornicated with each other around the perimeter of the dais.

Ariana, still nude and painted in drying blood, read something unintelligible from the book, as Jeremy ground his naked body atop Cindy. Her gag had been removed, and her screams rebounded and echoed through the chamber. But she couldn't get away from her torturer. Ariana had wound a strand of silver wire around Cindy's porcelain neck, and bound the other half around Jeremy's. Likewise, Cindy's bonds had been released so that her wrists could be bound to Jeremy's. Their ankles were similarly connected. He rode her as both captor and willing prisoner. They were truly the unified beast with two backs; neither could escape the other.

Joe saw several new slashes across Cindy's ribs and thighs, and a cut even crossed the bridge of her nose to end just below the eye . . . She cried tears of crimson that Jeremy lapped up, as wire about their necks dragged him tighter and tighter to union with his victim.

"The twentieth cut
Is the deepest cut

Yet it hurts the least," Ariana read.

She set the book down and moved from behind the dais to reach into her bag. She was so spackled in gore that blood hung from her like raindrops, beads of it ready to fall from even the thinnest hair of her sex as she bent over.

She returned to the dais with a long, curved silver knife. Then she whispered something in Jeremy's ear, and the man grinned, and sped up his pace. As his pale, hairy ass rose and fell like an obscene jackhammer and Cindy's screams turned hoarse, Ariana spoke another passage, from memory, as she raised the blade.

"And the bitch shall slay the dog
as the dog ruts in heat
she will lap up his life in ecstasy
and paint her pleasure with his pain."

She brought the blade down hard, two-handed. Jeremy screamed as it penetrated his ribs from behind.

"You missed," he cried, pulling against his bonds, but only succeeded in rolling both himself and Cindy to the very edge of the dais. He couldn't reach the knife.

"No," Ariana said. "I didn't."

She bent down and picked up the abandoned razors, and began to carve amid the dark pelt of hair on Jeremy's back.

S
A
C
R
I

He screamed and thrashed as she drew the knife cruelly across him, but he could not reach her as she finished the word.

F
I
C
E

"Come to me, Curburide," Ariana called, and bent to lick the blood from the word carved in living flesh.

Jeremy was coughing up blood on Cindy's face, but she didn't seem to care. The girl had ceased to make any noise at all.

"The twentieth cut only knicks the skin but releases a taste of the original sin," Ariana read.

With a wire cutter she then clipped the wires that held Cindy and Jeremy together. The man was now shuddering in horrible-looking spasms. He gasped loudly for breath, his eyes rolling back in his head until only the whites showed.

With a shove, Ariana rolled him over until he fell from the dais with a gagging scream to the floor. She reached a hand out to touch the new wound just below the nipple of Cindy's left breast and smiled. "The twentieth cut," she whispered.

The room was suddenly thick with shadows, and Ariana stood back and observed. The spectral Curburide crowded the room, waiting for the final stroke that would make them whole. Pleasure washed over Ariana in waves so powerful, she almost collapsed from the intensity. Ghostly, wicked children and ghastly lecherous old men slipped back and forth between her legs, licking and touching with unflinching, seductive attention. Women with breasts ripe and full as Vegas hookers inserted translucent fingers in her ass and bit and fingered her nipples. Their eyes glittered hellish bright and hard as diamonds. None of these creatures had substance, yet. And still they gave Ariana more pleasure than any human man or woman had ever given her. What would they give her when she set them all free?

Joe rolled himself end over end again across the room until he came face-to-face with Alex. His vision was hazy, obscured on one side by a black spot, and his head felt fiery and broken. Every blink of his eyes made him want to scream. But all he could think about was Alex, lying there unconscious now for . . . an hour? Two? It seemed like a day. Joe cried, as he lifted his head and bent over her, arms still behind his back, to kiss those bloody silent lips. They felt soft, and sticky. But still warm. As the spirits danced and cried out in guttural orgasms throughout the room, Joe leaned in to touch her lips in the most chaste kiss he'd ever given.

"I love you," he whispered. A tear dropped from his face to mingle with the blood on hers. It slipped down her cheek, a consummation of defeat.

Her eyes fluttered open, and her lips parted in a low moan.

"It hurts," she whispered. The white of her right eye was drowning in red, the pupil dilated black and wide. "How long was I out?"

"It's almost over," Joe said. "She's killed the boy, and her thug."

Alex groaned, and a bloody tear slipped from her eye.

"Can't see you very well," she said. "Blurry."

"I know, baby," he said. "He got you good."

"But I can see the opening. It's getting wider right now."

Joe followed her gaze, and saw the black ridge separating the electric blue crystals from each other. It stretched across the ceiling of the room, centering above the dais. A dark glow like black light emanated from its center, and as he watched, more and more ghostly, ghastly figures slipped from its nadir to join the thickening spectral crowd. The noise of twisted laughter commingled with deadly, unnatural sex grew louder every second.

"Can you draw on them?" Joe asked. "Can you loosen my rope so I can undo yours?"

Alex closed her eyes. A shiver passed over her body. When she opened them again, she whispered, "Joe, I'm scared."

"I'm with you," he said.

She closed her eyes again, and from somewhere nearby, a shriek of anger erupted.

A ghostly arm suddenly pointed in Alex's face as she opened her eyes. The creature grasped Alex's neck, but with a smile, the girl stared hard at the spirit, and it melted away.

"What was that?" Joe said.

"I stole something," Alex grinned. But her grin faded

quickly, as a blade of pain passed through her head. "Try your wrists," she whispered. "Hurry, before any others realize I've drawn on their power."

He pulled hard against the rope, and the strands seemed to slip off like silk, as if they'd never been tied.

"That's it!" he said, and went to work to undo his legs. Every time he bent and pulled at the knots, his head lanced with white-hot pain, but he forced himself to finish, and then, making sure that Ariana wasn't watching, he went to work on Alex.

"That's it," he said in a moment, lying next to her.

"That's great," Alex said. "There's just one thing."

"What's that?"

"I can't move."

Chapter Forty-six

Ariana was losing her grip. The Curburide were so entranced by her Calling that they'd not stopped with reaching inside her and pulling her G-strings to orgasm over and over again. She was so weak from pleasure, that she had fallen, knife still in hand, to her knees on the far side of the dais. Her breath came in heaving gasps, the orgasms coming as intense as childbirth labor. The air ripened with the smell of her, as she came again and again until her thighs glistened with sticky wetness.

A child approached her, eyes glowing green. The boy reached out chubby arms, and fastened them around her neck like a human toddler. But when she brought him close, he cuddled into her neck. And then bit her.

"Shit!" she screamed, and jumped away. She put a hand to her neck, and it came away wet. Bloody. The child still stood, unmoving, at the foot of the dais. "Bloody kisses," it grinned, showing its too-white teeth. "Set us free."

She nodded. It had only been a reminder of what she was here to do.

She raised the knife over Cindy's breast, and chanted the words of the 21st cut.

"Bittersweet and honey rage
Innocent and filthy sage
Under blade and under tow
To Curburide your life I throw."

* * *

"What do you mean you can't move?" Joe said.

"Nothing works," Alex cried. "I can't feel my feet. Or my arms. I can barely see. What did he do to me?"

"Hit you too hard in the head, baby," Joe said, and kissed her again. "Can you use your power to draw from the ghosts and stop her somehow?"

"I need help," Alex whispered.

"Shall I lift you?"

"No," she said. "I need Malachai."

"No," Joe said. "Too dangerous."

"It's the only way now, Joe. I need his help."

Joe closed his eyes. He'd once forbidden Malachai to speak to Cindy, for fear the demon would possess and use her again. The last thing he wanted was for Malachai to use Alex like a puppet. He had his suspicions that Malachai had caused Alex to kill her parents so that he could drag her into this gambit. Not that she didn't have reason, but the way the murders had happened, and only after the demon had taken possession of her . . .

Joe's thoughts stopped cold when he saw the blade. Ariana held it poised over Cindy's naked breast, and was mumbling some words of ritual. He could barely see her through the cloud of demons in the room.

"No!" he screamed, and jumped up, intending to jump across the dais and stop Ariana.

Instead, a half dozen wretched, rectal faces turned from their masturbating and fornicating celebration at the ring of the dais and shoved in unison at him. Rather than moving forward, Joe suddenly found himself being thrown forcibly back. He landed again in a heap at the wall, head screaming in pain.

"It's the only way," Alex yelled above the spectral screams and grunts of the Curburide orgy. "They are about to become flesh all around us. And if they do, we are lost anyway!"

"Malachai," Joe whispered, hating himself as he said the words. "Can you take possession of Alex, and help her stop this?"

If that is your wish, the demon said. *Though I do not desire it.*

"Help her stop them!"

Something warm and familiar slipped from Joe's brain, and in a second, Alex was climbing up from the floor.

You will need to direct the power, Malachai told her.

Alex nodded, ignoring the drops of blood that fell to the ground as she shook her hair. She walked through the demons without pause. They turned fearsome eyes and razor-nailed fingers to stop her just as they had Joe, but her very glare made them melt and wither.

Alex reached over the body of Cindy to grab the wrist of Ariana. Cindy's eyes had lolled back in her head as if she were already dead. Alex wasn't sure, but she guessed the girl still had to be alive, or the Curburide would have accepted the sacrifice as complete and the doorway would be open fully.

"Stop," Alex demanded.

Ariana laughed. "Girl, you can't stop this now. It's gone too far."

With that, the child Curburide who had stabbed at Alex earlier leapt atop Cindy's body and stared into Alex's eyes with its burning orbs. It laughed, a horrible sound of endless despair and malice. A dozen spirits grabbed onto his tiny arms, and they came at Alex in a phalanx, throwing her backwards before she could recover. As the younger witch stumbled, Ariana laughed and screamed, "With the twenty-first cut, I call thee, call thee, Curburide!"

Her blade punctured the soft flesh of Cindy's once beautiful left breast, and the girl shuddered once, twice on the dais. But her eyes never fully focused. With a final twitch, and a slight wheeze, she was gone.

Above them, the gap in the ceiling screeched with screams of death and ecstasy, and all around Alex, the transparent figures began to take full form. The child Curburide hopped up and down on the bloody belly and crotch of Cindy, and laughed as his body suddenly became opaque.

"Nooooo!" Alex screamed. "Malachai, I command you, close the door."

She lifted her hands, and pulled with all of her might at

whatever spiritual energy was in the room. She could feel it slip up her arms like a bolt of electricity; it tickled the balls of her feet like firecrackers.

Ariana leapt around the dais to attack Alex, but Joe had recovered enough to stand, and he was there to guard her back. He grabbed one of the razors from the floor and lashed out as Ariana came around to stab at Alex with the sacrificial blade.

The razor caught Ariana in the side, and her eyes widened in ultimate surprise. She buckled, and fell to the floor, but never took her eyes off of Joe. Her brow wrinkled in pain, and shock. How could this happen now? Now as they were at the final hour? she thought.

Joe didn't think at all, he just kicked her as hard as he could in the ribs, and she screamed the most horrifying sound he had ever heard a human being make, her voice cycling from an eardrum-piercing shriek to a gurgling wheeze. She rolled over and pointed the knife at Joe, but he pounced on her, holding her down with the weight of his body and wrestling her wrist until he pinned it to the ground above her head.

She gasped beneath him, unable to breathe, and he held the razor to her throat.

Behind him, Alex was chanting in a foreign tongue. Her voice seemed deeper than usual, and her head wavered in the air as if it were raised on a neck of jelly.

"*Dubrois ten et nu des* Curburide," she called.

"What are you doing?" he yelled. Above them, the ceiling looked like a maelstrom. The black door had turned to a shimmering oval of red and silver and black threads, all twining around and around in a whirlpool of ghostly faces and hands and legs.

We're closing the gate, Malachai said. *Drawing on Alex's natural power.*

"*Et nei renebras de farulte fasta nelti vie!*" she said. Then Alex stood on the dais itself, and raised her arms to the ceiling. Half-formed Curburide were ripping at her with their hands, but she could not be budged. Whether it was Malachai's protection or her natural power with spirits, Joe didn't know. But the creatures seemed to grow faint as they reached for her. Then their legs left the ground and they were sucked upwards stretching like angry taffy, into the whirlpool of dark light and ghostly limbs. Around them the blue crystals flickered and shuddered with power as Alex screamed the words of another tongue.

Lift the Caller to the dais with us, Malachai said in Joe's mind.

Joe didn't question the command; he dragged Ariana to her feet. Her face was purple, and she gagged and gasped for air. He didn't think he'd kicked her *that* hard, but maybe one of her ribs had punctured a lung. Joe didn't feel guilty about it.

Grabbing her around her blood-slicked waist, he hoisted Ariana up to stand between Cindy's legs, and then held the knife to her belly to keep her there. "Stand still," he commanded.

Around them the room blurred in a cyclone of white and gray. The Curburide were still trying to climb out of the hole between the worlds and into the cave; long fingers slipped out of the black beyond and scrabbled on this side of the divide for purchase. They gripped and slipped on the ice blue crystals above, but quickly their tenuous holds were broken, and trails of gray slime were left on the crystals as they were sucked back to wherever they were from. The spirits who had urged Ariana on were falling upwards now, as Alex intoned a spell and used their own power to send them skyward.

"Alve, nix etui re," she cried. Joe could see the sleeves of her shirt shaking in the psychic wind. She broke her concentration for just a moment, and her eyes met his.

"I love you, Joe," Alex said.

And then she said the last words Joe heard her say in that room:

"Ecsto ferni blatan Curburide palo no gon no. Neech!"

Alex reached her arms around Ariana and pulled the other woman close to her, in a strange hug between nemeses. Suddenly they were both rising in the air, spinning round and round as the waves of spirits and black otherworldly ether swirled in the room faster and faster to drain like a pool of water through a narrow hole.

The air filled with a hellish shriek and a sound that oscillated from the deep bass howl of a dying behemoth to an ear-piercing siren, and then with a vacuum howl and sucking, sloppy snap, the black crack of the door between worlds was gone, blue crystals of the strange room's ceiling seamlessly back in its place.

Gone also were Alex and Ariana. And as Joe called futilely, both in his mind and aloud, he realized that Malachai had been sucked into the void with them.

Joe slumped back against the dais, Cindy's dead hand hanging in the space above his shoulder. After a moment, he began to cry.

He waited there for a long time without moving. The silence of the room was palpable. Then Joe Kieran stood up, and looked at the blood-spattered face of Cindy, a girl he'd once saved from a demon. A girl that he had not saved from a murderess.

He stepped past the naked, bloody bodies of the boy, and the man, and picked up the book that Ariana had read from, where it lay bent and open on the ground. *The Book of the Curburide,* its cover read.

As he was starting to walk towards the exit, he saw fingers gripping the wall across the room. His heart leapt for a moment, thinking that Alex had only been thrown to the side, not sucked into the maelstrom. He ran to the alcove where Broderick Terrel had written and left his journal about the Calling of Malachai, and their defeat of the Curburide 100 years before.

"Alex," Joe called, and shined his flash into the small room. But the face he saw there wasn't hers. The light uncovered the silver hair and squinting, blinking eyes of Chief Harry Swartzky. The man was lying prone on the floor, his bound hands gripping at the wall to pull himself forward.

"Holy shit," Joe whispered, and bent to pull off the chief's gag. Then he began to untie the man's bindings. "You've been back here all this time?"

A tear slid from the chief's weary eyes as he looked out at the bodies and blood in the crystal room. He nodded.

"Yeah," he said in a voice lower than a train rumble. "And I couldn't do a thing to save 'em."

Joe stared at Cindy hanging limp half-off the dais, looking for the last time at the empty eyes of the girl he'd once loved. Her beautiful blonde hair was matted and tangled with gore, and her body sliced and broken in every possible place. He had to look away from the bloody hamburger they had made of that once-velvet place between her thighs that he'd kissed again and again. And when he did, he was forced to see the betrayed, frozen scowl on the face of her traitorous brother Ted, limbs akimbo on the cave floor, not so far from the carved back of the brawny man who'd been Ariana's helper. Blood from the letters she had carved deep in his back, SACRIFICE, had run from the corners of the S and the A and the C and all the rest in thin, dying rivers down his ribs to pool around him on the rock.

"I know," Joe said, and put his arm around the injured police chief, to help the older man limp towards the exit.

"This time, I couldn't either."

Finalist for the Bram Stoker Award!

JEFF STRAND

They first met in boarding school—Alex, shy and nervous, and Darren, constantly scribbling in his journal. They became best friends in college. Alex always knew Darren was a little odd. He didn't know his friend was murderously insane until Darren asked Alex to join him in his blood-soaked fun. They could be a team, hunting and slaughtering human prey. Alex doesn't want any part of it. He's no monster. But Darren is twisted, deadly… and determined. And he won't take no for an answer.

"MARVELOUSLY CREEPY!" —*Publishers Weekly*

PRESSURE

ISBN 13: 978-0-8439-6253-6

To order a book or to request a catalog call:
1-800-481-9191
Our books are also available at your local bookstore, or you can check out our Web site **www.dorchesterpub.com** where you can look up your favorite authors, read excerpts, glance at our discussion forum, and check out our digital content. Many of our books are now available as e-books!

JACK KETCHUM

AUTHOR OF *RED* AND *THE GIRL NEXT DOOR*

Lee is a veteran who came back from the war a changed man. He's haunted and scarred. And his grip on reality is weakening, especially since his wife and son left him. He keeps to himself, deep in the woods. But today he's not alone. A group of weekend campers have intruded on his fragile world. For Lee this means he's back in the war. For the unsuspecting visitors it means a fight to stay alive.

"Who's the scariest guy in America? Probably Jack Ketchum."
— STEPHEN KING

COVER

ISBN 13: 978-0-8439-6187-4

To order a book or to request a catalog call:
1-800-481-9191
Our books are also available at your local bookstore, or you can check out our Web site **www.dorchesterpub.com** where you can look up your favorite authors, read excerpts, glance at our discussion forum, and check out our digital content. Many of our books are now available as e-books!

"A voice reminiscent of Stephen King in the days of
'Salem's Lot." —Cemetery Dance

NATE KENYON

**Finalist for the Bram Stoker Award
and author of *The Reach***

The biggest news in the small northern town of
Jackson was the reopening of the local hydropow-
er plant. Until the deaths. First a farmer was found
horribly mutilated in his field. Then a little girl disappeared from her home. Deep in the woods a
deputy came upon a chamber of horrors straight
from a nightmare. And through it all, one child is
haunted by visions of the mysterious "blue man,"
a madman who brings with him blood and pain
and terror, a terror spawned by forces no one can
understand.

THE BONE FACTORY

ISBN 13: 978-0-8439-6287-1

To order a book or to request a catalog call:
1-800-481-9191
Our books are also available at your local bookstore, or you
can check out our Web site **www.dorchesterpub.com**
where you can look up your favorite authors, read excerpts,
glance at our discussion forum, and check out our digital
content. Many of our books are now available as e-books!

☐ **YES!**

Sign me up for the Leisure Horror Book Club and send my FREE BOOKS! If I choose to stay in the club, I will pay only $8.50* each month, a savings of $7.48!

NAME: _____

ADDRESS: _____

TELEPHONE: _____

EMAIL: _____

☐ I want to pay by credit card.

☐ **VISA**   ☐ **MasterCard.**   ☐ **DISCOVER**

ACCOUNT #: _____

EXPIRATION DATE: _____

SIGNATURE: _____

Mail this page along with $2.00 shipping and handling to:
Leisure Horror Book Club
PO Box 6640
Wayne, PA 19087
Or fax (must include credit card information) to:
610-995-9274

You can also sign up online at **www.dorchesterpub.com**.
*Plus $2.00 for shipping. Offer open to residents of the U.S. and Canada only.
Canadian residents please call 1-800-481-9191 for pricing information.
If under 18, a parent or guardian must sign. Terms, prices and conditions subject to change. Subscription subject to acceptance. Dorchester Publishing reserves the right to reject any order or cancel any subscription.

GET FREE BOOKS!

You can have the best fiction delivered to your door for less than what you'd pay in a bookstore or online. Sign up for one of our book clubs today, and we'll send you *FREE* BOOKS* just for trying it out... **with no obligation to buy, ever!**

As a member of the Leisure Horror Book Club, you'll receive books by authors such as **RICHARD LAYMON, JACK KETCHUM, JOHN SKIPP, BRIAN KEENE** and many more.

As a book club member you also receive the following special benefits:
- **30% off all orders!**
- **Exclusive access to special discounts!**
- **Convenient home delivery and 10 days to return any books you don't want to keep.**

Visit www.dorchesterpub.com or call 1-800-481-9191

There is no minimum number of books to buy, and you may cancel membership at any time.
*Please include $2.00 for shipping and handling.